D0098600

KINGDOM

of

SEA

and

STONE

Books by Mara Rutherford
available from Inkyard Press

Crown of Coral and Pearl
Kingdom of Sea and Stone

MARA RUTHERFORD

KINGDOM

of

SEA

and

STONE

inkyard
PRESS

ISBN-13: 978-1-335-14651-9

Kingdom of Sea and Stone

Inkyard Press
22 Adelaide St. West, 40th Floor
Toronto, Ontario M5H 4E3, Canada
www.InkyardPress.com

Printed in U.S.A.

To Jack, who dreams up all the best monsters.
And to Will, for making every day a plot twist.

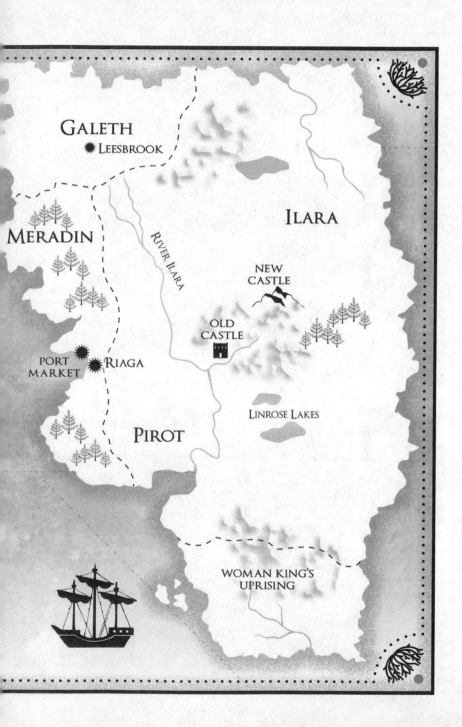

Prologue

On the day Zadie and I turned thirteen, Father surprised us with a trip to the floating market—our first glimpse of the world beyond Varenia.

I spent the journey perched on the bow of our family's boat, welcoming the cold ocean spray on my face and the wind in my tightly plaited hair. Zadie sat between Mother and Father, her knuckles white on the edge of the bench, her golden-brown eyes wide with anticipation.

As we approached, I eagerly took in the sight of the intricately carved wooden boats, with their colorful wares and raucous merchants. While Father traded our precious Varenian pearls for drinking water and food, Mother made Zadie and me sit next to each other near the front of the boat where everyone could see us. She had shown us off to every villager in Varenia a hundred times, but today an entirely new audience was at her disposal.

Men and women smiled at us as we floated past, likely because identical twins were a novelty.

"Lovely girls," one of the merchants said, and I watched as Mother swelled with pride like a pufferfish.

She thanked him and urged us to do the same. But just as I started to speak, the man craned his neck to get a look at the right side of my face.

"Pity about the scar, though."

I could feel Mother wilt behind me like a seaflower left out in the sun.

Zadie, embarrassed, settled into the bottom of the boat where no one could stare at us, but I stayed where I was, watching as Father looked over a basket. I was used to these kinds of comments by now, but it felt as though Mother would never accept that one of her daughters was a damaged good, just like the basket Father handed back to the merchant, gesturing to a hole in the bottom.

"Pssst."

I turned to see a young man—the son of the trader, presumably—motioning for Zadie and me to come closer.

Zadie eyed him suspiciously. Mother had warned us that Ilarean boys were beneath our notice. We were the most beautiful women in the world, after all; that was why we were considered worthy of marrying royalty.

But with my scar, I wasn't going to marry royalty, and I was curious to see what the boy wanted. I scooted to the edge of the boat. He looked like any boy in Varenia, though his clothing was finer and his hands were as smooth as Zadie's.

He glanced around to make sure no one was watching, then handed me a small glass bottle. "For you," he said.

I held it aloft for a better look. The contents were disappointing: sand, salt water, and a tiny yellow shell. All things I could find in Varenia, I thought glumly. But it was the only gift I'd ever received from a boy, and I politely thanked him.

When we returned home with our food and fresh water, I placed the bottle on a shelf.

"What's this?" Mother asked, immediately recognizing that there was a foreign object cluttering her kitchen.

"It's a wandering crab," Father replied, reaching into the bottle. For the first time, I noticed the tiny legs poking out from the shell. "They usually live closer to shore, but I've seen a few in my time. They find a discarded shell and make it their home, and when that one grows too small, they choose another, larger shell and move in."

I held out my hand, fascinated. Father passed the crab to me and it scuttled across my palm, tickling my skin. "It carries its home on its back?"

"That's right." Father gently took the crab from me before it could plummet to the floor. "It has everything it needs, right here."

I smiled, pleased with the idea of such an untethered, independent existence. "It can go anywhere it wants to." I glanced around our little house, which already felt too small for my imagination, and sighed wistfully. "Lucky."

"Nonsense." Mother plucked the crab deftly from Father's hand. Without ceremony, she flung it over the balcony, where it immediately sank below the surface of the water.

She ignored my startled cry. "You have everything you need right here in Varenia. Do you think they'd actually accept you out there, with your..." She trailed off, gesturing vaguely to my cheek. "Now hurry up and help me. This food isn't going to put itself away."

For a moment I thought Father might protest, but he simply retreated to the boat. Zadie frowned sympathetically.

I watched the spot where the crab had disappeared, knowing it was probably well on its way to somewhere new. It was only a crab, yet already it had seen more of the world than I ever would. I wondered if that was why the young man had given it to me, more of a cruel joke than a gift.

"Lucky," I whispered again, thinking not just of the crab but also the trader, his son, the ocean, and everything that had more freedom than a girl born in Varenia. Then I did as I was told.

"We're almost home," Zadie said, her teeth gritted against the strain of the oars. Our family's wooden boat crested a wave exactly like the hundreds before it, reminding me how vast the ocean was—and how quickly one could forget something they'd known their entire life.

"I can take over." I reached for the oars, but Zadie shook her head. There was a time, not long ago, when the soft skin of her palms would have torn open within just a few minutes of hard rowing, but that was before I left Ilara, before Prince Ceren cut off my family's drinking water, before our best friend, Sami, was banished.

Before, when I would have given anything to see the world beyond my floating village in the sea. Before I understood just how much I had to lose.

I gasped as Varenia finally came into sight. "It really is beautiful," I said to Zadie, taking in the stilt-legged houses painted in every shade of sunset, from palest yellow to deep red. "But then, you always knew that, didn't you?"

Zadie finally passed the oars to me and smiled despite her exhaustion. We'd been rowing all night, with nothing but the stars to guide us. I longed for the comfort of my old bed, but I also knew I wasn't returning to the same village I'd left behind.

"You loved it here, in your own way, Nor," Zadie said once she'd caught her breath.

Maybe she was right, but I had always wanted to leave. And I couldn't know if the people who had once wanted to see me banished would be willing to take me back, even if they learned just how far I had gone to protect them.

Zadie wiped the sweat from her brow with her sleeve. Now she was the one with suntanned skin, and I was pale from my time in New Castle. "Mother and Father will be so happy to see you."

I let out a wry laugh, grateful for the change in subject. "I'm not sure *happy* is the word I'd use, at least about Mother." She, along with most of Varenia, believed I had planned for Zadie to be injured by a maiden's hair jellyfish so that I could go to Ilara in her place.

I touched the scar on my right cheek absently. It seemed so insignificant, compared to the scars that twisted over Zadie's leg. The stain I had once used to cover the star-shaped blemish was forgotten back in the fortress I had lived in for the past few months. Compared to Mount Ayris, the cluster of houses before me seemed impossibly small and vulnerable, each one a tiny island huddled against the vastness of the ocean, as exposed as a cave creature in the sunlight.

"Mother will be happy," Zadie insisted. "She regrets not saying goodbye to you. I know it."

The village was as quiet as it always was this early in the morning, with only a few children scurrying along the docks that connected some of the houses. It didn't seem possible that things could be as drastically different as Zadie said; surely Mother would still be in bed next to Father at this hour, the house would be neat and tidy, and, however improbable, Sami would come by soon to ask Zadie and me if we wanted to go diving for oysters.

I secured the boat to one of the pillars beneath our house, waiting for my sister to enter first through the trapdoor. I wasn't sure I was ready to see the look on Mother's face when I appeared out of nowhere, like a spirit come back to haunt her.

I waited a moment, then several more, but there was no sign of life from inside the house, and I climbed quickly up the ladder, afraid something terrible had happened.

"They're out." Zadie's muffled voice came from the kitchen, where she was rummaging for something to eat.

"Out?" I looked around in confusion. "The sun just came up. Where could they be at this hour?"

"Fishing, I suppose." Zadie seemed unconcerned as she pulled a small basket off a shelf. "They're gone overnight sometimes, searching deeper waters. Sami and I were able to buy a larger boat." Her expression clouded over at the mention of her missing beloved, and I felt the loss as if it were my own. Nothing would be right until they had been reunited.

"We're going to find him, Zadie," I insisted. "And we're going to need to be well rested when we do."

I went to our room and collapsed onto the bed, wincing as my back hit the stiff straw mattress.

"Don't you want to eat something?" Zadie asked, coming to join me. "I know dried fish isn't exactly an Ilarean delicacy, but you must be starving."

"I'm all right." More than anything, I wanted to wash away the shame and fear that clung to me ever since I'd been locked in the New Castle dungeon. "I'm guessing we don't have enough fresh water to spare for a bath?"

"No baths these days, I'm afraid."

"Mother must be beside herself," I said, rolling my eyes. She smiled, but it seemed forced.

"What's wrong?"

"I just hope you'll give Mother a chance. She's making an effort. It hasn't been easy for her. It hasn't been easy for any of us."

I frowned, feeling chastened for a comment that would have rolled right off Zadie's back three months ago. "I'm sorry."

"I know." She let out a weary breath and closed her eyes. "I'm just tired."

"You rowed to land and back again the same day. That would exhaust even the strongest man."

She glanced at me and shook her head. "It's not the physical exhaustion, Nor. Losing you, then Sami, and having no idea if he's even alive… I can't fathom a future without him." She closed her eyes again. "I know that's probably hard to understand, too."

"Not so hard," I murmured. My longing for Talin, Prince Ceren's half brother, surged in my mind, but it felt selfish to mention my feelings for him when Zadie was hurting so much from Sami's loss. Talin and I weren't best friends like Zadie and Sami. We hadn't grown up together; we didn't even come from the same world. Still, Talin had given up the crown to save me, and I knew that if given the chance, the feelings that had blossomed in New Castle could grow into something special in their own right.

Zadie mumbled a few more words before her breathing

deepened, and I realized she had fallen asleep. I curled onto my side, watching her chest rise and fall. The furrow in her brow that I feared had become a permanent feature softened, her mouth relaxed, and she was once again the sweet, beautiful sister I had always known. Yes, things had changed, but surely there was nothing that couldn't be remedied if we were together. I took her hand and allowed myself to drift off to sleep, secure in one thing, at least.

I was home.

I was startled awake by Mother's shriek, as shrill as a gull's cry. For a moment I was sure I was back in New Castle, but then I saw my sister next to me. She rubbed the sleep from her eyes as I took a deep, shuddering breath.

"Is everything all right?" Zadie asked Mother around a yawn.

"Is everything all right?" Mother stared down at us like we'd appeared out of thin air. "You told me you were going to deliver a message to Nor, not bring her home with you! How did this happen?"

"Good morning, Mother," I said, before Zadie could answer.

Mother's mouth opened and closed like a fish as she glanced from me to Zadie to Father.

"Father!" I leaped from the bed and ran to him before he was fully through the trapdoor. I pulled him the rest of the way up and wrapped my arms around him as tight as I could. "I'm so happy to see you."

"Nor?" Father's voice cracked. "Am I dreaming?"

I smiled against his chest. "It's me, Father. I came back."

"How——?"

"Did something happen in Ilara?" Mother asked. "Why did Prince Ceren allow you to return?"

I had no idea how to answer their questions. I certainly couldn't start by telling them I'd left my blood coral blade behind in Ilara, still embedded in Ceren's chest. Even though I had killed him in self-defense, his final scream echoed in my ears, making what little sleep I got fitful at best. I could only hope that putting an ocean between myself and those awful memories would be enough.

I released Father reluctantly. "I'll explain everything. I promise. But I need to speak to Governor Kristos immediately."

"Oh, child, I wish you could," Father said. "But he won't see our family. Not after Sami's abduction." The pain Father felt at the loss of both Sami and his parents' friendship was etched in the lines of his face.

Zadie had explained to me that while Governor Kristos was furious at Alys's mother, Phaedra, and her cronies for abducting and abandoning Sami, he feared punishing the culprits would result in retaliation, given the fragile state of the village. Kristos had ordered the Varenians to pool their resources in an attempt to make sure everyone had adequate food and water, but some people rebelled and stopped diving altogether. Punishing Phaedra could backfire, given the large contingent of villagers on her side.

Mother and Father exchanged a look I couldn't interpret. "You can try," Mother said, surprising me. "He has always been fond of you. But we'll wait until after sundown, so you aren't seen. If Phaedra catches sight of you… Well, who knows what she's capable of?"

My eyebrows rose. "Does she really wield that much power?"

"When the emissary came to pay your bride price, Phaedra told him you had switched places with Zadie. Our water supply was cut off not long after. In the wake of that event, she convinced the villagers that your betrayal of the king caused all our hardships," Father said gently. "I don't think we can be too cautious."

I thought I saw the sheen of tears in Mother's eyes, but she blinked before I could be sure. "Zadie, come help me. I caught a sunfish, and I intend to make a feast of it."

Now it was my turn to gape. "You caught a fish?"

"Don't look so surprised," Mother snapped as she lifted the trapdoor. "Catching a fish is nothing compared to raising twin daughters."

As the hours passed, my worry about how Governor Kristos would perceive my presence in Varenia only grew, especially knowing that Sami had been banished for "conspiring" with me.

"What if Kristos refuses to see me?" I asked Zadie, who handed me another fishing net to mend. Normally I would have found any excuse to avoid such a boring task, but keeping busy was the best way to pass the time.

"We won't let him," Zadie said, though judging by the way she was pulverizing the fish for our supper, she was as anxious as I was.

"If only we had some way of knowing if Sami made it to land." I dropped the net and began pacing over the floorboards. Kristos would welcome me with open arms in that case.

"Surely he would have gone to see the kite seller if he had."

The kite seller. Of course. He was Sami's best contact on land, as far as we knew, and Sami trusted him to keep his secrets. "What exactly did the kite seller say to you when you saw him at the port market?"

"What do you mean?" she asked. "And for the love of Thalos, stop pacing! You're making me nervous."

I took a seat on one of our driftwood stools. "You said he gave you the rose, but did he say anything to you? Did he give you any hint that he might have seen Sami?"

She shook her head. "Not really. When I arrived at the tent, he was already packing away his kites for the day. He smiled when he saw me—he must have thought I was you— and handed me the rose."

I put my hand on my knee to stop it from bouncing. "You're right. He would have thought you were me," I mumbled. "Which means he thought he was giving me the rose. You're sure he didn't say anything?"

"I suppose he must have, but I was so worried about finding you." She chewed absently on a fingernail, an old habit I hadn't seen since Mother put bitter squid ink on Zadie's fingertips. "I do remember several Ilarean guards walking past us, which seemed to make him anxious. He was humming a tune over and over. It was familiar, but I couldn't place it."

I leaped up from the stool, too excited to sit still. "Try to remember it, Zadie. It's important. He wouldn't have been humming for no reason. It was a message, I'm sure of it."

Zadie still looked doubtful. "Why wouldn't he have just told me?"

"You said the market was crawling with guards. He had to be careful." I turned to look at my parents, who had just emerged from their room. "Sami was at the port market. He left a coded message for me."

Father scratched at his head, and Mother looked more skeptical than hopeful. "What message?"

"The rose, and a song, if Zadie can remember it."

"I could remember it much more easily if everyone would

be quiet!" Zadie had taken up my pacing and was still worrying at a jagged nail with her teeth. "It reminded me of our childhood," she added in a softer voice.

"A lullaby?" Mother suggested.

Zadie shook her head. "No, something more obscure than that. Maybe one of those songs Sami used to sing, the ones he picked up at market?"

I hopped in place, more certain than ever that I was on the right track. "The one about the goat and the donkey?" It hadn't been my favorite, since I had no idea what a goat or a donkey looked like, but Sami assured me it was funny.

"No, no. Something pretty, but with a melancholy tune."

I grabbed her arm and pulled her toward me. "'My horse has a mane of handspun gold, and hooves of finest silver?' That one?" It was a song that Sami had taught me when we were twelve or thirteen. I had never seen a horse then either, but Thalos knew I had imagined them a thousand times.

"Maybe. Can you sing it?"

I hummed the tune, then gasped as the final line came back to me. "'And roses red around her neck, for no other horse is finer.' Red roses, Zadie!"

I spun my bewildered sister in my arms. "I don't understand," she replied.

"Sami is alive!"

Zadie planted her feet to stop my spinning, and I waited for the room to come back into focus. "What if I'm wrong about the song?" Zadie asked. "What if it's just a coincidence?"

"It is not a coincidence," I insisted. "We have to tell the governor."

"I'm sorry, Nor, but you can't tell Kristos about the song," Mother said.

Father placed his hand on my shoulder. "I understand that you want to help. But it might give him false hope."

I hesitated. Maybe they were right. If I was wrong about this, Kristos would have even less reason to trust me. But hope was hope, and Varenia had been in short supply of it for too long. I couldn't go to the governor's house and prove to him that Ceren was dead and Varenia was free, but I could give him this.

"It's not false hope," I said, lifting the trapdoor. "Sami is alive. I know it."

I wouldn't give up on finding Sami, no matter what everyone else thought. Not only was he imperative to Zadie's happiness, but he had risked his life twice to see me at the port market, and it was his loyalty to Zadie and me that had made him an easy target for Phaedra. If the tables were turned, there was no question Sami would search for me.

The only real question was whether, once I found him, I could return to a place that had turned its back on me and the people I loved.

And more importantly, would I even want to?

2

"I can't believe they wouldn't even hear me out."

I sat on the bed next to Zadie, tears of frustration welling in my eyes. My conversation with Governor Kristos had gone horribly. In the past, I had been one of the only villagers allowed inside his house, thanks to the close relationship between him and my father. But today, I could barely get out my theory about Sami and the kite seller without Kristos speaking over me.

Far more painful than his dismissiveness was the realization that he didn't believe I had killed Ceren. Every time I spoke Ceren's name, I flashed back to my last moments with him, the warmth of his blood on my hands, the sheer hatred in his eyes. It was bad enough that I had stabbed him; the fact that no one believed me made it a hundred times worse.

Zadie brushed my hair with her fingers. "I'm so sorry, Nor. I know how much you sacrificed, and soon enough so will the rest of Varenia."

I sniffed and wiped my tears on my sleeve. Despite Zadie's warnings about the villagers' anger, in the back of my mind, I had still hoped for a peaceful homecoming. How could I have expected to be welcomed back when I was more despised here than ever?

"Let's get some rest. Surely we've earned that."

"I'll come to bed soon," I said. "I need some more time to think." I walked out to the balcony and picked up a ladle from the bucket of fresh water. It was distressingly low. Kristos and Elidi thought waiting for salvation was the prudent decision, but prudence hadn't filled our buckets or our bellies for years.

Once we had official word that Varenia was free—which the governor insisted on waiting for—I wondered how much things would actually change. I couldn't imagine the elders going to Ilara; even if they wanted to leave our village, the land sickness might kill them. And as much as I hated the term "wave children," our isolation in Varenia assured that we were as inexperienced as children when it came to life on land. Who would show them how to survive there?

Silver clouds obscured the moon, but the ocean was as still as glass tonight, reflecting the entire night sky. I may not have appreciated Varenia enough when I left it, but I had always felt reverence for the natural beauty of this place. I inhaled a deep breath and let it out in a long sigh, wishing I could capture this feeling in my chest: a tightness that was both longing and a sense of fulfillment. It made me feel small in a way that was oddly reassuring.

I placed my hands on the railing and hissed as the side of my right palm snagged on a splinter. A single droplet of blood appeared, and for a second I saw Ceren's face so clearly it was as if he were there with me. I staggered backward, directly into Father.

"Steady, child. Are you all right?"

I nodded, shaking away the thought of Ceren, and we leaned against the balustrade together. I was grateful for his warmth as he put his arm around me. Everything else may be a disaster, but this, at least, was right.

"What's troubling you?" he asked after a few minutes.

"I can't see my way forward anymore," I said, my voice thick with unshed tears.

"I know, child." He smoothed my hair off my forehead. "Your journey has never been an easy one. I fear it never will be."

"Why?" I asked, just like I had as a child, when I met every answer he gave with another question.

"Some of us are born knowing exactly who and what we are," he said. "Others have to search a little harder."

I chewed my lip, considering. "Zadie knows who she is, doesn't she?"

He nodded. "Yes. Your mother as well."

"And you?" I whispered.

"I think I knew, and I fought against fate for a while, and then I accepted it."

I wondered what he meant by that, but in the end, there was only one question that mattered. "Are you happy?"

"I'm content. I know I'm where I'm supposed to be."

"And people like me?"

There was a long, disconcerting silence. "I'm not sure you're looking for contentment, Nor."

I glanced up at the stars winking through the clouds. There was still so much I didn't understand, and though I'd risked everything to get back to Varenia, deep down, I knew a part of me would always wonder what else was out there.

"No," I conceded. "I suppose not."

Father was quiet for a few minutes, but finally he turned to me. "What happened to you in Ilara, Nor?"

I considered telling him about the bleedings, the dungeon, the monster, watching Lady Melina be pushed from a cliff and nearly meeting her same fate. But burdening Father with my struggles didn't feel fair. I knew it would only weigh him down, and we were all struggling to stay afloat these days. I told him the same story I'd told Elidi and Kristos, sparing everyone the most gruesome details.

Father was quiet as I spoke, his lips flattening into a thin line. I could see that he was sad, but also angry, and he was struggling to maintain his composure. When I was finished, he hugged me fiercely, as if he feared we might both fall apart.

"Should I leave in the morning?" I asked finally.

He vehemently shook his head. "You will stay as long as you choose."

At least Father still wanted me here. But I knew I would have to leave soon, not just to find Sami, but because my presence meant my family and I were at risk. I had no way of knowing if the decree barring Varenians from setting foot on land had been lifted yet. But if Phaedra discovered me, my family and I could soon share Sami's fate.

"You should sleep," Father said. "And so should I. Some of the men are going hunting tomorrow, much farther out to sea. I'll need my strength."

I looked up at him. "No, Father. That's too dangerous. Stay home with me. We can dive together."

He smiled sadly. "I wish I could. But there are too many hungry children to feed in this village. I see them in my dreams, their mouths gaping like baby birds'."

My heart ached for those children and for the responsibility Father felt. "It will get better," I said, though without the conviction I'd felt when I first reunited with Zadie. With so many people doubting me, it was becoming harder and harder not to wonder if they were right.

"Do you believe me, about Sami?" I pressed, even though I feared the answer.

Father sighed and looked up at the sky, then turned his dark gaze on me. "I will always believe in you, Nor." He was quiet for a moment. "You're going to search for him, aren't you?"

"I have to, Father. Zadie needs him, and so do his parents."

He nodded. "I know. But I hate to lose you again, when I just got you back."

I closed my eyes and felt the tears slip past my lashes. "I don't want to lose you, either."

"Just promise you'll wait until I return from my fishing trip."

"I promise." But even as I spoke, I wondered how long that would be. I had hoped coming home would calm the restless part of my soul that constantly yearned to move forward, the part of me that always wanted to be at the prow of the boat, the first one to reach the oyster.

But as comforted as I felt in my father's presence, I felt equally compelled to leave, rather than wait for the village to decide my fate for me. There was a familiarity in running toward something, rather than away from it.

Father kissed my forehead. "My girl, take heart. No journey worth taking was ever easy."

I hugged him and went to my room, where Zadie was already asleep. I slipped into bed next to her, letting the sound of her soft, even breathing calm my frayed nerves, saying silent prayers that *this* journey would prove worth the taking.

Father was gone before I woke the next morning, and Zadie was in the kitchen preparing food for the day. I changed into

one of my old tunics and borrowed skirts from Zadie before
joining her in the kitchen, relieved to find Mother was still
asleep. I wasn't sure if Father had told her what we'd discussed last night.

I had slept poorly, plagued by dreams of Ceren that felt
disturbingly real. Fleeting images came back to me while I
worked, of a teenaged Ceren sword-fighting with Talin and
of a much younger Ceren climbing onto his father's throne,
as if testing it out for size. Why did I keep thinking about
him, when he was the least of my worries now?

"What's troubling you?" Zadie gently took the spoon from
my hand. I hadn't even realized I'd stopped stirring our stew.

I leaned closer to Zadie. Mother had an uncanny ability to
ignore anything she didn't want to hear, but she could somehow pick up gossip from across the house. "Why haven't we
received word that Varenia is free yet? Talin must know how
worried I am. I left him days ago."

Zadie squeezed my shoulder reassuringly. "You said yourself that it would likely take time."

"But how much time? How long are we supposed to wait?"
I hadn't told Zadie yet that I was planning to search for Sami
as soon as Father returned. I was afraid she'd insist on coming, and someone needed to stay and make sure our parents
were safe.

I couldn't tell Zadie about my constant thoughts of Ceren,
either. It would only worry her, and she'd had more than her
share of worry lately. I forced a smile and went to the cutting
board to chop herbs. "Never mind me. I'm just restless. I wish
I could go for a swim to release some of this nervous energy."

"I wish you could, too. But it isn't safe to go out." A few
minutes later, she touched my shoulder on her way to gather
the wash. "I'm sorry it has to be this way," she said, but my

mind was already far away in New Castle, wondering just who was sitting on the throne.

Several minutes later, she came in without a word, the color high in her cheeks.

"What's the matter?" I asked as I set the knife down. "You're flushed."

"I was just thinking," she said, her voice pitched strangely, "that maybe you should go onto the deck and finish the wash."

I furrowed my brow in confusion. "Why?"

"I've been doing it for months on my own, that's all."

"You know I'm sorry about that." I resumed my chopping. "But you said yourself it isn't safe."

"There's no one around," she insisted. "I really think you should go."

I brushed the hair out of my face with the back of my hand. "What's gotten into you?"

"Nothing. I just really don't want to do it, all right?"

I let out an exasperated sigh. "Fine. I'll do it myself."

"Thank you." As I passed her, she reached out and tucked a stray strand of hair behind my ear. "I love you," she said, pressing a kiss to my cheek.

I shrank away, watching her suspiciously from the corner of my eye. "Um, I love you, too, you strange girl."

I walked outside, blinking at the brightness of the sunlight. Despite my annoyance with Zadie, I was so grateful for the feel of the sun on my skin that for a moment I stood with my arms outstretched and my eyes closed, drinking it in. I shook out the messy knot of my hair and spun in a slow circle, and when the light stopped burning my eyelids, I finally blinked them open.

The ocean was indigo and gold today, the waves glittering in the sunlight. I sighed as I knelt down to pick up the heap of wet clothing, wishing I could stare at the horizon a little longer, daydreaming of what lay beyond it.

As I pushed to my feet, movement at the end of the balcony caught my eye.

I closed my eyes again, sure it was some kind of illusion. But when I opened them, he was still there, his hair ruffling in the breeze, his cerulean eyes watching me.

Eyes I would know anywhere.

Talin.

It was like seeing him for the first time. His gaze held mine, making me physically aware of every inch of my body. At Old Castle, we had promised we would see each other again, but even then I hadn't fully believed it. And with every hour that passed in between, my doubt had only grown.

But he was in Varenia, wearing a white tunic tucked into black breeches and leather boots, once again completely overdressed for the environment. At least he'd left his doublet behind this time. If Talin was here, it could only mean that his mother was back in New Castle, that everything else was as it should be. Ceren really was dead, Zoi was alive and well, and Varenia was finally free.

And yet Talin did not look overjoyed to see me.

I slowly set the washing down and stepped toward him, unsure if I should smile when his expression remained so serious. "Talin," I said, because *hello* seemed wholly inadequate under the circumstances.

"Nor." He sighed heavily, as if he'd just remembered to breathe, and opened his arms for me.

Relieved, I ran to him, closing the space between us in just a few strides. He wrapped his arms around me, the warmth infinitely better than all the sunlight I'd just absorbed. I breathed in as deeply as I could and felt his chest rumble with laughter.

"What?" I leaned back to smirk at him. "You smell good."

"So do you," he said, pulling me closer. "I forgot just how good."

For a moment, we stood in each other's arms in silence, simply enjoying the feel of each other. But when he didn't speak, I knew I would have to ask. "Why do I have a terrible feeling it's not good news you've come to deliver?"

"I'm afraid it's not," he said, pressing a kiss to the top of my head. "But it can wait for just a minute longer."

I closed my eyes, trying to shut out the specter of whatever bad news had chased Talin here. "Zadie saw you, didn't she?" I remembered the funny look on her face when she'd told me to come out and do the wash.

I could feel his jaw shift into a smile against the top of my head. "Yes. I hoped it was you, from a distance. But the way she placed both hands over her mouth when she saw me convinced me immediately it wasn't."

"Why? Too ladylike?"

"Something like that," he murmured.

I punched him lightly in the side.

He let out a gentle *oof*, which was clearly feigned. "That's more like it."

I couldn't decide if I wanted to pinch him or kiss him, and I suspected that was what he liked about me. From the moment he'd first seen me, sodden hair and clothing dripping water onto Governor Kristos's floorboards, I'd been far from the model of feminine grace my mother had tried to mold.

"Don't tell me you made it all the way from Ilara in that," I said, noticing the prow of a small rowboat peeking out from below the balcony for the first time.

"My men have the ship. I thought it best if they waited farther out to sea." He held up a finger at my confused expression. "I promise I'll explain. Come on, you can show me how to wield the oars properly."

"I should stay here. Most of the village doesn't know I'm back yet."

Now it was his turn to look at me askance. "We need to talk, Nor. Preferably alone." He brushed my loose hair aside and kissed my neck, and just like that, I realized how badly I wanted time alone with him, too. It had been next to impossible to spend time together in Ilara, and now we had an entire ocean at our disposal.

"Of course," I said, momentarily allowing my fears to recede into the background. "Come on."

I rowed us far enough out that the odds of being discovered were slim. The water was a bit choppy and the horizon was thick with ominously dark clouds, but I kept the anchor up in case we needed to leave in a hurry. I sat on the bench next to Talin and let the rocking of the waves nudge me closer to him. The sleeves of his tunic were rolled up to the elbows, revealing tanned forearms corded with muscles. Hesitantly, I ran my fingers along the contours, still not quite believing he was real, and goose bumps erupted on his skin.

"I forgot about how ticklish you are," I murmured.

When he smiled, my stomach fluttered. I'd also forgotten how he could make me lose my head with just a glance. Back in Ilara, my attraction to Talin had gotten me into trouble more than once. But out here, with no one around to judge me, I could indulge myself, just a little.

"What?" Talin asked.

I'd been staring. I didn't care. "I missed you."

"I missed you, too." He twined his fingers through mine, bringing our hands up to brush his lips softly against my skin. This time I was the one to shiver. "I was afraid you were suffering, but when I saw you on the balcony, dancing in the sunlight…"

I laughed. "That was *not* dancing. You caught me in a brief moment of indulgence. I'm still trying to get the cold from New Castle out of my bones."

"But that's just it, Nor. Even when everything around you is falling apart, you manage to find those moments of joy."

I blushed and glanced away. "You're giving me far too much credit. I have done more than my share of complaining, I assure you."

I felt his finger curl under my chin, tugging it gently toward him. Slowly, I brought my eyes up to his. The last time I had seen Talin, everything had been urgent and desperate. I had just escaped New Castle, and he had revealed the secret of his mother and sister. And of course, I had stabbed Ceren. The world seemed far too complicated then.

But right now, it seemed so wonderfully simple. He tucked my hair behind my ears with callused fingers, cupping my face in his hands, and pressed a kiss to the scar on my right cheek. Then another, to my left cheek. I closed my eyes, dizzy with anticipation. "I'm so happy you're here," I murmured.

Talin's grip tightened almost imperceptibly, and I felt him lean back. "Nor?"

I opened my eyes to see that all the joy had evaporated from his face. Nothing was simple, I reminded myself. Not when it came to us. "What is it, Talin?"

He shook his head. "I'm so sorry for what I'm about to tell you."

My blood ran cold as he let his hands fall from my face, taking their warmth with them.

"Ceren is…" He swallowed thickly and forced himself to meet my eyes, though I could see it pained him. "My brother is still alive."

3

A sick, sinking feeling pulled my stomach toward the ocean beneath us. *No, no, no.* I couldn't accept that everything I'd sacrificed, everything I'd been through, had been for nothing.

"How?" I managed, my voice hardly more than a whisper.

Talin placed his hands firmly on my shoulders, grounding me. "You injured him gravely below the mountain. When his guards found him, they believed he was dead. They brought him up to his room, where the royal physician removed the knife. The wound had clotted around the blade. He was alive, but barely."

"My blood," I breathed. "It saved him."

"Yes."

Hot tears seeped out from between my closed eyes. All this time, I believed I had saved Ceren that day at the lake, only to kill him beneath the mountain. The truth was, I had stabbed Ceren, only for my own cursed blood to save him.

"There was a pearl in the hilt of the coral blade," Talin said after a moment. "A bright red pearl, I'm told. Ceren had it ground down. He consumed that as well. It helped significantly. He healed in two days."

The pearl had come from the oyster I'd been diving for the day of the incident, when I saved Zadie from drowning and sustained the injury that caused all of this. It made sense, I supposed. If a pink Varenian pearl had strong healing properties, a pearl like the one in the coral knife must be even more powerful. I should have pulled the blade back out when I ran that night. He would have bled out faster, and he wouldn't have had the pearl to help him heal.

Fear and anger built in my chest until I couldn't hold myself back any longer. "Damn it!" I shouted, slamming my fists against the bench.

Talin's grip on my shoulders never faltered. "I'm so sorry," he said quietly. "So very, very sorry."

I leaned forward and buried my face in his tunic. "*I'm* sorry," I whispered against the soft fabric. "I should be grateful I don't have his life on my conscience. But I can't be." My voice broke on a sob.

"He did unspeakable things to you, Nor. He brought all of his suffering on himself."

I nodded, more to ease his pain than my own. It had been difficult enough believing I had killed Ceren. Now I had to process his survival.

"What's going to happen?" I asked when my tears were spent.

Talin sighed heavily. "Ceren is King of Ilara."

"And you?"

"I am a wanted man."

My head jerked up. "What? Why?"

"For aiding a criminal."

I laughed mirthlessly. "Me, I suppose."

"I helped you escape," he said. "Ceren sent his guards after me as soon as he could speak. Grig and Osius came with me. They're on the boat, waiting."

"Thalos," I breathed. "And the rest of your men?"

"Most of them didn't know that I'd helped you. I can only hope Ceren spared them."

Fresh tears filled my eyes.

"It's not your fault," he insisted, taking my hand. "Even if I hadn't helped you escape, I'm wanted for 'conspiring with the woman king.'"

Woman king was a moniker people attributed to Talin's mother, Talia, who had fled New Castle after Ceren tried to kill her. She'd later given birth to Zoi, Talin's little sister, who was the rightful heir to the Ilarean throne and the true woman king. "He knows she's alive?"

Talin nodded. "I had sent word to my mother immediately after you left. For two days we believed Ceren was dead, and my mother and her forces were nearly at the Linrose Lakes. Then Ceren made his miraculous recovery, and everything changed. I had no choice but to flee."

How difficult it must have been, to get so close to victory, only to see it snatched away. "Where is your mother?"

"She halted her advance once she knew she wouldn't be able to take the throne uncontested. Some of her troops are in Pirot, and others are back in the south, waiting for their next orders."

I took a deep breath, releasing it slowly. This was bad, but not as bad as it could have been. Talin was alive, and so were his mother and sister. There was still a chance to regroup and defeat Ceren.

"Does your brother know where you are?"

"Osius, Grig, and I were able to make it across the border into Pirot, thanks to the soldiers there. Ceren still believed Lord Clifton's men were on his side. We lost Ceren's guards. I assume he thinks I joined my mother's army."

I tensed at his words. "But he might guess you came to Varenia, which means you aren't safe."

"And neither are you."

A chill ran over my scalp. "What do you mean?"

"He's told everyone you tried to kill him. There is a price on your capture, and mine."

I remembered Ceren's face when I stabbed him, his jaw drenched in blood, his eyes burning with sheer hatred. Even before that, my choices had been to marry him or die. "Is he coming after me?"

"I imagine he will, eventually. He's too busy preparing in case my mother decides to mobilize her army again."

I nodded, but I was lost. What was I going to tell Governor Kristos? What was he going to tell the council?

"Why did you come here?" I asked. "Why didn't you join your mother and sister? You could have had an entire army between you and your brother."

"I had to warn you about Ceren. And I can't go to my mother yet, not without reinforcements. Her army is large, but it's not skilled enough to mount an attack on New Castle." He took my hands in his, running his thumbs along my skin. "Besides, I needed to see you again."

I couldn't help smiling at that. "I'm not happy that you put yourself at risk, but I suppose I can't be mad at you, either."

His grip tightened. "Will you come with me, Nor?"

I blinked at the urgency of his request. "What?"

"I know you just got back, but we shouldn't stay in Varenia.

It's not safe for either of us, and I fear by remaining here, you could put your family in danger as well. We'll find more troops and join my mother in the south."

I had already been preparing myself to leave Varenia to look for Sami, but only because I believed my family would be safe and I would be able to go on land without fear of repri- sal. With Ceren alive, I no longer had those assurances. My heart began to race as my ribs constricted around my lungs, making it a struggle to draw a full breath. No matter what I did, the people I loved would be in danger. "Gods, this is impossible!"

"I know things look dire right now, but we'll think of something. Together." Talin pulled me closer, but even though I knew the gesture was intended to be comforting, I found myself more desperate for release.

I shrugged him off as delicately as I could. "I just…need a moment," I panted, and without another word, I plunged off the side of the boat.

The cold water helped immediately. Within a few seconds, my heart rate slowed as my body instinctively prepared for a dive, and my thoughts began to settle. Talin was right. We'd figure out a way to fix things, together.

I had just closed my eyes to rest for a few more moments when a strange light flashed across my vision. I opened my eyes, afraid lightning had struck the water, but the ocean was gone. I was staring at a man wearing a dark metal crown stud- ded with red stones. He was facing away from me, but I would have recognized his long white-blond hair anywhere. Ceren.

He was in his study, surrounded by vials and flasks. Slowly, he turned toward me, until I was looking directly at his face. His gray eyes widened, almost as if he was seeing me, too. And then I saw the blood on his pale mouth.

I gasped, inhaling seawater, and the vision vanished. I raced toward the sunlight above me, sputtering as I broke free of the surface.

I reached for the boat as I retched up water and bile, but my hands met empty air. The untethered boat must have drifted while I was under. I spun in a slow circle, trying to get my head above the waves, but I couldn't see Talin anywhere. I ducked back under for a better view, and that was when the first hint of panic crept in. There was no sign of the boat anywhere.

"Talin!" I shouted when I resurfaced, even though I knew how easily sound could be lost on the water. Talin wouldn't have left me. The idea was absurd. I must have drifted farther than I realized. The vision had only seemed to last a few seconds, but it could have been much longer.

"Talin!" I called again. There was nothing out here, no way to orient myself. Treading water seemed safer than trying to swim toward a boat that could be anywhere. Talin would have a better idea of where I'd gone than I did.

Unless he wasn't looking for me.

Unease tugged at the corners of my mind. What if Talin hadn't come to Varenia just to be with me? What if he hated me for allowing Ceren to live, twice? What if he thought my blood was the reason his mother was still in exile, rather than on her throne?

Pain pulsed in my rib cage as my muscles began to spasm. I was being ridiculous. I was the one who had jumped out of the boat, and Talin would be a fool to abandon his only guide back to land. He didn't know the first thing about navigating in the ocean.

The blood drained from my face. *Talin knew nothing about the ocean.* And no one else knew where I was.

Just as another stab of pain went through me, something grabbed my shoulder from behind. I screamed, inhaling another lungful of seawater, and found myself being pulled backward.

Into a boat.

"Good gods," Talin cried, looking down at me with sunlight surrounding him like a halo. "I thought I'd lost you! You were under for so long, and when I went in after you, you were gone."

"You—you what?" I sat up and took in his soaked clothing, his dripping hair.

"What happened, Nor? I was terrified!" He rubbed his hands on my arms, attempting to warm me.

"I'm so sorry. The current must have been stronger than I realized. And when I was coming up, I had a..."

His grip tightened in concern. "A what?"

A vision? It sounded like nonsense, even to me. It could have just as easily been a dream or hallucination. Maybe I'd been unconscious for a minute or two. "I don't know. It was as if I blacked out for a moment. But maybe it was longer than I realized."

"It must have been," he said, smoothing my wet hair off my forehead. "We should get back. You clearly need to rest. We'll get some food into you and warm you up."

I nodded, hoping he was right and I was simply exhausted and overwhelmed. But the vision had seemed so real. When Ceren turned to me, I could have sworn he saw me.

I shook the thought away and sat up a little in Talin's lap. I hated myself for doubting him, even if I had been momentarily lost at sea.

I rowed us back home, allowing the rhythm to settle my frayed nerves. But all too soon the house came into view, and we both knew that after we stepped inside, there would be no going back.

I reached up to tuck a sun-kissed strand of hair behind his ear. No matter what happened, I was glad he had come.

"I wish I could make this easier for you," he said, his voice so earnest it made my heart ache.

But he couldn't make any of this easier. He couldn't change the fact that Ceren was alive or give Varenia enough fresh water to ensure no one would die of thirst this month. He couldn't make any promises, and neither could I.

I blinked back my tears. We were too young to have such burdens hanging over us. But perhaps Father was right: some of us were not meant to have easy journeys.

So far, life had conspired against us at every opportunity, and I wasn't naive enough to think that was going to change anytime soon. But for now, I would take whatever moments I could get.

"Kiss me," I whispered.

His brow furrowed for a moment, as if he wished he had something more to give, before he finally pulled me toward him and lowered his lips to mine.

4

We entered the house hand in hand.

Zadie stood up from the table abruptly, nearly knocking over her stool.

Mother rose far more gracefully than Zadie. "Prince Talin," she said, inclining her head. Her hair was braided neatly, and she wore a fresh tunic and a lemon-yellow skirt. "Welcome back to Varenia."

He released my hand gently and bowed to Mother. "Thank you, my lady."

"I know it's not much," she replied, gesturing to the house around us, "but we are honored by your presence."

I had forgotten Talin had never been inside our home before. For one brief moment I saw the tiny living space through his eyes, the mismatched dishes in a stack on our salvaged wooden shelf, the tattered hems of our curtains. But we had worked hard to make this place a home, and I was proud of it, even if—

"Your home is lovely," Talin said, taking one of Mother's trembling hands in his and kissing the back of it, as he'd once done to me, and I felt my heart swell with gratitude as Mother's cheeks turned a flattering shade of pink.

"Thank you," she said. "Can I offer you something to drink? We have a little wine, and water, of course."

"Water would be perfect."

Mother nodded graciously, then turned away from Talin and shot my sister a vicious look. Zadie blinked, remembering herself, and quickly went to fetch a cup and some fresh water from the bucket. I had told Talin about Sami's banishment on our way back to the house, so he wouldn't ask Zadie about him. At least Talin seemed more optimistic than she did that the rose and the song were a message, though he also didn't know what they meant.

I showed Talin to our sturdiest stool, praying it wouldn't collapse beneath him, while Zadie set a pitcher of water—only slightly chipped—and a few oranges from her last trip to the floating market on the table. It wasn't much, but at least it was fresh.

"Please, sit," my sister said. "You must be tired from your journey."

"Thank you." Talin settled himself on the proffered stool, which stayed blessedly upright beneath him.

"Did you come alone, Your Highness?" Mother asked.

Talin chuckled politely. "Alas, my navigational skills do not extend to the ocean. My men are nearby, waiting for my signal. I thought it best I arrive quietly."

"I'm sure Governor Kristos will be eager to see you. Although we are deeply flattered you chose to grace us with your presence first. Aren't we, Nor?"

I struggled to keep my voice as serious as Mother's. "Oh, indeed."

Talin smirked at me, then looked back at Mother and cleared his throat. "I wanted to speak to your family before meeting with anyone else. Is your husband home?"

"Several of the men went on a fishing expedition," Mother explained. "We hope they'll return tonight, though it could take longer."

Talin nodded, his expression serious. "I see. Well, I wish this news could wait for his return, but I'm afraid it can't."

I was grateful that Talin recounted the story so I didn't have to. But when he got to the part about Ceren healing from the blood coral knife, I saw the confusion on Zadie's and Mother's faces.

"How did he survive such a wound?" Mother asked. "Nor nearly died from the tiniest scratch from a blood coral."

Talin glanced at me, and I nodded for him to continue. "When my brother imprisoned your daughter, he discovered the healing properties in her blood. He injured her, repeatedly, to gather her blood so that he could study it. Eventually he realized that by…consuming her blood, he could also heal himself."

"Consuming it?" Zadie's voice was as thin as seagrass. I hadn't told her that detail, only that Ceren had found a way to heal himself with my blood. It had seemed too awful to say the rest out loud.

Mother's voice was eerily flat when she spoke. "He drank her blood."

Talin nodded. "Yes."

I closed my eyes, but the silence that filled the room was so thick I was finally forced to look around. When I did, I saw that my mother's face was streaked with tears.

When I had been injured as a child, and when Zadie's legs had been scarred, Mother had wailed and moaned loud enough for the entire village to hear. I was accustomed to her histrionics, yet this silent display of grief was far more difficult to witness.

Talin took her hand and waited patiently while she collected herself. "I wanted to give you time to process all this before the rest of the villagers hear, but I think I should speak with Governor Kristos and the elders right away."

Mother glanced out the window just as the first drops of rain began to fall. "I understand your concern, but I'm afraid Kristos has joined the men on the fishing trip."

I turned to stare at her. Given the tension in the village, it seemed like a particularly dangerous time for Kristos to leave.

"He was criticized for his economic decisions," Mother explained to me. "He felt he needed to do more to contribute." She returned her attention to Talin and bowed her head. "I know our home is small, but we would be honored to have you stay with us tonight, Your Highness."

"What about Grig and Osius?" I asked, my eyes returning to the window, where the rain was already falling heavily. "They've never spent a night at sea before."

"They'll be all right," Talin said after a thoughtful moment. "Grig only gets mildly seasick."

At dinner, Talin managed to consume several bowls of watery fish stew and seemed to genuinely enjoy it. Mother had gone to bed early, claiming a headache, though I had a feeling she was still trying to process what Talin had told her. Zadie washed the dishes as I prepared a pallet for him in the living area of our house.

"I'm sorry it's not much," I said as I led him to our balcony, where I shook out one of our few blankets. The rain had eased, but every now and then the clouds lit up with distant lightning. "We've never had a guest spend the night before."

Talin leaned against the balustrade. "I'm honored to be the first."

"I still can't believe you're here," I said, folding the blanket over my arm. The light from the house spilled out onto the balcony, bathing Talin in its warm glow. A part of me didn't want to go to sleep tonight, because I was afraid I'd wake to find this had all been a dream.

Talin held out his hand, and I joined him at the railing, pressing into his warmth. "I don't know how we'll explain this to the governor," I said softly. "Not after I was so sure..."

He placed his hand on top of mine. "I hoped when I saw you again it would be to tell you that Varenia was free. Instead I've made your lives far worse."

"You haven't. If I'd never gone to Ilara in Zadie's place..." I trailed off, taking a ragged breath. "If I'd never met you—"

"Don't you dare finish that thought." He put a hand on my shoulder and turned me to face him. "Meeting you was the only good thing to happen to me since I found out my mother was still alive. And every moment I've spent with you after has been better than the one before. Even right now, when I have no idea what we're going to do, all I can think about is how badly I want to kiss you."

I blushed at his frankness. "Then why don't you?"

"Your mother is right inside the house, for one thing."

I stood on tiptoe until my lips were close to his ear. "My mother doesn't have to know."

Talin turned his face before I had lowered myself back down, his mouth finding mine instantly, stealing my breath. His hands moved from my shoulders into my hair, tipping my head farther back. I dropped the blanket and felt his lips curl in a smile against mine.

Just a few hours ago, I had wondered if I would ever see Talin again, and now he was here, holding me. For a moment, I let myself forget the horrible news that had brought him to Varenia and said a silent thank-you to the universe for giving us this time together.

We were so focused on each other that I almost didn't hear the tiny voice calling my name.

Talin and I froze, still intertwined.

"I only wanted to let you know that I've decided to sleep on the pallet," Zadie called softly from just inside the house. "It's too cold in our room," she added. "Um, good night."

A moment later, I let out a very unromantic snort of laughter, a mixture of embarrassment and relief. For the first time since we'd met, we could be together without fear or judgment. The only thing we risked hurting tonight was my mother's sense of propriety.

"Have I ever told you how much I like your sister?" Talin murmured. He picked me up and stumbled backward into my room until his knees buckled against the mattress and he landed with a heavy thud.

"Careful," I hissed. "We don't have your fancy feather mattresses here, you know."

Talin glanced behind him. "You don't have our fancy *doors*, either."

"Mmm. Pity, then, that you're so ticklish."

"You wouldn't dare," he said, inching away from me toward the edge of the bed.

I arched an eyebrow and flexed my fingers. "Wouldn't I?"

I leaped atop him, quickly discovering the places he was most ticklish and then doing my best to avoid them, in order not to wake my mother with his laughter.

"This isn't fair," he said through gritted teeth. "You're not ticklish."

I finally relented, letting him catch his breath for a few minutes while I disappeared behind the curtain and changed into a shift. When I returned, he had removed his boots and unlaced the top of his tunic, exposing a few inches of his smooth bronzed chest.

We both looked at the tiny bed at the same time. A furious blush bloomed in my cheeks.

"I'll sleep on the floor," he said quickly.

"Don't be ridiculous. You're our guest." I shuffled around him awkwardly and reached for the dropped blanket. "I'll take the floor. In the meantime, I thought maybe we could both sit on the bed and talk."

His arched a brow. "*Sit* and *talk*?"

"I'm sure we can manage to keep our hands off each other for a few minutes," I said, perching on the edge of the mattress. "You're a gentleman, after all."

He laughed and sat next to me, leaving a few inches between us. After a moment, his expression turned serious. "I'm not sure this is a good idea, Nor. It feels…dangerous."

I knew he was right, but I also knew this might be our last night together for a long time. Maybe forever. "Every moment we've ever spent together has been more dangerous than this. You can't be that afraid of my mother."

"It's not your mother I'm afraid of," he said, twining his little finger through mine.

I turned to face him. "It can't possibly be me."

He sighed and collapsed back on the bed. "Do you have any idea what torture it is to be this close to you, Nor?"

Teasingly, I scooted closer to him.

"I mean it. It's taking all of my strength not to kiss you again."

"Then kiss me." I leaned over him and blew out the lantern on the nightstand. "No one will know but us."

He only hesitated a moment before pulling me down to his chest. "When we're married—"

The word was like a cold bucket of water on the warmth spreading throughout my body. "Married?"

He sat up next to me. "I was hoping, when all of this is over..."

I twisted my braid over my shoulder, my stomach strangely unsettled. When I had been trapped in New Castle, doomed to a life with Ceren, the idea of marrying Talin seemed as lovely and improbable as a fairy tale. But we'd never spoken about it before, and I didn't want to imagine anything beyond this moment.

He let out a small puff of laughter when he saw my expression. "I don't mean tomorrow, Nor. Or even the week after. I just... I want to be with you." He ducked his head, avoiding my eyes. "I thought that was what you wanted, too."

"It is," I replied, before I had even gathered my thoughts. It was true. Gods, with his heat seeping through my thin shift and the scent of him all around me, I wanted it more than ever. But I would never go back to New Castle, where every dark corridor and cold chamber held another terrible memory, not even if Ceren was dead. And there was still so much of the world I hadn't seen...

"Hey." Talin brushed my hair off my shoulder and leaned down to kiss the exposed skin. "I can see that mind of yours racing. I'm sorry I said anything. Being with you right here, right now, is enough."

He lay back down, and I snuggled against him. "I'm sorry I reacted that way. You caught me off guard, that's all."

He sighed, a soft breeze against my cheek. "Then let's talk about something else. Whatever you want."

"Tell me about your childhood," I said, twining my fingers through his. "Tell me about what you were like as a boy."

As Talin told me stories of his childhood, the tension between us eased. His chest shook with laughter when he remembered the trouble he got into with his friends, and I found myself laughing along with him, sharing my own misadventures after the incident, when my scar had granted me the freedom to be more reckless.

Underlying everything was Talin's fierce loyalty to his mother, which made me respect him even more. After all, it was my loyalty to Zadie that had brought us together. I would do anything for the people I loved, and so would Talin.

As we held each other, our limbs tangled in the small bed, I wondered if this was what Talin envisioned for our future: long nights spent talking and laughing, sharing feelings and kisses and secret desires. I remembered what Father had said about contentment. In this moment, I thought I knew what that meant. It felt like safety and acceptance, and Thalos knew those were things I'd gone too long without.

But as I listened to Talin's heartbeat slow into sleep and watched the steady rise and fall of his chest, I had the nagging feeling that something was missing. I could envision our nights, but what about our days? Talin would be busy helping rule a kingdom, and where would that leave me? Knitting shawls and gossiping with the ladies at court? The thought made me shudder, and Talin's arms circled tighter around me.

I wriggled until he released me and I could breathe again, but sleep was as elusive as a golden nautilus. I couldn't fight the feeling that maybe Father was right.

Maybe contentment wasn't what I was searching for after all.

5

Exhaustion must have finally claimed me, because I woke in the morning to find Talin wasn't beside me. I could see him through the doorway leading to the balcony, framed by the golds and soft oranges of another perfect sunrise.

I pulled the blanket off the bed and went to join him, wrapping us both in the soft fabric. "It's a beautiful view, isn't it?"

Talin didn't respond, and I glanced up to see his eyes narrowed in concentration. I followed his gaze to a small dot on the horizon.

"Who is that?"

"Your father?" he ventured.

I ran inside to get the bronze spyglass I had salvaged from a shipwreck years ago and hurried back to his side.

"Too large," I said, raising the glass to my eye. "That ship has sails." I handed the spyglass to Talin. "Do you recognize it?"

He lowered the glass and placed a hand on my shoulder. "It's my ship."

I released my breath. "That's good news."

But Talin didn't look convinced. "Is it? They were supposed to wait for my signal, not come on their own."

"Maybe Grig gets more seasick than you thought," I joked, though my stomach was beginning to twist with worry. I went back into the house, where my mother and sister looked at us questioningly. "It's Talin's ship," I explained. "The two of us will take the boat out to meet them. They won't be able to get past the reef."

After Mother and Zadie agreed to stay behind in case Father returned, I rowed us out to the small sailing vessel. When we pulled alongside it, I looked up to see Grig and Osius leaning over the railing, waving.

"Come aboard," Osius called, tossing a rope ladder over the railing. "We have news."

Talin nodded and held the ladder steady for me so I could climb up ahead of him. As soon as I was on board, Grig and Osius bowed, though Grig couldn't hide his smile.

"Enough with the formalities," I said, pulling them both into a hug. They had always looked after me at New Castle, and I was genuinely happy to see them.

"My lady," Osius said, remaining his formal self even as I squeezed him tightly. "I'm glad to see you looking so well."

"And you." I glanced sympathetically at Grig, who had dark circles under his eyes. "Was it a terrible night?"

"I've slept better, my lady. But I'll be fine, just as soon as we return to solid ground." He extended a hand to Talin, who grasped it and stepped up onto the deck next to me.

"We worried when you didn't return yesterday," Osius said. "We were afraid something had happened to you."

Talin clapped him on the back, offering a sympathetic smile. "I'm sorry for worrying you, but I had a much better offer of accommodation for the night. And the company was too good to refuse." He smiled at me, but I caught the strain in his eyes as he turned back to Osius. "Did you just come to check on me, or do you have news?"

Grig looked to Osius, who cleared his throat. "One of the men we paid back at the port was just here. He rowed all night to tell us that Ceren and his men are looking to commandeer a ship."

My blood whooshed in my ears. I had known Ceren might come for us eventually, but I had hoped we'd have more time. I thought of the vision, of the blood staining Ceren's pale lips, and I knew this wasn't about Talin. Revenge could wait; he was coming for me.

"I suggest we leave immediately," Osius added. "While we still have the advantage of time."

"I have to go back!" I blurted. "I promised I wouldn't leave without saying goodbye to Father, and I can't go without telling Zadie."

A muscle ticked in Talin's jaw, but he nodded. "Very well, but we have to move quickly."

"Thank you," I said, squeezing his hand.

"Grig, Osius, you'll wait with the ship." Talin slipped into his role as commander seamlessly. "We'll be back as soon as possible. Be ready to sail when I return."

I rowed us back to Varenia as fast as I could, my mind racing as I thought through what I needed to gather and wondered how quickly we could get back to Talin's ship. In the end, there was really only one thing important enough to bring with me.

"I want my family to come with us," I told Talin.

His brow furrowed in response. "Nor, you saw how small the ship is. It can only carry five or six people safely. Between

the captain and the crew member, Osius, Grig, and me..."
He trailed off as my face began to fall.

I swallowed the lump in my throat. "My mother put on
a brave face for you, but the situation is more dire than you
know. There are babies starving. My father is out there risking his life to provide for us. I may not be able to help the
rest of Varenia, but I can't just leave them to die."

"Nor—"

Talin reached for me, but we were close to my house, and
I leaned away to grab on to a pillar. I rushed up the ladder,
convinced Talin was wrong. My family was small. We'd find
a way to fit.

"What is it?" Zadie asked as I pushed through the trapdoor.

"Ceren's men are close. We have to go to keep them from
coming to Varenia. But..." I looked to my mother, who
bravely lifted her chin without even knowing what I was
about to say. "Is Father back?"

Zadie shook her head. "Not yet."

My heart sank at the realization that I would not be able
to keep my promise to wait for Father. How could I leave
without saying goodbye?

Talin had emerged through the trapdoor behind me, and
he placed his hand gently on my shoulder. "I'm so sorry, but
we have to go."

I looked at him, sure he would change his mind about
bringing my family when he saw the anguish on my face.

"If we take them, we might not be able to outrun Ceren's
ship," he said quietly. "It would put them in even more danger."

Mother stepped closer to me and touched my forearm. "You
should go, Nor. Your father would want you to be safe." She
swallowed thickly. "*I* want you to be safe."

"I can't leave you," I said, my voice breaking.

She nodded. "Yes, you can." Tears streamed down her cheeks for the second time in as many days, and I felt the part of me that had hardened against Mother's cruelty begin to crack. She placed her forehead against mine. "I was wrong to doubt you before. I won't make that mistake again."

Tears welled in my eyes, and before she could stop me, I wrapped my arms around my mother and squeezed her as tight as I could. She hadn't embraced me since I was a child, but slowly, I felt her arms come up around me.

"I'll stay," she said. "And wait for your father. We'll be fine."

I released her and nodded, even though I knew we were both pretending. I could see my fear reflected in her eyes.

I reached for Zadie's hand and bit my lip to keep from sobbing. Leaving my parents was almost too much to bear; I could not go without my sister.

But Zadie's back was straight, her chin set at the same stubborn angle as Mother's, when she looked at Talin and said, "Nor and I together weigh little more than one man. I'm sure you can find room for both of us."

Mother stepped next to her and took a shuddering breath before nodding once.

To his credit, Talin didn't even attempt to argue. "All right."

"It's going to be dangerous," I said to Zadie, though relief coursed through me. "Ceren will come after me."

"I won't lose you again, Nor. Besides, I have to find Sami." She turned to Mother. "Are you sure you'll be all right without us?"

Mother, once again cool and self-possessed, folded her arms across her chest. "Of course we will."

Zadie and I each kissed one of her cheeks, and for a brief moment, she pressed her hand to my face, her finger brushing over my scar. It was the first time she'd touched me there since the incident. A soft sob escaped me as her hand fell away. I hadn't realized how much I'd needed that one simple gesture.

"Nor, please." Talin was already at the trapdoor, holding it open for us.

I nodded and turned away from Mother, afraid that if I looked back, I wouldn't be able to leave. Our relationship would never fully heal, but I was grateful that this time, at least, I had the chance to say goodbye.

As I dropped into the boat next to Zadie, I looked up at the horizon and gasped. Beyond Talin's tiny ship, a much larger ship loomed, and a fear I hadn't felt since I ran from New Castle washed over me.

Ceren's men had arrived.

"How did they get here so fast?" I asked.

"Ceren must have commandeered a galley manned by dozens of oarsmen—and paid handsomely for it," Talin said through gritted teeth as he rowed us toward his vessel. "It's far faster than a sailing ship."

Faster, I thought as I took over the rowing for Talin, but I could tell from its long, low design that the ship was not meant for sailing far out to sea. If they planned to chase us, they would be at a disadvantage, especially if we encountered any large swells.

Fortunately, Talin's men had brought his ship as close as possible, and we reached it quickly. Though I had just been aboard, I hadn't properly taken in how small it really was, a sloop with only one mainsail. Talin was right about one thing: we couldn't have taken any more passengers.

Within minutes of our boarding, the sails had been

trimmed, and we were pulling away from Varenia. I hadn't expected to leave again so soon, and I was filled with a mixture of regret and longing for a place that no longer felt like home. As I turned back to catch a final glimpse of the village, I saw someone emerge from the governor's house. I wished I'd had the chance to explain everything to Sami's parents. Instead, I would forever be a liar in Kristos's and Elidi's eyes. But we would find Sami, and perhaps that would be enough to prove I'd never meant to hurt them.

Osius approached Talin and handed him his spyglass. "You'd better take a look," he said, pointing toward Varenia.

"Damn it," Talin hissed, lowering the glass.

"What's wrong?" I asked. "What did you see?"

Talin handed me the spyglass wordlessly. I raised it and focused on Varenia. A boat containing about a dozen men had left the galley and was heading toward Governor Kristos's house. I focused in on the smaller vessel and gasped when I saw who was at the bow.

As if he'd heard me, Ceren's pale head swiveled toward our ship. Even from this distance, I had the sense that he knew I was watching him. And somehow, even without the spyglass, I had the strange feeling that I would have known he sensed my presence, too.

"Can we go any faster?" Talin shouted to the captain, but he only shook his head.

"Why would he come himself?" Zadie asked, clinging to the railing for support.

I could see that Talin was cursing himself for not leaving Varenia sooner. Any minute, Ceren would return to his ship and come after us, and we might not be able to outrun him.

But, to my surprise, Ceren's small vessel remained where it was, and several more boats had set out from the ship to join his. I was about to raise the glass again when something caught my attention in the corner of my eye. "No," I breathed, my stomach dropping. The Varenian fishing boats were returning.

Heart pounding, I found myself waiting—and suddenly *hoping*—for Ceren's boat to circle back to his ship, but, to my horror, he instead continued moving toward the dock. As he disembarked, I remembered too late that Governor Kristos was with Father, so the figure I'd seen come out of the house could only have been Elidi.

"What is he doing?" I shouted, running along the railing. "Turn us around! We have to go back."

In horror, I watched as several of Ceren's guards disembarked and began striking down Varenians. Moments later, they were herding the villagers into their small boats, as if...

"They're taking the Varenians!" I screamed.

"What?" Zadie ran up beside me. "Why? I thought he was coming for you and Talin."

"So did I." The fishing boats were getting close to Varenia. I groaned, wishing Father and the others would turn away. But of course they wouldn't, not now that they'd seen Elidi and the other Varenians were in danger. I turned to Talin and grabbed him by the front of his tunic. "Please, we have to go back."

Talin looked down at me, a muscle ticking in his jaw. "We can't, Nor. It's too dangerous."

I briefly contemplated wresting the ship's wheel out of the captain's hands before acknowledging that I would be quickly overpowered.

"Please," I cried. Realizing they weren't going to listen to me, I started to peel off my skirt, ready to leap from the ship and swim back to Varenia on my own.

It was Zadie who stopped me. "Nor," she shouted, grabbing my shoulders. "You can't go back. Even if you made it, Ceren would capture you and take you back to New Castle."

The thought made me weak in the knees, and I slid to the floor, bile burning the back of my throat. "But don't you see? He's taking *our parents.* He could throw them in the dungeon, just like he did to me. Gods, he could do even worse things."

Zadie sank down next to me. "We don't know that he has our parents. We have no idea what he's planning. But we can't stop him, not without help." She pulled me against her, cradling my head in her lap. "You did the right thing, Nor."

I shook my head, but she continued to shush me and stroke my hair. "All I've done is put everyone in danger, including you," I said.

"You didn't put me in danger. I chose to come."

I glanced up at her. "But you have no idea what you're getting yourself into."

"I know I'm heading toward Sami, and I'm with you. I also know Mother and Father are stronger than you give them credit for."

How could she be so calm about leaving the Varenians to face Ceren alone?

I studied my sister's hands, browned from the sun and callused from rowing. The village had turned their backs on her, and she had managed to help take care of our family despite severe injuries. She was not the girl she'd been, I reminded myself.

And neither was I.

6

Zadie and I passed the afternoon in silence. I didn't want to speculate on our parents' fate and cause her more worry, and I suspected she felt the same. As the sky grew dark, I glanced up at the stars to orient myself. We were heading northeast, toward the shore. Zadie had fallen asleep, and I rose carefully so as not to wake her, then went in search of Talin.

He stood at the prow, staring into the darkness, but he glanced back at my approach.

"Are we heading to the port?" I asked, stepping up next to him. "Everyone in Ilara will be looking for us."

He sighed heavily. "I know. But what choice do we have?"

He was right. The ship didn't have enough supplies for a long voyage, and anyway, Talin had to get back to his mother. "Where do you plan to look for troops?"

"We'll start in Meradin," he said. "It's well forested and fairly neutral territory. My father did a poor job of ensuring their loyalty, due to their proximity to shore."

"Speaking of loyalty, where is the crew from?" I asked. One man was at the wheel, the other trimming the sail.

"I hired them at the port market."

"Are they trustworthy?"

Talin glanced at the captain from the corner of his eye. "Only as far as they are greedy. I paid them half up front. They'll get the rest when they deliver us safely to shore."

I nodded and rubbed my arms to warm them against the cool night air.

"Are you cold?" He looked past me, to where Grig and Osius stood. "I have a cloak somewhere."

"I'm fine," I lied, not wanting to burden him more. Guilt for leaving my parents and fear for their safety soured my stomach. I glanced at Grig, who was clinging to the railing and trying valiantly not to be sick. I understood how he felt.

"We'll get you some traveling clothes at the market, along with the rest of the supplies we'll need," Talin assured me as Osius approached us.

"Apologies for the interruption, but I was thinking that we'll need to get to the horses right away." He turned to me. "I know you can ride, but what about Zadie?"

"She can't," I said. "She'll have to ride with someone else."

Osius nodded. "She can ride with me, but we'll need another horse, unless you'd prefer to ride with Prince Talin."

"I think I'd prefer my own horse," I admitted, hoping I didn't offend Talin. "Riding double isn't exactly comfortable."

Osius bowed. "Of course, my lady."

Talin and I stood in silence for several minutes, mulling over our own thoughts. "Nor," he said finally. "I'm sorry we couldn't take your family." He chewed the corner of his lip, then added, "I'm sorry we couldn't take *everyone*."

I leaned back against the railing. "I know it was impossible.

And my mother wouldn't have left without Father. But I can't help feeling like I abandoned them to a monster."

He ran his hands through his hair in an attempt to smooth it, but he quickly realized it was hopeless and let his arms fall. "I know, and I am sorry. I had no idea he wanted the Varenians. But even if I'd guessed his plan, we couldn't save them all. Believe me, if it were possible, I would have."

I knew he was telling the truth and that his remorse was genuine. But it didn't make leaving my parents behind any less painful. As much as I didn't want to fall back into Ceren's hands, it was almost more frightening that he hadn't immediately come after us, because now we had no idea what he would do next.

Tentatively, Talin reached toward me. "I promise I'll do everything in my power to make sure my brother never hurts another person again, Nor."

I looked up into his blue eyes and knew he meant it, even if it was a promise he couldn't keep. I placed my hand in his, and he released a sigh before pulling me against his chest. His warmth made me realize how silly I had been, stubbornly refusing his cloak.

"It will be a few more hours till we reach shore," he said. "You should sleep."

"I'd rather stay with you."

He rested his chin on my head. "Good."

Despite my best intentions, I was swaying on my feet within an hour. The nearly sleepless night with Talin, followed by the tumultuous day, had left me exhausted. Talin carried me back to Zadie and settled me next to her, where I slept until I heard the cries of so many birds it could only mean one thing: we had reached the port.

Zadie stirred beside me, her hair a knotted mess, her clothing damp and wrinkled. She pushed to her feet and rubbed the sleep from her eyes.

Grig, Osius, and Talin stood nearby. Talin helped me to my feet, smiling as I blinked blearily at him. At some point, he had draped cloaks over Zadie and me, somehow fastening the clasps without waking us. He pulled the hood up to shade my face, then did the same with his own. "We should be as inconspicuous as possible."

"I'm going to give the captain the rest of the payment," Osius said. He turned and bowed to Zadie. "I don't believe we've been formally introduced, my lady. I'm Osius, former captain of the king's guard and—current status as a wanted man notwithstanding—your humble servant."

She blushed and held out her hand for him to kiss. I couldn't help remembering the moment I had met him and how I'd found the gesture awkward and mildly humiliating. Zadie had always been better suited for this than I had.

Talin nudged me with his elbow as I took his arm. "My lady," he said with a grin. We approached the gangway arm in arm, with Zadie and Osius behind us and a very relieved Grig bringing up the rear.

I had never been to this part of the port before, and it was even more crowded and overwhelming than the market. I turned to Zadie, who was taking her very first steps on land, and my heart clenched at the uncertainty on her face. She had never expected to leave Varenia, not after I went in her place. She had never even wanted to. I recalled my own first steps, which had been overly cautious and unsteady—and I'd been in far more peaceful surroundings.

"You may be ill," I warned.

She smiled weakly. "I remember. Land sickness. But it's worth it to find Sami."

"This way." Talin escorted me away from the docks and into the street. "Our horses are stabled at an inn nearby. Grig will see to them while Osius procures weapons." He turned to Zadie. "Come with us," he said, holding his arm out. "We're going to find you ladies some proper attire."

He steered us through the busy streets, past a dress shop with beautiful silk and lace confections in the window. Zadie stared longingly at them as we passed. When we entered a different store, I watched with amusement as she took in her surroundings, her face falling.

"What are we doing at a men's tailor's shop?"

"We can't ride in gowns," I explained. "We need trousers, boots, and cloaks."

Talin nodded and turned to the shopkeeper, who took in Zadie's and my salt-stained clothing and arched a skeptical brow.

"Here." Talin set a sack of coins onto the counter with a loud clink. "You heard the lady."

The man nodded and immediately sprang forward with his tape measure.

"This is all well and good," Zadie whispered to me as the man inched toward her inseam. "But what about our undergarm— I beg your pardon!" she squeaked.

"Apologies, madam," the man said, hopping backward. "I believe I have everything I need. The ladies are the same size, are they not?"

I nodded.

"Very well. When will you need these by?" The man began to scribble notes on a piece of parchment.

"Within the hour," Talin replied.

The tailor's eyes goggled. "I'm afraid that's impossible, sir."

"Then find whatever you have ready-made that's as close as possible to their size. Perhaps something for a young lad. We are in the greatest of hurries, I'm afraid. I'll pay double for your best quality. We'll be back soon."

With that, Talin strode out, looking every bit the prince he was, as Zadie and I hurried to keep up.

We visited several other stores, purchasing the essentials for a week-long journey, as that was the most we could carry. It took everything I had not to stare slack-jawed at the sights around us. Riaga reminded me of the port market, only it was far, far larger. The streets were wide enough to accommodate two passing carriages, and people in all manner of dress crisscrossed the streets, hardly seeming to notice the horses rushing past them. Zadie gripped my arm as if she was afraid of getting swept up in the current. I didn't blame her.

As promised, within an hour, we were back in the tailor's shop. The man was wiping his bright red face with a handkerchief as a shop boy darted frantically around the cramped space, pulling various items off shelves.

"I believe these will fit," the tailor said with a bow. "Would the ladies like to try them?"

Talin shook his head. "We don't have time, unfortunately. We will take your word for it, sir."

The man looked relieved. "Very well. Shall I wrap them up?"

"No time for that, either." Talin pulled another sack of coins out of his tunic, dropped it on the counter, and asked the boys to gather up the garments. Zadie and I each took a pair of boots in our hands and followed Talin outside, where Grig and Osius waited with the horses and other supplies.

"We need to get out of the city as fast as possible," Osius

said when we joined them. "I saw several of Ceren's guards patrolling the streets. They must be waiting for the ship to come back."

I grabbed Talin's arm. "Wait. We should see the kite seller before we go."

"There's no time—"

I leveled him with my sternest glare. "If you think I'm not going to take every opportunity to search for Sami now that I'm on land, you clearly don't know me at all."

Talin's eyes darted to Osius, who looked like a fish caught in a net.

"Very well," Talin sighed. "Grig, see if you can find out where this kite seller lives."

Within a few minutes, Grig had learned of the kite seller's address from the tailor, who seemed happy to oblige after being paid so handsomely. We made our way to the outskirts of the city, where we stopped in front of a small house set back from the street. There were kites dangling from the eaves on fishing line.

"Nor, Zadie, do you want to go in?" Talin asked. "We'll stay outside and keep watch. Please, be quick."

We nodded and handed our bundles of clothing to Grig and Osius, then made our way up the stone walkway to the front door. As sure as I'd been that the rose and song were a sign, my stomach was twisting itself in knots. If I was wrong, if Sami hadn't made it...

Zadie took my hand and looked at me, and I could see in her eyes she was struggling with her own fear and doubt. I squeezed her hand and knocked on the door.

A moment later, it opened as if on its own. It wasn't until I glanced down that I realized a small girl had opened it.

"Who are you?" she asked, glancing between Zadie and me.

I leaned down to look her in the eye. "I'm a friend of your father's. Is he home?"

She turned and moved into the house without a word, then returned a moment later with a man who looked to be my father's age. "Who are you?" he asked, in the same mildly curious tone as the child.

I blushed, realizing my mistake. "I'm sorry. I believe I know *your* father," I said to the man. "The kite seller?" I added hopefully.

"I see." The man shook his head and motioned for us to follow him inside. "My father is full of surprises lately."

Zadie pressed closer to me, her nervous energy radiating through our linked hands. "What do you mean?" I asked.

He shrugged and held the door wider. "You're the second stranger to show up at our door this month."

7

The kite seller sat at the head of a long rectangular table, his family members clustered behind our chairs. I could feel them pressing in closer, clearly curious about us. There were a dozen of them all told, including seven grandchildren, living in a house not that much larger than my family's home. Yet, somehow, it didn't feel crowded. It felt warm and safe, and I wondered what it would be like to have a place where you could be completely yourself.

"I was wondering when you would come," the kite seller said. His name was Rollo, and he was nearly eighty years old, though he looked as old as Varenia's centenarians. "I know my message wasn't entirely clear, but I had to protect our friend."

"So Sami is alive?" Zadie asked, her face lit up with hope in a way I hadn't seen since I returned.

"He was when I saw him last, but that was weeks ago."

"But he made it to land," I said to Zadie. "That's what we

were most worried about." I turned back to Rollo. "Did he say where he was going?"

Rollo smiled. "I had hoped you might guess from the song."

Of course, I realized suddenly. A song about horses would have come from the place we talked about most as children. "He went to Galeth!"

Rollo patted Zadie's hand. "He was with a Galethian when I saw him last, yes. But I can't say for certain that's where he went."

"Then we'll start by going to Galeth," I said to Zadie. "And if he isn't there, we'll search the entire continent until we find him."

Zadie looked like she didn't know whether to smile or cry. "But...Galeth? Isn't that far away, in the north?"

Rollo nodded. "It is. And you'll need to be very cautious. It's not safe for two young ladies alone on the road, even when the kingdom isn't preparing for war."

"We'll be careful, I promise. Thank you so much for your help." I glanced at Zadie. "We should get on the road as soon as possible."

Rollo stood, and his family members parted to let us cross the room toward the door. "Oh, one more thing." He went to rummage in a trunk for a moment and came back bearing a crimson cloth neatly rolled.

I took it from his outstretched hands. "What is it?"

"It's a Galethian flag. Hold it up when you reach the border, and if you're lucky, you won't be killed on sight."

Zadie and I glanced at each other, our faces mirror images of concern. We had little to go on when it came to Galeth, just the stories Sami had told us growing up, which included the fact that every man, woman, and child was a member of their cavalry. We may share common ancestry with the Galethians, but that didn't mean they would allow me, a wanted criminal, across the border.

"Thank you again," I said as we crossed the threshold. "Not only for helping us, but also for helping Sami. I know it was a risk for you and your family."

The old man smiled. "Samiel has been a good friend to me. He gave me a Varenian pearl when my kites were destroyed in a fire. It saved my family, and I have never forgotten his generosity."

Suddenly, Zadie turned and embraced Rollo, who looked as startled as I was by the gesture. "Thank you," she said. "Thank you for giving me hope."

"Of course, child." He held her at arm's length so he could look into her eyes. "Hope is like a kite. Hold on to it tight enough, and even the fiercest storm can't claim it."

We made our way out of the city, finally stopping once we'd reached the forest. Behind the cover of trees, Grig and Osius laid out all our supplies and made an inventory while Talin, Zadie, and I discussed what we'd learned at Rollo's house.

"Galeth," Talin said, rubbing his chin thoughtfully. "I admit it's not the first place I would have looked for more troops. The Galethians are notorious for refusing to take sides, and it will take days to get there and back. Days we may not have. But so be it."

"What are you saying?" I asked. "That you'll come with us?"

Talin blinked in confusion. "Don't tell me you thought you'd go on your own."

"Of course I did. Zadie and I have to find Sami, but I know

you need to join your mother as quickly as possible. I would never ask you to go north when your destination is the south."

Talin inhaled and slowly released his breath. "I don't know whether to be proud of your resolve or offended that you think I wouldn't help you."

I flashed a guilty smile. "Resolve" was Talin's sweet way of saying "stubborn as a barnacle," as Sami had once called me. We would be far safer with trained soldiers at our side, and gods knew I didn't want to leave Talin. "But you said yourself you have no idea if the Galethians would help you. You can't afford to waste precious time on a chance."

"There's no guarantee that *anyone* will be willing to help us. But if I'm going to attempt to enlist more soldiers, I might as well start with the best cavalry in the world, even if they tend to keep to themselves."

I hugged him so fiercely he staggered backward, then wrapped his arms around me. "Thank you." The kite seller had made it clear that Galeth wasn't safe for outsiders, including Sami. If that was indeed where he'd gone, we had no time to lose. "Zadie and I would have gone on our own if we had to, but I would much rather travel with you alongside us."

He kissed the top of my head. "We should hurry. There's only a few hours of daylight left, and I'd like to make use of it."

"What are we going to do about the Varenians?" Zadie asked me as we headed toward the horses. "I want to know that Sami is safe and well more than anything, but if our parents are also in imminent danger, perhaps we should be trying to help them first."

"I had the same thought," I said. "But if Ceren wanted them dead, he could have killed them in Varenia, or simply cut off all access to fresh water. He took them, which means he has a plan for them." He didn't need them to dive for pearls anymore. Not when he had my blood to make him strong. But whatever he was planning, it didn't seem to involve killing the Varenians. At least not yet.

"Besides," I continued. "We can't help them on our own. We're just going to have to convince the Galethians to help us."

We reached the supplies and gathered clothing to change into behind a stand of trees.

Zadie held up a pair of leather leggings, her nose wrinkled in displeasure. "Are these necessary?"

"Spend one hour in a saddle while wearing a skirt," I said, gesturing to one of the horses, "and you'll realize just how necessary they are."

She poked her toes gingerly into one pant leg. "It doesn't seem proper."

"Forget about being proper, Zadie. We're going to be riding all day, sleeping on the ground, and likely not bathing for a week."

She bit her lip, frowning. "Mother would be horrified."

I was about to remind her that Mother wasn't here, but then I remembered where she likely was, and I held my tongue. "Here," I said, handing her a pair of wool breeches. "These will be more comfortable."

Zadie still looked doubtful, but she managed to smile and took the breeches from me. "Thank you."

I pulled on the leather leggings myself. They were clearly meant for a boy—the fit was off in the thigh and waist—but they would do. I donned one of the shirts, far nicer than any of the clothing we had in Varenia, and a short velvet jacket. The boots were made of soft, supple leather. I tied my hair up in a braided bun, then helped Zadie with the rest of her clothing.

"You look lovely," I assured her. She glanced at me skeptically but didn't argue.

When we were finished, we tied up the rest of our new belongings in tidy bundles and returned to the men.

Talin took in our new attire and smiled approvingly. "Ready?"

I nodded. "Is this my horse?" I walked up to the only one I didn't recognize, a long-legged mare with a shiny coat so dark brown it was nearly black. Talin had brought his gray stallion, Xander, who had faithfully carried me to Zadie just recently.

"She is," Talin said. "Her name is Titania."

Grig patted her on the rump. "A big name for a little horse."

She turned to eye him warily.

"I like it." I took the reins from Talin and stroked Titania's velveteen nose. The only marking on her was a tiny swirl of white fur in the middle of her forehead, but it was hidden by her long forelock. "Where did she come from?"

"The innkeeper said she was left by a traveler who never returned for her. He gave me a good price. She's sound," Grig added, seeing the concern on Talin's face. "But I can't speak to how easy she'll be to ride."

"That sounds promising," I said wryly.

Grig held up his hands. "Apologies, my lady. We were in a hurry."

I gathered the reins and found a large rock to mount from. "I'm sure it will be fine."

"See?" Grig said to Talin.

I flashed a sweet smile. "If not, I'll trade with you."

Grig's posture stiffened, but he nodded in agreement.

When we were all mounted—Zadie sitting behind Osius

with her eyes squeezed shut and her arms wrapped around him so tightly it was a wonder he could breathe—we headed north to the main road through Meradin.

"Shouldn't we stay hidden?" I asked Talin, riding up beside him.

"I would love to, but we'll make terrible time if we don't use the road, and we need to hurry. For Sami's sake, and my mother's. Our best option is to ride as fast as we can for Galeth and pray we can outrun Ceren."

The little mare danced beneath me as we made our way through the trees, her gait light and buoyant. It was clear she was well trained; the slightest touch on the reins and she reacted, almost too much. If I so much as brushed her sides with my heels, she broke into a trot or canter. It was a good thing one of the men hadn't tried to ride her. I doubted they had a light enough touch.

Gently, I patted her neck, whispering words of reassurance in her gracefully curved ears, which flicked toward me in response. Eventually, I relaxed into my seat, and she seemed to get used to the feel of my weight on her back.

Once we reached the road, we rode hard to put as much distance between the port and our party as possible. I was afraid for our parents, for Sami, and for myself, but the exertion of riding gave me something else to think about. There were even brief moments where I forgot why we were fleeing and could concentrate on nothing but the feel of the wind in my hair, the tension in my muscles, and the road ahead.

Despite the potential danger, I couldn't help imagining what it would be like to finally see Galeth. I had dreamed of going there one day, ever since Sami told us the story of the Varenians who had been brave enough to escape and eventually create a society that revolved around horses. Now that I knew how to ride, the idea was even more fascinating.

Which wasn't to say that horses didn't intimidate me; they were enormous and powerful creatures, and it often seemed that our control over them was a mere illusion—a small bar of metal between his teeth was not going to keep Talin's stallion, Xander, from bucking me into the next kingdom if he chose. That was why the idea of a partnership between man and beast was so intriguing. Galethians were not considered masters of their horses but equals.

An hour after sunset, we made camp among the trees. We had seen few people on the road, fortunately. It seemed everyone was hunkering down, preparing for war. We had covered more ground than expected, and the horses were still fresh, as the early autumn weather was ideal for riding.

"You did well," Osius said as he helped Zadie down from his horse's back.

She landed with a small groan. "Really? All I did was hold on."

He smiled, blue-gray eyes crinkling at the corners. I'd always liked Osius. He had been kind to me from the start, though somewhat removed, unlike Grig, who felt like a big brother in some ways. I had noticed a relationship blossoming between Grig and Ebb, my lady's maid, before I left, but I doubted they'd seen each other since. The thought of Ebb, who had been my only friend in New Castle, sent a pang of worry through me. I hoped she was all right.

"You held on well," Osius amended. "Let me help you get settled."

Zadie demurred politely. "You should see to the horse, surely. I'll help make the camp."

She went to clear the campsite of rocks and debris while

I unpacked our saddlebags. If she was experiencing any land sickness, she was doing a remarkably good job of hiding it. I glanced back at Osius, who was still observing my sister, as if he wanted to make sure she was truly all right before he tended to the horses.

"You noticed it, too, then," Talin said, startling me.

"What?"

"I believe your fair sister may have caught the eye of our captain."

I turned to stare at him. "Osius? Impossible. He's all business."

Osius had moved on to the horses, but he stole repeated glances at Zadie, who was gathering firewood.

"Oh dear," I said. "I think you may be right. He does know she's in love with Sami, doesn't he? That's why she's here."

"He knows. And I don't think Osius has any plans to marry. Most members of the king's guard don't."

"If he thinks she's the kind of girl who would betray—"

Talin chuckled and patted my shoulder. "Calm down. He doesn't. I think he's just protective."

"He never behaved that way toward me," I muttered as we walked to the campsite.

Talin smirked. "But you were never really in need of protection."

"Hmph."

"Besides," he added, tucking me against his side, "he knew all along that if anyone was going to attempt to protect you, it was going to be me."

I smiled and kissed his cheek. "I may not need protection, but I am in dire need of a shoulder rub."

"That," he said with a grin, "I can manage."

8

By the fourth day, Zadie had adapted to life on land. She had never been sick to her stomach the way I was, which could have been because I was forced to travel in a closed coach with no access to fresh air. She was always eager to cook when we made camp at night, while I preferred to un-saddle the horses and rub them down. I took particular care with Titania, who had proven herself to be an unusually in-telligent and loyal animal.

"It's unnatural," Grig grumbled, pointing as Titania fol-lowed me around camp, which she had taken to doing in the evenings. I suspected she would have happily slept next to me, though even Talin objected to that. He reasoned that she could roll over in the night and crush me, but I knew it had more to do with the fact that it was our only time to be together. He didn't want to share me, not even with a horse.

"Leave her alone." I held out an apple core to Titania. "She just likes me."

"You wouldn't think anything of it if she were a dog," Osius said to Grig. "Besides, you'd better get used to it. Where we're going, I've heard the horses practically live in the houses."

Zadie lifted her head from the cook fire, eyes wide. "What?"

"It's not true," I assured her. "Is it?" I whispered to Talin. He shrugged. All any of us had to go on were rumors.

"What if they turn us away?" Grig asked, poking at the fire with a stick. "Where will we go then?"

"If I can't find reinforcements in Galeth, I'll join my mother and sister in the south and pray for a miracle. But I would understand if you chose to journey onward." He glanced at me. "All of you."

I was surprised that he was already discussing the possibility of going separate ways. Only a short while ago, he had scoffed at the suggestion that Zadie and I head north alone. Then again, I had closed up like a clam when he mentioned marriage.

"There's no reason to cry storm when the sky is clear," Zadie said, as if sensing my discomfort. "Let us wait and see."

I patted Titania's neck. "I'm going to tie her up for the night with the other horses. Would you help me, Zadie?"

She nodded and hurried to my side.

"What is it?" Zadie asked when we had reached the horses. "Aside from all the obvious answers."

Titania arched her neck and gazed down her long nose at me, as if to say, *Do you really expect me to spend the night with these three again?* I ignored her and tied her lead rope to a branch a short distance from the two geldings and Xander.

Zadie and I had spent very little time together on the journey. She rode with Osius every day while I generally rode next to Talin, unless the road only permitted for single file.

During those solitary times, I was alone with my thoughts, which seemed to be caught in a whirlpool of fear and doubt.

We'd been riding later and later each night, afraid that we were taking longer than we should. There was no way to know if Ceren's guards were following us, or what had become of the Varenians we'd left behind, and every day away I grew less certain that we'd made the right decision by heading north. Then, of course, there was...

"Talin," I responded. "Sometimes I feel as if he truly loves me, and other times I can't tell what he's feeling."

Zadie sat down on a mossy tree stump, leaving enough room for me to join her.

"I imagine he's feeling quite torn, Nor. He cares about you greatly. There is no question in my mind. But he also loves his mother and sister. You can't expect him to choose you over them."

I winced at the suggestion. "No, of course not."

"I think he was trying to give you a way out, so you don't have to make a choice between staying with him or going your own way, either."

I unraveled my braid and combed it out with my fingers. "You're probably right. I'm just feeling insecure."

"That's natural," she said, helping untangle my hair. "I've felt insecure with Sami, too."

"You have?" I gazed at her with wide eyes. We were born only minutes apart (Mother would never tell us who was first, saying it didn't matter; I secretly suspected she'd mixed us up and didn't remember) but Zadie had always seemed wiser and more mature.

"Of course," she said with a soft laugh. "After the scarring, I had no idea if he would marry me. But even before that, when I found out he was betrothed to you, I thought he was fine with that outcome. It was terrible."

I felt selfish for not realizing what that must have been like for her. "I'm so sorry I didn't see it."

She was about to speak when we heard rustling in the brush behind us. I reached for the knife Talin had purchased for me back in the city, which I kept tucked in my boot, and Zadie grabbed hold of a sturdy branch.

"Who's there?" I called into the shadows.

Two strangers stepped out of the darkness.

"What do you want?" I demanded, but the man already had his hands in the air, and the girl looked like she was about to cry.

"We're just looking for shelter for the night." The man was dressed in clothing that had once been fine but looked well-worn from travel. The girl had the same green eyes and brown hair as the man, who had his arm protectively around her shoulders. She couldn't have been over twelve or thirteen.

"What are you doing all the way out here?" I asked. We hadn't passed a town in miles.

"We're on the road, like you. We saw your fire when we were searching for a campsite."

I cursed under my breath. We needed to be more careful when we chose where to camp.

I heard the girl giggle and realized I hadn't been as quiet as I'd intended. "I'm sorry. We don't have any shelter, just our bedrolls." I studied the two of them more carefully. They didn't appear to be carrying any weapons, other than a small knife at the man's waist, which he hadn't reached for. Despite the giggle, the girl was reeling on her feet, utterly exhausted. Talin wouldn't like it, but we couldn't leave them out here to wander in the dark. "You're welcome to join our camp for the night."

The man sighed in relief. "Thank you. We saw the men back there but were afraid to approach them. When we heard your voices, we thought asking you for help might be safe."

"You're safe," Zadie said, reaching for the girl's hand. "Come and meet our friends. One of them is a prince," she whispered.

"I'm Nor," I said to the man. "That's my sister, Zadie."

"I'm Shale. My daughter's name is Ella."

I shook his hand. "It's nice to meet you, Shale."

When we reached the outskirts of the campsite, Talin, Grig, and Osius rose. Their posture was relaxed, but all three men had their hands on the hilts of their swords.

I gave a tight shake of my head to indicate the weapons were unnecessary. I didn't want to frighten Ella. "This is Shale and Ella. They're heading…"

Shale shrugged and waved in the general direction of north.

"Anywhere in particular?" Talin gestured for Shale to take a seat by the fire, though his hand never strayed from his sword. Ella was with Zadie, receiving a bowl of the stew we'd eaten for supper. We wouldn't have any left for breakfast, but we would manage.

"Anywhere the woman king isn't," Shale said. He glanced up as Zadie handed him a bowl of stew and thanked her.

"What do you mean?" I asked before Talin could respond. I didn't need to see his face to know he was offended.

"We're from just south of Linrose Lakes. The uprising has been simmering in the south for years, but we thought we were safe, living as far north as we were. But in the past few weeks, it has become untenable. She started conscripting every able-bodied male between the ages of fifteen and forty. Ella is just thirteen, and my wife is gone." Shale glanced at Ella. "I can't leave her alone."

Talin took a seat, softening a bit. "I'm sure there will be exceptions made for special circumstances."

Shale shook his head. "I'm afraid not. We were told to report for duty one morning, no exceptions. Ella and I ran that night."

I looked across the fire at Talin. He was staring into the flames, his expression unreadable. "Surely you can stop running," I said. "Meradin is neutral territory, and the woman king won't be coming this far north."

"Perhaps. But once we started moving, I wasn't really sure when to stop. We have no other family. It seems as if the entire kingdom is at war, or about to be." He took a few bites of stew, stretching his long legs out in front of him. "What about you? Where are you heading?"

"To Galeth," Talin said, surprising me. I wasn't sure if he would reveal our destination to a stranger.

Shale's forehead wrinkled in confusion. "Is that where you're from?"

"No. We're Ilarean."

Shale looked at Zadie and me. "Not these two."

I smiled. "No, not us."

"Where are you from?" Ella asked Zadie. My sister had always been the more maternal of the two of us, and Ella had gravitated to her like a moth to a lantern.

"We're from a place called Varenia," Zadie told her. "We're refugees, just like you."

"Varenia?" Ella asked. "Where the princesses come from?"

Zadie nodded. "That's right. It's a small village in the middle of the Alathian Sea."

"But you don't really live in the ocean, do you?" Ella

looked at her father for confirmation. He nodded, and she turned back to Zadie, eyes narrowed. "I thought only mermaids lived in the ocean."

Zadie and I chuckled. "Our mother always said my sister is half fish."

"Is that so?" Talin grinned at me, finally relaxing.

I wiggled my feet in the air in front of me. "A quarter fish, at most."

Ella laughed, and in that moment, we were all friends traveling the same road together. As we settled down for the night in our bedrolls, our bellies full of stew, my heart still light with Ella's laughter, I turned to Talin.

"Good night," I said sleepily.

His hands were folded behind his head and he was staring up at the night sky, wide awake. "Good night, Nor."

"What's the matter?" I scooted closer. Osius was standing first watch, and everyone else was already asleep, or close to it.

"I can't stop thinking about what Shale said about my mother." Talin rolled to his side, propping his head on his hand. His cheeks were shadowed with stubble, which made him look older, less like a princeling and more like the fugitive he had become.

"He wasn't talking about your mother," I said gently. "Not really. The people have built this woman king up in their minds. She's become some mythical creature, when in reality she's your four-year-old sister."

"If that's true, it's only because my mother allowed it. Encouraged it."

"I'm sure she felt like she had to. How else would she get people to join her cause?"

Talin stared at me for a few moments, but I knew he wasn't

really seeing me. "Do you think she's actually forcing people to join her army?"

I could see the fear in Talin's eyes, his concern that his mother had become someone he didn't know in the past four years. I shared his apprehension. It was easier for me to believe she had changed, having never known her in the first place. But he didn't need me to add to his worries. He needed my support.

"I think," I said finally, reaching for his hand, "that there are two sides to every story. I'm sure Shale isn't lying, but I also don't believe your mother is behind whatever forced him to flee. She's doing all of this for her own children, after all. She wouldn't be that cruel. No one who raised you could be."

His smile almost reached his eyes. "Thank you. You're probably right. I'm letting my fears get the best of me."

"Understandably." I glanced at the forest around us. The fire had died down, and despite the moonlight, there was something about the trees that made me uneasy. I preferred the wide open skies of Varenia, where it was much more difficult for something to sneak up on you.

Talin smiled and patted the ground next to him. "For warmth."

I only hesitated for a moment. Everyone knew how Talin and I felt about each other. What did it matter if we slept closer to one another?

I dragged my bedroll next to his and tucked myself under his outstretched arm, which started to close around me. When he felt me flinch, he lowered his arm until his hand just rested on my hip.

"What is it?" he asked.

I closed my eyes, not even sure myself why I didn't like the feel of his strong arms around my chest. Gods knew I had, once. "It's nothing."

Within moments, I could feel Talin's breath on the back of my neck, deep and even, and I was glad that my presence calmed him, even if I couldn't relax in his arms. I didn't know what awaited us around the next bend in the road, but our fears had not gotten the best of us yet.

The best was here, in the space between us, soft and warm and safe.

9

The next morning, we left Shale and Ella on the road, wishing them a safe journey. They were on foot, and we couldn't afford to wait for them. I hoped they found a place to settle where they could live in peace. It seemed like such a simple thing to wish for.

The fifth day of our journey was uneventful, though we were all growing weary of the road. While I had developed calluses on my hands from rowing so much in Varenia, they had softened during my time in Ilara, and my palms were raw from gripping the reins. Every morning when I went to saddle Titania, she lowered her head and exhaled heavily through her nostrils, the equine equivalent of a sigh.

On the evening of the sixth day, when by all accounts we should have been close to the Galethian border, Osius pulled out his map of the continent and spread it on a large rock.

"Why is Galeth blank?" I asked, peering over Talin's shoulder at the map. "Surely the mapmaker knows what the geography is like there."

Talin glanced at me with a knowing smile. "Perhaps. But this is an Ilarean map. Whoever commissioned it, probably my grandfather, would have told the mapmaker to leave it blank. It's still a sore spot that the Galethians took that piece of land from us."

"What is it like?"

"I'm not sure," Talin admitted. "But judging by these foothills," he said, gesturing north, "I'd say mountainous."

Grig muttered a curse. "That means it will likely be cold as well."

"The hardier the Galethians are, the better for us," Talin said, patting Grig on the back. "Assuming they'll help us, of course."

We all knew what a big assumption that was, and the closer we grew to Galeth, the more I worried they would refuse. If we came all this way and abandoned our parents to Ceren for nothing, I didn't know how I'd ever forgive myself.

"Do you need any help, my lady?" Osius asked Zadie, who was using a branch to sweep a small clearing for our bedrolls.

She wiped the sweat from her brow, smiling. "No, thank you. We're just about ready."

Zadie had grown used to the trousers and boots, though we both longed for a bath. Even our bodies were changing. I had always been strong from swimming, but this was the first time I was both exercising and getting enough to eat. When I removed my tunic to change into my shift at night, I was shocked to see muscles in my upper abdomen where I had once only seen ribs.

"I'm going to check on the horses one last time before heading to bed," I told the group. Titania and I had developed a bond that even I could tell was unusual. She had taken to kneeling down so I could mount without a boost from Talin or a rock. She anticipated my needs, so I rarely had to signal with my hands or legs. Most of the time, I didn't even need to use my voice or adjust my weight. She was one step ahead of me, the smartest horse any of the men had ever seen.

"There you are." I held out a handful of grass that I'd plucked on my way over. She was perfectly capable of getting her own, but I liked feeding her. She had the softest muzzle, and she never nipped. She lifted her face to mine, blowing softly against my skin, tickling me with her whiskers.

Then, without warning, she swung her body to the side, standing rigid and alert.

"What is it, girl?" I couldn't hear anything but the usual nighttime sounds. The other horses were still munching contentedly on the tall grass, and the birds and insects still chittered.

But I trusted Titania. If she felt something was wrong, I wouldn't ignore her. Reaching for the knife in my boot, I knelt down and crept toward the road. We were far back, having learned our lesson after Shale and Ella found us. Feeling foolish, I pressed my ear to the ground as Osius had taught me, not sure what I was expecting to hear.

I walked back to Titania, who was still straining against her lead. Afraid she would hurt herself, I untied her and started back to camp, when I heard a high-pitched whistle in the distance. It was so quiet I almost wasn't sure if I'd heard it, but Titania's ears were pricked as far forward as they could go, and I knew I hadn't imagined it.

A moment later, I heard another whistle, followed two seconds later by another.

Without me having to ask, Titania knelt down and I scrambled onto her back. My fingers had barely wound themselves in her mane before she took off toward camp. We had been found.

We burst into camp a moment later, nearly knocking Osius off his feet.

"Gods, Nor! What are you doing?" Talin shouted. "You could have hurt someone!"

Breathless, I swung down from Titania's back. "There are riders out there."

His hand flew to his sword hilt. "What? How do you know?"

"I heard them signaling to each other. At least three people."

Zadie was already grabbing our belongings. "How much time?" she asked.

"I don't know. I couldn't tell. I just know they're close."

Talin and I threw our most necessary belongings into our saddlebags and rushed back to the horses. I tried to be as gentle as possible while saddling Titania, but my heart was pounding and my hands were clumsy. Fortunately, she was as solid as a stone, not even flinching when I tightened the girth.

Finally, the sound of hoofbeats on the road reached our ears, unmistakable. There had to be twenty horses, at least. That many people could only mean one thing: Ceren's guards had caught up with us.

"Can we outrun them?" Grig asked.

"We have to try," Talin said with a grunt as he swung into his saddle.

Osius mounted, and Zadie climbed up behind him. Within moments, we were flying through the woods toward the road. Our route would give our pursuers an advantage, but we had no choice. I hoped the fact that they had clearly been riding hard for a while would help make up the difference. We had been making good time, but not at the expense of our horses' health.

I glanced over my shoulder. I still couldn't see the men, but there was no question we were being pursued. "What if the Galethians won't let us cross the border?" I cried.

"Then we're doomed." Talin freed the Galethian flag from his saddlebag, dug his heels into Xander, and surged ahead. The other horses followed.

We'd been galloping for several miles when I glanced back and saw the first rider behind us. They were gaining. It was one of Ceren's guards, clad in black armor with the Ilarean crest—the profile of a young woman inside a heart, with two daggers crossed behind it—on the breastplate. Titania was breathing hard, but only sweating lightly. I could see that the other horses were struggling, though, as the elevation increased. The road was getting worse, too, as if it was rarely used or maintained.

Talin looked back and swore. "Maybe the men and I should turn and fight," he said, lifting the Galethian flag above his head. "You and Zadie could make it at least."

"No! That's out of the question, Talin."

We were winding our way up a mountain pass, and I could see why the Galethians had chosen this as their border. They could funnel anyone attempting to cross through this pass and pick them off from above.

I looked up at the mountains on either side of us. "This is a trap, Talin."

"I know. But not for us, I don't think."

"What makes you say that?"

Talin jerked his head to the left. We were moving so fast

I barely caught a glimpse of the rider among the rocks on a gray horse. She had a crossbow fitted against her shoulder, but she hadn't fired at us.

I risked a glance back just as she loosed the arrow, picking off Ceren's first guard.

"Who are they?" I called to Talin, who was ahead of me now that the road had narrowed.

"Galethians, if I had to guess."

"Why are they helping us?"

"I have no idea, but I'm not going to question it."

Another rider appeared, then a third. Soon, they had filled the road behind us. I stopped Titania and turned her around. Two guards lay dead in the road. I squinted to see if more would come, but only one rider came forward, slowly.

Ceren sat on a pitch-black horse, its coat providing a stark contrast to his pale skin and hair, as did his black armor and that dark metal circlet inset with gems atop his head. The red stones seemed to glow faintly in the moonlight. He looked larger than I remembered, his shoulders broader than his brother's now, and there was color in his cheeks and lips.

He wouldn't come closer. That much was clear. From this angle, I could see the Galethians scattered across the mountain, all clad in gray and mounted on gray horses to blend in with the terrain. At least a dozen crossbows were trained on Ceren.

Talin had ridden ahead and disappeared around a curve in the trail. The Galethians had started to fill in the road behind me, riding backward with their bows still aimed at Ceren's heart. And still he sat impassively below the mountain, staring at me as if to say that he would see me again soon.

Titania snorted and stamped a hoof, breaking the spell, and Ceren turned away, leaving his dead guards behind to rot.

10

The Galethian riders surrounded our party without a word, escorting us the rest of the way up the mountain and down the other side. I was relieved to see that it was not the start of a mountain range, but instead the entrance to a wide valley that stretched as far as I could see, at least in the dark. The Galethians were like ghosts beside us, absolutely silent due to their lack of tack of any kind: no bridles, no saddles. The men and women were all dressed the same, in gray tunics and leather trousers. But though it was clear we were under their guard, they didn't keep their crossbows aimed at us, and I felt safer than I had in ages. Even Ceren didn't dare attack these people.

We crossed the lush valley single file. I could make out the shapes of horses in the dark, grazing. Behind us, on the mountaintop, was a stone fortress, but we were moving away from it. If I squinted, I could make out tiny twinkling lights scattered far ahead of us. Houses on a hillside, from the look of it.

"Where are you taking us?" Talin asked finally.

"To bed," one of the women said, her tone as dry as sun-bleached fish bones.

Talin coughed. "Excuse me?"

A moment later, all of the riders burst out laughing. Even Osius snickered.

The woman responded to Talin when everyone had settled down. "You'll stay in a cottage for the night. It's late, and we're all tired. In the morning we'll take you to the fortress to meet our commander."

"I see," Talin said flatly. I shared his confusion, but I was so delighted by the idea of staying in an actual house that I nearly wept in relief.

Several of the riders broke off as we approached a hillside, apparently returning to their own homes, until the woman who had spoken was the last one to remain. She led us up to the front of a little stone cottage lit with lanterns on the outside. A stone barn stood off to one side.

"You'll sleep here tonight," she said. "There is hay for your horses." She looked at Titania, then me. "Tomorrow you can explain how you ended up with Landrey's horse."

"I— What?"

She ignored the confused look on my face. "My name is Kester, by the way. I'll be back at dawn to collect you."

When she was gone, we all shared incredulous looks and dismounted.

"I don't understand," Zadie said. "Why are they treating us so well?"

Talin shook his head. "My only guess is they saw the flag from the kite seller and decided we must be friends. I suppose we'll have to wait till morning to find out for certain. Nor and I will take the horses. Zadie, if you wouldn't mind seeing if there's anything to eat? Grig, tend to the fire. Osius, make sure the house is secure."

The men nodded and set out to begin their tasks. I led Titania and Osius's gelding toward the barn. It was as tidy and cozy as the cottage itself. I removed Titania's saddle and bridle, patting her damp neck. "Welcome home," I whispered in her ear. "No wonder you're so perfect."

"It does make sense," Talin said, untacking the other horses and leading them into the small stalls. It was the first night the horses had had fresh hay since we left the port, and they all eagerly buried their noses in the piles.

I took a seat on a low bench, stretching my aching legs. "They'll probably make me give her back to this Landrey, won't they?"

"We'll get you another horse."

"Not one like Titania," I pouted. I had never developed a bond with an animal before, and her large, warm presence had become an unexpected reassurance during our journey.

Talin sat next to me and lowered his head into his hands. "I still can't believe my brother came all the way to the Galethian border. I know he despises me, but I didn't think he was foolish enough to abandon New Castle for so long."

After seeing Ceren take the Varenians prisoner, I had believed I was no longer his target. But I couldn't deny that the visions and dreams had taken on a new meaning, now that I knew he had tracked us here. I should have told Talin sooner, but how could I explain something I didn't understand myself?

I took a deep breath and released it heavily. "I don't think your brother came for you."

"You think he came for you? But why…" His furrowed brow rose slowly in understanding. "You mean you still think he wants your blood?"

I nodded.

Talin considered for a moment. "But why does he need more of it? He's healthy, isn't he?"

He had certainly looked healthy, and the fact that he had chased us after capturing the Varenians meant he was stronger than we had imagined. "I don't know. But the day you came to Varenia, when you lost me in the water? I had some kind of vision. I thought it was a dream or a hallucination, but there was blood on Ceren's mouth, and I think... I think he could see me, too."

Talin stared at me for a moment. "I don't understand."

"Neither do I. There was another time, before you arrived in Varenia, when I cut my hand on a splinter, and for a moment I thought Ceren was right there with me. And then I've had nightmares while we've been traveling, and they always seem so real."

He cupped my face in his hand. "Why didn't you tell me about your suspicions, Nor?"

"I thought it was just a result of my experiences in New Castle. I thought it was normal to have nightmares after something like that." And I didn't want to believe that I was somehow linked to the man who had caused me so much pain and suffering.

I was afraid Talin would be angry with me for not telling him—or at least be skeptical about the trustworthiness of potential hallucinations—but he only stroked my cheek with his thumb. "In these...visions—did he seem angry?"

"No. At least, not to the extent I would imagine he would be if he was coming to kill me."

"And you think he saw you, too?"

"Yes. I know it doesn't make sense. I have no idea what he wants from me. But I know that whatever I've been experiencing is more than just nightmares."

Talin took my hand and kissed the back of it. "We're safe for the moment at least." He rose and helped me to my feet. "Let's get some rest and see what the Galethians have to say in the morning. The fact that they helped us cross the border seems like a good sign to me."

I could only hope he was right as I moved on stiff legs back to the house.

Inside the cottage, Grig had a fire going in the stone hearth, and Zadie was making stew with the ingredients she'd found in the pantry. It wasn't much, but it would fill our bellies until morning.

"There's a ewer and pitcher in the bedroom upstairs, Nor," Zadie said as she stirred. When she looked over her shoulder and saw me, she set the spoon aside and wiped her hands on her tunic. "You're exhausted, Nor. Why don't you go wash upstairs? I'll call you when supper is ready."

I thanked her and made my way up the narrow staircase, my knees creaking with every step.

The house was small, with only the single upstairs bedroom, but clean and cozy. The men had generously offered to take the downstairs floor to give Zadie and me a night in a real bed. Everything was decorated in shades of blue, from the wooden nightstand to the ewer and pitcher, reminding me oddly of home, despite the fact that we were miles from the ocean. The bed was made up with a soft quilt that had clearly been sewn by loving hands.

I removed my sweat-stained tunic and trousers, eager to wash myself. By the time I was finished, the water in the bowl was brown from all the dirt on my skin. I started at a light knock on the door, but Zadie's soft voice followed immediately after.

"It's just me."

"Come in," I said, digging in my bag for my last clean shift.

"I thought we might have supper in here." She was carrying a small tray bearing two bowls and spoons, plus a chunk of crusty bread.

"Thank you. Having a meal by ourselves sounds perfect right now."

She held out a comb, offering to brush my hair for me, and I gladly let her. It had grown horribly knotted over our week on the road.

"I think this was Landrey's house," she said as she worked.

"Why?"

"Just a feeling, and the way Kester spoke of Landrey. This house clearly belonged to someone." She stroked the quilt tenderly. "Look how much care went into this."

Selfishly, I wondered again if this meant I would have to give up Titania. "You don't think something happened to Landrey, do you?"

"Possibly. Why else would we be allowed to stay here?"

I ate my stew and bread while Zadie continued to comb my hair, humming a Varenian lullaby as she worked. Normally, her singing calmed me, but I was still shaken up from our encounter with Ceren. Sharing my concerns with Talin made me feel less alone, but it didn't change anything. Was Ceren waiting for us at the border, or would he return to New Castle and take out his anger on the Varenians?

"I would love to live in a house like this someday," Zadie mused, setting the comb aside to braid my hair.

I smiled. "Mother and Father would never live on land, and I'm not sure I like the idea of being surrounded by mountains."

She chuckled. "I meant with Sami. I don't think our husbands would appreciate all of us living together. We'd need a larger house at the very least."

The hair on the back of my neck prickled, but I told myself it was because Zadie's fingers brushed my nape as she worked the comb through some particularly difficult tangles. "Talin and I aren't even engaged."

"Neither are Sami and I. At least not formally. But you will be, someday. And I intend to marry Sami as soon as possible, gods willing."

That had always been the plan, so it shouldn't have surprised me. But with everything we'd been through recently, I hadn't imagined marriage was at the forefront of Zadie's thoughts. "What about our parents?" I asked.

"We're going to save them, Nor," she assured me. "I truly believe that. But I will marry Sami without their blessing, if I have to. I can handle anything with him by my side."

It took me a moment to find my voice. "Of course."

"Nor, that's not what I—"

I set my tray down, finding my appetite had diminished rapidly. "I think I'll go to bed, if that's all right."

She finished my braid and said with forced cheerfulness, "Good idea. We have to be up early." She rose and went to the door. "Do you need anything else? I'll come up to bed as soon as the dishes are put away."

I faked a yawn. "I'm fine. Just tired."

She started to open the door, then turned back to me. "You do know how much I love you, Nor. Don't you?"

"Of course," I said, and I meant it. But I still couldn't stop myself from thinking that Father was right; Zadie, my wise, practical twin sister, knew exactly who she was and what she wanted.

Part of me wished I were as sure about everything as Zadie

was. I wished the idea of marrying and settling down in a cottage like this one sounded appealing. It wasn't that I didn't want to be loved and accepted by others; if anything, I wanted that more than ever. Why else would I have returned to Varenia, if I hadn't believed I might finally belong?

But in this house that Zadie found so cozy, I couldn't fight the feeling that the stone walls were closing in on me, that the roof over my head was a barrier, not protection.

That I may never find a place that truly felt like home.

11

Kester was there at first light, as promised. I had slept like the dead, with not a single nightmare to disturb me, and there was no news of Ceren from the border. But if he wasn't here, he could be anywhere, and somehow that was almost as terrifying.

We filed back across the valley on our horses. It seemed Galeth, or at least the part we'd seen, was designed entirely for travel by horseback. The valley would have taken well over an hour to cross on foot, and there were hitching posts and mounting blocks next to every cottage.

Titania clearly remembered her home. She knew the way without any help on my part, and she seemed more at ease than she ever had on the road. As we made our way up the mountain path to the fortress overlooking the valley on one side and the mountain pass we'd used to escape Ceren on the other, she picked her way daintily around stones and cracks.

"So, how did you come by Landrey's horse?" Kester asked me. "The last time we saw Landrey, she was heading south."

"Talin purchased Titania from an innkeeper in Riaga," I explained. "All they said was that she'd been left there, and no one ever came to claim her."

Kester frowned. "Landrey never would have left her behind. She must have been stolen."

"And Landrey? Is she all right?"

There was a long pause. "I have no idea."

Unease crept over me like crabs scuttling on a rock. "That's whose house we're staying in, isn't it?"

Kester nodded. She was clad in an undyed tunic and black breeches today, riding a chestnut gelding. She looked to be in her mid-forties, with skin weathered by the sun and hair cut short to her chin. "She wouldn't mind," she said, gentler than I would have expected. "Besides, you'll be relocated tonight."

"Relocated?" Talin asked.

"Roan will explain everything," Kester said, ending the conversation.

The fortress was a large stone edifice running along the top of the mountain. It was narrow, with a walkway on top for archers and cannons, and little in the way of living quarters by the look of things. Galethians were posted at intervals on the wall. They weren't mounted, but there were horses stationed at the bottom, ready to deploy if necessary.

A man on the hairiest horse I'd ever seen was waiting for us at the top. He appeared to be a few years older than Talin, with close-cropped auburn hair and piercing brown eyes above a slightly aquiline nose. A scar cut through one eyebrow, adding to his already rugged appearance. "Welcome to Galeth," he said. "I'm Roan. I trust you slept well last night."

He was speaking to all of us, which surprised me. Perhaps it wasn't clear who was in charge.

"We recognized you girls based on your friend Samiel's description," Roan continued. "Without the flag, the rest of you would have been shot on sight."

"Is Sami here?" Zadie looked around eagerly. She had been given her own horse this morning, brought over by Kester, who hadn't seemed to like the idea of her riding double with Osius.

"He's farther north," Roan said. "You'll see him soon."

Zadie deflated a little, and I bristled on her behalf. I didn't like the way Roan seemed to be withholding information. We weren't the enemy.

Talin was similarly frustrated. He dismounted and approached Roan on foot and bowed, no small gesture from a royal. "I'm Prince Talin, second son of the late King Xyrus of Ilara. That was my brother, Ceren, who chased us to the border. He exiled me and—"

Roan held up a hand, cutting him off. "There will be plenty of time for that later, when our council convenes."

"I'm sorry," Talin said. "I was under the impression you were..."

He arched an eyebrow. "The King of Galeth?"

Kester snickered and Roan grinned, but there was no mirth in his eyes. "We don't have a monarchy. We rule by council. I command the cavalry at Fort Crag simply because I am the best rider. Kester is my second-in-command, and she will be taking over while I escort you to our capital, because I also sit on that council."

"Apologies," Talin said, looking chagrined. I wished he wouldn't. Roan didn't strike me as the kind of person who would be impressed by Talin's courtly manners.

"Never mind. We'll get you properly outfitted and set out right away. Just as soon as we find a new mount for the girl." He was staring directly at me.

I stared back. I didn't like this *boy* at all. He was brusque and demanding, and Titania belonged with me. "No."

He tilted his head to the side. "No?"

"Kester said Landrey hasn't returned. We purchased Titania, and she has bonded with me."

His lips twisted in another humorless grin. "If that's the case, she won't let me take her from you."

Titania's dark ears flickered back and forth, listening. "Very well," I said finally. "Come and try."

"Nor." Talin had remounted and stood next to me on Xander, and there was a note of warning in his voice.

"It's fine," I said. "The worst that'll happen is I'll get another horse."

"Something tells me that's not the worst that could happen," Talin muttered from the side of his mouth.

Roan was approaching on his shaggy steed, more mountain goat than horse. I had no idea what to expect. Surely he didn't plan to take Titania from me while I was still mounted?

"Move," Kester commanded, motioning the rest of our party to back up. Talin did so reluctantly.

Roan dismounted, and his horse wandered several feet away, picking at a few scraggly blades of grass that had managed to find sunlight between the rocks. "Titania," he said. Her ears pricked forward immediately. "To me." He made a flicking gesture with his wrist. I could feel her body tense beneath me, but she didn't move.

Roan's eyes narrowed almost imperceptibly. He made the same motion again, but when I didn't respond to the gesture, Titania ignored him, instead scraping at one front leg with her teeth.

"I'm afraid I don't understand what's supposed to happen," I said, scratching absently at my own arm. I couldn't deny I was enjoying this.

Roan frowned. "All our horses are trained to obey their commanders if their riders fall. Landrey was in my unit. Titania should respond to me in her absence." He made another half-hearted flick of his wrist.

"I told you she was bonded to me. We've spent the past week on the road together. She alerted me when Ceren's guards were approaching. She would sleep with me if she could."

"Of course she would. That's what our horses are trained to do on the road."

I had to restrain myself from giving Talin an I-told-you-so smirk.

"Very well," Roan said with a shrug. "You can keep her for the time being, at least until Landrey comes for her. She will never forsake her First Rider."

"I understand." Or at least, I thought I did. But what if Landrey never returned? Would Titania remain mine? I patted her neck, grateful she hadn't gone to Roan. I would have let her go if I had to, but I wasn't sure how I could ride another horse after Titania.

Roan escorted us into a supply room in the base of the fortress, where we were outfitted with Galethian saddles and heavier clothing for cold nights.

"This should fit you," Roan said, handing me a fur vest that looked suspiciously like his horse's coat. Talin and Grig were sifting through weapons with Kester, and Zadie was being taught more of her horse's commands by another Galethian.

I took the vest and rolled it up, tying it to one of the many straps on the high-pommeled Galethian saddle. "Thank you. And thank you for letting me keep Titania for now. She has made this journey far easier than it could have been."

"I didn't let you do anything," he replied, patting Titania's cheek. "She chose for herself." She nuzzled my shoulder, and Roan laughed. "She has good taste."

I shot him a sharp look, but he had already turned away. "I know why your sister is here. She's betrothed to Samiel. But I don't know your story."

"My story?" I flipped through a pile of saddle blankets for something softer. "I don't have a story."

"Everyone has a story." He leaned up against the wall, folding his arms and watching me intently. He had more scars crisscrossing his forearms, and I couldn't help thinking that they would be a source of shame back in Varenia.

"All right, then," I asked, mildly discomfited. "What's yours?"

Roan didn't seem ruffled in the slightest. "I was born and raised in Galeth. I come from the eastern border, where I quickly became the best rider in the region." He wasn't boasting, I realized, just relaying the facts. "When I was ten, I was sent to the capital to train, and at seventeen I became the commander of Fort Crag. I've been there three, nearly four years."

"Ah, that kind of story. Yes, I suppose I do have one of those."

Talin approached before I could continue, his expression curious, though his tone was more suspicious. "Everything all right?"

"Of course," Roan said, pushing off from the wall. "I think we're all set to leave. Aren't we, Nor?"

I ignored him. I'd seen this kind of male posturing between

Talin and Ceren back in New Castle, and I knew that my participation had very little to do with it. We all mounted, and I was happy to find that Zadie's gelding got along well with Titania. It seemed a bit of a risk having a mare in the group, but Xander was a well-trained stallion and Titania was not the kind of mare to put up with unwanted attention. The other horses were all geldings and posed no competition to Xander.

We rode back across the valley, over the foothills where we'd spent the night, and into a small mountain range that fortunately didn't ever seem to grow to its full potential. Roan was the only Galethian to accompany us, and our numbers were even now, with four men and two women. We rode two abreast for most of the day, but Titania often seemed to gravitate to Roan's gelding, to my frustration.

"Are you feeding her treats when I'm not looking?" I blurted at one point. We were making our way through a dry riverbed, and Titania hung back as if deliberately waiting.

"She knows Duster, that's all," Roan explained. "Landrey and I were lovers."

My cheeks reddened instantly at his frank declaration, but I forced myself not to look away. He was obviously trying to shock me.

I could hear him chuckling, and my embarrassment was quickly replaced with annoyance. I tried to kick Titania forward, but she only flicked her ears back at me.

"You wouldn't like it if someone was thumping you in the rib cage either, Nor."

"Fine." I dropped my reins and folded my arms across my chest. "So, you and Landrey were *lovers*. You don't seem particularly concerned for her."

"Landrey can take care of herself. She was going to be made commander of Fort Blight before she left."

I wrinkled my nose. "Your forts certainly have charming names."

"We're not trying to attract visitors," Roan said dryly.

"Why was Landrey in Riaga?" I asked, sensing there was very little that offended Roan.

"I'm not sure. To trade, maybe. We sell our leather goods there, but she could have been hoping to buy something, or learn more about the situation in Ilara. We don't get a lot of information this far north. At least not until Samiel arrived."

"Is he all right?" I asked. "My sister has—"

"He's fine. We would have told you if he wasn't."

I glared at him. "You haven't told us much of anything."

"We don't even know you," he said. "You're lucky we let you in at all. We rarely allow strangers across our border."

"You let Sami in." I turned to look at him. His profile was as chiseled as a rock face. "Why?"

"He was brought by one of our men. Sami knew more about King Xyrus and the Ilareans than we ever could, and we knew he'd be killed if he remained in Ilara."

He hadn't said that Sami was free, but at least he was safe. "Thank you."

Roan turned his dark eyes on me, his gaze disturbingly hawklike. "For what?"

"For letting us across the border, and for protecting us."

He nodded. "You and your sister are welcome in Galeth. Talin and the Ilarean guards will have to face the council."

I was about to say something in Talin's defense but bit my lip at Roan's hard expression. My pleas on his behalf were worthless.

"Are you lovers?"

I turned back to face Roan, only to find he was looking ahead at the trail again. "Wh-what?" I sputtered.

"You and Talin. I thought I detected something between you, but perhaps I read the signals wrong."

I was so flustered it took me a moment to find words. Of course there was something between us, but it wasn't defined. And whether or not we were lovers was none of Roan's business. "No. I mean yes. You're wrong."

He arched an eyebrow and laughed before clucking lightly to Duster. "Come on. We have a lot of ground to cover before nightfall."

We reached a large rustic cabin just before dark. I had spent the rest of the ride next to Zadie, avoiding Roan's amused glance. I had the feeling that whatever he meant by *lovers* was not the same thing I did. Or at least, it was not considered taboo or forbidden before marriage the way it was in Varenia and Ilara. Yes, Talin and I had kissed and slept side by side, but we hadn't done anything beyond that. He had made it clear he wouldn't until we were wed, and considering we hadn't been alone together in days, romance was the last thing on my mind. Or had been, until now.

After leaving the horses in a stable stocked with hay and grain, we entered the log cabin. It was enormous inside, with a massive fireplace and a dozen small beds lined up against one wall. There were cupboards full of supplies and even a large metal tub for bathing, though I noticed it lacked any kind of privacy.

"These cabins are all over Galeth," Roan explained as we unpacked our bags. "Travelers can stay here whenever they wish. The idea is to replace the supplies you use the next time you pass through."

"And it's safe?" Grig peered around the open space, as if someone might be lurking in the shadows.

Roan puffed out a sardonic laugh. "Of course."

"Everyone in Galeth is good and honest?" I asked skeptically. "There are no bandits or robbers in the entire country?"

"I wouldn't say that." Roan pulled off his boots and sat down on one of the beds. I noted the location so I could pick one as far away as possible. "But there isn't much worth stealing. And if they need something that badly, none of us would deny them anyway."

I remembered what the kite seller and Talin had said about women traveling alone in Ilara. But in Galeth, where the women seemed just as capable as the men, I wondered if that was still a concern. If I had been trained to ride and fight from birth, things at New Castle might have gone very differently. "That's nice," I said, eliciting a strange look from Talin. "I only mean it's nice that you help each other." In Varenia, we had always looked after family, but everyone else was competition for dwindling resources.

Roan nodded and rose to his feet. "Right. I'll get the supper started. Zadie, Nor, do you want to get us some firewood? It looks like the stock is a little low. You boys can help me."

Talin, Osius, and Grig blinked at Roan as if he'd just spoken a foreign language. Grig, who had helped Zadie cook during our journey, moved toward the kitchen, but Osius shook his head.

"It's dark out, and we're in a foreign land. The ladies should stay inside while we get the firewood."

"The *ladies* look perfectly capable to me," Roan said. Talin's cheeks turned a shade I'd never seen before, and I grabbed Zadie's hand and hurried out before he exploded.

"What was that all about?" Zadie asked when we reached the side of the house where the firewood was stacked.

"I have no idea. Roan asked if Talin and I were..." I trailed off, embarrassed. Zadie and I hadn't ever talked about this before.

"If you were what?" she asked.

"Lovers," I muttered.

"Lovers? As in, if you aren't, then he'd like you to be his?" Her eyebrows had risen to her hairline. "That was brazen of him."

I twisted my lips to the side. "Maybe? Although I suspect that's perfectly normal here. I suppose we shouldn't assume that customs are the same as what we're used to everywhere."

"I suppose not," Zadie said, clearly lost in thought.

I nodded for her to step farther from the house with me. "What about you and Sami?" I asked. "Are you...you know?" It felt like something I should know about my own twin, but things had changed since I'd left, as Zadie often reminded me.

She smiled, blushing. "We're not ready for a child, if that's what you're asking. But we've done other things."

"Where? How?"

She shrugged. "The boat."

"Zadie!" I nearly dropped the wood I was gathering. "Weren't you afraid that Mother would find out?" Mother had always made it clear that our "virtue" was one of the considerations for being the chosen girl, and even after, that it was to be saved for marriage.

"Nor, after everything that Sami and I have been through in the past few months, I'm not afraid of anything anymore. As soon as I have him in my arms again, I don't plan to ever let go."

I flushed and stared at my sister with new eyes. "I see."

She started toward the log cabin, glancing once over her shoulder at me with a knowing smile that only made me blush harder. "You don't yet. But you will soon enough."

I stared after her, wondering what exactly she meant. Did she assume that Talin and I were headed down the same path she and Sami were on? Did Talin? Before I left Varenia the first time, I hadn't given much thought to my future there. My daydreams were all about the world beyond my village. And since then, I hadn't dreamed about anything beyond a secure future for the people I loved.

I hefted the wood in my arms and told myself there was no point in speculating about my own future. After all, I'd spent years imagining Ilara, and look how wrong I'd turned out to be. But something about our conversation nagged at me as I made my way back to the cabin.

How could Zadie and Talin know where I was headed, if I didn't even know myself?

12

Leesbrook, the capital of Galeth, was located in the center of the country. We traveled along acres of farmland with rich, dark soil, worked by heavy draft horses and their owners, who waved to us as we passed. I noticed that all of the roads were far softer and better maintained than any I'd seen before, which Roan explained was an initiative to protect the horses' feet. Their manure was also used to fertilize the pastures, which in turn grew the lush green grass that became the hay they ate. There were herds of free-roaming horses in the mountains, but here they were pastured, to protect the soil from their hooves.

We entered Leesbrook in the late afternoon. It was clearly the hub of commerce in Galeth; the streets were wide enough for carriages and lined with shops of all kinds. Horses were tied to hitching posts up and down the street. Young boys and girls waited with shovels and pails, charging a nickel a pile.

They heaped the manure onto wagons that carried it out to the countryside for fertilizer.

"The council meets at nightfall," Roan told us as we wound through the city streets toward a timber inn. "These are your lodgings. I'll come for you when it's time."

He left without a backward glance, disappearing among the crowds. A girl ran out to take our horses to the stables, collecting a coin from Talin that she tested with her teeth before pocketing.

Inside, the inn was dark and smoky, and I was glad when we were shown immediately to our rooms upstairs. Zadie and I were down the hall from the men, and I was grateful for the time alone with my sister.

"I can't believe I'm going to see Sami soon," she said, instantly stripping out of her riding clothing and searching in her bag for the one gown Talin had permitted us each to purchase in Riaga. "Help me change, would you?"

"We have hours." I sat down on the bed with a sigh. Last night I had been so relieved to be safe, and so exhausted from the road, that my fear for our parents had eased a little. But I was growing restless. "We're wasting time. We don't even know what's happening in Ilara. I hate that they don't get any news this far north."

Zadie seemed hardly to hear me, so I continued to think out loud.

"And I'm worried about this council. Roan said Talin, Osius, and Grig would have to face them, as if they're on trial or something."

Zadie held her gown up in front of the mirror, twisting back and forth. "They allowed Sami to stay."

"Did they allow it?" I couldn't keep the edge out of my voice.

"Or is he being forced to stay? Besides, Sami isn't Ilarean. And he's not a prince."

She came to sit next to me in her shift. "Try not to fret. Roan seems like a fair leader."

"He's not a leader. Not the only leader, anyway. These people aren't at all bothered with what happens outside their borders. It seems impossible they'll agree to help us."

"A few days ago, it would have seemed impossible that we would even make it to Galeth, Nor. But we're here, and we're safe."

Maybe we were safe, for the moment. And I knew it was a miracle that Sami had survived and we would get to see him soon. But that was only one battle in a looming war. We had no idea what was happening to our parents, and every day here was undoubtedly another day of suffering for them.

I startled at a knock on the door. "It's Talin. May I come in?"

"Just a moment." Zadie snatched her cloak off the bed and wrapped it around herself, then called Talin in.

He peeked gingerly around the door. "I'm sorry to disturb you. I was going to find something to eat. I thought you might like to join me."

"I'm too anxious to eat," Zadie said. "I'm going to see about a bath. But you go, Nor. Bring something back for me."

I pressed a quick kiss to her cheek before following Talin into the hall. "Where are we really going?" I asked once we were outside. I was fairly certain we could have gotten a meal at the inn if he was that hungry.

He smiled at me. "You know me too well. I just wanted to get the lay of the land. I don't like that we've been completely at the mercy of the Galethians since we arrived." He took my hand and brought it to his lips, kissing the back of it. "And I wanted to spend some time with you."

I was filthy from the road and full of anxious jitters, but Talin's calm demeanor helped ease my mind. "I'm glad you came," I said. "I needed the distraction."

"Good. So," he said, swinging our hands between us, "what do you make of Galeth so far?"

I glanced around the bustling street, hoping Talin was keeping track of our progress, since I hadn't been. Leesbrook was just as overwhelming as Riaga, and I wasn't sure I'd be able to find my way back to the inn on my own. "I don't know yet how I feel about this city, but I like certain things about Galeth."

"Hm?"

"The way women seem to have so much freedom, for example."

When Talin didn't respond, I turned to see his expression. He was looking at me, one eyebrow raised.

"What?"

"Did Roan say something to you?" he asked.

My scar tingled as my cheeks heated. "About what?"

"About us."

I glanced away. "What about us?"

"If we were betrothed. I noticed the way he looks at you. Not that I can say I blame him."

I stopped in front of a shop selling gloves, but these gloves appeared specially designed for riding, unlike the knit gloves I'd seen in New Castle, or the fine ladies' gloves in the shop windows of Riaga. "He asked if we were lovers," I admitted, though my face was threatening to melt off from embarrassment.

I was slightly appeased when Talin spluttered the way I had at the question.

"I told him we weren't, of course," I continued.

There was another long pause. "Oh."

I turned toward him. "What was I supposed to say?"

His eyes were fixed on the display in the shop window. "Nothing. He shouldn't have asked you such a personal question. I just worry you gave him the impression that we aren't attached in any way."

I had grown used to seeing Talin with a beard on the road, but he had shaved at the stone cottage, and with his smooth cheeks and tousled hair falling over his forehead, he seemed younger, more vulnerable.

"I didn't mean to hurt you," I said, stepping closer to him. "But we aren't attached. Not formally, at least. And you made it clear on the road that your priority is restoring the throne."

"Nor—"

"I understand," I said, taking his hand and forcing him to look at me. My heart still stuttered in my chest every time his eyes met mine. It seemed quite possible he would always have that effect on me. "My priority is helping my family, too. And I don't want either of us to feel beholden to anything. Not when there's still so much uncertainty."

For a moment I thought he might try to argue with me. A part of me hoped he would. But he only nodded and turned back to the street. "Let's find something to eat," he said. "I really am starving."

I spent the rest of the day wondering what I should have said differently to Talin. I didn't want him to think I was pulling away from him because I was interested in Roan or my feelings had waned. But maybe it was easier to let him believe that than try to explain that I wasn't sure yet what I wanted, that his vision of our future together might not match mine.

I helped Zadie brush out her long, dark hair, which hung in shining waves to the small of her back, and laced her into the corset of her new dress. It wasn't nearly as fine as the gowns I'd worn at New Castle, the silks and taffetas and rich velvets that had felt more like shiny cages than clothing. But aside from the pink gown she'd worn for the choosing ceremony, it was the finest garment she'd ever owned, and she looked lovely.

I was not in the mood for corsets and lace. I chose a pair of black leather leggings and a black tunic with embroidery along the cuffs and collar, as well as the fur vest from Roan. Zadie helped me fashion my hair into a braided crown.

"Are you sure you wouldn't rather wear that?" She glanced wistfully at the gown Talin had purchased for me. It was simple, like Zadie's, made of moss-green velvet, with only a bit of delicate lace at the cuffs and collar.

But while Zadie's thoughts were on Sami, I knew that we had a battle ahead in convincing the Galethians to join our cause. This wasn't the time for delicacy.

Roan came for us at nightfall, as promised, and we followed him on horseback through Leesbrook until the shops began to dwindle and the bustling crowds thinned. The houses were larger and freestanding, with lush pastures surrounding them. A herd of beautiful black-and-white horses with flowing manes and shaggy fetlocks galloped along the road, following us.

"Who lives out here?" I asked Roan, who had once again found his place beside me. He had changed into a sleeveless leather jacket with buckles down the front over a clean tunic.

"Trainers, instructors, and veterinarians, mostly. They need larger facilities to accommodate the horses."

"I see." I wasn't sure I did, and I definitely didn't know what a veterinarian was, but I didn't like admitting my ignorance to Roan. "Why are horses so important to Galethians?" I asked after a few moments of silence, my curiosity getting the better of me.

He shrugged. "The Varenians who escaped all those generations ago never would have made it here without the stolen horses. And they couldn't have cultivated this land without them, either. The reason Galeth was easy to take was because no one wanted it. The soil was rocky, the mountains difficult to cross, the valleys vast, and the winters harsh. Without our horses, life would have been unsustainable."

"But surely once you'd tamed the land, you could have given up the horses. Or at least not maintained such a reliance on them."

He was riding Duster bareback, and he leaned back until he was lying on the horse's wide rump, staring up at the stars. The shaggy horse didn't even flinch. Roan had explained that they only used saddles on their horses when necessary—on rough terrain, for example, when a rider needed better control, or to help carry gear. "I don't see this as a reliance, Nor. Duster is my partner. I take care of him, and he takes care of me. I would no sooner 'give him up' than you would give up your sister."

"You're comparing my sister to a horse?" I asked, though I wasn't really offended. I could see he genuinely loved Duster.

"Well, she's much prettier than a horse." He rose to a sitting position without using his arms for balance or support. His abdomen must be solid muscle, I mused, then blushed at the image. "But I don't have any siblings, so perhaps it's not a fair comparison."

"No brothers or sisters?"

"No. None that made it past infancy, anyhow."

His self-assuredness made more sense, knowing he'd never had a sibling to put him in his place. "And your parents?"

"They're still in the east. I haven't seen them in years, but we write every now and then. Yours?"

"Ceren came to our village as we made our escape. I thought he would follow me and leave our people alone, but he appeared to be taking them prisoner. I can only assume my parents are at New Castle. As soon as we get Sami back, I'm going to find them."

I hadn't realized I intended to go directly to New Castle until I said it out loud. But I knew in my heart it was right. We had lost enough time as it was, and while I couldn't help Talin and his mother win this war, I could at least make sure my parents were alive. Traveling with a large party would attract notice, but alone, I might be able to slip away.

Roan's expression hardened, something I hadn't thought possible. "Why didn't you tell me sooner?"

"You wanted to wait until we were in front of the council," I said, my eyes meeting his.

"I'm sorry. I didn't realize what was at stake. Sami didn't say."

"Sami doesn't know."

Roan swallowed but didn't respond. It was the first time I'd seen him look uncomfortable, and part of me was glad I'd finally managed to unnerve him. I barely squeezed Titania with my knees, and she trotted ahead to where Talin rode with Osius and Grig.

"Everything all right, my lady?" Osius asked.

"Fine," I lied. I forced my eyes on the road ahead, rather

than glancing back at Roan. I wasn't even annoyed with him; I was angry with myself for not keeping my focus where it mattered most. "I just hope we're not too late."

The council meetinghouse looked like a fortress, complete with a moat and drawbridge. This was where the leaders from every outpost convened, and the building was built to be the last stronghold of Galeth in the event of an invasion.

The council consisted of eleven people, six women and five men. They ranged in age from eighteen to sixty. Since riding ability was the main determining factor in being chosen as a councilmember, most members were on the younger side, but at twenty, Roan was still one of the youngest members.

The moment we entered the meeting room, Zadie let out a shriek and flew to Sami before I'd even spotted him.

"Samiel," she gasped, falling into his arms. He caught her instantly, gripping her to him with such intensity I was afraid he might hurt her. But she was weeping tears of pure elation.

The rest of the councilmembers watched their reunion with no hint of sympathy or interest. Something told me these kinds of emotional displays weren't common in Galeth.

Fortunately, Roan broke the awkward silence. "Councilmembers, I've brought our newest arrivals from Ilara." He introduced us one by one. "Zadie is Samiel's betrothed, as you can probably tell."

A few members chuckled, but most remained impassive. Zadie and Sami turned to face the rest of the room, sheepishly straightening their hair and clothing.

I ignored the strangers and walked to Sami, pulling him into a hug. "I'm so glad you're all right," I said against his chest. He was dressed like a Galethian, but he was the same

Sami I'd always known, with his perfect smile and messy brown hair. "We've missed you."

"Thalos, I'm so happy to see you." He nodded past my shoulder to Talin and the others. "I wasn't sure I'd ever see you again."

"I know the feeling. Have they treated you well?" I asked quietly. Zadie was stuck to his side like a barnacle, her vow to never let him go already well under way.

"They've been incredibly generous, given the circumstances." He took in Grig's, Osius's, and Talin's hard expressions and lowered his voice. "Why do I get the impression your reception has been less friendly?"

"We'll talk later," I said. "We should probably sit down."

There were only seats for the councilmembers at the table, but there was a row of chairs against one wall for the rest of us. We sat down like dutiful children awaiting punishment. I could tell Talin didn't like being treated this way, but he wisely kept his mouth shut.

"Thank you, Roan, for bringing the Ilareans to us," one of the women said. She had a shorn head, save a two-inch long strip of red hair down the middle. "I trust they didn't give you too much trouble."

"Not too much," he said, then had the nerve to glance at me.

The woman gave a satisfied nod. "Good. And Ceren?"

"He turned away at the border, once we killed two of his guards. He sent another later that night, but we captured him quite easily."

"What?" Talin and I exclaimed in unison.

"Why didn't you tell us?" Talin asked.

"Because we captured him," Roan said.

"Alive?"

Roan turned to him, a disgusted look on his face. "I don't consider it capture if the prisoner is dead. Do you?"

"I would like the opportunity to question him." There was a deadly calm in Talin's voice that even I didn't recognize.

"Considering you're a prisoner here yourself," the woman said, "I hardly think that would be appropriate."

At that, Osius and Grig both placed their hands on the hilts of their swords and rose to their feet. "I'd ask you to mind your tongue when speaking to Prince Talin of Ilara," Osius rumbled.

The woman scowled. "He's no prince in Galeth."

Roan held up a hand. "I don't believe they mean us any harm, Yana. Nor believes Ceren has captured the Varenians, and Talin is clearly their ally."

"Nor?" Yana asked, arching one red brow.

I rose and stepped forward. "I'm Nor. Zadie's sister, and Samiel's friend."

"Ah yes, one of the twins we've heard so much about." Yana gestured me forward. For a society that didn't have leaders, she certainly seemed to do a lot of the talking. "Explain."

Zadie held Sami as I told the council about Ceren's attack on Varenia, but I could see him trembling with rage from the corner of my eye.

"What does Ceren want with the Varenians?" Yana asked.

Talin and I exchanged a glance, and he nodded for me to answer. "We're not sure," I admitted. "It could be he's holding them hostage to get to me."

"And what would the King of Ilara want with a girl like you?"

I hesitated. I wasn't sure if I should tell them about my blood. I didn't even know for certain that was what Ceren wanted. Talin had believed me about the visions, but these people didn't even know me.

"Ceren was betrothed to Nor," Talin said. "Nor tried to kill him. He wants revenge."

Yana looked to Roan. "A pity, then, that he didn't take her at the border. We could have washed our hands of this matter."

Yana's cold detachment made it hard to take her words personally, but I could see that Talin's composure was slipping. "*This matter* involves everyone," he ground out. "It would be very dangerous for all of us if Nor were to fall into Ceren's hands."

I gently touched his arm to calm him, silently reminding him that he was hoping to enlist the help of the Galethians, though I had to admit that seemed unlikely.

"In the meantime," Yana continued as if Talin hadn't spoken, "we must decide what to do with the men."

A chill crept over my scalp and I pressed closer to Talin. They had referred to him as their prisoner, after all, and I had no idea what Galethian treatment of prisoners was like.

"You," Yana said to Talin. "Ceren is your brother, correct?"

"My half brother, yes. We share a father, the late King Xyrus."

"And Ceren is king now?"

"He believes he is. The rightful ruler is my mother, Queen Talia, whom Ceren tried to murder four years ago. She survived and gave birth to my sister, Zoi, who will be ruler of Ilara when she comes of age. Ilarean succession runs through female lines, or did, before the males began killing off the female heirs."

This caused quite a stir, and I felt a swelling of pride. Talin was the only male Ilarean royal who had dared to admit this for hundreds of years.

"Are you sure?" another councilmember asked. "Is there proof?"

"My mother is proof," Talin said. "As for the murdered female heirs, no, I can't prove that. Not yet, anyhow. But there is no denying that my sister is the rightful heir."

"Why are you here?" It was the eldest councilmember who spoke, a gray-haired man who looked to be in his forties, though Roan had told us he was sixty-three.

"To find Samiel," Zadie said, the first time she'd spoken since the meeting began.

The man turned to her. "I know that's why you're here, and I respect that you came for your man. Rest assured, he is not a prisoner. But I'm talking about the princeling and his guards. They want something from us. And I can almost assure them they aren't going to get it."

I knew Talin wanted to ask for the Galethians' help, but it was clear to me that this wasn't the time. He would be swiftly denied—and potentially kicked out of Galeth. As far as we knew, Ceren had guards waiting for us just outside the border. Talin needed more time to make them understand the severity of the situation.

Talin cleared his throat "We want—"

"To stay in Galeth," I blurted, cutting him off. Everyone in the room turned to stare at me.

"What?" Talin asked, along with the old man and several of the other councilmembers. I could feel Roan's eyes on me, and I had a very annoying feeling he was smirking.

"We've had a difficult journey," I began, "and our horses need rest before we can ride out again." I figured if the Galethians would respond to anything, it was the welfare of our mounts. "If Ceren took the Varenians to New Castle, we will need a strategy to rescue them," I added, glancing at Sami. "Varenians aren't legally allowed on land, and Talin and his men are fugitives. Ceren was pursuing them as much as me. We are so grateful that you allowed us to cross your border to safety. All we're asking for is a day or two to figure out our next move."

Yana and Roan exchanged a glance.

"Leave us," Yana said. "The council will vote. We'll call you back in when we've made our decision."

I breathed a sigh of relief and hurried out of the room, the rest of our group on my heels. When we'd reached the little antechamber, Talin and Sami rounded on me.

Talin's feathers weren't easily ruffled, but it was clear I had angered him in the meeting. "We can't stay here, Nor. You know that."

"Our families are likely suffering," Sami added. "Have you gone mad?"

"Quiet!" Zadie cried, silencing both of them. "Can't you see that Nor was buying us time? Those councilmembers despise royalty, Talin. They were going to escort you straight to the border, where Ceren's guards are probably circling like sharks at a chum bucket. And, Sami, I know you want to help our families, but Ceren has men all over Ilara hunting for Nor. The moment they spot us, we'll be captured or killed, and what good will we be then? We need a plan, and time to get the Galethians on our side. Honestly. Think!"

I mouthed a thank-you to Zadie as the men sat down on a bench and stared at their boots, shamefaced. A few minutes later, Roan appeared at the entrance to the hallway and waved us back toward the meeting room. His expression was so stony I was sure we were about to be told this was our last night in Galeth.

The councilmembers rose in unison when we entered, but

Yana was the one to speak. "The vote was six to five. Personally, I voted against it. I think you'll bring us nothing but trouble, and we have no good reason to allow this. It's certainly never been done before in the history of our people, and I don't see why we should start with you."

"Yana," Roan said under his breath.

"Oh, very well," she growled. "Congratulations, outsiders. And welcome to Galeth."

13

As the council broke up for the night, Roan led us back into Leesbrook. "Yana seems to think I'm responsible for you lot," he said. "First we're going to get some ale, and then I'm going to explain what your life in Galeth will look like for the time being."

I was grateful we would have more time to formulate a plan, but I had the distinct impression that we weren't going to be able to convince the Galethians to help us in the next couple of days, if at all. I also knew that my idea to escape alone and look for my parents was flawed, potentially fatally so. I told myself I would give it three days. After that, I would leave no matter what.

We entered the inn together, receiving strange looks from some of the other patrons, until they saw Roan and nodded in recognition. Physically, Galethians were as diverse in appearance as Varenians, but there was something about us that marked us as outsiders. Probably the way we clung to Roan like whale calves to their mother.

He pointed to a table in the corner and went off to get us a pitcher of ale, trusting us to manage without him for a few minutes.

"I hope you know what you're doing," Talin whispered to me as we sat down.

"I'm improvising," I whispered back. "Besides, I didn't see anyone else coming up with a better idea."

"Here we are." Roan set the pitcher down between us and passed out a half dozen cups that looked disturbingly like horse hooves. "Help yourselves to the ale. It's on me." He took a long swig, wiped his mouth with the back of his hand, and settled into his chair like he hadn't a care in the world.

"Now then. Talin, Osius, and Grig: you're military men and strong riders. I want you to join me at Fort Crag. I could use the help now that we know this Ceren fellow might be paying extra attention to our border. If you agree, you'll be given the same living quarters as the rest of my riders. No special treatment, just a bed in a barracks and two hot meals a day."

Osius and Grig nodded. They were used to that kind of living, but they wouldn't speak until their leader did.

"What about the others?" Talin asked.

"I'm getting there." Roan took another swig of ale, taking obvious pleasure in dragging this out. "Samiel can sort things out with Hoff, since they made an arrangement when he came."

I glanced questioningly at Sami. "Who's Hoff?"

"When I first reached land after I was banished, I met a Galethian at the port market," Sami explained. "He saw me hiding in an alley, clearly suffering, and bought me a meal.

It was a risk, trusting him, but I was desperate. After he heard my story, he offered to bring me to Galeth, knowing I couldn't stay in Ilara. He found me a job with Hoff, the eldest member of the council."

There was a sadness in Sami's brown eyes I didn't recognize. He turned to Zadie, gripping her hands tightly in his. "I'm so sorry. I hated leaving the port, knowing you would worry about me. That was why I left the message with the kite seller. I planned to come back to you, just as soon as it was safe."

"I know," she said softly. "I'm just glad you're all right."

"I am." Sami looked healthier than he had in years, probably because he was finally getting enough to eat, but I knew that he had to have suffered greatly from being kidnapped and banished, both physically and mentally. "Zadie can stay with me," Sami said to Roan.

Roan nodded and turned to me. "You're a good rider, Nor, and Titania makes up for what you lack. You're welcome to join us at Fort Crag, or you can stay with your sister if you prefer."

What I wanted was for us all to stay together so we could decide what our next move would be. If Talin really believed he could convince the Galethians to help, then he needed to do it quickly. And Zadie, Sami, and I had to figure out the best way to help our parents. What we needed was someone who could tell us what Ceren was planning, and if there were any chinks in his armor.

"I'd like to speak to the captured guard," I said suddenly.

Roan's eyebrows rose above his cup. "Oh?"

"Tomorrow morning, if possible. I will decide where to stay after."

I expected Roan to argue, but instead he shrugged and

drained his ale. "I'll see what I can do. Get some sleep. You look like you need it."

I scowled at his retreating back and rose, waiting for Zadie to follow. She glanced at Sami, then at me. I realized with a blush that she wanted to go with him tonight. "I'll see you in the morning, then."

I went up to my room and changed quickly. A soft knock sounded on the door just as I was about to blow out my candle for bed. I was tempted to ignore it, but I padded to the door in my shift and cracked it open. A pair of sea glass eyes waited for me in the dim hallway.

"I'm sorry," Talin said as I closed the door behind him.

"I wasn't trying to undermine you, you know. I was just afraid you'd ask for the Galethians' help and they'd refuse you, and we would be out of options before we'd even started."

"You were right. That's exactly what would have happened, Nor." He took my hand and led me to the bed. "I'm used to being the one in charge, whether I want to be or not. But I'm smart enough to recognize when I'm wrong."

I cupped his cheek in my hand, running my thumb over the smooth bronze skin. "I wish this wasn't so complicated."

"I know." He pressed his forehead to mine. "As much as I don't want to be apart from you, I completely understand if you want to stay with Zadie."

"Sami and Zadie need time alone together," I said. "At least as much as they can get before we're on the road again."

"I'll support whatever you decide." He leaned forward and brushed his mouth, warm and tasting of ale, against mine. I hummed in pleasure and drew him closer.

"Maybe you should come to Fort Crag after all?" Talin teased, his lips as soft as feathers on my neck.

I bit my lip as his mouth moved to my shoulder, nuzzling

my shift out of the way. "I don't think," I breathed as my hands slipped under his tunic and along the muscular planes of his back, "that they allow this in the barracks."

He laughed, and I was relieved that we could still be silly with each other, even when everything was so bleak. "I should go," he said finally.

I almost protested. I would have liked another night like the one in Varenia, where we had talked and cuddled under some semblance of normalcy. But until I knew if my vision of the future matched Talin's, it didn't feel like a good idea to ask him to stay.

"Good night," I said, rising from the bed.

He followed suit and paused at the door, looking at me in a way I had never seen before. There was a mixture of hope and fear in his eyes, like he wanted to ask me something but was afraid of the answer.

Finally, he smiled. "Good night, Nor."

When he was gone, I released a breath, and I realized that I had been afraid of the question.

Somehow, Roan was able to convince the other council-members to let us speak with the captured guard the following morning. Considering that Yana had made it clear she wouldn't have minded if Ceren had killed me at the border, I was surprised they were giving us access to the prisoner. Until I saw him for myself.

I didn't recognize the prisoner from my time in New Castle. More surprisingly, neither did Talin, Grig, or Osius. A man in his early twenties with olive skin and black hair, he was shackled at the wrists and ankles, but he didn't look frightened or angry. I wondered if he was even making the conscious decision not to cooperate. He looked sleepy or drunk, not resolved.

"He's been like this since we captured him," a rider from Fort Crag explained. He kicked at the guard's shackled legs. The man let out a grunt but otherwise didn't react. "The only time he made any sign that he was even conscious was when we tried to take that."

The Galethian pointed to a chain hanging around the man's neck. Dangling from the end was a red jewel the color of fresh blood.

I took a step closer. "Where did he get that?"

"Why?" Roan asked. "Do you recognize it?"

"I don't know," I admitted. "But it looks like the stones I saw in the tunnels below New Castle—and the ones in Ceren's crown."

Talin placed a hand on my shoulder. "You think it's a bloodstone?"

"The bloodstones are gone," Yana said. "That's what we've always been told."

My mouth had gone dry, and I swallowed thickly. "They were believed gone, yes. But when I escaped, I saw a vein with my own eyes."

Ebb had told me about the bloodstones once, how they were believed to be the frozen blood of giants. *They were said to make the wearer so powerful, she could command armies to certain death if she chose.* Lady Melina had said the stones were only visible to Varenian eyes, but Ceren had Varenian blood in his veins now. Mine.

A groan escaped me. If Ceren had bloodstones at his disposal, what did that mean for Talia and her army?

"Do you know how the stones work?" Roan asked me.

I shook my head. "No, only that they make the wearer stronger."

Talin glanced at the guard, who clearly didn't appear strong, and frowned. "We always believed the stones were similar to blood coral. The mines were below the royal crypt."

"You think the stones come from the dead bodies of Ilarean royals?" Zadie asked.

"Just like the blood corals grows from the bodies of dead Varenians." I tried to remember everything Ebb had told me about bloodstones, but it had been such a short conversation. "The stones don't work the same way as the Varenian pearls, though. Do they?"

"You mean by healing people?" Talin asked. "No, I don't believe so."

"What happened when you tried to take the bloodstone?" Yana had combed her strip of hair up off her head, which made her look even fiercer than yesterday.

"He went berserk," the man from Fort Crag replied. "Screaming and flailing like a yearling with a horsefly on his—"

"Thank you," Yana said curtly. "You can return to your post." It seemed to me Roan should give that order, considering the rider was one of his, but Yana went on. "Well, should we vote? Interrogate the prisoner or take the stone by force?"

"I get the impression an interrogation won't yield much in the way of answers," Roan said. "Not unless we plan to use torture. We should send for Adriel. She might have a better idea."

I glanced questioningly at Roan, but he didn't respond.

Yana murmured something to a young Galethian woman and she dashed off, seemingly to send for this Adriel person.

"We'll consult with the council," Yana said. "The outsiders

can wait in the antechamber." She walked away without another word.

I stared after her, wondering where she got the nerve to
speak to people that way.

"You don't like her, do you?" Roan asked as he escorted us
to a waiting room. I noticed that his rider hadn't left, but he
was staying as far from Yana as possible. "Why not?"

"She's abrasive," I blurted. "And rude."

"She's forceful. It's an important quality in a leader."

Talin and his men were conversing across the room, while
Zadie and Sami were whispering into each other's ears. Judging from the blush creeping up Sami's neck, they weren't talking about the bloodstones. "I thought you were all equal,"
I said, genuinely confused. "But she seems to be in charge."

"We are all equal when it comes to voting, but Yana is the
best rider in Galeth. That garners a certain amount of respect
around here."

I tried to imagine what my mother would make of a woman
like Yana. She was not feminine by any Varenian standard;
most of her hair was shorter than Roan's, and her arms were
as muscular as Sami's. There was nothing soft or demure about
her. But she was clearly well regarded, a respected leader with
the battle scars to prove it.

"What does that look mean?" Roan said, studying me.

"That I'm learning, I suppose." I smiled ruefully. "She despises me, doesn't she?"

"Yana?" He patted my arm. "Yana doesn't like anyone. But
if you speak your mind, she just might come to respect you."

We all turned as the Galethian Yana had sent off entered
and asked us to follow her to the meeting room, where the rest
of the councilmembers were waiting for us. Another young
woman had joined them. She wasn't dressed in riding cloth-

ing, like almost everyone else I'd seen in Galeth, but instead wore a garnet velvet dress with split skirts. She had a spattering of dark freckles across her nose, in stark contrast to her pale skin, and her black hair was loose around her shoulders.

"You're lucky you caught me." Her voice was throaty and rich, an interesting contrast to her wide blue eyes and small, pert nose. "I was just about to head home."

Yana inclined her head. "Thank you for joining us. We know how busy you are." She was being genuine, I realized. Whoever this Adriel was, she was in Yana's good graces.

"I'd like you to meet our new friends," Roan said. "Talin, Osius, Grig, Sami, Zadie, and last but not least, Nor. She's the one I told you about."

I glanced at him. When had he had time for that, and what could he possibly have told her about me?

Adriel turned to me and smiled. Something about her clear blue gaze was disarming. I felt as if she was seeing directly into my head, gleaning thoughts I wasn't even conscious of. I smiled back, but she didn't look away, and my smile faltered. Why wasn't she looking at anyone else? What had Roan told her about me?

"The guard refuses to give up the bloodstone," Yana said, finally taking Adriel's focus away from me.

"That's hardly surprising," Adriel remarked as she approached the Ilarean, who had been brought into the council chamber, with a slow, swaying stride. She was curvaceous in a way I suspected many women in Varenia would be, if it weren't for the lack of food. "The bloodstone has him under its control. Well, under the control of the person who wields the stone."

"Ceren?" I asked. Several heads swiveled toward me.

"Is he the Ilarean king?" Adriel asked.

"For now," Talin grunted.

"I've never seen a bloodstone in person before." Adriel stopped just in front of the guard. He dragged his eyes up slowly to hers, but his expression remained dazed and unfocused.

Adriel made no move toward the stone, just leaned down until she was at eye level with it. "I only know the information that was passed down to me by my teacher. But my understanding is that only the Ilarean royals can wield them, since the stones are infused with the power of royal blood. Whoever wears a bloodstone given to them by the royal is under their command. If the king is giving them to his guards, then he will have full control over them."

Yana folded her muscular arms across her chest. "Full control?"

"There is literally nothing they wouldn't do for him. They'd even die if he commanded it."

I shuddered at the thought. How would anyone defeat an army like that? I knew better than most that Ceren had no problem killing people who stood in his way, and he would be all too happy to use others to do his dirty work for him.

"And what if we were to take the stone from him?" Talin asked. "What happens then?"

"I'm not sure," Adriel said over her shoulder. "It may kill him. Or it may break the control of the stone. Or perhaps it will transfer Ceren's control onto whomever takes the stone. Personally, I don't want to be the one to test it."

Yana rubbed her chin for a moment. "Do you think you can learn more safely?"

"I can try, although without a bloodstone to study, it will be difficult. And you know I don't like to mess with blood magic, Yana. It's messy, to say the least."

I remembered how we'd compared bloodstones to blood coral. Was that what my healing capabilities were? Blood magic? And was that why I'd had the visions of Ceren and those strange dreams that felt all too real? Messy didn't even begin to cover it.

"There were two more guards killed outside the border," I said. "It's possible they were wearing stones as well. Do we know what happened to their bodies?"

Roan and the rider from Fort Crag put their heads together for a moment.

"We recovered the bodies," Roan said. "They were burned, but we did collect their belongings. We'll have to search them to see if there's a bloodstone. We don't recall seeing one."

I nodded. Naturally, they would have noticed if there had been a beautiful red jewel among the guard's belongings.

"It was a good thought, Nor." Yana inclined her head when I looked at her before turning to Adriel. "We'll put the man in the dungeon. Let's see if you can discover anything else about the bloodstones. I'd like to spare his life, if possible. More importantly, I'd like to question him. He has useful information in there, somewhere."

"Can I help?" I asked, sensing we were about to be dismissed.

Yana's gaze darted to mine. "Help?"

"With the questioning. I have some things I'd like to ask, too." I glanced at the others and added quickly, "In case the guard knows something that can help us rescue our families."

Yana narrowed her eyes at me but didn't press. "Very well. If Adriel can figure out a way to make him talk."

As the councilmembers disbanded, Talin fell in step next to me. "Have you decided where you'd like to stay? There's no pressure. I just want to make sure you'll be safe."

Before I could respond, Roan appeared on my other side, oblivious to the fact that Talin and I were trying to have a private conversation. "I was thinking about you last night, you know."

Not oblivious, I realized. Just a troublemaker. Talin muttered something under his breath.

"About where you could stay," Roan added, smiling innocently. His eyes went to Adriel, who was walking ahead of us. "You should stay with Adriel. She lives between Leesbrook and Fort Crag, so you wouldn't be too far from your friends or your sister," Roan continued. "And Adriel could probably use some help figuring out those bloodstones. Couldn't you, Adriel?"

She turned and blinked slowly, her lips curved in a secretive smile. "I could."

As much as I disliked the idea of staying with a stranger, it was clear Adriel knew more about the bloodstones than anyone else. She might even understand the link between Ceren and me. I was afraid we were wasting time here in Galeth, time my parents might not have, but until I knew more about Ceren's plans, rushing off to New Castle alone was likely to do more harm than good.

"That does sound like a reasonable compromise," I said, glancing up at Talin.

He smiled and nodded, but I could tell he was holding something back.

I reached for his hand. "It's just for a few days."

"Good. Then it's settled." Roan clapped his hands together in satisfaction. "We should get on the road. There's a storm coming."

"But what about my belongings?" I asked, unmoored by the sudden turn of events.

"I'll have them sent." Roan turned to Talin, Osius, and Grig. "Are you ready?"

I hadn't been prepared to say goodbye to everyone right away. I stepped closer to Talin and lowered my voice so Roan wouldn't overhear. "Are you sure this is all right? I don't want to be away from you or Zadie, but Adriel might know something that can help us."

"Of course it's all right," he said, pressing a chaste kiss to my cheek. "Just be careful."

"I will." I turned to find my sister, feeling a sudden pang of regret. We had only just gotten each other back. Maybe separating was a bad idea.

"It's okay, Nor," she whispered in my ear, because of course she could sense my hesitation. "It's only for a day or two, and then we'll go find our parents, and we'll all be together again."

I embraced her, wishing I shared her sense of certainty. Then Adriel was leading me back outside to where Titania waited in the courtyard.

"Don't worry," Adriel said as she mounted her own horse, a blood bay mare with a black tail so long and luxurious it dragged on the ground. "I don't bite."

I climbed onto Titania, glad I would at least have one friend with me on this new phase of my journey.

"Adriel," I asked as I followed her down the road away from Leesbrook. "I was wondering if you could tell me a bit more about what it is you do."

"Didn't Roan tell you?" she called over her shoulder. "I'm a witch."

14

I stared after Adriel. The only witch I'd ever heard of was the one in Samiel's stories, an evil temptress who caused rogue waves that sank ships and drowned sailors, and she had been a myth. At least, I had always believed she was.

"What do you mean?" I called, trotting to catch up.

She glanced at me, a grin lifting one side of her mouth. "What, you don't have witches in Varenia?"

Ceren had once mentioned that the Ilareans thought I was a witch after I saved him from drowning. "Do you mean people who can do things that defy the laws of nature? At least, nature as people understand it?"

Her grin widened. "That's an interesting way of defining magic. I'll have to remember that."

"You didn't answer the question," I said, but she turned back to the road and didn't speak again for the rest of the journey.

We arrived at Adriel's home just as the storm broke. Tucked

into the green hills beyond the pastures we'd passed on our way to Leesbrook, it was a lovely little stone cottage with a wavy thatched roof that gave it the appearance of a toadstool.

"You live out here all alone?" I asked as we led our horses to a barn behind the house. It had two stalls separated by a small tack room, which was just as well; our mares didn't seem overly fond of each other.

"Why shouldn't I?" Adriel asked. She showed me where to hang my cloak and led me across the small yard, which had been cultivated into a tidy little garden. "It's perfectly safe."

"Don't you get lonely?" I ducked under the low door frame after her. Inside, the cottage was as cozy as it appeared from the outside, consisting of one room with a stove and a hearth on one end and a bed at the other. In the middle was a little wooden table covered in various herbs and several books.

"I don't have time to get lonely," Adriel said.

We certainly wouldn't be lonely now; in fact, I didn't see how there was room for me. The dwelling was smaller than my house in Varenia.

"It's all right," she said, sensing my concern. "You can sleep in my workshop. I'll move my things in here. Roan said he'd have a bed brought from Leesburg later today, so you'll be comfortable there."

It seemed like a lot of trouble to go through, considering I only planned to stay for a few days at the most. "Thank you. You didn't have to do that."

She glanced up from the hearth, where she was arranging kindling for a fire. "Roan said you needed somewhere to stay. Was he lying? I wouldn't put it past him. Especially not when a pretty face is involved."

I ignored the teasing smile on her face. "I could have gone

to Fort Crag with Talin or stayed with my sister in Lees-brook."

"But you chose to come with me. Interesting." She fin-ished building the fire and rose. "Come on, I'll show you the workshop. I have a feeling you'll like it." She led me through a door at the side of the house, across a small covered walk-way, and into an even more diminutive structure.

There was a long wooden table covered in bottles and jars filled with various liquids, reminding me vaguely of Ceren's workshop. But the similarities ended there. There were plenty of windows, which, when the storm cleared, would let in lots of sunlight. Lacy white curtains hung next to them, creating pretty shadows on the clean whitewashed walls, which were decorated with bouquets of dried flowers. Crystals and col-orful stones had been collected in little handmade clay bowls, and a striped orange animal I'd never seen before—a cat, ac-cording to Adriel—lay curled in an armchair in the corner.

"What do you think?" she asked.

"It's lovely, Adriel. But I can't ask you to clean it out for me. I can sleep in the corner, on my bedroll. Or in the barn, if that's easier. I won't be staying long."

"Nonsense. You're welcome as long as you like."

I almost insisted again that I would be leaving soon, but I knew it would be more to reassure myself than her. "Thank you. That's very kind." I went to look through one of the bowls of polished stones. "I understand that you're a witch, but what exactly do you do?"

"I'm a hedge witch," she said. "I work with plants. Healing, medicine, that sort of thing. Women come to me when they have cramps from their monthlies, or if their children have the croup. I create salves for chafed skin and teas for sore throats."

"We have a healer in Varenia." I wondered where Elder

Nemea was and if Ceren had even spared the elders. I picked up a chunk of blue crystal that reminded me of Talin's eyes and twisted it in my fingers. The storm was picking up; raindrops plinked against the windows, and the door rattled on its hinges.

"I've heard about your pearls. I've never had the opportunity to study them."

Her words made me think of Ceren. "Maybe some things are better left a mystery. Like the bloodstones." I looked up at her then, our eyes meeting across the room.

"What did I say about blood magic that upset you so much back in the council meeting?" Adriel missed nothing, I realized.

I shrugged. "I suppose it was the way you said that it's messy."

"And that troubles you?"

Of course it did. But I didn't know this woman, and I wasn't comfortable telling her about my abilities, not when she was clearly so curious about the blood coral and Varenian pearls.

When I looked up, Adriel had turned to remove a leatherbound book from a shelf. She blew on the cover, sending a cloud of dust into the air. "Perhaps you'll find something in this book that I missed. If it were up to me, we'd forget about the bloodstone."

"And the guard?"

She waved dismissively. "He can stay in the dungeon until he decides to talk."

"You saw him," I said, taking the book from her. "I don't think it's his decision to make."

"Perhaps not. Either way, I don't want to get involved." She pulled a bouquet of dried flowers off the wall, took them to the long table and began to crush them with her fist. Not a decoration, then.

"Some of us don't have a choice," I mumbled, turning the book over in my hands. There were no words on the red leather cover, only an engraving of a tree with long, skeletal branches.

A knock sounded on the door, causing me to nearly drop the book.

"That will be Roan," Adriel said, setting aside her herbs. "Come in," she called.

"How are you getting on?" Roan asked as he entered the cottage. Behind him, Talin, Osius, and Grig stood in the rain, their cloaks soaked through. "We came to deliver your belongings on our way to Fort Crag, Nor. Your bed will come after the storm passes."

"Go on inside and warm up," Adriel said to Roan. "But take your cloaks and boots off first."

I hadn't realized I'd get another chance to see Talin, and I eagerly followed them into the cottage. There wasn't enough room for all of us there either, but fortunately Osius and Grig decided to wait in the barn.

Roan looked back over his shoulder at the sky. "We should keep going. I'm hoping we can outride the worst of the weather."

"I'd like a few minutes alone with Talin," I said, taking him by the hand and leading him back to the little workshop before Roan could argue.

"How are you?" I pushed his dripping hair out of his eyes. "This all feels so strange and sudden."

"Are you having second thoughts?"

"And third and fourth and—"

He leaned down and kissed me, his lips much colder than

they'd been last night. I wanted to remove his rain-soaked clothing and warm him myself, but I knew we didn't have much time.

"It's not too late to change your mind," he said.

"I know, but I won't be any use at Fort Crag. I think I might be able to learn how Ceren is using the bloodstones here." I glanced at the book, which I'd set on the long wooden table. It was thicker than any book I'd ever read. But if it could explain the bond I seemed to have with Ceren, and if there was any way I could use it to understand his plans, I had to try.

Talin tucked my hair behind my ears. "Are you sure you'll be all right?"

Back in New Castle, I had been scared and worried a hundred times, but I had been sure of my decisions. Saving Ceren at the lake had been the right thing to do, just like escaping by any means necessary had been.

But since my return to Varenia, I wasn't sure about anything. Had leaving my parents in Varenia been the right thing to do? Had I been foolish to let Talin come to Galeth with us, when it seemed highly unlikely he'd get the troops he needed? Should I try to save my parents right away, rather than potentially waste more time?

I couldn't answer any of those questions. Instead, I pulled Talin's mouth back to mine, kissing him.

"Time to go, lovebirds."

We broke apart at the sound of Roan's voice. He was watching us from the doorway without a hint of shame. "Terribly sorry to interrupt, but we really do need to get going."

I glared at him. "Has anyone ever told you you're the worst?"

Roan shrugged and turned to leave, but not before I caught an amused glint in his eye.

When he was gone, Talin dropped one last kiss onto my lips, whispered goodbye, and followed Roan into the rain. I watched him go, a pit forming in my stomach at the realization that as uncertain as the future was, it was guaranteed to be full of more painful farewells.

And for the first time since leaving Varenia, I sat down on the floor and cried.

My tears subsided along with the rain, and I could no longer ignore the pangs of hunger in my empty stomach. I knocked sheepishly on Adriel's door, opening it a crack when there was no answer.

She was stirring a pot of something that smelled spicy and delicious, and when she turned toward me, her smile was warm and open. "I thought you'd get hungry eventually."

"I'm sorry," I said, removing my boots and setting them by the fire to dry properly. "I think I'm just tired."

"You don't need to apologize. You're allowed to be sad, or tired, or even just annoyed with Roan."

I snorted and rubbed at my cheeks, which were tight from my dried tears. "It's not just that. Ceren attacked Varenia when we escaped. I have no idea what happened to my family, and it feels as if time is slipping through my fingers like water."

"Here." She placed two bowls of soup on the table and gestured for me to sit. "This will help."

"Why?" I eyed the spoonful in my hand skeptically. "Did you put something in it?"

She laughed. "Yes, if you count chicken, potatoes, carrots, and leeks as 'something.'"

"Oh," I said, embarrassed. "I'm sorry. I don't really understand how magic works, I guess."

She raised a quizzical brow.

"Not your kind of magic, anyway."

"They say Varenians live longer than any other people," she said, watching me take a sip of broth. It was so delicious I almost groaned. "That you heal remarkably fast. That your waters make you healthy and strong."

I nodded. "That's all true."

"And you don't think that's magic?"

I chewed on a chunk of potato, considering. "I suppose I always thought of that as nature. We die, our bodies nourish the blood coral, which in turn nourishes the ocean, which then nourishes us. It's a cycle of life and death, not magic."

"Hmm," she said, still watching me.

I realized I'd eaten nearly half my bowl of soup and set my spoon down. She hadn't taken a single bite. "Do *you* consider that magic?"

"I think the world is full of magic. It's in the air and the water and the soil and the trees. But only some of us are capable of harnessing it. I sense you are one of those people, Nor. I think that's why Roan told you about me."

I blushed, staring into my bowl of soup. "What would give Roan that impression? He hardly knows me."

"Because Roan's mother was a healer, like me. And because he's an empath, believe it or not. He hides behind sarcasm and crude humor, but he's far more perceptive than people give him credit for. He sensed you were searching for something that you might find here. I think he was right."

I dug back into my soup to avoid responding. I wasn't ready to talk about my healing powers or the fact that Ceren needed my blood, and more importantly, I didn't want to admit that Roan might actually be perceptive, despite his smug exterior.

By the time we finished eating, the storm had blown away, leaving an innocent blue sky in its wake. A man with a cart came by with my little wooden bed, which was placed in a corner of Adriel's workshop. I was about to sit down and start reading the book Adriel gave me when she knocked on the door.

"Come on," she said, tossing my still-damp cloak at me.

"Where are we going?" I asked, slightly cranky at being interrupted. I didn't have much time to figure out how the bloodstones worked, and Adriel's constant questioning made me anxious.

"I'm taking you to see the bone trees," she said, and disappeared outside before I had a chance to respond.

15

Adriel and I left the house on foot and headed for the forest that began less than a mile away. Since the ground was soft from the rain and our boots got stuck in the muddy road, we kept to the fields, tromping through the damp grass and wildflowers. Every now and then, Adriel would stop to pluck a specimen and place it in a satchel she wore across her body.

"Tell me about Talin," she said after we'd been walking in silence for a while. "Roan said you told him you aren't lovers, but somehow I don't believe that's entirely true."

"What is it with Galethians and personal questions?" I stepped over a rotted branch as we entered the forest. "My relationship with Talin isn't any of your concern."

Adriel cast me a questioning glance. "Apologies. I didn't realize that was considered personal where you come from."

"It is," I huffed. "I haven't asked you about your relationships, have I?"

"I wouldn't mind if you did. Although my last lover moved

to Leesbrook over a year ago. She wanted to become a black-smith's apprentice, and I couldn't very well move to the city."

"Oh." I blinked in surprise.

She rolled her eyes. "Don't tell me only men and women are allowed to be lovers in Varenia. I know how strict the Ilarean royals can be when it comes to marriage and procreation, but I thought the Varenians were a little more evolved than that."

"It isn't that," I said, shaking my head. Varenian girls were groomed to marry a prince, whose sexual preference was irrelevant as far as the crown was concerned. His duty was to carry on the royal bloodline, and he would have to marry accordingly. But if we weren't chosen, we could marry freely, as long as our parents and the elders approved the match. "I just assumed you and Roan were lovers."

Adriel laughed. "My tastes are far more discerning than you give me credit for."

"And the woman who left?"

"Ana." She pushed a branch aside and waited for me to pass. "I loved her, but the truth is that most hedge witches live alone. I knew she wouldn't stay forever."

I mulled over her words over for a moment. "Do Galethians marry?"

"Some do. It's more of a formality than anything, though. Are you and Talin going to marry?"

I should have been prepared for the blunt question, but it still caught me off guard. "I don't know," I said honestly. "I was betrothed to his brother, Ceren. But I never loved him." I told her the story of how Zadie had been chosen to marry Ceren and I'd gone in her place, elaborating on how Talin had helped me while I was at New Castle.

"It sounds as if he would do anything for you," Adriel said after I'd finished. "Do you love him?"

I knew that I did, but it felt strange to admit that to someone I barely knew before I had told Talin. I nodded instead. "But his goal is to help his mother overthrow Ceren, and I have to make sure my family is safe. It's hard to even think about marriage."

"Is that why you came? To ask the Galethians to help you?"

We had reached a clearing. In the center was a grove of the strangest trees I'd ever seen. Tall and skeletal, without a single leaf on their slender white branches, they looked more like dead coral than trees.

I turned to Adriel. I knew she was close to Roan, and I didn't want her going to him before we'd had time to come up with a strategy. "Do you think the Galethians would help us if we asked?"

"That all depends on why you think the Galethians *should* help, I suppose. This is not their fight, Nor."

From what I knew of Ceren, this would be the entire continent's fight eventually, but my thoughts had snagged on something else. "What do you mean by *their*?"

She walked into the clearing, the light streaming down onto her dark hair. She was objectively beautiful by Varenian standards, but it was her lack of self-consciousness that set her apart from any woman I'd met before.

"My ancestors came from the Penery Islands, to the west. They arrived on these shores back when this land was still part of Ilara and began a small settlement. These trees are all that remain of them."

I followed her into the clearing. "What do you mean?"

"Just like your blood coral, the bone trees grew from the bodies of my ancestors. When I die, I will be buried here, and my bones will nourish the roots of a new tree. The last tree, unless I choose to have a child someday." She placed her hands on the nearest trunk and looked up at the bare branches. "They flowered, once upon a time. The fruit was poisonous, if eaten straight, but the seeds could be made into teas and elixirs with healing properties, just like your pearls."

"Why did they stop blooming?" I asked. The wind picked up, and the branches rattling overhead sounded eerily like dried bones. A chill ran through my body, and I suddenly had the feeling we were in the presence of spirits.

"When the Galethians came, they drove my ancestors out of the region, back to the islands where they'd come from. A few stayed, but it wasn't enough to sustain the grove."

"You said Roan's mother was a healer as well. Does that mean he shares your ancestry?"

"Only on his mother's side." She sat beneath the trees, finding a space for herself amid the roots, as if she already longed to be among them.

I stayed where I was, in the space between the forest and the grove. "If the Galethians were Varenians once, then what happens when they bury their dead? Do they grow some other kind of tree?"

She smiled sadly and looked up, past the branches into the sky. "The Galethians don't bury their dead, Nor. They burn them."

Her words sent another chill through me. "And the ashes?"

"Scattered on the wind."

"Meaning they don't return to the earth."

Adriel's eyes were shiny with tears. "And the cycle of magic—nature, whatever you want to call it—is broken."

I could tell she considered this a genuine tragedy, and under other circumstances I would have agreed. But if the Ilarean royals really were linked to the bloodstones the way Varenians were linked to the pearls, then it might mean there was a way to break *that* cycle as well. Without the blood of a royal, the stones would lose their power.

And there was only one full-blooded Ilarean royal left: Ceren.

That night, I lay awake in my new bed in the little workshop, which Adriel had cleaned up for me, despite my protests. I liked the smell of the herbs, the books and crystals and even the cat, whose name I had learned was Fox (short for foxglove, a flower that Adriel said could either be medicinal or poisonous depending how it was used). Fox had come to sleep at the foot of my bed, curled up and making a strange rumbling sound that Adriel called purring. She assured me it meant he liked me, but I had my doubts.

I opened the book Adriel had given me, the one with the bone tree on the cover. It had come from her ancestors, she said, passed down through generations, and might help me to understand the connection between blood and nature. Though, she warned me, the language was deliberately confusing and arcane to prevent anyone who wasn't a witch from using it, and she had given up on it long ago.

"Be careful," she had warned before retiring for the evening. "Blood magic is—"

"Messy," I'd finished for her. "I'm not planning on doing any, I promise."

She had smiled, lingering in the doorway for a moment as if there was something more she wanted to say. I had breathed a sigh of relief when she'd turned and closed the door behind her.

But she hadn't been wrong about the book being confusing. I hadn't made it more than two pages before I was lost among the words, rereading the same lines several times before giving up and moving on. The writer used tall, narrow script, so uniform that as my eyes grew tired, the letters all began to bleed together, making it difficult to discern an *L* from an *I* and a *U* from a *V.* After a while, I started to wonder if the letters were actually rearranging themselves on purpose to trick me.

I set the book aside, still not sleepy, and forced myself to close my eyes. My thoughts turned instantly to Zadie. I didn't like being away from her after everything I'd been through to get back to her, but I knew I'd done the right thing in giving her and Sami space. Something told me that they would soon cross the line to lovers, marriage or no marriage. The thought was oddly painful, a deep ache in my chest. I was happy for them, but I couldn't help feeling like I was being left behind, that Zadie was moving past me into something that I might never be able to understand.

And there was something about Galeth that didn't feel right to me. Not dangerous, per se, but almost as if it were a bit rotten around the edges, like a seaflower beginning to wilt. I admired the true equality of its citizens, how much freedom women had in choosing their own paths, though even that was something of an illusion. Otherwise, Adriel would not be an outcast, something I could empathize with all too well. And while passing down leadership through the father the way we did in Varenia or Ilara had always seemed arbitrary and unwise, being the strongest rider in your region didn't seem to be the best qualifier, either.

My restless thoughts turned to Talin, who was probably sound asleep after a hard day of riding. He wouldn't mind sleeping in a barracks with other soldiers. He'd had his own living quarters at Old Castle, but he never put himself above his men, other than to lead them. While Ceren believed the throne was his by right and anyone standing in his way was merely an obstacle, Talin followed a moral compass that pointed due north.

I wished he was with me. Another squall had rolled in, and a sudden burst of rain pelted the windows, making Fox sit up. Lightning flashed somewhere in the distance, followed several heartbeats later by the sound of thunder. The candle had burned down, and the total darkness reminded me too much of the New Castle dungeon.

I was used to storms since I grew up at sea. Once, a massive wave had nearly taken off our entire roof. Some of our belongings had washed away, and other families had lost their boats and docks. I wasn't nearly as vulnerable on land, I reminded myself.

Then a burst of lightning came at the same time as the loudest clap of thunder I'd ever heard, and I sat bolt upright, sending Fox darting into the shadows. Heart pounding, I was half tempted to run to Adriel. She was probably used to this, living out here all alone. I could feel an all-too-familiar tightening in my chest, the kind that would normally be quelled by submerging myself in water. But I wasn't going to get that now.

Without thinking, I flew out of bed, pulled on my riding boots, and sprinted out into the rain in my shift. I thought perhaps just being outside would release some of my rising panic, but it was the movement that seemed to help, strangely. I was strong from riding, and though my boots weren't designed for it and my shift was soaked through and clinging to me, I found that running came easily.

A blinding flash of white came out of nowhere. For a moment, I was sure I had been struck by lightning. But there was no pain following the light. It was as if I had left the rainy fields and was inside New Castle. In Ceren's study, specifically. He was hunched over his desk, his back to me, scribbling madly on a piece of paper. A half-drunk vial of blood sat next to him on the desk, and red stones, both polished and raw, filled a bowl nearby, the way the Varenian pearls had just weeks ago. His own arm was bleeding over a silver bowl, and with his free hand, Ceren picked up a stone, turning it over in his long white fingers before throwing it aside in frustration.

"Such a child," I said, and then he turned, as if he'd heard me.

His gray eyes darted around the room searchingly. He looked so different than I remembered, and not just because his nose wasn't broken and bleeding. His once deathly pale cheeks were pink, as were the full lips, which were so like his brother's. Whatever the mountain had taken from him, my blood seemed to have given it all back and then some. He was beautiful, in his own way. And the fact that I could acknowledge it after all he'd done to me made my stomach churn.

"Ceren," I said, and his pupils dilated instantly as he focused on me.

"You're really there."

I knew he couldn't hurt me through the vision, but my heart still raced, even as I told myself not to be afraid. I could feel my body in the field, the rain pouring down my frozen limbs, but a part of me was there in that study that I had always hated.

A smug grin played on his lips. "Enjoying your time in Galeth, are you? You look like a drowned rat."

"We have one of your guards," I ground out, ignoring his jibe.

He waved a pale hand. "I have a hundred more."

This was the Ceren I knew so well, the one to whom human life meant nothing. "Why did you follow us here?"

His eyes darted to the vial of blood unconsciously. My blood.

"Why do you still need my blood?" I blurted. "And why are we connected whenever you drink it?"

He shook his head but didn't answer. He had a weakness, it seemed, but he wasn't going to reveal it to me. I wasn't surprised, of course, but I didn't know when I would have another chance to ask, and he might let something slip in his arrogance.

"Where are my parents, Ceren?"

He cocked his head like a strange white bird. "They're in New Castle. All your people are."

"Why?" I growled in frustration, nearly taking myself out of the vision. Somewhere in the distance I could hear thunder, feel my entire body shaking with cold. "What do you want from them?"

He stared into the empty space before him for a moment, as if he wasn't sure how to answer.

I was about to ask again when I felt a hand clamp around my arm. For one brief moment, Ceren's gaze sharpened, and then the vision broke and I was standing in a field with Adriel, who was shaking me with a look of wild fear in her eyes.

"Nor! Wake up!"

I sputtered, pushing ropes of wet hair out of my face with my free hand. "I'm here."

"What are you doing?" Her tone was sharp, but she pulled me toward her and threw her cloak around both of us as well as she could.

I shivered so hard I stumbled. "I don't know. I was afraid of the storm, and I panicked."

She half pulled, half carried me across the field until we reached her house. Inside, she sat me down in front of the fire and pulled my soaked shift off over my head before throwing a heavy blanket around me.

"Get warm," she said. "I'm going to make you some tea. If it hadn't been for Fox mewling at my door, I wouldn't have even known you were missing. What possessed you to go out into a lightning storm? Surely a girl from the ocean knows better than that."

She was talking to herself more than me, and my teeth were chattering far too hard for me to answer anyway. Foxglove appeared and began to roll on the floor in front of me, exposing the tufts of soft white fur on his belly and twisting his head at me as if to say, *Did you forget about me, outsider?*

I reached out with one chilled arm and scratched behind his ears, which set him to making that strange rumbling sound again. Perhaps he really did like me.

"Here," Adriel said, squatting down beside me and handing me a steaming cup. "This will help warm and calm you. I didn't realize you had such a fear of storms."

"I don't, normally." My violent shivering had finally slowed to the occasional twitch. "I think it's just that I was on my own. I've never lived by myself before."

She gazed at me with a sad, pitying sort of smile. "You were hardly alone, Nor. I was right here."

"I didn't want to wake you."

"I would have preferred that to finding you talking to yourself in a field."

My cheeks flushed. "I'm sorry."

"You weren't talking to yourself, though. Were you?" Adriel pulled a stool over and sat down next to me with her own cup of tea. I was a little relieved to see she was drinking it, too.

She was studying me again in that unnerving way, and while it made me want to curl in on myself, I knew that if anyone might understand my link to Ceren, it was Adriel. Her interest in bloodstones and pearls had worried me at first, but of course she would be interested; they were linked to her heritage, too, via the bone trees. And she had taken me to the grove, a place that was clearly meaningful to her. Maybe it was time for me to be vulnerable, too.

I took a sip of the tea, which had a light berry flavor. "No, I wasn't talking to myself."

"Care to tell me about it?"

I told her about the visions and dreams, how twice I'd seen Ceren drinking my blood, which might help explain our link. "I spoke to him this time," I added. "And he responded. He said he has the Varenians, but he wouldn't tell me what he plans to do with them."

She watched me intently, and I couldn't fight the feeling that she was gathering up my thoughts like she would gather herbs, as if they were ingredients in some potion I couldn't fathom.

"I understand your fascination with blood magic now," she said when I'd finished.

I snorted. "I wouldn't call it a fascination. It's more of a necessary interest."

"Fair enough." She took my cup from me and rose to her feet, stretching. "As I said before, I know very little about blood magic. The bond that you and Ceren have... I can't say I've never heard of anything like it, but I have no experience with it. And for now, it sounds like it might be useful."

I raised my eyebrows and pulled the blanket closer around me. "How so?"

"You're able to communicate with him. Perhaps, if you learned to control it, you could even spy on him."

I shook my head. "I tried my hand at spying once. It didn't go well."

"Roan was right about you," she said with a twist of her lips. "You are an enigma."

I laughed dryly in response.

"You disagree? You're a girl from a tiny village in the sea who should never have set foot on land, and here you are communicating through visions with the king of Ilara and telling me you've already tried your hand at spying. I'd say that makes you something of a riddle."

Maybe she understood me better than I wanted to admit. Riddles were in want of answers, and Thalos knew I was in short supply of those these days. Ever since I'd returned to Varenia, all I'd felt was doubt and uncertainty.

She handed me a dry shift. "Here. This belonged to Ana. She left it behind, and it doesn't fit me."

"Thank you." I pulled it quickly over my head. It was a bit long on me, but it would do. "I'll return it to you as soon as mine is dry."

"Keep it," she said as she helped me to my feet. "It isn't as if she's coming back for it."

She said it matter-of-factly, but there was hurt there, clearly. She had taken a lover knowing she wouldn't stay, and yet she still missed her.

"There's something I don't understand, something from my vision," I mused aloud after a moment. "Why did Ceren take all the Varenians? If it was only my blood he wanted, he could simply have taken my parents hostage and lured me to him that way."

"They must have something Ceren wants," she said. "Or more importantly, something he needs. More soldiers for his army, perhaps?"

I shook my head. "They're malnourished. And they'll never fight for Ceren willingly. He would have to use bloodstones to control them." Was that his plan? To lead his soldiers with his mind? The thin vein I'd seen in the tunnels below New Castle wouldn't yield enough stones for an entire army. "There must be more bloodstones in the flooded mine," I said, more to myself than Adriel.

"And?" she asked.

A horrible thought struck me, sending chills over my entire body. "He doesn't need the Varenians to dive for pearls anymore." I sat down again as the room began to spin around me. "But he still needs the Varenians to dive."

16

I couldn't know for sure if Ceren had captured the Varenians to mine for him, but I also couldn't think of another good reason for bringing them to New Castle. Adriel agreed that it was a likely explanation, so I was eager to share the theory with Talin, Zadie, and Sami. If Ceren really did need the Varenians to dive, he wouldn't kill them, which bought us a little time. But I wouldn't know anything for sure until we went to New Castle, and I had no idea if Talin was having any luck enlisting the Galethians' help.

The old Nor would have already been on the road south, armed with a half-formulated plan and driven solely by the need to act. I thought of my time in New Castle, where I'd been alone and without allies, until I made the decision to trust Lady Melina, Ebb, and finally Talin. I wasn't without allies now, and I was going to have to trust that we had the best odds of helping the Varenians together.

Adriel herself had become the most unlikely ally of all.

Sensing my anxiety, she put me to work to keep my mind occupied. She concocted remedies and tinctures from herbs, wildflowers, mushrooms, berries, and other unidentifiable substances she kept in glass vials for the people who came by the cottage. At one point, she sent me out with a book filled with drawings and descriptions to fetch a special kind of mushroom for a tea. I managed to bring back several poisonous mushrooms along with the correct ones, and the berries I picked on a whim gave me a rash. Fortunately, Adriel had a cure for that, too.

"Have you found anything useful?" she asked the following morning, nodding to the book in my hands. I'd spent all last night reading it and was fairly certain I'd actually *lost* intelligence in the process.

"No," I huffed, nearly tripping over a stone as we crossed a field. Adriel was gathering a rare herb that only bloomed one week each year. Lungflower, it was called, or godsbreath, a small, innocuous plant with tiny white buds as soft as down. I would never have noticed it if Adriel hadn't pointed it out. She gathered the buds, leaving the stems to die and regrow again next year. The buds would be dried and used in tea to ease a sick patient's congestion.

"Come now," she said, taking my arm so I didn't trip again. "You must have learned something."

Our horses were grazing in the field nearby, and the sun was warm despite the crispness in the early autumn air, but I was too exasperated to appreciate it. "Every time I think I'm getting somewhere, the book tries to trick me."

She glanced at me from the corner of her eye. "What do you mean?"

"Take this, for example. 'Bloodstone magic royals keep; bonds of death that run skin-deep.' Does that mean that the bloodstone only works as long as it's in contact with the wearer's skin? Or does that mean that once the bloodstone is removed, the wearer dies?"

She shook her head, lips curled in an amused smile.

"I'm glad you find my frustration comical." I flipped to another page. "And this. 'Bloodstone wearers willing are; control is weakened from afar.' That seems to mean Ceren can't control his guards from far away, which would make sense, considering how easily the captured guard was taken. And it explains why he would have come to Varenia and Galeth himself. But I could be reading that completely wrong. I just don't see why the entire thing has to be written in riddles. Aren't books supposed to be helpful?"

Adriel placed a gentle hand on my shoulder. "Breathe, Nor."

"Meanwhile," I continued, "Ceren has an entire village of Varenians at his disposal, and a mine's worth of bloodstones he could force them to extract."

Her grip tightened. "We don't know that yet."

I tried to take a deep breath, but I felt like I was wearing a corset. We didn't *know* anything, which was the problem. If Ceren could bring on the visions by drinking my blood, then I could be transported back to New Castle at any minute. The visions and dreams had been scary enough when I believed it was my own subconscious controlling them. Being under Ceren's control was far more terrifying.

"Let me see," Adriel said, holding her hand out. I passed the book to her, open to the page I'd been studying. I'd alternated between reading each line as closely as possible and skipping around, hoping I might stumble upon something that made sense. The book was filled with a lot of information that had nothing to do with bloodstones or blood bonds, too, and sifting that out took additional time and effort.

"Look at this next line," she said, leaning closer to me. "'Wearers linked by mind and soul; power gives but takes its toll.'"

I rubbed at my temples. "And?"

"Ceren controls the people who wear the bloodstones with his mind, correct?"

"We assume so."

"But it's taking a toll on him. It has to. No magic comes without cost, especially magic of that magnitude. His power is also his weakness."

And in order to combat that weakness, he was drinking my blood. The fact that he had come after me could only mean he needed more. "Should we be focusing on Ceren instead of his guards?" I asked. "The mind controlling the body?"

She shrugged. "Perhaps?"

"But we can't do that from here."

"Can't we?"

Before I could respond, we heard the pounding of hooves and looked beyond the field to the road.

Talin.

I rose to my feet, worry coursing through me as I waved at him. When Talin neared us, I ran forward to greet him the moment he dismounted. To my relief, he was smiling.

He picked me up by the waist and spun me around, then set me gently on my feet before looking me over from head to toe, like he was checking for injuries. His eyes flicked up to my hairline and a lopsided grin quirked his lips. "Pardon, Your Highness. I didn't realize I was in the presence of royalty." He bowed deeply, glancing up at me with twinkling eyes.

I laughed, completely having forgotten the daisy crown

Adriel had made for me earlier that morning. "A fool's mistake. How should I punish you?"

"Time away from you was surely punishment enough." I glanced behind Talin to Grig, who had just reached us. "Grig wouldn't let me travel alone," he explained.

"Good man," I said with a smile, waving to Grig. "But what are you doing here?"

"Your hunch was right, Nor. The Ilarean guards who died at the border had bloodstones."

My pulse sped up. Finally, something useful. "They did? How did you find them?"

"One of the Galethians who had helped recover the bodies had the stones. Roan discovered them when he noticed the woman was acting strangely."

I sucked in a breath. "No."

"She didn't know what they were, only that they appeared valuable. But Roan was furious."

I could imagine that easily enough.

"What will happen to the woman who stole them?" Adriel asked.

Talin glanced at her, clearly uneasy. "I get the sense that if it's up to Yana, she'll be banished to Ilara."

"What? Why?" I looked from Talin to Adriel.

"Yana doesn't suffer fools, or traitors," Adriel said.

I felt something inside of me grow cold. "What does 'banished' mean?"

"Sent south. She will never be allowed to live in Galeth again."

I couldn't judge too harshly. It was a better fate than Varenian banishment, and certainly better than being put to death, but after what had happened to Sami, I wasn't sure if it was just, either. "Where are the stones?" I asked Talin.

"On the way to Leesbrook."

"Roan could have brought them to me," Adriel said. "He knows I don't like going there." She was mostly talking to herself, but Talin and I exchanged a glance. "Besides, the stones on their own aren't much use. All this tells us is that Ceren is using the stones to control his men, which we already know."

Talin shook his head. "That's not entirely true. The Galethian with the stolen necklace seemed listless, half-asleep, just like the captured guard in Leesbrook. She didn't struggle when Roan approached her, so he decided to try taking the necklace. Whatever hold the stone had on her was gone. It didn't kill her. It was as if she woke up from a dream. She remembered nothing after she'd taken it."

"Now we know what skin-deep means," I said. Talin looked at me questioningly, and I explained Adriel's book and the lines about bloodstones. "It seems that wearing the stone, having any kind of physical contact with it, causes the bond to form. Which means we can take it from the captured guard, and it won't harm him. If anything, it will help him."

"Exactly."

I smiled at Adriel, but she didn't seem as pleased with the news.

"When are we leaving?" she asked Talin.

"Immediately. Roan and the others already rode ahead. I stopped to collect the two of you."

Adriel folded her arms across her chest. "Collect us? Like specimens?"

"I'm sorry?" Talin looked at me, clearly confused.

I shrugged, but Adriel only hitched her bag on her shoulder. "I need to go back to the cottage and leave a note for my patrons. I can catch up with you if you want to go with them, Nor."

Talin smiled at me encouragingly, clearly eager to spend time with me, but I didn't feel right leaving Adriel to finish up our work alone.

"You ride ahead," I said to Talin. "We'll be right behind you."

I was relieved when he didn't argue. "We're meeting at the fort. I'll see you soon."

I kissed him lightly on the cheek and watched him ride back to the road leading to Leesbrook with Grig.

"What's wrong?" I asked Adriel as we gathered our belongings. "This is a good thing. We might actually learn something useful about the bloodstones and Ceren's goals."

"You forget," she said, mounting her mare. "I don't actually care about Ceren or the bloodstones. Your prince's cause is not my cause."

I flinched, stung by her tone, but my hurt was quickly followed by anger. "None of you understand," I said under my breath.

"Understand what?"

"Understand what's at stake! If Ceren defeats Talia's army, do you think he'll just let the people he's controlling go? Do you think he'll let my parents go?" Hot tears pricked my eyes. "Ceren was close to stripping Varenia bare of pearls. He'll take all the bloodstones he can, and if he finds something else he thinks will give him an advantage, he'll take that, too. Everyone is so focused on their own concerns, they aren't seeing the bigger picture."

Adriel's brow furrowed. "And what's that?"

"Varenians are Ilareans, and Galethians are Varenians. The freedom of both groups depends on the other's. Perhaps Ceren wasn't willing to waste his men on breaching the Galethian border now, but once he has thousands of mindless soldiers? What will stop him then?"

"I'm sorry," Adriel began, but I clucked my tongue to Titania, who immediately broke into a canter toward the barn.

At the workshop, I changed into a pair of thicker riding breeches for the trip to Leesbrook. Foxglove sat on the wooden table where Adriel kept her herbs, licking his paws and watching me with one eye.

"What?" I demanded.

He blinked lazily in response.

Adriel knocked on my door a short while later, already dressed for the trip. "I'm sorry," she said again, before I could speak. "You're right. I should care about the bloodstones and Ceren's plans. And I do. But I also live alone in the woods for a reason, Nor. The citizens of Galeth only like me insofar as I am useful to them. Beyond that, they think I'm strange, even frightening."

"You're frightening on purpose," I said, only half joking.

That elicited a half smile. "Only because it's easier to pretend that's why they don't like me." She patted Fox on the head, running his tufted ears through her fingers. "I think you know what it's like to be misunderstood, to feel out of place wherever you go."

I lowered my gaze, already feeling the tears welling. She was right, of course. I had found plenty of places I didn't belong, but not yet one where I did.

"I tried to live in Leesbrook with Ana," she continued. "But it only took a few months before the whispered insults about 'the witch' started to take their toll. Ana was defensive on my behalf, but no one would visit my shop. Far easier to come to me out in the middle of nowhere, where no one will overhear if they ask for a cure for a personal problem or a way to prevent pregnancy."

I raised my eyes. "They ask for those things?"

She nodded. "I don't judge them, Nor. They are the ones who judge themselves."

"Are you afraid you'll see her?" I ventured after a few moments of silence. "Ana."

Adriel started to head for the door. "I'm not afraid. I pray for it every time I go. And that's the problem. She's married, with a child. Those are things I'll never have. Not because I don't want them, but because no one wants them with a witch."

It was my natural inclination to explain all the ways she was wrong, but I could tell that she would have a counterargument for anything I said. Besides, she knew her life. I was a stranger here. What could I possibly know that she didn't?

Instead, I placed a hand on her shoulder. "You're right, Adriel. I do know what it's like to be misunderstood, to feel like you don't belong anywhere. And I don't know how to make it better. But I do know one thing."

"What's that?" she asked.

I smiled. "You're not alone."

Zadie and Sami were already at the meetinghouse when we arrived, and I ran to my sister the moment I saw her. She practically glowed with health and happiness, and I felt an unfamiliar stab of jealousy toward Sami, knowing that her happiness had very little to do with me.

While the councilmembers assembled, Zadie led me to an alcove so we could talk. "How are you?" she asked.

"I'm fine," I assured her. "I have so much to tell you. But first tell me how things are with you and Sami."

She blushed and looked down at her hands, twisting a bit of the lace edge of her sleeve. "We're good, Nor. I can't tell you how good it feels to hold him, to know he's safe." Her smile faltered. "And then I feel guilty because I know the people we love are suffering."

"Our parents are at New Castle," I said. "All the Varenians are."

Her eyes widened in shock. "What? How do you know?"

I hadn't told Zadie about the visions and dreams yet, in part because I hadn't understood them, but also because I hadn't wanted to frighten her. "I'll explain everything to you, I promise. But for now, I just need you to trust me."

"Let's get this meeting started, shall we?"

I turned at the sound of Yana's voice.

"The prisoner is ready for us. He's been tied down, so we should have no problem removing the stone." She glanced at Roan. "I'd like to lead the interrogation."

None of the other councilmembers protested, but Talin stepped forward. "With all due respect, Yana, I know far more about Ilara, New Castle, and my brother than anyone else. I believe I can get the most useful information out of him the fastest."

"And with all due respect, Talin, he is our prisoner, captured trying to cross our border." Yana looked out over her fellow councilmembers. "Anyone opposed to me questioning the prisoner, say aye."

"Aye," Roan said immediately, earning a glare from Yana.

I studied the other members, several of whom moved uncomfortably in their seats, but they kept their hands down.

"Wouldn't a vote be fairer?" I blurted.

"What do you think this is?" Yana said, turning her blistering glare on me.

It was hard not to be cowed by her, but I remembered what Roan had said, that Yana would only respect me if I spoke my mind. I stuck out my chin stubbornly. "Perhaps if it was a blind vote, people may be more inclined to show their real preference."

All of the councilmembers turned to stare at me as if I'd grown a second head. But I knew I was right. That was how things were done in Varenia when the elders held a vote.

They wrote their decisions down on a piece of parchment and placed it in a box. Governor Kristos gathered the votes and read the decision when they were finished.

"That was the way we did it before," Roan said.

Before what? Several of the councilmembers were nodding their agreement. Yana's face was pale beneath her freckles.

"Very well," she ground out. "We'll do it by secret ballot."

I exhaled in relief. I had been prepared for a fight, but Yana only studied me coolly.

After the votes were tallied, they came back five in favor of Yana, five in favor of Talin. Yana wasn't allowed to vote since she clearly had a vested interest.

"Who has the deciding vote?" I whispered to Roan.

"Generally, it falls to the eldest member. His vote counts twice."

I glanced at Hoff, who was one of the few people who didn't seem intimidated by Yana. He rose from his chair. "I voted in favor of Talin," he proclaimed.

Yana's expression remained flat, but I could see that the nod of agreement she gave didn't come easily.

"Don't get too cocky," Roan said in my ear, and I realized I was grinning. "No one holds a grudge quite like Yana."

My smile vanished as Talin, Zadie, Adriel, and I followed him toward the dungeon, where the prisoner was being held. Yana and Hoff were also in attendance, while the rest of the councilmembers stayed behind.

At least there were windows, I thought, unlike the New Castle dungeon. But it was still a prison, designed to hold people in, not make them comfortable, and I couldn't stop the memories of my own captivity from flooding back. I'd spent days alone in the dark, living in my own filth, subsisting on moldy bread and thick, metallic-tasting liver stew.

Ceren had come to visit me only when he wanted more of my blood. And the last time he'd come, I had only managed to escape by stabbing him.

Ceren's guard sat in a heavy wooden chair, restrained with leather straps. His skin was sallow and gray. We were doing him a favor by taking away the stone, though with the way he screamed and struggled as soon as Roan touched the necklace, it was clear he didn't think so.

Fortunately, the straps held, and the prisoner's color began to return almost as soon as the stone was off his skin. Roan, who wore thick leather gloves, immediately dropped it into a metal tray, where it couldn't influence anyone else.

The guard blinked and shook his head as if he was waking from a dream, exactly as Talin had said.

"Where am I?" the man asked, looking from Talin, who stood directly in front of him, to Zadie and me. He seemed to relax a little when he saw there were women present.

"You're in Galeth," Talin said calmly. "You were captured and imprisoned when you attempted to follow us across the border."

He stared blankly at Talin, as if the words meant nothing to him.

"What is the last thing you remember?" I asked, coming to kneel in front of him. It must be terribly disorienting to find yourself restrained in a room full of strangers, and so far, he wasn't even struggling.

He closed his eyes. "I was in my village. The king had come to test all the strongest men, to see if we were worthy of being chosen."

"Chosen for what?" Talin asked.

"To be a member of his guard. To receive one of his bloodstones. He told us they would bring us unimaginable power."

His face colored as he glanced between us. "I know it sounds foolish, but I'd seen the king before with my own eyes. He'd always been weak and sickly, but he looked like a completely different person. He said it was because of the stones."

"And you were chosen?" I asked.

"Yes. So were my brothers. I haven't seen them since." He squinted a bit, looking at Talin. "You're the king's brother."

"I am."

The man bowed his head. "Your Highness. The king told us we were to find you and capture you. I don't remember why."

Talin sighed. "I'm fairly certain he didn't actually give you a reason."

The Ilarean sagged a little in his restraints. "Am I going to be executed?"

"Of course not," Talin said. "You weren't in control of your actions. We just need to know a few things."

He licked his lips nervously. "What kinds of things?"

"Everything you know about the bloodstones and my brother's plans."

The man looked crestfallen. He seemed eager to cooperate—or at least to not be punished. "I don't know." His eyes darted from Talin to Roan. "The king wore a crown full of stones like those," he said, glancing at the necklace in the tray.

"He placed that on me himself," the man said. "That's the last thing I remember."

"How many stones has he given out?" Talin asked.

"I wish I knew. Hundreds, at least. Ours wasn't the first village he visited."

"And he's only recruiting men?"

"I—I believe so?"

Zadie appeared at the guard's side so quietly I hadn't seen

her move. She held a cup of water to his lips, and he drank eagerly, nodding in thanks when he'd finished.

"Did he tell you why he was growing his army?" It was the first time Roan had spoken.

"He said he was going to restore Ilara to its former glory," the man said. "That we would no longer allow territories to secede, like Pirot and Meradin. That we would defeat the so-called woman king. He said he wouldn't allow us to remain weak, that he wasn't like his father."

Talin's mouth flattened into a line. "Was there anything else?"

The guard couldn't meet Talin's eyes. "He…he promised us that those who stood in his way would be executed, but those who served him would be rewarded with land and other riches."

"I can't speak for my brother," Talin said. "But I believe it was his intention to let you all die, if need be. I'm sorry. It seems he controlled you completely while you wore that stone."

Rage and disgust for Ceren coursed through me. Once, he had used his power to intimidate others. Now, he could literally control them like puppets, and he did so remorselessly, with no regard for anyone but himself. How many people could he control at once, I wondered? A hundred? A thousand? An entire army?

I could see the guard was on the verge of tears. "What became of my brothers?" he asked.

"I don't know." Talin placed his hand on the man's shoulder. "What's your name?"

"Jerem."

"I hope we'll find your brothers, Jerem."

Roan stepped forward. "We'll need to vote, but as far as I'm concerned, you can leave Galeth with Talin and his men."

Talin nodded his thanks. "You'll be free once we reach Ilara. You can go your own way, or you can join my side and fight against my brother. It's your choice to make."

The man's eyes darted around the small room, taking us all in as if he suspected this was a trap. "What is your side?" he asked finally.

"I fight for the woman king," Talin answered, and Roan's eyes narrowed almost imperceptibly. "And I am here to ask the Galethians to join me."

Yana looked like she was ready to kill Talin, but Hoff managed to escort her back to the meeting room while Roan led us to another part of the fortress. There was a large sitting room decorated with tapestries and carved furniture, similar to what I'd seen in New Castle. Roan collapsed into an overstuffed chair and flicked his hand at us, indicating we should all sit.

"I'm sorry," Talin said, still standing. "I didn't want to ask for your help before you understood the magnitude of what we were up against."

"Do you take me for a fool?" Roan asked, sitting up. "I knew your purpose from the start. Why else would you elect to stay, when your mother is about to start a war?"

I wasn't entirely surprised Roan had guessed our plans. "You understand why we didn't mention it to the rest of the council, though, don't you?" I said. "We couldn't risk being thrown out of Galeth."

"I do understand. What I can't figure out," Roan went on, "is why you didn't tell me you were on the side of the woman king." He was looking at me when he said this, but Talin answered.

"I did. I told you my mother and sister were alive and my sister was the rightful heir of Ilara."

"But you didn't tell me she *was* the woman king."

"I'm sorry," Talin said, blinking. "I thought that part was obvious."

Roan sighed in exasperation. "It wasn't. And besides, do you know what this so-called woman king—I imagine that refers to your mother, since your sister is barely out of her swaddling clothes—is doing?"

My thoughts went immediately to Shale and Ella. I had wanted to believe that they were wrong about Talin's mother, but if Roan had heard something similar, it would be harder to dismiss.

"I've heard rumors," Talin said, his voice hardening. "But they are just that, rumors."

"Most rumors have some truth to them," Roan retorted. "Even if she isn't conscripting everyone to her army, why should we side with her any more than Ceren? We're not interested in a monarchy, whether it's a kingdom or a queendom."

"I would think some people would be very fond of the idea," I mumbled.

Roan smirked. "Yana likes to believe she's in charge. She's not."

"I can assure you that my mother is nothing like Ceren," Talin said. "She's the gentlest woman I've ever known."

My eyebrows rose at that, but I kept my mouth shut. Talia had survived a murder attempt, escaped New Castle while pregnant, and raised a child—and an army—in exile.

I doubted anyone who knew her now would describe her as gentle. But Talin had only known her as his mother.

"Gentle women don't command armies," Roan said. "And we won't commit our forces to hers. You were delusional for thinking we would."

"Even after what that Jerem said?" Talin asked, his voice rising with anger.

"He told us what Ceren wants to do, not what he's actually doing. We've protected our borders without breach for decades. If we send our fighters south, how will we do that?"

"You don't need to send everyone," Talin said. "A thousand riders would—"

Roan laughed, a deep, booming chuckle that rang completely false. "You'd be lucky if we gave you a dozen."

Talin turned and ran his hands through his hair in frustration.

"Listen," I said, stepping next to him. "A dozen riders wouldn't help your mother, but it might be enough to get us to New Castle."

"You know we can't go there yet—not without the backing of my mother and her army. We'll be slaughtered if we attempt to rescue the Varenians on our own."

I raised my voice so the others would be able to hear. "What if we didn't need to launch a full-scale attack on New Castle? What if we could get right to the source of all of our problems?"

"You mean Ceren?" Talin asked. "Are you suggesting we assassinate him?"

"Cut off the head to kill the body," Roan said. "It makes more sense than trying to face his army."

"New Castle is a thousand times harder to penetrate than Fort Crag," Talin countered. "There is only one way up the mountain. Ceren will have sealed up the exit you used by now, Nor."

I'd already considered that, of course. But on the ride here, a new plan had begun to formulate in my mind. Now that I knew exactly what Ceren wanted, and why, the solution seemed almost too simple. I knew Talin wouldn't like the next part of my plan, but if I could learn to trust the people around me, he would have to do the same.

"What if we could lure the eel out of his cave, rather than try to enter it?"

Roan and Talin both turned to look at me. "What?"

I took a deep breath. "Ceren still needs my blood. Why else would he chase us here? He's using a lot of magic to control minds with the bloodstones, and I believe my blood is giving him the strength he needs to wield it."

Roan looked horrified, but it was Talin who spoke up. "You're not going anywhere near New Castle."

"Believe me, I have no intention of ever going there again. I was thinking more of using me as bait."

Talin frowned. "How is that supposed to make me feel better?"

"He can track me," I said, "through the visions."

Zadie, Sami, and Roan turned to stare at me, but I held up a hand to quiet them. "If I leave the safety of Galeth's borders, I believe Ceren will come for me."

Talin folded his arms. "I know I can beat him one on one, even with his newfound strength."

"Thank you, but I wasn't finished." I took a deep breath. "I think we should split up."

Now it was Talin's turn to stare at me, but I continued on before he could protest. "If I'm reading Adriel's book correctly—"

"That's a big if, Nor," Adriel interjected.

"*If* I'm reading the book correctly, then Ceren can't control people who are far away from him. It explains why he came to Varenia and Galeth himself, and why the guards he left behind are essentially mindless. Which means New Castle would be vulnerable. You could potentially take it on your own, without Talia's army." I knew it was all a risk, but it might prevent a massive war and give us the chance to rescue my parents much sooner.

"There would be no guarantee you could outrun Ceren," Talin said. "Or that I'd be able to breach New Castle."

"Do you have another idea?" I asked.

He gave an almost imperceptible shake of his head.

There was one more thing we needed, and unfortunately, it would depend on the last person I wanted to ask for a favor. "Do you really think you can get us a dozen riders, Roan?"

"I know I can. I'll choose them myself."

"You mean riders from Fort Crag?" Talin asked. "That's too risky. You're Galeth's first line of defense. Surely one of the other forts can spare them."

"Perhaps. But I wouldn't trust riders I haven't trained."

My mouth fell open in shock. "What are you saying?"

He grinned. "You didn't think I was going to let you have all the fun without me, did you?"

18

"We should come with you," I argued as Roan started to close the door behind him. He had escorted us outsiders to a sitting room so he could explain what he'd learned to the rest of the councilmembers.

"What, so you can get in another fight with Yana?" He clucked his tongue. "I'd sooner put two dominant mares in the same pasture."

I wrinkled my nose at the analogy just as he slammed the door in my face.

He returned an hour or so later, face beaming in triumph even as Yana followed him through the door.

"What are you thinking?" she demanded. "Sacrificing Galethians for this spoiled princeling and his girlfriend? Or were you perhaps hoping this would impress her enough to pick you instead?"

I rose from my chair, indignant, but Roan cut me off with a sharp glance.

"Do you really think I'd endanger my own men and women for a girl? Be reasonable, Yana. If you still can."

Her face had turned nearly the same shade of red as her hair. "What's that supposed to mean?"

"You know exactly what it means. We've given you the benefit of the doubt because we know how difficult it was when Landrey left, but we voted on this. One soldier from each fort will replace my men and women at Fort Crag. Twelve including me. The decision is made."

For the first time since I'd met her, Yana appeared at a loss for words. I watched as the color leeched from her face, and she sank into a chair, suddenly looking exhausted.

There was a long, heavy silence, and then she tilted her face up to Roan. "You think this is because of Landrey?" Her usually powerful voice was raw with emotion, and just like with Mother, I found it difficult to witness. There was something about seeing the cracks in a seemingly impenetrable veneer that cut straight to my heart.

Roan placed a hand on her hunched shoulder. I expected her to recoil at his touch, but she remained slumped in defeat. "Of course it is," he soothed with surprising gentleness. "She's your sister. I know how hard it was for you to see her banished."

I covered my mouth with my palm to stifle a gasp.

"You have no idea how hard it is," she whispered, but there was no anger in her voice. Whatever fight she'd put up in the meeting room had finally left her. "And to see that child riding Titania is even worse." Her eyes traveled to me as she said it, but she seemed resigned rather than bitter.

"Titania chose Nor," Roan said. "Believe me, I was as shocked as you were. But that horse doesn't make false moves.

And I believe Landrey would be glad to know Titania's with a rider she chose."

Yana made a small noise in her throat. The rest of us looked at each other, having no idea what would happen next.

After a few moments of silence, she sat up straighter and placed her hands on her knees. "Right. Well, you can't all ride straight for New Castle. Ceren will see you coming and crush the lot of you." She stood up and began to pace the room. "It seems to me that if it's Nor he wants, she should travel directly south with you and your soldiers."

Roan's eyebrows twitched. "Then you and Nor are in agreement. She was already planning to split up with the others." He lowered his voice and leaned in closer. "You'd know that if you hadn't stormed out of the meeting."

Yana looked sheepish for a split second before her eyes darted to me. "Talin and his men should go east and cut south along the shore. They can take the old road to New Castle," she continued.

Roan tapped his chin thoughtfully. "Not a bad idea."

"Nor," Talin said, placing his hand on my arm. "I don't like this. If anything happens and I'm not there to protect you…"

I pursed my lips. "I thought we agreed I don't need protecting."

"That was before I knew my brother wanted more of your blood."

Roan rolled his eyes at the two of us. "We'll ride slowly as a large group. You'll make far better time without us. And the sooner you reach New Castle, the better the odds you'll be able to infiltrate it while Ceren is away."

"It's a risky plan," Yana said. She glanced at me, one eyebrow raised. "The best plans usually are."

I smiled at the unexpected approval. "Thank you."

Roan looked to Talin and his men. "You should leave right away. We'll hang back a day to give you a head start."

Osius and Grig nodded, but Talin turned to me. "Can we talk for a minute?"

"Of course." I followed him into the hallway, where we had more privacy. "What's wrong?"

"I hate the idea of separating from you. I know you don't need my protection, but I want to be sure that you're safe."

I cupped his face with my palm. "I don't like it, either. But there was no way we were ever going to stop Ceren without putting ourselves at risk. Danger was always going to be inherent to the plan."

"I hate the plan," he murmured into my hair. "Just promise me one thing."

"What?"

He sighed, a soft puff of air against my skin. "That when you're in a position to do something bold and reckless and Nor-ish, you remember how much I love you."

It was the first time he'd said it out loud, and the words spread warmth throughout my chest. "Fine," I said, smiling. "But you have to promise me something, too."

He nodded.

"That when you decide to do something heroic and brash and Talin-ish, that you remember that I love you, too."

He leaned back to look me in the eye, and there was so much hope and fear there that my heart swelled with tenderness. His voice was almost too quiet to hear when he asked, "Are you sure?"

I rolled my eyes. "Honestly, Talin, the nonsense that comes out of your mouth."

His lips twitched in a grin. "Do you remember what happened the last time you said that to me?"

"I do indeed. So what are you waiting for this time?"

When he kissed me, I knew he didn't actually doubt my love for him. And I knew that I didn't doubt it, either. I wanted to stay there with him forever, but the rest of the group was waiting for our decision. We walked back in the room hand in hand, and Roan smiled.

"I knew you'd do the right thing," he said, and I wasn't sure if he was talking to Talin or me.

Talin, Grig, Osius, and Ceren's guard headed east that afternoon so they could cross the border into Ilara under cover of darkness. The odds that Ceren would have men watching that border were slim—it led into far northern Ilara, which was uninhabited—but the Galethians had promised to help them cross the border safely, with the councilmember from the nearest fort escorting them.

I watched them go from the top of a hill, clutching Zadie's hand as they disappeared around a curve in the road. Until I left Varenia the first time, I didn't have any practice with goodbyes. Now I understood that they wouldn't get easier. Difficult things, I was learning, never did. You simply got stronger.

"Is this a stupid plan?" I asked Zadie. "Should we have stayed together?"

She shook her head. "It's not a stupid plan. But I understand why you're questioning it." She sat down on the grass and motioned for me to join her. "When were you going to tell me about Ceren and the visions?" she asked. There was no accusation in her voice, only hurt.

"I'm sorry, Zadie. I should have told you when I told Talin. I was just afraid of worrying you unnecessarily, when I didn't even know what they meant."

"Silly Nor. Don't you know I was worried about you any-way? I always know when you're keeping something from me. I didn't push you because I knew you'd tell me when you were ready. But I can't help wishing you'd told me sooner. Not that it would have changed the outcome, but because I might have at least offered you some comfort."

I stared down at my hands folded in my lap. "I just feel like I'm constantly bringing trouble to the people I love, when all I ever wanted was for you to be happy."

She placed one of her hands over mine. "I know that, Nor. And so do Talin and Sami. Father knows, and even Mother, I think."

I raised my eyes to hers. "Then stay in Galeth with Sami. Stay so I'll know that at least two of the people I love will be safe."

"Nor—"

"You and Sami could have a good life here," I insisted. "This journey will be dangerous, and there's nothing you and Sami can do that the Galethians and I can't. It's me that Ceren wants. There's no reason for you and Sami to risk yourselves."

I trailed off when I saw that her expression hadn't changed a bit.

"Are you finished?" she asked.

"I don't know. I suppose so."

"Good. Now it's my turn. When you went to Ilara, I ex-perienced the worst pain I'd ever felt. The sting from the maiden's hair jellyfish was nothing compared to the agony of your loss. I put on a brave face because I didn't want you to leave thinking I wouldn't be all right without you. But even Sami's banishment didn't hurt me as much, perhaps because I'd already become numb. I don't know."

"Zadie—"

She started to raise a hand to cover my mouth in warning, and I pressed my lips closed.

"Look, Nor. I know you think you have to be the brave one all the time, that you're the leader and I follow. That you have to be everything for me. And it's my fault more than anyone's. But there was one good thing that came from you leaving." She took my hands in hers. "I learned I can be brave, too."

I shook my head. "I know. I've always known."

"Yes," she said, her golden-brown eyes welling with tears. "But I didn't. And I would sooner die than let you leave without me again."

I bit my lower lip to keep it from trembling. "I'm so sorry, Zadie."

"After you left, things in Varenia were bad. Worse than I've let on. I had told myself that I'd done what I'd done not just so I could be with Sami, but also so that you could go to Ilara and live the life you dreamed of. I couldn't think of another way. And I've never forgiven myself for asking you to help me that night."

"I have never held it against you. I know you thought it was your only option."

"But I struggled with the guilt, with my own selfishness. I told Sami everything, and he said he understood, but I don't know if he did. I think a part of him would have found it nobler if I had gone to Ilara anyway, despite the fact that he loved me. I dishonored myself by lying and allowing you to take my punishment, and I don't know that he'll ever see me the same way as he did before."

"That's not fair," I said, my anger growing on her behalf. "It's not like he was doing anything to help!"

"He has guilt of his own, believe me. That's why he tried to convince his father and the elders of your innocence after he saw you in the port market. He risked his standing in the community for both of us, and it cost him everything." She looked away. "He isn't the same since the banishment, Nor. It took something from him."

We sat in silence for a few minutes. "What happened out there on the ocean?" I asked gently.

She shook her head. "I don't know exactly. He doesn't like to talk about those three nights at sea. He was able to create a makeshift paddle from the benches on the boat and row to shore on the fourth day. But I don't think it was being at sea that traumatized him; it was the kidnapping, the way people he had known his entire life turned on him. He never wants to go back to Varenia. I don't, either. Once we free our parents, we plan to go somewhere else to settle. I can't look those people in the eyes anymore."

Questions I couldn't bear to consider popped into my mind without warning. Were those people still alive? Was there even a Varenia left to go back to? "I understand, Zadie."

I wiped her tears away with my thumbs before they could fall, and she did the same to me. After a minute, she sniffed and set her chin.

"In conclusion, while I appreciate your speech, and I know it's coming from a place of love, kindly shut up on the subject of this journey."

I blinked in shock. "Wh-what?"

She rose and brushed the grass from her skirts. "I don't want to hear about it again. Sami and I are in complete agreement on this, so don't think going to him behind my back will help. His parents are in just as much peril as ours."

"I know that," I said, still reeling as I climbed to my feet. "And I know that you're brave, Zadie. But selfishly, I want to keep you safe. I couldn't bear losing you again."

"And you think I can?"

I shook my head, unable to speak.

"We came into this world together, Nor. And that's the only way I plan on going out. Do you understand me?"

I nodded. "Yes."

"Good." She pulled me to her, and for the first time in my life, she didn't feel small in my arms. It wasn't my job to protect her anymore. We would protect each other.

19

"Come with us," I pleaded as Adriel helped gather my be-longings from her cottage. "Please."

She glanced at me over her shoulder. "I would only slow you down. I'm not a natural horsewoman, Nor."

"We're not going to travel fast. And your knowledge would be invaluable on the road if anyone gets sick or injured."

She glanced at Foxglove, who was licking his outstretched hind leg, one ear flicked toward us. "Who would take care of him?"

"He's been taking care of himself just fine, from what I can tell." The cat came and went when he felt like it, sneaking in through a cracked window when he wanted shelter and warmth. Even when he slept on my bed at night, I got the sense it was because he desired somewhere soft to rest and a hand to pet him, not because he needed companionship.

"And what if I don't make it back?" Adriel asked. She was convincing herself not to come. I'd seen the same tactic in

Zadie a hundred times, when I tried to get her to go diving against Mother's wishes. But I had a knack for knowing
when to leave her alone and when to push just a little harder.

"Bring him with us," I said.

She turned to look at me, her blue eyes wide with incre-
dulity. "What?"

Fox slowly lowered his leg mid-lick, his pink tongue still
partially extended, as if he was keen to hear this explanation, too.

"He can ride in a basket behind your saddle. He'll like it."

She laughed. "He'll hate it."

"Fine, he'll hate it. But if it convinces you to come with
us, it's worth it."

She sat down on the edge of my bed. "Why do you want
me to come so badly?"

I could have said that I wanted her help with the book and
understanding the blood bond between Ceren and me or re-
iterated that I thought she would be useful on the road. But
I genuinely cared for Adriel, and I knew she wasn't happy,
despite her bravado.

"Because," I said, coming to sit down beside her. "I think
you and I met for a reason. And I don't think our journey
is meant to end here. You've never felt accepted in Galeth.
I know what that's like. But if there's one thing I've learned
from everything that's happened lately, it's that we don't have
to accept things just because of where we happened to be
born."

She was quiet for a moment. "Wave child," she said finally.
"That's what they call you, isn't it?"

I nodded. "The Ilareans do, yes."

"We were called all sorts of things by the Galethians. I've
heard people refer to me as the Hedge Hag when they think

I can't hear. They learned to put up with those of us who re-mained because we were useful to them, but they never fully accepted us."

I nodded in understanding. "Oh yes, I know all about that. We Varenians were never good enough to come to land, and yet somehow we were good enough to marry the Ilarean princes."

She gave a wry snort. "Tell me, Nor. What did you hope to find when you left Varenia? I imagine with your limited experience in the world, you couldn't have had any idea what to expect. But what were you hoping for?"

I sighed and leaned back on my elbows. "I told myself I wanted adventure, to see things that I'd never even dreamed of. But it was about more than that." I touched the scar on my cheek absently. "After I was injured as a child, I could tell that I had lost value not just as a potential bride, but as a daugh-ter. My father always made me feel loved, but my mother... I wanted to prove to her, to everyone in Varenia, that I was worth more than my appearance."

Adriel's brow wrinkled in confusion. "All that over a tiny scar?"

I nodded. "I tried to contribute to our family by diving deeper and more often than most girls. But all my mother saw was my salt-dried hair and dull skin. When Zadie was injured and couldn't go to Ilara, I asked to go in her place because I thought I could make a difference. But the village accused me of deliberately hurting her for my own selfish aims. And when I found out what Ceren was doing to the Varenians and tried to warn them, they ended up banishing Sami for con-spiring with me. The entire village despises me."

"Then why do you want to help them?" Adriel asked.

"They're still my people," I said weakly.

Adriel cocked her head, clearly not satisfied with my answer. "And?"

I should be angry with them, I knew. They had turned their backs on my family and nearly killed Sami. But despite everything… "I suppose I still want them to accept me."

Adriel was quiet for a long moment.

I tucked in an errant sleeve on the folded tunic beside me and placed it on top of my small stack of clothing. "Adriel, I don't want you to do anything you aren't comfortable with. I just want you to know that I would love for you to join us, if you want to. If not, then I will hope we meet again, in this life or the next."

She glanced at Foxglove, who had returned to sunning himself in the window. "I can't bring a cat on the road, Nor."

"No. I suppose not."

"I'll ask one of my customers to look after him for me while I'm gone. Just promise me that you won't leave me behind."

I leaped up, toppling my stack of folded clothing, and hugged her. "Never."

We joined the rest of our traveling party at Fort Crag that evening. Roan seemed surprised to see Adriel with me, but he didn't question it. There were eleven other Galethian soldiers, their mounts saddled and ready, waiting outside the fortress. Sami, still learning to ride, had been loaned Duster, who was so wide and cushiony that Sami said he felt more like a sofa than a horse.

Roan looked powerful atop a stocky, muscular gelding with a golden coat, dark mane and tail, and a dark stripe down his back. I could tell immediately this was a special animal, one that seemed far more fitting for a commander than Duster ever had. I wondered if he rode Duster just to show that he didn't need a fancy horse to be the best rider in his region.

"I'd like to go over a few ground rules before we set out," Roan said. "First, Nor, Zadie, Sami, and Adriel should be in the center of our group at all times. If I ever find one of them riding first or last, I'm going to make sure your next few days of riding are incredibly uncomfortable."

A few of the soldiers winced, as if they'd experienced the alluded-to punishment before and weren't eager to try it again.

"We will be walking and trotting for most of the journey. We're not going for speed. This is about safety, first and foremost. I know, I know," he said to the grumbling riders. "Not the most exciting. But we don't know what to expect, what Ceren has planned, or even what the terrain will be like. Our mission is to see our guests safely through to the woman king's camp, not to have an adventure." He paused and grinned. "All right, I'm hoping for a little adventure along the way, too."

The soldiers whooped and cheered. It was clear they both respected and liked their leader, similar to the way Talin's men regarded him. There were five female soldiers in the group and seven men including Roan. There didn't seem to be any hierarchy among them. They trained, ate, and slept together. Most of the women had shaved heads or close-cropped hair, like the men. To avoid the spread of lice, Adriel told me. But it also made them look fierce; Varenian standards of beauty— grace, delicacy, softness—had no place here. These women were tanned and muscular, unadorned and rough around the edges. But the way they moved with their horses, as if they were one with the animal, was far more graceful than any curtsy I'd ever seen.

One rider, a tall woman with short blond hair that matched

her palomino's mane almost perfectly, had found her way over to where Adriel and I stood.

"You should take a saddle pad from the supply room before we go," she said quietly to Adriel. "Your mare needs a riser to counterbalance her flat withers."

Adriel arched a dark eyebrow. "You think I don't know what my mare needs?"

"I can tell you've never ridden her for more than a few hours at a time," the woman said, but there was nothing accusatory about her tone. She was merely stating the facts. "And I can tell you care for her and wouldn't want her to suffer on our journey."

Adriel nodded. "Would you show me which one would work best?"

The woman escorted Adriel to the tack room while the others made their final preparations.

I mounted Titania, checking her girth one final time.

"Are you nervous?" Roan asked, his gelding earning a skeptical eye from Titania.

I cut him a similar glance. "About what?"

"Getting back on the road. You have no idea what you're facing."

"No," I retorted. "But then, neither do you. Isn't this your first time leaving Galeth?"

We started filing down the mountain from the fortress to the pass that would lead us back into Ilara. According to the scouts, they hadn't seen any of Ceren's guards since the first night, but the archers would keep watch from the fortress until we were out of range. Then we were on our own.

"I haven't," he admitted. "But there isn't a man alive who can outride me."

"Ah, but what about a woman? I believe you said Yana was the best rider in Galeth."

He flashed one of his wry grins. "I haven't challenged her in a while."

"Why did you really agree to come on this mission?" I asked. The border pass was just up ahead. Soon we would need to ride single file.

"What if I said it was because I wanted to spend time alone with you?"

I rolled my eyes. "I would say you are a flirt and a liar."

He chuckled. "Fine. I volunteered because I don't believe that Galeth should continue to cut itself off from the rest of the world the way it has. We would benefit from a safe continent with more open borders between countries."

"How?" I asked, my curiosity piqued. "It seems to me that most Galethians are very happy."

"We're people just like you, Nor. Some are happy, some aren't. And our strict borders don't just keep foreigners out. They keep us in. I would like my children to see the rest of the continent someday, if they so choose." He paused as if waiting for me to challenge him.

"I agree with all of that. And I'm glad you're joining us."

"Why?" he asked as his horse pulled ahead to lead the way. "Afraid you'd miss me?"

"Hardly," I said, driving Titania forward at the last second to cut him off before we entered the pass.

"Thanks," he called from behind me. "The view is much better from back here."

We crossed the border without incident and soon found ourselves back on the road. The forest was dense on either side of the road, and Roan's soldiers were extremely vigilant, surrounding us civilians to ensure we were in the middle of the herd. Zadie and I were pressed close together, which Titania wasn't particularly fond of. Sami and Adriel, who both had slower-moving horses, had naturally fallen in line with each other and were talking behind us, too quiet to hear. I could see Roan's dun up ahead. He was riding with the tall blonde, Shiloh, who appeared to be the second-in-command since Kester had remained behind at Fort Crag.

We had gotten a late start, and the sun was already dipping below the trees. "When do you think we'll make camp?" Zadie asked me. She was back in her riding clothes, her gowns and petticoats left behind.

"Soon, I hope. We're not in a hurry. I think Roan just wants to get beyond these trees."

Just as I finished speaking, I heard the sound of rushing air, followed by a startled grunt.

Titania and Zadie's mare were instantly on high alert, as were the rest of the horses. The riders pressed in closer around us, turning their backs to us and drawing their weapons. Some had swords, others crossbows.

I glanced around, wondering if Sami and Adriel were all right, and saw an arrow sticking out of the thigh of one of the men closest to me. Beyond the grunt, he hadn't made a noise.

Zadie and I shared a horrified glance just as another arrow came flying through the air, landing at the feet of one of the other horses. It didn't flinch, and neither did the rider.

"There," someone called, pointing to the woods. Just as the riders had turned their attention to that place, a third arrow flew toward us, followed swiftly by a fourth and fifth.

We were being ambushed. Roan whistled between his teeth, one long note followed by a short one, and the horses turned as if one animal and began galloping south. It happened so quickly I barely had time to gather my reins before we were flying down the road, more arrows than I could count whizzing overhead.

"I thought they wanted you alive!" Zadie screamed. "What are they doing?"

"I have no idea," I shouted, stealing furtive glances behind me. Despite their laziness earlier, Adriel's and Sami's horses were having no problem keeping up with the herd. I saw an arrow pierce the flank of one of the horses, but it didn't falter, even as blood began to seep from the wound.

I looked farther back on the trail and saw a group of five or six guards clad in black armor. Ceren's men. The arrows had ceased, with only a few having found their mark, but we were weighed down with more supplies and more riders, and the guards were gaining.

"We're not going to outrun them," Zadie said, just as Roan whistled three times. The horses to our left came to an abrupt halt as the rest of us kept going. As I looked back, I saw that the Galethians had turned on their heels and were riding toward Ceren's guards.

I expected the Ilareans to fan out or turn around, as anyone would when faced with six Galethian war horses and an array of weaponry coming toward them at high speeds. But Ceren's men rode straight ahead, colliding with the Galethian troops in a clash of horseflesh and swords.

Roan whistled again and two more Galethians peeled off the back of our group to help their comrades. A moment later, Roan yanked his horse to a halt, and our mounts followed.

"Surround the outsiders," he ordered. There were only a few Galethians left, but they did it immediately, without hesitation. I had taken a short sword from the armory at Roan's insistence, and I drew it now, though I had absolutely no idea how to fight with it.

"Easy there," Roan said to me as he brought his dun up beside Titania. "I don't think you're going to need to kill anyone just yet."

From where we stood, we could hear shouts and the sound of fighting, with the occasional scream from a horse that froze my blood.

"Shouldn't you help them?" I asked as more time passed and no one returned.

"I trust my riders," he said, though his jaw was tight and his own sword was drawn.

Even though I knew the members of the Galethian cavalry could match any Ilarean guard under normal circumstances, I couldn't help but worry. Ceren's guards were fearless in the face of danger thanks to the bloodstones. They would mindlessly throw themselves off a cliff if Ceren commanded it. I scanned the woods, wondering where he was. If my theory was correct, Ceren couldn't be far.

A moment later, the first of the riders appeared, and I found myself breathing a sigh of enormous relief. The rest followed in quick succession, bloodied and battered but alive.

I waited for Ceren's guards, but the lead Galethian gave Roan a quick shake of his head. "We killed several, but the rest fled. We decided it wasn't worth the chase."

"Did you search the bodies?"

"Yes," a rider said. "No bloodstones that we saw."

"That explains why the guards retreated," I said, relieved that Ceren wasn't controlling everyone around him with the bloodstones. "The good news is we know they aren't nearly as loyal when they're free to make their own decisions."

"The bad news is, Ceren isn't following us," Roan added.

"Not yet, anyway."

"We can only hope those who escaped will tell him we crossed the border." Roan dismounted and helped take stock of the injuries. Aside from the man who'd been shot in the leg, the horses were the only ones who had shed blood.

"We should get off the road and set up a camp for the night," Shiloh said. The sun was already below the treetops. "Adriel can tend to the wounded when we're settled."

I glanced at the man with the arrow still protruding from his thigh. He wore thick leather breeches, so the arrowhead didn't appear to have gone deep, but I could see Zadie going a little green around the gills at the sight.

Roan nodded and sent several riders off into the forest to look for a camping spot. By the time a place had been settled on, it was completely dark, and exhaustion had replaced the adrenaline that had rushed through my bloodstream earlier.

The horses were allowed to graze—they knew not to stray far—while we made camp. Zadie, Sami, and several of the Galethians began to prepare supper while others made the fire and scouted the area to make sure there were no more guards waiting to ambush us.

"Care to help me?" Adriel asked. She had a satchel full of healing supplies slung over her arm.

I nodded, grateful to have something to do. We approached the man with the arrow wound first, but he shook his head when he saw Adriel's bag.

She rolled her eyes. "Don't tell me you're going to refuse treatment because I'm a—"

"It's not that," he blurted. "I'd just rather you treat the horses first."

She blinked, clearly surprised by his request. "I'm not an

expert in horse healing, but I promise I will check on the animals. First, however, we need to remove that arrow."

He was young, with shaggy brown hair and a crooked nose, and he seemed as intimidated by Adriel as I had been when we first met. "Yes, miss. Er, ma'am?"

Adriel arched an eyebrow as she reached for a knife. "Call me Adriel. I'm going to need to cut off your breeches. Nor, I need boiled water and clean linens. I don't think the wound is deep, but we'll need to keep it well wrapped to prevent infection."

I watched in awe as she worked methodically, maintaining perfect composure even as she pulled the arrow out of the man's flesh. He was remarkably stoic, but the arrow was designed to inflict damage on the way in and out. When I saw sweat breaking out on his forehead as Adriel doused the wound in alcohol and used a knife to widen the opening in his flesh, I held out my hand. He gripped it so hard I worried he might shatter the bones, but I could tell it helped to have something else to focus on.

Afterward, when the wound had been cleaned and the soldier rested, we went to check on the injured horses. Adriel cleaned their scrapes and placed a salve on their wounds.

"What is it made of?" I asked.

She handed me the small pot so I could smell it. It had a strong herbal scent. "Calendula flower, for pain and swelling. It helps prevent infection, too. Comfrey, to stop the bleeding and aid the healing. Beeswax to bind it."

I studied her for a few minutes. She had a calming effect on the horses, I noticed. They lowered their noses to the ground as she ran her hands over their muscles, checking for soreness. When she'd finished, I followed her to the stream, where she rinsed off her hands and instruments.

"Adriel," I said, coming to sit beside her on a rock. "What you're doing—healing, I mean—it isn't magic, is it?"

She glanced at me as she dried off her knives. "No, Nor. It isn't."

"Then why do the Galethians call you a witch?"

"Not everything I do is healing, although the vast majority of it is. You've seen the spells in that book of blood magic. That goes far beyond herbs and flowers."

"But you said you don't do blood magic."

She pushed her dark hair off her face and leaned back against the rock. "I said I don't *like* to do it."

"Then you know how?"

She turned to face me, her eyes glittering in the moonlight. "I can't help you if you don't tell me what you're dealing with, Nor."

I nodded and reached for one of her clean blades. "I think it would be easier if I show you."

20

"What are you doing?" Adriel grabbed for the blade, trying to stop me, but I had already stepped out of her reach.

"Don't worry," I said as I dragged the blade slowly across my forearm, doing my best not to wince at the sharp bite of pain. For the span of several heartbeats, I saw Ceren's face, just like I had the time I caught my hand on the splinter, but it was gone before I could make out where he was or what he was doing.

"Nor!" Adriel reached for one of her clean cloths and grabbed my arm, clamping the cloth onto the wound. "What were you thinking?"

I shook my head to clear it. If it wasn't just drinking my blood that brought about the visions—if I really could bring them on myself by bleeding—then I might have more control in this situation than I'd thought. "I'm fine," I said to Adriel. "Go ahead and remove the cloth."

"I have to staunch the bleeding. Honestly, I would never

have considered taking you on as an apprentice if I'd known how careless you are."

I placed my hand over hers until she looked up at me. "You were going to make me your apprentice?"

She shook her head in annoyance. "I had considered it, yes. But now..."

Gently, I pushed her hand aside. As the cloth moved, it wiped the blood away, revealing my already healed arm.

Her eyes flashed to mine. "What is this?"

I shrugged, unable to keep the lopsided grin from tugging at the corners of my mouth. "Magic."

"How?" She pulled my arm closer, struggling to see in the dark.

"I'll tell you everything. But first I need to know something."

She nodded, eyes still wide with surprise and fascination. "All right."

"If I asked you to do blood magic for me, would you?"

She ran her fingers over my forearm where the cut had been. The skin was as smooth as if nothing had happened. "I don't know, Nor. As far as I can tell, you've already dabbled in it yourself."

"I haven't," I assured her. "This came to me naturally, from a blood coral." I told her about the incident when I was ten, how I'd cut my cheek on the blood coral saving Zadie. "No one ever understood why I can heal the way I do. As far as I know, no one else has sustained that kind of injury and survived, let alone gained powers from it."

"I suppose it could work in the same way some medicine does," she said.

"What do you mean?"

"Take foxglove, for example. The plant, not the cat," she

clarified with a laugh. "The entire plant is toxic, including the roots and seeds. If ingested, it can cause vomiting, hallucinations, delirium, convulsions, and even death. It's sometimes known as dead man's bells or witch's gloves."

I shuddered. "That's what you chose to name your cat after?"

She grinned. "That's just it. If used in properly controlled doses, various parts of foxglove can also be used to treat internal bleeding, regulate an erratic heartbeat, and cure dropsy."

I raised a questioning brow.

"Swelling from fluid buildup. In other words, a substance that can be deadly in large doses can be beneficial when diluted."

I thought about the connection between the blood coral and the Varenian pearls. No one understood how it worked; we only knew that one was deadly and the other healing. But if the toxins released by the blood coral were diluted by enough seawater, as Adriel said, then perhaps whatever was beneficial in it accumulated safely in the pearls. Or, in my case, in my blood.

"You said the fruit of the bone trees was poisonous, but the seeds could be made into healing teas and tinctures, right?"

She nodded. "I never heard of anyone eating the fruit and surviving, but I suppose it's possible. Perhaps they had powers like yours, too."

There was a strange comfort in the idea of someone else out there being like me. "There's something else," I said. "When Ceren drank my blood, it gave him my healing abilities. I stabbed him with a blood coral blade and he survived. What if…" My voice trailed off. I was too afraid to say it out loud.

Adriel took my hand. "What's the matter?"

"If a wound of that magnitude didn't kill him, I'm not sure what can."

"What are you saying? That he's immortal?"

I shrugged. "I don't know. Perhaps."

I couldn't voice the last part, the part I hadn't ever wanted to consider. Because if Ceren was immortal, what did that make me?

Unlike when we had camped on the journey to Galeth, on our way south the horses stayed with us through the night. Each rider rolled out their bedding near their horse, who lay down next to their rider. Titania seemed relieved when I didn't try to tie her up to a tree branch.

"What if they roll over?" I asked Roan, remembering Talin's concern. The dun gelding had chosen a spot right near my mare, to my dismay.

"They won't," he said, tucking his hands behind his head. "In twenty years, I've never heard of it happening."

"How do you train them?" I asked, turning on my side to face him. His features were so chiseled that I sometimes couldn't read his expression.

"Any Galethian horse that is going to belong to a soldier is taken from its mother the day it's born."

"That seems cruel," I said. "Surely they need their mothers."

"Their rider becomes a mother figure to them. We feed them from bottles and sleep in their stalls with them. Those first few weeks are the most important. If the rider and horse don't bond immediately, they'll never form the kind of connection they need to fight together."

I glanced up at Titania, who seemed to be watching me in the dark. "Never?"

Roan smiled. "Titania is well trained. But if it came down to it, I can't say whether she would lay down her life for you."

"And your horse would?"

Roan reached behind him and the gelding immediately placed his muzzle in Roan's palm. "Kosmos? Without question."

"What about your other horse, the one who looks like he's part fur seal?"

He laughed. "Is that how you think of him? Duster has a disease that means he doesn't shed, among other things. He's getting old, but he was my first bonded horse. I got him when I was three years old."

My mouth dropped open in shock. "You learned to ride when you were three?"

Roan eyed me strangely, like maybe I was joking. "I could ride before I could walk, Nor."

"Oh." I rolled onto my back, staring up at the stars. I wondered what my life would have been like if I'd been born in Galeth instead of Varenia. I would have had my own horse like Titania, of course, and I would have been trained in combat rather than the art of wooing a husband.

"What were you and Adriel discussing earlier?" he asked. "I saw you talking by the river."

"Medicine, mostly. She said she wants to make me her apprentice."

Roan sat up a bit. "What, in Galeth?"

I shrugged. "I have no idea."

He watched me for a moment. "And what do you think of that?"

A deep sense of exhaustion washed over me, and I released a heavy sigh. "I was raised to be beautiful, to be a good wife, to be a mother someday, perhaps."

"What about what you want?"

I turned my face toward him. "I *wanted* to leave Varenia, to see the world and experience all it has to offer." And in doing so, I had caused pain and hardship for the people I loved.

"Has that changed?"

"How can I think about what I want when I have to save my parents, to make sure that Ceren is stopped from hurting more people?"

"We all have things we *have* to do, Nor. But once everyone is safe, surely your parents will be able to look after themselves. Zadie has Samiel. And Talin and his mother and sister will be there to keep the kingdom safe."

I considered his words for a moment. I had envisioned that future, yes.

"And in that case..." he continued "...what will you do?"

I closed my eyes, frustrated that he once again seemed to know what I was thinking. "I'm trying to take things one day at a time right now. I could be dead from an arrow tomorrow."

"I'd never let that happen."

I opened my eyes and turned to him. "Oh no? You're going to prevent any possible harm from coming to me until I arrive safely in the south?"

I could see his jaw feathering in frustration. "That's why I'm here, isn't it?"

"I don't know why you agreed to come."

He was quiet for a few minutes, and I wondered if he had fallen asleep.

"I understand taking things one day at a time better than most," he said softly. "After I left home to join the elite cavalry training, all I did was try to survive one day, and then the next, and the one after that. I didn't think about my future or becoming the head of a fort. I didn't like to think about the future at all."

I waited, listening to the soft sounds of breathing coming from the other humans and animals around the fire. Roan didn't seem to need anyone, but Adriel had said he felt emotions more strongly than most. Of course it would have been hard to leave his family.

"It's obvious that Talin loves you, Nor. And if he does win this war and return to his life as a royal, I'm sure he will marry you and be happy to keep you at his side like the trophy you were raised to be." There was nothing cruel in his tone, but I could feel tears at the back of my throat. "But somehow I don't see that making you happy."

"You have no idea what will make me happy," I whispered.

"You're right, Nor. I don't. But the real question is, do you?"

Sometime that night, I dreamed of Ceren.

He was just a boy, but I recognized him immediately. He looked to be no older than ten, his white-blond hair brushing his shoulders. His skin was so fair he seemed translucent, like some deep-sea creature not made for the sunlight, which suited him well to life at New Castle. He was playing in what looked like a nursery, based on the toys surrounding him. He picked up a wooden practice sword and spoke to a child on the other side of the room.

Talin was a little smaller than Ceren, but not as much as he perhaps should have been considering he was two years younger. His hair was a mass of glossy brown curls, and his blue-green eyes cut quickly to Ceren before darting away. Ceren had asked him to play. And Talin had said no.

Ceren looked disappointed but not surprised. He rose from

where he was sitting and went to answer the door. A beautiful young woman with olive skin and golden-brown curls falling to the small of her back stood in the shadows. Her green eyes instantly landed on Talin, a smile spreading across her face that seemed like sunshine itself.

Talin rose and ran to her, and she dropped to her knees to embrace him.

Ceren stood next to the doorway watching, no expression in his pale eyes. Talia rose and took Talin's hand, leading him out of the playroom. Talin raised a hand to his half brother, but Ceren didn't wave in return.

The door closed. A moment later, Ceren returned to the wooden practice sword, picked it up with his long, delicate fingers, and beat it against the wall until it broke in two.

When he was finished, Ceren sat down on the floor of the playroom. His cheeks were pink from the exertion of destroying the sword, and purple bruises were blooming on his arms where he'd inadvertently struck himself, but his gray eyes were just as empty as they had been before.

As the dream faded, I woke with cold tears snaking down my cheeks. I understood now why Talin had refused his brother; Ceren was so delicate that he was likely not allowed to play with the wooden swords. And he wasn't allowed to go wherever it was Talin had gone with his mother, either.

Roan was awake and watching me. I wondered if I'd made some noise in my sleep. I wanted to get up and leave, my tears threatening to spill over, but I was afraid I'd wake the others.

"Nightmare?" Roan mouthed to me.

I nodded, because it was simpler than the truth: that what I had seen was likely one of many similar memories Ceren had from his childhood. The visions had been disturbing enough, but this was far worse. Because even after all the terrible things he had done, I had seen a small glimpse of what had shaped him, and how could I want to kill someone who had been so broken inside from such a young age?

All of my frustration from last night had turned into a sorrow so heavy I knew I had to release it. As quietly as I could, I slipped out of my bedroll and made my way to the river. Mist rolled on the surface of the water in the pre-dawn light. I sat on the same rock I'd sat on with Adriel last night and let the tears come, weeping silently as the forest began to wake around me.

At the sound of soft footsteps behind me, I whipped around, hand flying to my waist before I remembered I had left my knife under my pillow.

Roan raised his hands. "It's just me," he said.

I groaned and wiped my tears on my tunic. "I'm fine. I needed to be alone."

"You don't look fine." He approached the rock slowly. "If this is about what I said to you last night..."

I rolled my eyes and turned away from him. "This has nothing to do with you, Roan."

"Okay." He sat down next to me, and I scooted as far from him as I could. "What was the nightmare about?"

"It wasn't really a nightmare," I said. "It was one of Ceren's memories, and it was heartbreaking."

"You're sure it was a memory? Is it possible he gave you some kind of false vision?"

I shook my head. "No. I don't know how I know, but I'm sure it was real."

"Empathy can be overwhelming at times. I can't imagine what it would be like to experience someone else's painful memories like that."

"Is that why you were so patient with Yana?" I asked. "Because you can empathize with her pain?"

"I suppose so. But I've also known her since I was a child, and I know she's a good person. Even good people can do bad things when they're suffering."

I thought of Ceren, staring into nothing though the pain he'd caused himself had to be excruciating. "I'm worried about the queen," I said. "Talia. I know Talin loves her and that she was a wonderful mother to him, but what if she's not the person he remembers? In this memory, she was so callous toward Ceren. He was just a child."

Roan nodded. "I can understand your concern."

"It's just...what if the person Talin is risking everything to help is no better than the person we're trying to stop?"

"I don't know," Roan said. "But I suppose we'll find out soon enough."

21

Over the course of the next few days, we encountered travelers heading north on the road, but they all gave us a wide berth and sent suspicious looks our way. I doubted such a large number of Galethians had been seen together south of their border before, and it was clear that Sami, Zadie, and I were not Galethians despite our escort.

Thankfully, there were no more signs of Ceren's soldiers, and I didn't dream of him again. But the image of his thin, bruised arms and empty eyes haunted me just the same.

On the one hand, I was glad Ceren hadn't caught up with us, but I had a terrible feeling that meant he had never left New Castle. Which meant Talin would have had no chance to rescue the Varenians. Regardless, our plan had been to meet Talin and the others in the south, where Talia's army was.

We reached the outskirts of Riaga on the evening of the sixth day, planning to remain in the area only long enough to replenish our supplies at the port market the following morning. The mood in the city had changed since we were here last. We overheard people speculating that the woman king's army had reached the southern end of the River Ilara, and mercenaries roamed the streets with their weapons slung prominently on their hips or backs.

"Sell swords," Shiloh explained. "They'll work for the highest bidder."

"I don't get the impression that the woman king and Ceren are leaving people much of a choice," I said.

"No," Shiloh said. "But Pirot has its own army."

"Pirot swore to help Talin's mother."

"If they're smart, they'll wait until they see who has the upper hand before sending troops." Roan dismounted and passed his reins to Shiloh. "I'm going to see about finding us rooms for the night."

It took me a moment to realize that the seedy-looking building with poorly dressed men and women smoking out front was an inn.

"Here?" I asked. "Talin gave me some money. We can find something better."

"We're not looking for fancy," Roan said. "We're looking for something that will have enough rooms for all of us."

He disappeared inside and came out a few minutes later, looking extremely angry.

"They won't let rooms to Galethians," he said, swinging onto his horse. "They said no one in Riaga will."

Sami shook his head. "Surely coin is coin. I've never had any problem trading, as long as I have something they want."

"That was before the war reached Riaga. The innkeepers said they won't take sides."

"But the Galethians are not on a side," I said.

"He seemed to think our presence proves otherwise. He

slammed the door in my face when I tried to argue. In the meantime, you should rest, eat, and bathe. My soldiers and I will get whatever supplies we need at the market tomorrow and meet you at the southern end of the city at dusk."

"No. We're not splitting up, Roan."

"I'm afraid we don't have a choice. Not if you want a chance to recover. Shiloh will stand guard outside the inn, to make sure you don't get into any trouble." He looked at me as he added this last bit, but I'd learned not to take his teasing seriously.

"Ceren could have soldiers in Riaga looking for us." The idea was to lure Ceren out, not run into him when we were without an escort.

"Exactly. And we'll be a lot easier to spot if we're together. As long as you stay in the inn, there shouldn't be a problem."

"I have contacts at the market," Sami said. "I should go with you to trade, surely."

"We'll take care of the supplies." Roan glanced at me. "You just take care of each other."

Adriel scowled as he rounded up his soldiers and headed south, out of Riaga. "If they weren't going to stay with us, they could have found us better accommodations."

"At least you'll get a bath and a meal," Shiloh said. "I'll be out here if you need me."

"I can't help with the bath, but we'll bring you something to eat," Adriel promised. "I'm sorry you have to stay with us."

Shiloh tossed her blond hair out of her eyes and grinned. "I'm not."

Adriel's pale cheeks pinked beneath her freckles. I'd never seen her blush before.

Inside, the inn was even worse than it looked from the outside. The carpets were threadbare, the wallpaper dingy with years of smoke, and there was a damp, rotten smell permeating the air. It was clear most people hadn't come for the ambiance.

"This way," the innkeeper, an older woman in a stained dress, said to us, leading us upstairs to the third floor of the building. The stairs creaked ominously beneath us.

"Your friend paid for two rooms," she said, indicating two doors next to each other. The roof was gabled and Sami had to duck to enter. "Don't matter to me how you split up. Bathroom's at the end of the hall. Hot water costs extra."

Zadie and I shared a glance, and I immediately fished one of the coins Talin had given me out of my purse. "We'll take enough for all of us," I said. "And something to eat for our friend outside."

"You'll have to take it to her yourself. I won't serve a flea-ridden horse lover."

I was about to say something when Adriel cut me off with a sharp look. "Don't get involved," she said when the woman had gone. "It's better not to call attention to ourselves. The innkeeper might call the guards." She pointed to the room on the left. "Nor and I will take this room. We can reconvene when we've all bathed and rested a bit."

The bathroom, it turned out, consisted of one metal tub filled with tepid water that had a brownish tinge to it even before I got in. But it was the first time my entire body had been immersed in water since I left Varenia, and I was grateful. I scrubbed the filth off my skin with the bar of soap provided by the innkeeper, then worked it through my long hair, which had been braided throughout the journey to keep it from getting tangled.

When I'd finished, I changed into my last remaining clean item, the dress Talin had purchased for me from the Riaga tailor before we went to Galeth. It felt strange to wear a gown again after spending so long in trousers, and the corset felt restrictive even though it lacked the boning that my New Castle gowns had.

When I returned to our room, Adriel sat up on the bed and smiled. "I'd forgotten what you looked like under all that dirt."

"Me, too." I dug a comb out of my bag, then began the long, tedious task of combing my hair. I was tempted to ask Zadie for help, but she and Sami hadn't had a moment alone together in a week.

"Let me," Adriel said, sitting behind me on the bed. She soaked up the remaining moisture from my hair with a towel and began to comb gently from the bottom. "Soon you'll be walking on your hair if you're not careful," she said. "I could cut it for you, if you like."

"I've never cut my hair," I admitted. "Neither has Zadie."

"Then I'd say you're about fifteen years overdue."

I chuckled. "Mother said long hair was a sign of femininity. The longer we grew it, the more alluring we'd be."

"Nonsense," Adriel said. "Shiloh's hair barely reaches her ears, and I'd say she's plenty alluring."

I turned to glance at her. "Really?"

"It's not about hair, Nor."

I shrugged. "I know. But it's hard to let go of something that was ingrained in me from infancy."

"And you wonder why you still want acceptance from the Varenians? You've tried so hard to escape that way of thinking, but it still controls you subconsciously. Real beauty can't be painted on with cosmetics or pinned up onto your head. I know you know that."

I remembered what Zadie had told me before I left for Varenia, how it was my inner strength that made me beautiful.

But maybe Adriel was right. Maybe, deep down, I hadn't let go of all the stupid rules I'd spent so many years trying to break.

"I like my hair," I said finally. "Even if it's because some part of me believes it's feminine, or because it's the same as Zadie's. I don't want to cut it."

"Good," Adriel said. "I like it, too. Now if you'll excuse me, I'm going to take a bath myself before this dirt decides it's happy where it is and chooses to take up permanent residence."

The innkeeper's idea of supper turned out to be a thin soup that looked frighteningly similar to the bathwater.

"That will be another of those gold coins," she said, setting a tray down on the wobbly and suspiciously sticky table in our room.

Adriel and I looked at each other and burst out laughing.

The innkeeper sniffed and looked down her crooked nose at us as if gravely offended. "You're lucky I took you in at all. No one else in this city is open-minded as I am. I could report you just for being on land," she added, looking directly at me.

"What?" I asked, my stomach twisting.

"I know who you are." She lifted her pointy chin with an impressive degree of imperiousness. "And I know *what* you are."

The blood drained from my face. There was nothing about my appearance that marked me as a Varenian, which meant Ceren must have put the word out about us. "What do you want?"

"Coin," she said with a gap-toothed sneer. "Or I'll call the king's guard myself."

"Do it," Adriel whispered to me.

I removed the small coin purse from my waist and handed it to the woman, who hefted it greedily. "Enjoy your dinner," she said and closed the door behind her.

"We have to leave," I said the moment she was gone. "I don't trust that the innkeeper won't call the guard anyway. Not if there's any kind of reward involved."

Adriel was already stuffing her belongings back into her bag. "I'll finish packing. Get Zadie and Samiel."

I nodded and opened the door a crack, listening. The only sounds were coming from the common area downstairs, along with a faint creaking from one of the rooms down the hall. I darted out and knocked briskly on my sister's door.

There was no answer. Heart pounding, I tried the door and found it locked. "Zadie," I hissed. "Open up."

I was just beginning to panic when the door opened to reveal a shirtless Sami, blinking sleepily. He scratched at his bare torso. "What is it? We just fell asleep."

"The innkeeper knows who we are," I said, pushing past him. "We have to go, now."

Zadie sat up. She was clad in only her shift, her hair in loose waves around her. "What's wrong, Nor?"

"Just get dressed and meet us in the alley behind the inn. Quickly."

I returned to my room and grabbed my pack, motioning for Adriel to hurry. "We're meeting them in the alley. Let's go."

We made our way down the stairs slowly, but they groaned beneath us anyway. Fortunately, whatever was happening in the common room seemed to be wildly entertaining, judging by the whoops and howls of laughter.

I pulled my cloak up over my head and opened the front door of the inn, peeking outside. People were going about their business in the fading daylight. There was no sign of Ceren or his guards.

"Come on," I said, waving Adriel behind me. I glanced around, looking for Shiloh. She was leaning against her horse to the side of the building, smoking a pipe. When she saw Adriel and me, she straightened immediately.

"What are you doing out here?"

"The innkeeper knows who I am," I said. "We need to head for the woods."

Shiloh nodded. "I'll get the horses and meet you there. You should get moving. It might take me a while."

"Thank you." I took Adriel's hand and headed back into the alley. Straight into one of Ceren's guards.

I would have known he was one of Ceren's even without the black armor and the bloodstone hanging from the chain around his neck. He had that same dazed, stupefied look in his eyes as the captive in Galeth. But the moment he saw me, his pupils shrunk to pinpricks in his blue eyes, as if some part of his brain had just activated.

"Halt in the name of the king," the guard said, but Adriel and I had already turned back and were moving toward the front of the inn. I heard the man shout something behind us, and another guard stepped out from a shop, his eyes finding mine instantly.

"Thalos," I breathed. "Where are Sami and Zadie?"

"I'll wait for them," Adriel said. "You should go."

"We are not splitting up."

"Yes, we are." She shoved me aside as the guard's pace quickened toward us.

"Halt in the name of the king," the men said in unison, one in front and one behind.

"I'll catch up," Adriel shouted as I broke into a run, heading into the streets of Riaga.

I had no idea where I was, and I couldn't have been dressed worse for the occasion. My stride was restricted by my skirts, and the corset made it difficult to fill my lungs. The streets were less crowded than they'd been earlier, but no one moved out of my path as I tore past the shops and stalls where merchants were hoping to sell off the last of their goods.

"Stop her," the guards called from behind me. Fortunately, no one seemed to understand they were referring to me until I was past them, and I was small enough to slip through cracks they couldn't.

But they were gaining regardless, and my breaths were coming in ragged gasps, the way they had when I ran from New Castle. Memories of that night were the last thing I needed. Desperate, I ducked into an alleyway, hoping my pursuers hadn't seen me turn and I could catch my breath for a few moments.

I realized quickly I'd stumbled upon the back of a blacksmith's shop. I could hear hammering from somewhere on the other side of the building. My knife was strapped to my thigh, and I started to lift my skirts when the end of the alley darkened with shadows.

"Halt in the name of the king!" the guards said, their voices eerily identical.

I cursed and dropped my hem, reaching into a pile of metal scraps for a hatchet with a crooked handle. I hefted it in front of me, knowing I had no chance against two fully grown men but refusing to go down without a fight. I had hurt someone before, and I would do it again if I had to.

Ceren wouldn't have told them to kill me, I thought desperately as the nearest man grabbed me. I struggled in his grip, but one of his hands was on my throat in seconds, causing me to drop the hatchet. He pushed me up against the wall, and as I scrabbled at the fingers around my neck, he brought up a knife with his free hand. I felt the bite of steel against my chin, felt my blood seep out from the wound.

There was a blinding flash of light that made my stomach churn, and then everything around me faded, and I was staring at Ceren.

He recognized me immediately this time. "Nor."

"Call off your men!" I gasped.

His brows knit in confusion, and then I saw the bloodstones on the chain around his neck begin to pulsate with light. He wasn't in his study from what I could see, and there was no vial of blood nearby. His face was paler than the last time I'd seen him, with dark circles beneath his eyes. Somewhere far away, I felt the steel bite further into my skin.

Help me! I screamed silently before I was wrenched out of the vision by the pain at my throat. My hands flew up to my neck, slick with blood, and I had the terrible thought that this wound was too deep for my healing magic. I watched wide-eyed as the bloodstone at the man's throat pulsed like a heartbeat, and his pupils dilated rapidly, the black swallowing the blue.

He released me so suddenly I fell to my knees. I fumbled for the hatchet I'd dropped, but the guards were already turning on their heels. They walked slowly out of the alley, as if I wasn't even there.

I gasped for air, still clutching at my bleeding neck, and attempted to stand, but my legs were too weak to support me.

I wasn't sure how much time had passed when I heard footsteps approaching.

"Nor!" Zadie was at my side, gently brushing my hair away

from my neck. I could feel the wound healing, but it was deep enough that it hadn't stopped bleeding yet. "We saw the guards come out of the alley. What happened?"

"Ceren called them off," I croaked.

Sami's strong hands were beneath my arms, helping me to my feet. "Why would he do that?"

"They would have killed me if he hadn't intervened, and Ceren wants me alive." But why hadn't he ordered them to capture me instead? All I could think of was how sickly he'd looked, how bone-weary. It must be incredibly taxing to control an entire army with his mind, particularly with men spread out all over Ilara.

Zadie pulled me into a hug. "It's okay. We're here now."

"Let me look at her," Adriel said.

I peered behind Zadie at the sound of her voice. "Thank Thalos you found each other. Where's Shiloh?"

Adriel was examining my neck for bruising, but the pain had subsided considerably. "Hopefully waiting for us in the woods with the horses. Are you all right?"

I nodded, though my tears hadn't dried. I hated how vulnerable I'd been against those men, even armed.

With Sami next to me for support, we made it out of Riaga without incident and found Shiloh waiting for us on the edge of the woods, along with the rest of the Galethians. By now I had fully healed, though that didn't stop Roan from asking us a dozen questions about our encounter with the guards.

As I assured him for the tenth time that I was fine, my eyes snagged on a small figure standing among the horses, her pale skin and hair luminous in the darkness. She stepped forward, her sky-blue eyes welling with tears.

I was having another vision, I thought wildly. It was the

only explanation for why my former lady's maid from New Castle could possibly be standing in front of me.

I rubbed my eyes and she was still there, and then I was running into her arms, crying and laughing. "Is it really you, Ebb?" I asked, holding her thin shoulders in my hands.

"It's really me. And thank the gods I'm here," she said, taking in my disheveled hair and torn skirts. "You're clearly in desperate need of my help."

22

Roan apologized for leaving us in Riaga, but I was grateful we'd split up in the end. If we had all stayed at the inn, Ebb might not have found us. Our party ventured farther into the woods, away from Riaga, to set up camp for the night. Ebb and I sat together on a fallen log a short distance from the others.

"How did you make it here?" I asked as I passed her my waterskin.

Ebb thanked me and took a long drink. "After Ceren returned from Varenia, I questioned the other servants to see if any of them had seen you. Only a few of us were allowed near your people—they're being kept in the caves closest to the mine. No one had seen a set of identical twins among the captured. I couldn't just sit by wondering where you were, so I snuck out in a wagon of dirty linens."

"Do you know how the Varenians are doing?" Zadie asked.

Ebb frowned. "I don't. Your guess was correct though,"

she said to me. "Grig told me you thought he was using your people to mine the bloodstones."

It wasn't a surprise, but the thought of my parents being forced to dive repeatedly in the freezing underground lake reignited my fury toward Ceren.

"Many of the nobles left when Ceren recovered from his injuries, knowing war was on the horizon." Her features twisted in disgust. "He promised wealth and power to any who stayed. Those who did were given bloodstones that they fashioned into rings and necklaces, not realizing they would be under Ceren's control as soon as they put the jewelry on."

"He's enslaving the nobility, too?" I asked.

Ebb nodded. "He's even done it to some of the servants. It's like a castle full of ghosts. The only people who aren't under his control are his war council and those too far below his notice to bother with."

New Castle had always been full of ghosts. I shuddered at the thought of those dark halls, made even more haunted by the presence of mindless royals. "Lady Hyacinth?" I asked, remembering the cold woman who had been a part of the war council when I was at New Castle. She was young and beautiful, using her charms to act the coquette one minute, while silently plotting against you the next. She had no doubt been a part of the capture of my people.

"She heads the war council. Some say she's in love with Ceren."

I scoffed. "Good luck to her, then."

Ebb took my hand. "He's been looking for you, Nor. When I crossed the river to reach Queen Talia's camp, the border was crawling with Ilarean soldiers."

After this last vision, Ceren definitely knew where I was.

The only question was whether he'd risk coming out to get me. "What were you doing at Talia's camp?"

"I was hoping to find Grig," she said, blushing. "I thought that if he and Talin were still alive, that's where they would have gone, and they were the most likely to know what had become of you."

"And?" I asked anxiously. If Ceren had never left New Castle, Talin would have ridden south to his mother, unless something had happened to him.

"I found them," she said, smiling, and relief flooded through me. "Talin couldn't leave the camp, but he said you and the Galethians might be passing through. He sent a soldier with me to intercept you." She gestured to the stranger standing a few meters behind us.

I embraced her again. "Thank you for looking for me. It must have been terrifying."

"Fortunately, the soldiers and mercenaries aren't conscripting or capturing people like me. I'm clearly too weak to fight."

She did look weak, I had to admit. Perhaps it was just that I'd gotten stronger since I'd seen her last, but her arms were as thin as branch coral, and there were purple smudges below her eyes.

"What about your brother?" I asked. He'd been a prisoner in New Castle since before I had arrived.

Ebb bowed her head like a wilted flower. "He's still in the dungeon as far as I know. The alternative is too grim to consider."

"We'll rescue him when we free the Varenians," I said hopefully.

A shadow passed over her pale eyes. "I wish it were going to be possible, Nor, but I don't see how. All the secret routes the servants used to get around the castle have been cut off. The passage you escaped through was sealed up after the bloodstones were extracted. You might be able to smuggle in one or two people the way I escaped, but Ceren is surrounded by guards at every moment. As long as he lives, you'll never defeat his army."

Seeing the utter hopelessness on her face made my stomach twist with unease, but I did my best to hide it. I made my way to where the horses were grazing. Titania's black coat was difficult to see in the dark, but she whickered when she heard me approaching.

"There you are, girl," I said, handing her a small lump of sugar I'd pocketed back at the inn. "I missed you."

"She missed you, too." Roan stepped out from behind his gelding, materializing like a wraith in the dark. "Apologies if I startled you. I was just checking Kosmos's hoof. He bruised it earlier."

"Hello, Roan. I figured you'd be here when I didn't see you at the campfire."

He came to stand beside me as I ran my hands over Titania's legs, checking for any heat or injuries.

"I really am sorry," he said after the silence began to grow uncomfortable. "I shouldn't have left you alone in Galeth. It was foolish of me."

I straightened to look at him. "You couldn't have known. Besides, you didn't have a choice."

His profile was even sharper in the moonlight, as if he'd been carved from stone. "There is always a choice."

I scratched behind Titania's ears. "And what will you choose now? We're almost to Talia's camp. You can head back to Galeth at any time."

"I thought we might meet with this woman king," he said. "Or girl king, as the case may be."

"I think you'd be meeting with her mother. Zoi is only four."

"You can tell a lot about a person when they're four."

I laughed. "Oh really? Beyond their favorite color or food?"

"I'll know not to trust her if her favorite food is spinach. And of course, I'll meet with her mother, too, if she'll agree to see us."

"Talin will make sure she does."

He was silent for a few moments. "Nor, I know you were hoping to free the Varenians before any fighting starts. But from what everyone has told me, that's going to be impossible."

I started to weave Titania's forelock into a braid, then brushed it out again with my fingers. "It was also impossible that I would survive cutting myself on a blood coral or that a girl with a scar would leave Varenia to marry the prince. It was impossible to escape New Castle and make it home again, and it was impossible that I'd visit Galeth and learn about healing from a witch." I fed the last granules of sugar to Titania. "Everything I've done for the past seven years is impossible, depending on who you ask."

"So what's your plan?"

"My plan hasn't changed. I just need to figure out how to get Ceren away from New Castle."

I expected Roan to ask me how, but instead he glanced up at the sky, and I was glad I didn't have to answer. A plan was beginning to take shape, but it was desperate to say the least, and I knew if I had to defend it now, it would crumble.

I leaned against Titania and looked up, trying to picture the future, but all I saw was the same thing I'd seen every night of my life in Varenia: a black sky studded with stars, each one a possibility that I hadn't yet imagined.

"Good night, Roan," I said, and left him staring up at the stars.

★ ★ ★

By the time we reached the border the following day, Talia's soldiers had already claimed the crossing. There was no one to stop us from reaching her camp; those who might have yesterday were all dead.

The camp was a field of tents as far as the eye could see. Whatever her methods of building her army, Talia had certainly been effective. The camp was huge, with men and women, and even some children, all busily bustling from one place to another.

"Ceren's army can't possibly be bigger than this," I said to Ebb as we were escorted to the largest of the tents. Talia's headquarters, apparently.

"Perhaps not," Roan said. "But Ceren can be assured of his soldiers' loyalty. Who knows if the same can be said of Talia?"

"Let's try to be open minded. If she's who Talin says she is, we have no reason to doubt her."

We all fell silent as a figure emerged from the tent. She was tall and elegant, her waist nipped tight by a leather corset over an emerald gown. Her hair cascaded to the middle of her back in golden-brown waves, her tanned skin still flawless, though she was at least forty. She didn't wear a crown, but she didn't need to; anyone with eyes could see that she was the leader.

"Welcome, friends," Talia said, arms spread wide as she floated toward us. The lessons she'd learned in Varenia had clearly never been forgotten; she was the picture of grace and beauty.

But there was a sharpness in her green eyes that I hadn't seen in her portrait in New Castle. I knew this woman probably had very little in common with the girl who grew up in Varenia, as eager to please as Zadie had been. She'd been through so much since then. But I hoped the woman who had raised Talin was still in there somewhere.

"My son has told me so much about you all. I know you've had a difficult journey."

Roan lowered his chin, as close to a bow as he was willing to give. "We have indeed."

I glanced around anxiously, afraid someone would point out his lack of courtesy. He hadn't used any form of address.

"I have accommodations ready for you," Talia said, ignoring the slight if she noticed it. "My soldiers will take care of your horses while we get to know each other."

Roan's posture remained rigid. "My soldiers will stay with their horses. I will be happy to meet with you for a short time, but we won't be needing accommodations."

"No?" Talia arched her fine eyebrows. "I had hoped you might stay a bit longer. I know my son made it clear to you that we could use your help."

"We haven't decided yet," Roan said. "Perhaps after we've met the woman king, we will have a better sense."

A shadow passed over Talia's expression, but it was gone in an instant. "Of course. Come with me… What did you say your name was?"

"Roan. And how should I address you?"

I struggled not to roll my eyes. Why did he have to be so arrogant?

"You may call me Talia, of course." She turned with an amused grin and a swish of her skirts, reentering the tent. Zadie, Sami, Adriel, Ebb, Roan, and I followed. As soon as we were inside, I spotted Talin, seated at a long table with a bunch of other men.

"Nor!" He rose and crossed the tent in a few strides, pulling me into his arms. "Thank the gods. I was afraid you wouldn't make it."

I extricated myself gently, fully aware of his mother's eyes on us. "I'm happy to see you, too," I whispered.

He seemed to remember himself and turned toward Talia. "Mother, this is Nor, the woman I told you about."

Talia's lips curled in a smile. "I knew it the moment I saw her. My son tells me you helped make our reunion possible. I am eternally grateful."

I dropped into a curtsy. "It's an honor, Your Majesty."

When I rose, she was still staring at me, her expression a mixture of curiosity and something I couldn't decipher. "And who are your companions?"

"My sister, Zadie; Governor Kristos's son, Samiel; and our friend from Galeth, Adriel. I believe you already know Ebb."

Talia inclined her head to Sami. "And what is the governor's son doing so far from home?"

Sami bowed at the waist. "I tried to warn the Varenians about Ceren, Your Majesty. Some of our people thought I was a liar, that I was conspiring with Nor against the king." He gave a tight smile. "They decided I no longer belonged in Varenia."

"I see. And how did you survive banishment?"

"I was fortunate to make it to shore near the port market. I had friends there willing to help me."

Talia cocked her head, a grin playing on her lips. "You can tell me how you happened to have friends at the port market another time. But you must be famished. I'll have some food and drink brought to your tents."

A man stepped forward and gestured for us to follow.

"Roan and Nor will stay," Talia said. "We have much to discuss."

The others looked at me questioningly, but I nodded for them to go. I was exhausted and hungry, but that could wait. What I wanted most was to talk to Talin alone, but it seemed that would have to wait as well.

When we were all seated at the table, Talia rose and waved her hand over the large map spread in front of us. "We were just discussing our plans for crossing into Ilara, now that my son has taken the border."

I glanced at Talin. I knew he was a soldier; he had been the head of the king's guard when I arrived at New Castle, after all. But the thought of him fighting in a war was something I hadn't really allowed myself to dwell on.

"We're close to Old Castle," Talin said as he rose from his chair. "If we can take it, we'll have a much more secure place to camp and plan our next attack."

"Do we know if Ceren has soldiers posted there?" I asked. "It seems unlikely he'd leave it wide open for the taking."

"He does," Talin said. "Ebb was able to tell us that much, fortunately. I sent Osius to scout it out this morning. We'll know more when he returns."

"Once we take Old Castle," Talia said, "we can plan our assault on New Castle."

"Assault?" I asked, earning a surprised look from Talia.

"Do you prefer a different term, child?"

I glanced at Talin, wondering if he'd told his mother our original plan. "I'm sorry. I just thought that New Castle was impenetrable."

Talia flashed another one of her tight smiles. "I lived in that castle for years. My son grew up there. Do you know something about New Castle that we don't?"

Roan stepped in before I could answer. "We'd like to know

more about your strategy before we decide if we'll join your efforts."

Talin glanced at me before returning his gaze to Roan. "I thought you'd already made your decision," he said.

"I want to meet the woman king before I decide anything."

"Zoi isn't here," Talia said with a laugh. "And she's four years old. She doesn't generally attend our council meetings."

"Funny, you didn't mention Zoi's absence when I brought it up earlier. And considering you're doing all this in her name, I would think she has some idea of what's happening."

"Roan," I hissed, but he ignored me.

"If you plan to rule in her stead," he said, "then I believe I can make my decision now." He rose to his feet. "Thank you for your hospitality, Talia. Nor, Talin, I hope to see you again someday."

He waited for one of Talia's soldiers to get out of his way before ducking back through the tent door. I looked at Talin, my eyes wide with concern.

"Excuse me, Your Majesty," I said, rising before executing a quick curtsy. "I'd like to speak to Roan before he leaves."

She merely blinked, which I took as a yes, so I ran out of the tent in search of Roan. I found him preparing to mount Kosmos, his riders clustered around him.

"What are you doing?" I shouted.

Roan said something to the Galethians before striding back to me. "You should go back inside, Nor."

"Why are you leaving? We just arrived."

"I've seen enough. I won't risk Galethian lives to serve that tyrant."

"She's leading an entire army. If she wasn't strong, no one would respect her. Isn't that what you said about Yana?"

Roan closed the last few feet between us. "The Galethians

escaped Varenia so they would never again have their lives dictated by a single ruler. Everything we stand for, everything we believe in, grew out of that vow. If you want to help her defeat Ceren, I won't stand in your way. But as far as I'm concerned, one is no better than the other."

"How can you say that? Ceren is using human beings like puppets to do his bidding. They just tried to kill me, remember?"

His jaw clenched stubbornly. "Galeth won't be getting involved."

He started to turn away, but I grabbed his arm, pulling him back toward me. "You're already involved, whether you like it or not."

He stared down at me, his mouth twisted in a scowl. "No, I'm not."

My face fell at the coldness in his voice. "I thought you cared about us."

"Listen, Nor. If you or Zadie or Samiel need me, I will be there for you. All you have to do is ask."

I searched his eyes, but they were impossible to read. "I'm asking now. Stay here. We need your help."

"With what? Strategy? I don't know how to plan the kind of assault Talia wants. I defend Fort Crag; that's all."

He was right. Talia didn't need him. She didn't even like him. But the thought of Roan leaving made me feel hollow inside. Despite his teasing and constant pushing, I respected him, and it scared me that he thought Talia was a tyrant. Having the Galethians present meant we weren't alone, that we were doing the right thing. Once, I wouldn't have needed anyone else to tell me what that was.

"I just..."

"What, Nor?" He placed a hand on my arm, his eyes

searching mine. I knew in that moment that if I told him to stay because I wanted him to, he would. I'd been fooling my-self to pretend that his teasing wasn't hiding something else. But if I asked him to stay, it would be purely selfish. I val-ued his friendship, but I knew deep down that wasn't what he wanted from me.

I clenched my jaw and stepped back. His hand slipped away.

"Goodbye," he said as I turned back toward Talia's tent.

Talin was standing in the entrance, watching us. I blinked away my tears and smiled at him. He didn't smile back.

23

I didn't see Talin again until that night. I had been assigned a tent with Ebb, Adriel, and Zadie, but as soon as I'd eaten and changed, I asked a soldier for directions to Talin's tent and slipped inside to wait.

I was asleep on his pallet when a cool breeze woke me. It was dark inside, the candle having burned out hours ago. I sat up, waiting for my eyes to adjust.

"What are you doing here?" Talin asked.

I pulled the blanket up to cover myself, feeling more exposed by the coldness in his voice than the night air. "I was waiting for you."

He sighed and removed his leather jerkin, then relit the candle. "I'm sorry. I didn't realize how late it had gotten. Osius returned after nightfall."

"Did he learn anything?"

"Yes, though nothing particularly promising."

I waited for him to continue, but he sat down on the edge

of the pallet and put his head in his hands. He clearly didn't want to talk about it anymore tonight.

I crawled over to him, placing my hands on his shoulders. "I missed you."

"I missed you, too. I was so worried something had happened to you. I underestimated just how slow you would travel."

"So did we, but it worked as a distraction, at least. You didn't encounter any problems on your way south?"

He shook his head. "I'm sorry about your parents. We staked out New Castle for a couple of days, but if Ceren was gone, he wasn't far enough away. His sentries were on strict orders not to let anyone enter. Even the Ilarean we brought from Galeth couldn't get in. We decided we were better off joining my mother and telling her what we'd learned, even without reinforcements."

I told him about our journey, how we'd been attacked by Ceren's men and the guards in Riaga. "I'm just glad we're all together again," I said, kneading the stiff muscles in his shoulders.

Talin groaned and leaned into my touch. "I didn't realize how sore I was. The battle yesterday took more out of me than I thought."

After a few minutes, he placed his hands on mine and pulled me around to face him.

"I know you saw me talking to Roan," I said. "It upset you."

"He had his hand on your arm, Nor. It looked like more than a friendly goodbye. I know you spent a lot of time together on the road. It wouldn't surprise me if something happened. But..."

I placed a finger on his lips. "Nothing happened, Talin.

Roan and I are friends. At this point, I'm not even sure you can call us that."

He raised his eyebrows. "Why?"

I considered telling him what Roan said about Talia, but when I looked into his eyes and saw how exhausted he was, I couldn't add to his burden. "Nothing important," I said. "I'm just disappointed the Galethians won't help."

"I don't think we'll need them," Talin said. "Mother's army is massive. There are over a thousand men in this camp alone. When the other troops join us, she'll have close to three thousand."

I blinked. "How does she have so many?"

He was quiet for a moment, and in that silence my doubts began to swell like a rising tide. "It doesn't matter," he said finally. "I met Zoi. She's wonderful. So smart for her age, and funny, too."

I smiled, genuinely happy for him. "I hope I'll get to meet her soon."

"You will. She's coming from one of the other camps to-morrow."

"Is that safe? Shouldn't she stay far away from the fighting?"

"She will be," Talin said, though I thought I heard some doubt in his voice. "And so will you, just in case you had any ideas."

I laughed softly. "You know me too well."

He took my chin in his fingers, tilting it so I would look him in the eye. "I'm serious, Nor. Promise me you'll stay in the camp."

"I have a stake in this, too, Talin."

He lowered his hand. "I know that. Of course you do. But you can't help on the battlefield. Promise me you'll stay here, so I can rescue your parents without worrying about your safety."

I hated the idea of sitting around and waiting while others were in danger, but I could see genuine fear in his eyes, and I knew he only wanted me to stay safe. I leaned forward, stopping just before our lips touched.

Talin's breath caught, his eyes glittering in the dark. His hands moved to my shoulders, and I could feel my heart beginning to race in anticipation. I was wearing only my shift, my skin bare beneath his hands.

Slowly, Talin moved one hand up to cup the back of my neck, the rough calluses of his palms sending chills down my spine.

"Do you remember the first time we saw each other?" he said softly. "In Governor Kristos's house?"

I grinned. "How could I forget?"

He dragged his lips along my collarbone. "You were beautiful, of course. I knew to expect that when I came to Varenia."

"I was soaking wet and dripping water all over the governor's floor," I reminded him.

He smiled. "That only added to your charm. But it wasn't your beauty that stole my breath."

"No?" I managed, feeling a bit breathless myself.

He pulled his mouth away to look at me. "It was the way you'd spoken to Sami."

I laughed. "So you heard all of that, did you?"

"I heard all of it, yes."

"You must have thought me the rudest, most improper girl in the world."

"Rude, improper, and brave," he said. "There was so much conviction in your words. I didn't know what you were talk-

ing about, but I could tell that whatever it was, you were willing to confront the governor over it."

I shook my head. "My mother would have killed me if
she saw."

"Your mother valued you for all the wrong reasons."

I blushed, grateful for his words but finding it difficult to
believe them.

Talin continued, his hands taking mine. "And then over
the course of the meal, as everything began to fall into place
for me, I saw how much you had wanted to protect Zadie."

"Of course I did. She's my sister."

He leaned back a bit more. "And Ceren is my brother. And
I wish I had even half as much certainty about what to do
next as you do. You always know what's right."

"But I don't," I said. "Not anymore. I'm as unsure as you
are. But if you think your mother is wrong—"

"I don't," he said, cutting me off. "Ceren *can't* be king,
Nor. He's too dangerous. I just…"

Talin loved his brother, and he hated him. He felt guilty
for not being kinder and for not stopping Ceren when he
became too cruel. He couldn't win in this scenario. But he
didn't need me to say that. He already knew.

"Get some rest," I said instead, helping him out of his tunic.
"Everything will be clearer in the morning."

He sighed as he lay back on the pillows. I nestled in beside him, absorbing the warmth from his body. "That's what
I tell myself every night. And every morning I wake up just
as confused as I was the night before."

"There must be something you're sure of," I said, smoothing his hair back from his temples. In the candlelight, his skin
glowed, my bronze sculpture come to life.

He looked up at me, his eyebrows furrowed. "I want to be," he whispered.

Talin was going to do what his mother thought was best, and Zadie was right: I couldn't expect him to choose between us. But that didn't mean I couldn't make a choice of my own.

I leaned over him, my hair forming a curtain around us, and kissed him softly. "I love you," I said. "Whatever happens in the days to come, don't ever doubt that."

Zoi arrived the next day. She came with the other two thousand troops Talin had promised, riding a white pony who looked like a miniature version of her mother's horse.

Zoi looked like her mother, too. She was small for her age, with her mother's olive skin and her father's lighter hair. Her face lit up when she saw Talin, who picked her up and spun her around as soon as she dismounted. It was such a purely happy moment that I felt my heart swell at the sight.

"It's like they were never apart, isn't it?" Talia stood beside me, watching the siblings' reunion. "For the past four years, this is all I have wanted."

"I'm very happy for you. For Talin and Zoi, too."

She nodded. "Thank you. My son has grown into a fine young man since I was left for dead by my stepson. I don't know that I could have improved him had I been there."

"You should be proud," I said, glancing at her from the corner of my eye. "Without a solid foundation, a house isn't strong enough to withstand a storm."

She was silent for a moment, watching Talin lift Zoi onto Xander's back, then mount behind her. The child was fearless on the massive stallion. Or perhaps it was simply that she trusted her brother.

"You're not like the Varenian girls I grew up with," she said finally.

"I'm not like the girls I grew up with, either."

She laughed throatily. "No, I imagine you're not. I can see why my son likes you. He was never interested in the young ladies at court, though they were trying to catch his eye from the time he was twelve. He knew he could never trust their motives. But you were engaged to his brother, and still you risked everything to be with him."

"Talin was one of very few people I could trust in New Castle."

She turned toward me. "But you didn't know that when you first got there. And something tells me you don't just like him for his handsome face."

"Maybe I'm good at reading people," I said. "Or maybe, after I was scarred, the people around me stopped pretending to be anything other than what they were. I wasn't someone worthy of impressing anymore in Varenia."

Talia reached toward my face, and I flinched back. She ran her fingers over my scar anyway. "Talin told me it was from a blood coral. That you can heal from any wound."

For a moment, I was angry that Talin had told her my most privately guarded secret, but I reminded myself that Ceren wouldn't be what he was if it weren't for my blood. I nodded. "Yes. As can Ceren."

"Is there any way to undo the magic?" she asked.

"Not that I've found. But Adriel, the woman who came with us from Galeth, is trying to help me find a way."

She arched a brow. "She's a witch?"

"A healer."

Zoi was running toward her mother, and Talia bent down to scoop her up in her arms without hesitation. She held the child tightly to her chest, kissed the top of her head, and set her gently back on her feet.

"Zoi, I'd like you to meet your brother's friend, Nor."

"She's more than a friend," Talin said with a glance at his mother.

But Zoi was staring at her brother, her voice full of awe when she spoke. "Are you going to marry her?"

Talin looked at me, something I couldn't read passing over his features, before turning back to Zoi. "Aren't you a bit young to be talking about marriage?" he said, avoiding the question and ruffling Zoi's hair. "Nor came on a Galethian warhorse."

Zoi reached for my free hand, fearless. "Does she perform tricks?"

I wondered what Roan would say if someone asked him if Duster performed tricks. Probably nothing kind. "Titania is very well trained," I said. "Would you like to meet her?"

Before Zoi could respond, Talia took the child's outstretched hand. "That sounds delightful, but this little girl needs to take her nap." She turned to Talin. "And I need your help in the war tent, if that's all right."

Zoi's lower lip began to tremble, but it stopped when her nursemaid appeared and scooped her up. Talin kissed Zoi goodbye and turned to me.

"Come find me later?" I asked.

He nodded and kissed my cheek before following his mother. I watched him go, oddly unsettled by his response to Zoi's question. I knew I had made it clear I couldn't make any promises yet, but his certainty about us had been a reassurance I now realized I'd taken for granted.

Shaking my head to clear it, I headed back toward my tent. Adriel was on her pallet, reading the spell book. We'd passed it around the camp at night on the road, hoping someone might be able to decipher the most confusing passages, but it had proved futile.

"Find anything useful?" I asked, sitting down next to her.

She stretched and yawned, as languorous as Fox after a nap. "Possibly? There's a page that seems to be talking about a blood bond, but the ink is smeared and I'm not quite sure I'm reading it correctly."

She passed me the book and pointed to the verse she was referring to. "It either says, 'Bonds of blood will not be broken, 'less the blood spell…'" She chewed on her lip for a moment. "That could say 'spill,' though."

"What's the rest of the line?" I asked, squinting at the slanted writing.

"I'm not sure. Something about 'twice is spoken.'"

"It must be 'spell,' then. You can't speak a spill." I handed the book back to her. "But we don't know what the blood spell is, do we?"

"There are a dozen blood spells in this book," Adriel said. "I've only done a very simple one, a long time ago, and I wouldn't do it again."

"What was it?" I leaned in, morbidly curious.

"It was a love spell, where the lovers cut their hands and tied them together with a cloth. I said the spell, and when the cloth was removed, they were supposed to be bound on a deeper level."

"And did it work?"

She wrinkled her nose. "I suppose so. When the man believed his wife was having an affair, he nearly killed her."

I shrank back in horror.

"Like I said, messy."

I looked down at the book again. "Can a spell like that be undone?"

"Sometimes. In that case, I could have torn the fabric apart and recited another spell, and that should have undone it. But there's never a guarantee a spell can be broken."

The thought of being tied to Ceren like this forever was untenable. "Well, this one has to be."

"Even if I do manage to break the spell," Adriel replied, "it won't stop him from wielding the bloodstones. He doesn't need your blood to do that."

"No, but as long as he has my healing abilities, he's going to be extremely difficult to stop. And besides, I want the link between us severed as soon as possible. I don't want to be in his head anymore, and I certainly don't want him in mine."

Adriel sighed. "It sounds like Talia's plan is to overtake Old Castle tomorrow, then attack New Castle, regardless of what you and I accomplish with this book."

"You should have left with Roan's soldiers when you had the chance," I said, angry with myself for endangering another person I cared about. "Now you're stuck here with me."

"I could have left, Nor. I chose not to. Despite Roan's misgivings about Talia—which, by the way, I happen to share—I wasn't going to leave without a solution to your blood spell problem. Besides, the thought of another seven days in the saddle was horrifying. And Shiloh promised to check on Foxglove for me, so there was no rush to get home."

I smiled, relieved that this friendship, at least, wasn't complicated.

The tent flap stirred, and a second later Zadie's head appeared. "There you are," she said to me. "We were looking everywhere."

Sami entered after her. "Any word from Queen Talia?"

"I wasn't invited to the strategy meeting. Where were you two?"

"Ebb took us with her to see Grig and Osius. They weren't invited to the strategy meeting, either."

"How can that be?" I asked. "Osius is the only one who has seen Old Castle."

"He reported back and was dismissed," Sami said. "Ebb was going to see if she could speak to Grig in private. Osius seemed reluctant to talk about it with us."

"He's a soldier," I ventured. "We're not."

"Fair enough, but we have as much stake in this as the rest of them. More, if you ask me. And if they're planning an assault on New Castle that could potentially endanger our parents, I think we have a right to know."

Zadie placed a calming hand on his shoulder. "I happen to agree with Sami. I don't like that we're being kept in the dark."

I nodded. "I'll talk to Talin later."

The tent flap rustled again, admitting Grig and Ebb this time.

"I only have a few minutes," Grig panted. "Osius needs me, but I want to tell you what he saw at Old Castle."

"It's about the Varenians," Ebb added.

"Some of them are being held at Old Castle. Those who weren't fit to work in the mines."

Hope sparked in my chest. "My parents?"

"Not among them, from what Osius could see. It was mostly elders and children, about twenty of them. They were in the armory, making jewelry out of the bloodstones. Some of them appeared to be wearing the bloodstones themselves."

The spark sputtered out. "Ceren must be using the gems

to control the Varenians. Which means he could be doing the same to those in the mines."

Ebb nodded. "It wouldn't surprise me. Rescuing them is going to be even more difficult than we thought."

"How is Talia planning to protect the Varenian prisoners when she takes New Castle?" I asked. "What if they get caught in the cross fire?"

"That's what I wanted to tell you," Grig said. "Talia seems to thinks the Varenians will come to her side and fight."

"Women and children? The elderly?" I shook my head. "That can't be true."

"I've seen her troops, Nor. It's not just able-bodied men. I saw some boys and girls who couldn't be over thirteen. It's the only way she can get the sheer numbers she needs to fight Ceren."

I remembered Shale's words, how the woman king would make no exceptions. "We have to talk to Talin. If that's true, he wouldn't stand for it."

Grig sighed. "Listen, Talin is a good man, the best I've ever known. And I know he doesn't condone his mother's methods. But he's spent the past four years trying to get her back, and I don't think he's going to go against her now. She keeps him so close it's difficult to even talk to him."

"Grig?" Osius lifted the tent flap. "You need to come quickly. It's time."

"For what?" I asked.

Osius's steady gaze met mine. "To launch our attack on Old Castle."

24

They launched their attack in the hour before dawn and took Old Castle by late afternoon. Talin came back from the battlefield that night battered and bruised but with a tired smile on his face. When he finally made it back to his tent, I helped him with the buckles on his armor and filled the washbasin with water from the ewer, soaked a cloth, and brought it to him.

"Let me," I said as I started to clean the dirt and gore off his face. He closed his eyes and sighed wearily, as if he hadn't taken a proper breath all day.

"What happened?" I asked.

"Ceren's troops were waiting, as we knew they would be. It was a matter of numbers, and we had more. But that's only because he's got the majority of his troops surrounding New Castle."

I finished cleaning his face and went to rinse out the cloth. "Can I ask you something?"

"Of course. But I can't guarantee a coherent answer. I'm exhausted."

I wrung out the cloth and handed it back to him. "Grig said there are children in your mother's army."

His eyes met mine briefly before darting away. "No one under the age of twelve."

"Twelve!" I couldn't keep the horror from my voice. I hadn't wanted to believe it was true.

"I know," he said as he collapsed on his pallet. "But Ceren has far more men at his disposal. We couldn't have won if we only sent in our adult males."

"And the Varenians?" I asked, trying to quell my growing sense of unease.

"We saved most of them. I'm afraid we lost a dozen or so in the skirmish."

My stomach sank as I shrank back against the tent wall. "A dozen Varenians?" Many of my people had turned against me and the people I loved, but in that moment, I couldn't imagine a single one of them whose loss I could bear.

"It's nothing compared to the hundreds of Ilareans we killed, Nor. Most of them weren't even aware of what they were doing. And we lost far more of our troops, too. This is war. People die. I'm not sure what you expected."

His coldness was like a punch in the gut. "Talin."

He pulled off his tunic and threw it on the floor. "If you came to make me feel bad about myself, you shouldn't have bothered. I don't need any help with that."

All of the adrenaline and thrill of victory had clearly run its course, and Talin's guilt was physically evident in the slump of his shoulders and the frown tugging at his lips. My heart ached for him, but I couldn't pretend that I agreed with any of this.

"There has to be another way," I said quietly. "A peaceful way."

His eyes flashed in the candlelight. "War is the opposite of peace, Nor. Diplomacy isn't going to work with my brother. You of all people should understand that."

"Was he there? On the battlefield?"

"Yes."

"Did you talk to him?"

His eyebrows rose, and I immediately felt foolish. "What do you think happens on a battlefield, Nor?"

"I'm sorry. I'm clearly making things worse. I'll go."

I was nearly at the flap when he grabbed my elbow. His voice was thick when he spoke. "Wait, please. Today was difficult, Nor. It's only going to get harder from here. I need to know that I have your support. I can't go into battle knowing you don't believe in me."

I placed my hand over his. "I believe in *you*, Talin. I always will. But this war... I'm just not sure I believe it's the only option. Do you know why your mother wants the throne so badly?"

His brow furrowed in confusion. "What do you mean? You know how Ilarean succession works."

"I know that she believes Zoi *should* be queen. But she has wanted to see one of her children on the throne even before Ceren became what he is. It can't simply be about birthright. Shouldn't what's best for the people matter most?"

"I'm surprised you of all people would question my mother's motives," Talin said. "She grew up under Ilarean rule, just like you did. She wants to make sure her people are safe. And she wants a peaceful Ilara."

I could understand that, of course. It was the same thing I wanted. But there was a part of me that feared Talia had lost sight of her true aim. She was so focused on the throne she could no longer see all the people she would damage on her way to seizing it.

Rather than press the point with Talin, I said a half-hearted goodbye and stepped out into the night. Most people were celebrating Talia's victory as I passed through the camp, but I went straight back to my tent to talk to Adriel. She was in her bed, trying to sleep but clearly frustrated by all the noise outside.

"Do you remember the vision I had in Riaga?" I asked her as I perched on the edge of her bed.

She sat up and glanced at my neck. "Of course."

"Ceren wasn't drinking my blood in that vision. I think it happened because my own blood was being spilled."

She arched an eyebrow. "And?"

"He looked completely worn out and exhausted, as I told you. And that was before the battle. I have a feeling he's out of blood."

"Good. That should make him easier to defeat."

"It should also make him desperate to get more of my blood."

She eyed me suspiciously. "What are you suggesting, Nor?"

"Talin only believes diplomacy won't work with Ceren because he isn't willing to give up the one thing Ceren wants."

Adriel folded her arms across her chest and stared at me. "You mean you, don't you?"

My doubts about this plan had plagued me since I arrived at Talia's camp. If I was wrong, I could foil her plans and put the Varenians in more danger. Even if I was right, I would still be forced to confront the source of so much fear and pain. How could I trust myself now, when every big decision I'd made leading up to this point felt like a mistake?

"I'm so lost, Adriel. I wish I had a compass to guide me."
"You do, Nor." She smiled and pointed to the center of
my chest. "And as far as I can tell, it has never led you astray."

We moved camp the next day, thousands of us packing up
and crossing the distance to Old Castle. It was heavily guarded
by Talia's strongest troops, the ones who were actually trained
soldiers. Some of us were moved into the castle itself, while
the vast majority camped in tents outside the castle walls.

Old Castle had once been filled with nobles and royalty,
but that had been decades ago, and it looked like what it
had been for the interim: a garrison, mostly. The rooms we
were given were full of faded furniture and dust. Those who
couldn't fight were tasked with making the place habitable,
but there was only so much that could be done.

Adriel and I were given a room together since Zadie was
with Sami. I hadn't seen Talin after our argument, and I hated
parting on bad terms. But I hadn't been invited to any of the
war council's meetings, and neither had Grig and Osius. I
could only assume that Talia's plans remained unchanged,
and for now, so did mine.

I went in search of the rescued Varenians as soon as we
were settled. I didn't know any of them well, but it was good
to see familiar faces. One, a girl who had been in our choosing ceremony, seemed eager to speak with me. I invited her
to have tea with Zadie and me, hoping she might be able to
tell us something I could use in the coming days.

Blaise sipped her tea carefully. She'd had poor vision from
birth, and therefore couldn't dive for the bloodstones, which
was why she was at Old Castle and not the mines. "The Ilareans who came for us had swords and arrows," she said,
bringing back painful memories of that day for all of us. "A

few men fought back, but they were killed immediately. After that, everyone went into the boats willingly."

"Was anyone left behind?" Zadie asked.

"A few people hid, I think. Some of the elders, and maybe a few of the youngest children. But almost everyone was taken, as far as I know."

I wasn't sure which fate was worse, to be a prisoner in New Castle, or to be left behind without food or water. "What happened when you were on the ship?"

"They chained the men and the strongest women. The rest of us stayed with our families. A man put those bloodstones on anyone who resisted, and it was like it turned them into sleepwalkers. Those with the jewels did everything they were told then, and the rest of us just went along with them. We were scared we'd be killed otherwise."

"The man who put the bloodstones on the others. Was it Prince Ceren?" I asked.

Blaise shuddered. "He had long white hair and the palest skin I've ever seen."

"That was him. Did he talk to anyone?"

"Not that I saw. He kept mostly to himself, I think. He didn't tell us anything until we got to Old Castle. Once we arrived, most of us were weak and dehydrated, but he divided us into those who could dive and those who couldn't. The others were taken away within a few hours. We've had no word of them since."

"Your family?" I asked.

"They were all taken. Do you know if they're all right?"

I sighed. "I wish we did. I'm afraid we have very little information about the rest of the Varenians. Our parents are there as well."

"You're going to save them, right?"

Zadie and I exchanged a glance. "We're going to try."

Blaise was quiet for a while, then turned to Zadie. "My mother said Nor scarred you so she could go to Varenia in your place. She said we shouldn't trust Nor, that she's wicked. But I saw you two throughout the choosing ceremony. You clearly love each other so much." She looked at me again. "Why would you ever want to hurt your sister?"

Zadie placed a gentle hand over Blaise's. "I made Nor help me so that I wouldn't have to leave Varenia. It was the most selfish thing I've ever done."

I shook my head. "Zadie—"

"I've waited a long time to have someone finally *want* to hear the truth," she said to me before turning back to Blaise. "I told myself I was doing it to help my sister, too, because she wanted to go to Ilara. And maybe if I'd managed to do it myself, I could have made that true. But I was weak, and I made her help me against her will." Zadie dropped her gaze to her empty cup as she spoke. "If anyone should have been punished, it was me. I thought sacrificing my beauty was the bravest thing I could have done, but I should have done it long before the ceremony."

"But then someone else would have had to marry that awful Ceren," Blaise said.

I took my sister's hand. "And nothing would have changed. We'd still be dying of thirst and starvation. Ceren would have finished his devices and forced the Varenians to dive. You did what you believed was right at the time, and no one can fault you for that."

Zadie blinked, releasing tears onto her cheeks. "You always see the best in people, Nor. I wish you could do the same for yourself."

I smiled and wiped her tears away with my thumbs. "I'm trying."

★ ★ ★

Late that night, Adriel was lying back on her bed, reading, when she suddenly let out a startled shout. She'd fallen asleep, and the book had landed square on her nose.

"Are you all right?" I asked, trying not to laugh at the disgruntled look on her face.

"I told you this book was dangerous," she said, rubbing the bridge of her freckled nose. Her eyes narrowed as she squinted at something on the page the book had fallen open to. "Wait. Did we read this before?"

"We've read every page in that book at least three times, Adriel."

"Maybe it's because I was just hit in the head with a heavy object, but this looks different to me. 'To break a bond that blood has made, the price must once again be paid. Drink the blood of both as one, until the magic is undone.'"

"*You* have to drink our blood?" I asked, sitting up. "That can't be right. Wouldn't that just bind you to both of us?"

"Not if I say the right spell, apparently. But I would have to have Ceren's blood to do it. If we're close enough to Ceren to get his blood, that means we're close enough to kill him and put all this to an end."

"Not necessarily," I said. "In the vision I had during the storm, Ceren was bleeding himself. It's possible he has blood already available for the taking."

"That would require sneaking into New Castle. We've already determined that's impossible."

"We have three days until Talia attacks New Castle. Thousands will die, and there's a very strong possibility Ceren will come out victorious. It seems to me it's worth at least trying to talk with him. If we send out an emissary to negotiate, someone he's unlikely to harm—"

"Talin will never allow it, Nor."

"No," I conceded. "But his mother might. I have to at least ask."

"You can't go behind his back like that. You'd be pitting him against not only you, but his mother as well. He'll feel like you've betrayed his trust. You will have!"

"I know," I sighed. I understood that trying to fix everything on my own was not necessarily the right way to do things, but I also hadn't heard an alternative other than all-out war. "Ceren won't kill me, not if he wants my blood. If there's any chance I can reason with him, I have to try."

I pulled on a robe and stepped into the hallway. The castle was dark at this time of night, with a few soldiers posted in the halls, but they knew me by now. I walked toward the wing where Talin and his mother were staying. The soldiers would probably assume I was on my way to see Talin, but I was beyond the point of caring.

I passed his room and found the largest chamber at the end of the hall, guarded by two armed men.

"I need to speak to Queen Talia," I said. "It's a matter of urgency."

"The queen is sleeping," one of the men replied.

"It can't wait until morning," I insisted.

They looked at each other. "Wait here," one man said as he disappeared into the chambers. He returned a few moments later and gestured for me to enter. Talia wasn't sleeping, as it turned out. She was poring over a map while her daughter slept soundly in their large bed.

"I'm sorry to disturb you," I said as quietly as I could. "I didn't realize Zoi was here."

"She hasn't wanted to leave my side lately." Talia looked at her daughter and sighed. She wore a simple nightgown, her hair pulled back in a braid, looking more like the mother I imagined Talin had grown up with than the warrior queen she'd become.

"That's probably natural," I said. "She must worry about you."

"It's all too much for a small child, I know. I would have left her back in the south if I'd trusted anyone to protect her as well as I can." She rolled up the map and gestured for me to sit in the chair across from her. "What can I do for you at this hour, Nor?"

I took a deep, steadying breath. "I'd like your permission to attempt to speak with Ceren tomorrow. I know it's unlikely he'll be willing to discuss surrender, but I think it's worth trying."

"My son would never allow it," Talia said, echoing Adriel. "And while I may not approve of his relationship with you, I also won't go behind his back."

"You don't approve?"

Her head tilted, a sympathetic smile on her lips. "You're both so young."

"No younger than you were when you married."

"That wasn't by choice. And as much as I hate to say it, I'm afraid Talin may not be free to choose, either. To strengthen Ilara, Talin will need to marry a princess from another kingdom. Otherwise we'll remain as weak as we've been for centuries."

I couldn't believe what I was hearing. "You married into the royal family," I said. "Your lineage is no better than mine."

"Of course not. But look where that got us. I'm fortunate my children grew up healthy, given how weak their father was, but we need to make ties with other kingdoms to improve our standing in the world. Kuven, perhaps, might have a suitable match for my son."

Seeing Zoi on the throne was never going to be enough

for her, I realized. She wanted power, just like every other Ilarean royal. The echoes of the Varenian origin story—of Princess Ilara, being forced to marry a neighboring ruler for power and wealth, rather than the prince she loved—were so strong she couldn't fail to see them. "Talin will never forgive you if you force him into a marriage he doesn't want."

She was quiet for a moment. "I'll make a deal with you, child. I'll allow you to meet with Ceren tomorrow, with a dozen soldiers to protect you, behind my only son's back."

"If?"

"If you promise to let him go."

I shrank back at her words. I wasn't sure I was ready for marriage, but I also wasn't ready to bargain away my future with Talin. "I can't make that promise. I won't."

"I know I'm asking a lot of you. It's clear to me that you love him. But do you really want to spend the rest of your life as a royal wife, with no real freedom of your own?"

I flinched involuntarily, and she eagerly seized on my weakness.

"Any girl who dares what you have dared, who risks everything for the possibility of adventure, isn't going to be happy spending her time in a cage, no matter how beautiful it may be."

"Talin wouldn't ask that of me," I whispered, my eyes pricking with tears.

"Talin will do what it takes to ensure his kingdom's future." She reached out for my hand. I was too stunned to stop her. "Sleep on it. If we're going to arrange a meeting with Ceren, it needs to be tomorrow." She glanced at Zoi, who had slept soundly through our conversation. "Let me know your decision by noon tomorrow, Nor. Otherwise we'll have no choice but to attack New Castle, and once the battle has begun, I can't guarantee that *anyone* will be safe."

25

I didn't sleep for the rest of the night, but I didn't go to Talin, either. How could I force him to choose between his mother and me when he'd risked so much to get both of us back?

I woke Zadie before dawn and asked her to come speak with me in the courtyard. I needed her advice before I made any decisions.

"You can't go through with this, you know." Zadie watched me as I picked up a pebble from the gravel courtyard and threw it as hard as I could. It bounced harmlessly off a stone wall, as ineffective as I would be if I went up against Talia.

"I can't just let Talia attack New Castle, not when there's even the slightest chance that I can prevent it."

"Talin will be crushed by the betrayal. And besides, it isn't safe." Zadie wore a new gown that Ebb had found for her, and her hair was braided in one of the intricate styles she'd worn back in Varenia. I couldn't help noticing that she looked more herself than I'd ever seen her.

I'd settled for a simple dress with split skirts and a soft corset. Gowns felt restrictive and wrong, but I didn't feel right strutting around in riding leathers like a Galethian. At least I could ride or run, if I had to.

"Talia said she'd send a dozen of her soldiers with me. I can't imagine even Ceren would attack an emissary on the battlefield."

She arched an eyebrow. "Can't you?"

I threw another pebble, wishing I could shut out my emotions for once. Every time I tried to imagine Ceren as I'd seen him in our last face-to-face encounter, bloodied and raging in the crypt, all I could visualize was Ceren as a child, sitting alone in a room full of broken toys.

"Talk to Talin, Nor. Tell him what you're planning. Going behind his back and making secret deals with his mother will only drive a wedge between you. If you love him as much as I think you do, trust me on this."

"I'm not even sure he wants to talk to me," I said. "We fought the other night, and I've barely seen him since."

She touched my arm gently. "Nor, people fight, and the people we love the most fight the hardest because they care the most." She took the last pebble from my hand and dropped it on the ground. "Which is why I will fight you tooth and nail before I let you do something foolish tomorrow."

I shrugged away from her touch. "I have no idea what you mean."

She took my face in her hand and turned it toward her. "I have known you since you took your first breath. Do you really think I don't know when you're scheming?"

I batted her hand away, but it was half-hearted. "If I tell you, you'll never let me go."

"You think I'll let you go if you don't tell me? Please, Nor.

If you're going to do something foolish, at least one person should be in on it. Otherwise, there won't be anyone to help you when the whole thing goes awry."

We glared at each other for a long moment before I finally broke. "Oh, very well. But you have to promise not to tell anyone. *Especially* Talin."

Zadie and I had talked for over an hour, and by the end of our conversation, we were both in tears. But we had a plan, and, admittedly, it was a better one than mine had been. Still, Zadie made me swear to tell Talin that I was going to see Ceren, and because she didn't trust me, she arranged the meeting herself.

The library was as deserted as the rest of the castle, the furniture covered in dust sheets, the leather book bindings cracked and dry. I ran my fingers over the spines absently, my mind too focused on what I'd say to Talin to appreciate the titles. A clock chimed ten times somewhere, and I began to fear he wouldn't come. I paced the length of the room, worrying at my lip with my teeth.

"I thought I told you to be gentle with that lip," Talin said from the doorway.

I grinned at the memory of our time on the road together, before I'd left New Castle. We hadn't kissed yet, but we were both anticipating it. I'd been anxious about finding Sami at the port market, but Talin knew who I really was, and though there were still many secrets between us, I had trusted him.

He approached me slowly. He had shaved again for the first time in days, and his hair had been properly washed and combed.

My stomach fluttered, as if we really had gone back in time and were near-strangers to each other. In some ways, we still were. There were so many years of memories we hadn't shared, all the experiences that had formed us as people before we met. How could I expect him to make any decisions based on my desires when we'd known each other for such a short time?

"I was told to meet my men in the library," he said, gently folding a cloth covering one of the couches to keep the dust from flying. He gestured for me to sit. "But I'm afraid I see only you."

"Afraid?"

He sat down on the sofa, leaving enough room for another person between us, and fixed me with a meaningful gaze. I had to force myself not to fiddle with the lace at my cuffs. It was absurd how nervous I felt, when Talin and I had been through so much together. But in the past week, a distance had grown between us that wasn't just physical.

He smiled and moved closer to me. "I could never be afraid of you. What did you want to talk with me about?"

"You're still planning to attack New Castle, I take it?"

He took my hand. "I know it isn't what you want to hear, but this is the way it has to be."

"What if it isn't?"

His eyes searched mine. "What do you mean?"

I wrestled with telling him my plan. I didn't want to cause a fight with him, not when I might fail and Talin could end up going to battle anyway. If something happened to him and his last memory of me was an unhappy one...

He brought my knuckles to his lips and brushed a kiss against them, the faked formality gone. "Please don't worry, Nor. Everything will be fine. I'll make sure your family is safe."

Reluctantly, I pulled my hand away. "I want to negotiate with Ceren. I already spoke with your mother, and she agreed." I didn't tell him what her terms had been. That would only hurt him.

He shook his head, but I held up my hand before he could speak. "I'm not asking for permission, Talin. I'm only telling you because I didn't want to do this behind your back."

"I can't believe my mother would agree to this," he said, rising. "She must know how I feel about you—and how important your safety is to me."

"I think she does. But our relationship is not her priority, and it can't be ours, either," I added softly.

Hurt washed over his features. "What are you saying?"

"I'm only saying that until all of this is over, we can't keep putting our concern for each other above everything and everyone else." I stood up and took his hands. "I'm only going to talk to him, Talin. With an armed escort."

He gazed down at me, his expression vacillating between frustration and pride. "I'm not going to change your mind about this, am I?"

I shook my head. "No."

He pressed his forehead to mine. "Let me at least come with you."

I only hesitated for a moment. "All right."

He tilted his head until our lips met, and for a moment I forgot about Ceren and Talia, about my parents and the battle ahead. Every mingled breath, each brush of his fingers, felt like an oath. I was his, and he was mine, and nothing was going to change that.

"There you are."

I turned my head to hide my flaming cheeks as Talia entered the library. To my surprise, Talin didn't disentangle himself completely.

"Were you looking for me, Mother?"

"You said you were meeting your captain. Unless he's al-tered his appearance drastically since yesterday, I must assume you were lying."

Her tone was cold, but Talin smiled. "I thought I was meet-ing my captain. Nor's presence was a very welcome surprise."

Talia's voice softened. "Of course, my son. I remember what it was like to be young. But you're a general. Your coun-cil is waiting for you."

"I'll be there in a few minutes. My council can wait."

I felt a brief surge of hope. Talin wouldn't cast me aside just because his mother wanted him to. Perhaps that meant there was hope he wouldn't let her dictate how this war went.

Talin's hand squeezed mine for one second before his fin-gers fell away. "I'll tell Mother the plan."

I nodded and watched him go, but Talia's green eyes were focused on me as she followed him from the room. She smiled, but there was a warning in her gaze as venomous as a sea snake's. *Do not come between us*, it said. *Or there will be conse-quences.*

The next morning, I dressed in my riding leathers and went directly to the stables. A groom had already saddled Titania, and Talin was there with a dozen trained and well-armed soldiers. I was relieved to see his mother wasn't joining us.

Talin handed me a white flag. "Raise this as soon as we reach the field. We sent a messenger last night. Since he re-turned unharmed, I'm reasonably confident Ceren will obey the rules of warfare. Perhaps you're right, and he'll agree to some sort of truce. I hope so, anyway."

I mounted Titania, then followed the soldiers out of the sta-bles. The drawbridge was lowered to let us out, and Titania's hooves clomped over the wood onto the road. A moment after we'd crossed, I heard the creaking of wheels as the bridge was drawn up behind us.

It was a two-hour ride to New Castle from Old Castle, but within an hour we could see the sprawl of tents in the fields before it. Ceren's scouts would have seen us approaching by now. From the top of Mount Ayris, they had the best view in the kingdom.

Finally, we spotted a small party riding toward us on the road. Ceren was unmistakable even from a distance. He rode the same black horse he'd ridden when we saw him at Galeth's border, a beast of a stallion even larger than Xander. Ceren had never been able to ride before, but my blood must have healed any lingering weakness. His long blond hair hung loose over his black armor, which matched the uniform his soldiers wore. The bloodstones at their throats pulsed in time with the ones in his crown, steady as a heartbeat.

The realization that I was about to confront Ceren face-to-face for the first time since I left New Castle struck me, and I felt my own heart rate speed up. I told myself I wasn't afraid of him, that I would never again be his prisoner, but my body was unconvinced. My hands grew clammy on the reins, and my mouth was so dry it was an effort to swallow.

Ceren called his men to a halt, and Talin ordered his soldiers to stop as well. He turned to look at me, a question in his blue-green eyes. I nodded, feigning confidence. We were just going to talk. I was not alone and without allies anymore.

I urged Titania forward. She didn't balk at the massive stallion, even though he outweighed her by half at least. We halted with a dozen feet between us, close enough to talk but not close enough to be in danger. He had a sword at his waist but no crossbow.

From this distance, I couldn't see the dark circles under his eyes or the weariness in his gaze, but I knew they were likely there since I'd noticed the signs of fatigue in my last vision. Still, he was larger than I remembered, and he sat as straight as a mast in the saddle. All the insecurity that once weighted him down appeared to have been washed away. There was a smirk on his face that I wanted to smack off, but I managed to maintain my composure.

"Thank you for agreeing to meet with me," I said.

He dipped his head in the slightest nod. "I admit, I was curious to hear what you had to say. You must know I'm not going to surrender. After what you did to me, I should kill you where you stand."

My eyes flicked back, toward Talin, but we were far enough apart that he couldn't have heard the threat. "Without my blood, you wouldn't be here at all."

His lips curled in a smile. "You can't credit yourself with my very existence, Nor."

"No, just its prolongation." I took a deep breath and exhaled slowly. "I didn't come to exchange unpleasantries with you, Ceren. I want you to free the Varenians. You have enough bloodstones for your army. Let them go."

He laughed. "And what do I get in return? Queen Talia will give up her pursuit of the crown? We both know that won't happen. You have nothing to bargain with."

"I have myself."

"I don't need you anymore," he said, though something in his expression had shifted.

"Wielding the bloodstones is weakening you. I could see it in the visions." If I wasn't completely sure before, the way his eyes narrowed confirmed my suspicions. "You need more of my blood."

"And you're offering it?"

This was the part I had kept from Talin. But if giving a little more of my blood to Ceren would free my parents, it was worth the risk. If I couldn't prevent the war entirely, at least I could make sure the Varenians were safe. I had considered asking Ceren for some of his blood in exchange, but I didn't want to alert him to the fact that we knew how to break the blood bond. Besides, if the plan Zadie and I had come up with worked, we wouldn't need it.

"In exchange for the Varenians—*all* the Varenians—yes."

"I must say, I'm surprised you're so loyal to those people. They have nothing kind to say about you."

I hated that the words stung, but I hated even more that I had questioned my own loyalty to them prior to this. Talking to Blaise and seeing the other Varenians at Old Castle had reminded me that just because some of them had turned their backs on me didn't mean I should do the same in return. At the end of the day, I was the one who would live with my choices, and I chose to follow the same compass that had guided me to this moment.

"You're one to talk about loyalty, Ceren. What would your soldiers say about you if you removed the bloodstones?"

He laughed dryly. "That's the difference between us, Nor. I don't care what they think."

I wanted to believe it was a bluff. The dream-memory belied his words. But he had been a child then. I had to remember that the years since had warped him. "Is there nothing I can say to prevent this war? No truce you would agree to?"

He almost looked sorry for me. "This was inevitable, Nor. Talia was always going to try to claim the throne in the name of her children, and I was never going to allow it to happen."

"Even though you're not the rightful heir? You haven't

turned twenty-one yet, and you know how Ilarean succession works. Your little sister is your father's heir."

"Ah yes, Princess Zoi. How is the little brat?"

"She's four years old. You can't possibly resent a child."

He tossed his hair over his shoulder. "My father would still be alive if it weren't for that *child* and her conniving mother." He stared past me, to where Talin and the other soldiers waited. "I can see my brother hasn't changed. Still watching over you like a hawk."

"He wouldn't have to if you could be trusted."

He arched an eyebrow. "I have been honorable, haven't I?"

Today, I thought bitterly. There had been nothing honorable about his treatment of me in New Castle.

"So those are your terms? Your blood in exchange for the Varenians?" His tone was nonchalant, but if he was considering the deal, he must need my blood even more than I'd realized.

I nodded. "Yes."

"And how will we make this proposed exchange?"

"Tomorrow, same place, same time." I took a deep breath, hoping Ceren couldn't see the sweat dripping from my forehead. "You can cut my arm and collect a single bowl of blood."

"In exchange for all of the Varenians? That hardly seems like a fair trade."

"Fair trade" was not a term Ceren had any right to throw around. "If you're so intent on this war and so sure you're going to win it, then one more bowl of blood should be all you need."

Something gleamed in his eyes, and I had the terrible feeling he had tricks up his sleeve I couldn't anticipate. "Fine," he bit out. "I'll agree to your terms. Tomorrow, same time, same place. Once the deal is complete, the truce is off. By the end of this week, Ilara's fate will be sealed."

I nodded. "Very well. I'll relay the terms to Talia."

He started to turn, then reined his horse back around. "One more thing, Nor. I need to know if it works both ways."

I narrowed my eyes. "What do you mean?"

"Can you see my memories in your dreams, or do I alone hold that honor?"

My blood ran cold at his words. "What?"

"Little Nor, writhing in agony from the wound on your cheek." He touched his face where my scar was. "Being scolded by your mother for your sister's failings. You want to be loved so badly, Nor, and that will always be your greatest weakness."

Ceren had violated me many times before: touching me without permission, locking me up, stealing my blood. But somehow this was worse. "Stay out of my head, Ceren."

"Why would I do that, when I enjoy watching you suffer so much?"

I nudged Titania away, refusing to let him know how much his words disturbed me. "I've seen you, too, Ceren," I said over my shoulder. "And you are as much of a child now as you were then."

26

With the first part of my plan in place, we rode back to New Castle. Talin asked me repeatedly what deal we had made, but I wouldn't tell him anything until Zadie, Sami, Ebb, Adriel, Osius, and Grig were present. This plan affected all of us.

A part of me still couldn't believe I had agreed to Zadie's idea. When I'd told her that I planned to offer my blood in exchange for the Varenians, her protests had begun even before I finished speaking.

"I won't let you offer yourself up to Ceren like a fish on a platter," she had said in the courtyard, her amber eyes blazing with anger. "I can't believe you thought you could get away with this."

"I'm not going to tell Talin, and neither are you. You promised."

She folded her arms across her chest. "That was before I knew you'd completely lost your mind."

"Zadie, offering Ceren a little of my blood in exchange for the Varenians is a good deal. Frankly, we'll be lucky if he even agrees to it."

Zadie and I had argued back and forth for nearly half an hour, neither one of us backing down. "Even if I trusted Ceren not to hurt you," Zadie said, "you'd be winning the battle just to lose the war."

"And what do you propose?" I had shot back, exasperated. "If we do nothing and Talia marches on New Castle, Ceren will have the Varenians to use however he sees fit: as troops, cannon fodder, or collateral. And I'm not sure Talia cares enough about them to let that stop her."

She had paced for a few minutes, considering. "What if we only let Ceren *believe* he was getting your blood?"

I shook my head. "Ceren isn't stupid. He'll want to collect the blood from my arm himself."

That was when Zadie had proposed her idea, and our arguing had only escalated from there. But I had recognized the same determination in her eyes I'd seen the night she scarred herself. I had always been known as the stubborn one, but when it came down to it, Zadie was even more obstinate than I was.

Now, as Zadie explained to the gathering what we had agreed upon, it was Samiel who exploded in a fit of rage.

"I can't believe I'm hearing this!" he shouted, practically leaping from his chair. "We can't send Zadie in Nor's place. Assuming Ceren even falls for it, she doesn't have Nor's healing abilities. If he cuts too deep or too hard—"

"He never has before," Zadie said calmly.

I turned to Talin, who was staring at me with silent, seething anger. "Say something," I pleaded. I hadn't expected him to like the idea of me offering my blood in exchange for the

Varenians, but I had hoped he would at least understand why I did it.

"I can't believe you made a deal with Ceren without consulting me first," he said finally.

"I knew you'd never agree to it. Anyway, you *should* be thanking me. We needed to lure Ceren out of New Castle, and we have. There is a place where the forest grows relatively close to Ceren's camp. You can ride there under cover of darkness tonight with your troops. When we make the exchange, we'll give a signal. By the time Ceren realizes what we've done, you'll have cut him off from New Castle and the rest of his army."

I was afraid Talin would dismiss the deal outright, but he closed his eyes for a moment before speaking. "I need to discuss this with my mother. We'll meet again in an hour." When he opened his eyes, they went straight to me, and I half hoped he would ask me to stay so we could talk through this. Instead, he dismissed us all with a wave of his hand.

Sami and Zadie disappeared to their room to argue in private. Adriel followed me back to our room in silence. Once the door was closed, she had plenty of say.

"I hope you know what you're doing." She flopped down on her bed, arms and legs stretched out like a starfish. "Because I have absolutely no idea."

"Zadie wants to do this, Adriel. And I'd be a hypocrite if I wouldn't let her do the very thing I proposed. She asked me to trust her, and believe me, knowingly putting my sister in harm's way is one of the hardest things I've ever had to do. But she's braver than people realize—than *I* realized—and I believe she can do this."

"And what if Ceren realizes what you've done? He could kill her, Nor."

It was the very same point I'd made to Zadie, but she'd had a counterargument. "Ceren knows he would never get my blood if he killed Zadie."

"And if he drinks the blood right away? He'll expect a vision."

"Which is why I'm going to be there, hidden. If he won't wait until Zadie is back with our troops, I'll cut myself the moment he drinks it."

She shook her head again but finally scooted over enough for me to sit on her bed. "I don't like it. I know you want to protect the Varenians, but we both know they wouldn't do the same for you."

I lay down next to her. "Would the people of Galeth heal you if you were the ailing one?"

"I doubt it."

"Exactly. And yet you work for them anyway."

"At least I get paid."

I turned to face her. "You know that's not the reason you do it. I know in my heart this is right, Adriel."

She sighed, resigned, and reached onto her nightstand for the leather book. "There's a spell written in Penery. My mother only taught me a few words in the language, but I found a book in the library that helped me translate it."

I sat up. "Really?"

She nodded and handed me the book, opened to a page near the end.

I scooted closer. "What does it say?"

"'Two hearts beating now as one; the bond must break to come undone. Free them from the spell they're under. What was made now tear asunder.'"

It was possible I had skimmed over the spell when I didn't recognize the language, though the page itself didn't look familiar, and once again I had the feeling it had kept itself hidden on purpose. "You drink our blood and say those words?"

She nodded. "I believe that's all there is to it."

I sighed and lay back down. "If only I could have gotten Ceren's blood. It would have saved us from having to make the exchange tomorrow. Our only hope is that Talin can get to Ceren while he's exposed on the field. If I'm right, he's already weakened, and his hold over his soldiers should be slipping."

She was quiet for a long time, and I felt my eyelids growing heavy in the silence. "There is one more thing I wanted to talk to you about," she said finally. "The dreams you and Ceren shared?"

I blinked sleepily. "What about them?"

"From everything I know of blood magic, it stands to reason that Ceren drinking your blood connects him to you mentally. And it follows that you can create that same bridge by cutting yourself. But the dreams... Nor, a blood bond can't be formed in just one person's body."

I shook my head, too exhausted to make sense of what she'd just said. "So?"

"So, you would have to have Ceren's blood in your system to complete the bond."

She still wasn't making sense. "Ceren never gave me his blood."

"Are you sure about that?"

I thought back to my time at the castle. The only time I'd seen him bleed was the night I escaped. There was no way I had his blood in my system. "I'm sure."

Adriel curled onto her side. "I suppose I'm wrong then. You know, I could come to the field with you tomorrow for moral support."

I turned to face her. "Thank you for offering, but I'll feel better knowing you're safe."

"When are you going to learn that this works two ways, Nor?" She shook her head. "You can't always be the one riding off to face danger. There are a lot of people who would be devastated if something happened to you, including me."

I knew there were people who would miss me if I was gone, but there was something about hearing Adriel say it that made my heart clench. She wasn't a relative or a lover; she was simply a friend. The best friend I'd ever had. "I'm sorry, Adriel. I know it's selfish to always want to be the one who goes ahead. I think I believed that if I made sacrifices on behalf of the people I loved, they'd see how much I loved them, too. And there was the very real possibility that if I didn't jump first, I'd have to see if anyone else would jump for me." I couldn't meet her eyes anymore. "I think I'm afraid of what would happen to me if I were the one left behind."

"We have that fear in common."

I glanced into her blue eyes and remembered what Ceren had said on the field about how my desire to be loved was my greatest weakness. Maybe he was right. But everyone needed to be loved, even Ceren. He had allowed that need to twist into something ugly and hateful, but that didn't mean it wasn't a weakness. I just had to figure out how to use it against him.

To Talin's dismay, Talia agreed to the plan. Talin and his men had left at midnight, riding for the forest closest to Ceren's camp, where they would wait until our signal. After another sleepless night, Zadie and I rode out in the morning with a dozen soldiers led by Grig. Zadie was dressed in my clothing from yesterday, while I wore the same leather armor as the soldiers. From far away, there was no reason

Ceren would recognize me, especially with my hair pinned up tightly on my head. Zadie's hair was down, which helped hide her features. Even Sami had been momentarily fooled when we showed him the disguise.

"That's him, isn't it?" Zadie asked.

Ceren's pale hair was always his giveaway. The bloodstones in his crown glowed faintly, pulsing, I realized with a start, in time with my heartbeat. "Yes."

Zadie's voice was tight with fear, and I saw her fingers start to lift to the star-shaped scar we'd painted on her cheek. "I'm starting to think this was a bad idea, Nor."

She was mounted on Titania, who fortunately was as calm and steady for Zadie as she was for me. I rode a borrowed mare who, while perfectly well trained, could never compare to my Galethian steed.

"Just breathe," I said to Zadie. "Don't speak unless it's absolutely necessary, but remember, Ceren has never met you before. He has no reason to think you would come in my place."

She nodded briskly. "It's going to be fine."

"It is," I assured her, though my scalp prickled with cold fear as Zadie continued forward while the rest of us remained behind.

They stopped just a few feet from each other. I couldn't hear their conversation from where we waited, but they dismounted simultaneously. Ceren barely glanced at one of his men, who raised his arm at what I could only assume was a mental command. At the signal, one by one, the Varenians began to emerge from the tented camp.

I breathed a little easier, knowing he had held up his end of the bargain. Maybe it was wrong to deceive Ceren when he had been honorable, but I couldn't care. Not when I knew what he was capable of.

Mount Ayris loomed behind the camp, its peak shrouded in mist. It took longer than I expected for all of the Varenians to gather on the field. There were somewhere between four and five hundred men, women, and children, and I couldn't make out individual faces, though I scanned the crowd for my mother and father anyway.

I flashed back to when I'd returned to Varenia and how vulnerable the village had looked. Seeing all my people together as one, I had hoped they would look as strong as I knew them to be individually. But New Castle had taken something from them, just as it had me. Even from here, they looked like they'd been set adrift. How would we ever recover from this?

Ceren took a couple of items from his guard, what I could only assume were a silver bowl and a knife, and my gaze snapped back to Zadie. My heart was pounding so loud I was sure Grig could hear it. I pulled out my own small blade and pressed it to my exposed wrist, ready to draw blood as soon as I saw Zadie turn to look at us, the signal that Ceren was about to cut her.

When she turned, I immediately ran the knife across my skin. There was a long enough delay that I was convinced it wouldn't work, but then light flashed across my eyes and it was as if I were in Zadie's head, with Ceren standing just before me. It took an agonizing minute for Ceren to gather the bowlful of blood, but when he had finished, Grig reached over and gripped my shoulder tightly to bring me out of the vision. I could see Zadie press a cloth to the wound in her arm, and then the signal was given for the Varenians to cross the field toward us.

Zadie walked to Titania as our group began to move forward. But before she could mount, Ceren approached her.

While she fumbled with the stirrup, he reached for her wounded arm and the cloth covering her skin.

My stomach sank. We had known this was a possibility, but we had hoped Zadie would mount and leave fast enough. My gaze flickered between the Varenians moving far too slowly across the field and Zadie struggling in Ceren's grasp. Grig shifted in his seat. From the corner of my eye, I saw a soldier lift the red flag that was the signal for Talin and his troops to attack.

Ceren released Zadie, and I thought we might have pulled it off.

But then his eyes flicked to us, and I knew something was wrong. I dug my heels into my mare's sides and galloped forward while Titania raced toward us, Zadie clinging to her mane. Ceren wasn't chasing her, thank Thalos.

Instead, he turned to face the Varenians. I scanned the horizon for some sign of Talin's troops, but I saw nothing in the camp. And then I watched in horror as red jewels began to pulsate on every single Varenian neck.

"What's happening?" I shrieked as Zadie and I reached each other.

"It's a trap," Zadie breathed, dismounting from Titania just before I leaped from my mare into Titania's saddle.

"I can see that! Are you hurt? How is your arm?"

"It's fine. Don't worry about me. Where are Talin and his men? Shouldn't they be here?"

I looked across the field, where the Varenians stood in even rows, knives and other makeshift weapons in their hands, waiting for Ceren's command. Grig and his men had pulled up their horses and circled back to us as soon as they realized what was happening.

Where *was* Talin? He should have arrived by now. What

if Ceren had spotted them and they'd already been defeated? What if Ceren had seen through all our plans and beaten us at our own game?

"I'm so sorry, Nor," Zadie said. "I wanted to help, and I've only gone and made things worse."

"You're wrong, Zadie. Ceren was planning this regardless of which one of us came."

Grig and his men had clustered around us. "We should retreat to Old Castle. We can't defeat that many people, regardless of their lack of training."

The thought of even trying to fight people I'd known my whole life, including small children, was horrifying. I was about to turn Titania back toward the castle when I saw one of the Varenians step forward from the others.

He walked to Ceren and knelt down. I couldn't make out the man's features, but he was fair-haired. Not Father or Kristos. As we watched, Ceren pulled out a blade and ran it across the kneeling man's throat. He collapsed onto the field without any sign of struggle. Zadie screamed, but I was frozen with fear. The other Varenians hadn't even moved.

Ceren turned to look at me then, and I felt something horrible pass between us, something I had no control over. He wanted me to know what he was capable of, that this wasn't a game. I clutched at my head, wishing I could tear him free of it.

Suddenly, a rider burst out of the trees behind us. For a moment, I was afraid Ceren had planned an ambush, but I recognized the horse immediately as Xander. What was Talin doing behind us?

He reached us quickly, pulling Xander up alongside Titania.

"What happened?" I demanded. "Why didn't you attack?"

"I'm sorry, Nor. We watched in the early morning hours as Ceren brought out the Varenians from the bottom of the mountain and led them into the tents. But when we saw they were wearing the bloodstones, we knew that if we attacked, Ceren could order them to do anything. We sent a scout to warn you, but I'm assuming he was intercepted."

While Talin spoke, Ceren had called another Varenian forward, this one a woman.

Zadie gasped. "Thalos, is that—"

"Phaedra," I said, recognizing her by the bright red, curly hair that went down to her waist.

"No!" I screamed as Ceren once again lifted his blade, slashing her throat. I had despised Phaedra for what she did to my family, but she was a mother, a daughter, a sister, a friend. She meant something to the people in her life, and she didn't deserve to die this way. No one did.

Zadie moaned and turned away. "I can't watch. Someone has to do something."

Talin looked up at me, despair in his eyes. "If I send my men in to attack, we could lose all of the Varenians."

I nodded, a numbness washing over me at the realization of what I had to do. There was only one thing that was going to make Ceren stop this madness.

Talin must have seen the resolve in my face. "Wait, no. Nor, that's not what I meant." He tried to reach for me, but I had already moved out of his grasp.

"Nor!" Zadie cried, her voice full of anguish.

I glanced at Ceren. This time, the man kneeling in front of him had bronze skin, dark hair, and a noble forehead. *Father.*

"I'm so sorry," I said to Zadie, to Talin, to myself. I had sworn I would never again be a prisoner, that I wouldn't go back to New Castle if my life depended on it. But Ceren was right. Love was my weakness, and I could not stand by and watch my father die. I gripped the reins and squeezed Titania with my heels, and she broke into a full gallop, the protests of Talin and Zadie lost in the rush of blood in my ears.

"Ceren!" I screamed, but he was already looking at me. The knife was still raised to my father's throat.

Titania flew across the field like an arrow, and within what felt like a handful of heartbeats, I was pulling her to a halt in front of Ceren. My father didn't register my presence, but Ceren had at least moved the knife away from his throat. I tried not to look at Phaedra and the blond man, who lay in pools of their own blood.

"I'm here. You got what you wanted." My hair had come loose as I rode across the field, but I was grateful for the armor. It made me feel less vulnerable. "Let them go."

Ceren glared up at me. "Why should I? You lied to me, Nor. Though I must admit, I never expected you to put your precious sister in harm's way." He tapped his chin with the tip of the knife. "The elders were right, you know. She is prettier than you."

"Enough!" I screamed, grateful that my voice wasn't as weak as I felt. "Let them go, or so help me I'll cut my own throat, and you'll never get a drop of my blood again." I raised my sword and pressed it to the skin at my neck until I felt the bite of steel.

"Oh, very well," he said. "No need to be so dramatic. I'll let them go. But none of this 'one bowl of blood' nonsense. You'll come with me to New Castle and remain there as long as I have need of you."

I wanted to cry at the thought of going back to the dungeon, but I lowered the blade and sheathed it. "You'll let all of the Varenians go, alive and unharmed."

He gave a mocking bow. "Of course."

I glanced back to my party. Talin and Zadie had ridden forward a bit, but they had stopped when they realized they wouldn't catch me. At this point my safety was in question if they came closer. Ceren would get to me long before they did.

"I would have kept my end of the bargain, you know." Ceren waited for me to dismount and approach him. "If you hadn't sent your sister in your place, I would have let the Varenians go."

"I will never again believe a word you say."

He grabbed me by the arm and began to lead me back to the castle.

"Wait." I tied Titania's reins into a knot so she wouldn't trip and took her head between my hands, pressing a kiss to the white star in the center of her forehead. She nuzzled me, expecting treats, but I released her, making the signal that Roan had taught me. Without hesitating, she turned and galloped back to join the others. Even though it was exactly what she'd been trained to do, a part of me wished she would have stayed.

Ceren pulled me roughly toward New Castle and my father rose silently, following behind us. I glanced back at him helplessly. When we were through the tented camp and had begun the climb up the stone steps carved into the mountain, Ceren turned and ordered his guards to remove the bloodstones from the Varenians. Alys was there, I knew. She would see her mother's body any second.

When the screams began, I pressed my hands to my ears. Realizing they were free, the Varenians began to run toward Talin and Zadie. Not one turned to see Ceren and me watching them from above.

I nodded toward my father. "And now him," I said.

"I'm afraid I can't do that. If I let him go, I'll have no guarantee that you won't try to sneak out or hurt yourself."

I had thought I was numb, but his words hit me like a knife in the gut. "You promised you'd release them all!"

"And I will release him. Once he's safely tucked away in the dungeon."

I swallowed back the lump rising in my throat. "You can't do this."

"Or what? You'll abandon your father?" He clucked his tongue. "Of course you won't. I know you better than anyone, Nor. Remember that."

I wished I could be numb, but fear and shame filled me as I resumed my climb up the mountain, wondering if maybe Ceren was right.

27

The climb up the stone steps carved into Mount Ayris was just as grueling as I remembered, though at least I wasn't as weak as I'd been the first time I'd made the trek. I was grateful Ceren didn't attempt to speak to me as we walked. I may be at his mercy, but I didn't have it in me to be cordial.

I glanced back at Father occasionally to make sure he was all right. Though he breathed heavily with exertion, his expression remained neutral. He wasn't injured, as far as I could tell, but he was thin and clearly weakened from his time in the mountain. I had to fight every instinct in my body to turn and embrace him. I had wanted so badly to see him, but not like this.

Finally, we reached the top of the mountain. It was even more heavily defended than when I'd lived here. As we stepped through the massive doors into the main hall, my entire body went cold, despite the blazing fires. The iron-

stone throne that had sat empty for my entire time at New
Castle somehow looked more lived in.

Everywhere we passed, guards, servants, and nobles bowed
to Ceren. Murmurs of "Your Highness" and "Sire" followed
in his wake. I had forgotten that to these people, he was King
Ceren now. Almost everyone I saw wore a bloodstone, and I
couldn't help noticing how they came alive as he passed, before quickly slipping back into their coma-like trances. Ceren
had shown me a hundred times how much evil he was capable
of, but it still shook me to my core to witness it.

"I hope you've enjoyed your time playing warrior," Ceren
said, nodding at my armor. "I'm afraid it's back to corsets and
gowns for you."

I wrinkled my nose in disgust. "Why bother when I'm
going to be spending my time in a dungeon?"

"Do you really think so little of my hospitality? You'll be
staying in your old room, of course."

I stopped, and Father bumped into my back. "No, I'm not."

"I can prepare a different chamber, if you prefer."

"I'll stay in the dungeon with my father."

Ceren shook his head. The bloodstones in his crown pulsed
faintly, still in time to my own heartbeat. "That's completely
unnecessary. I know you won't go anywhere while your
father is in a cell, and I need you to be healthy."

I swallowed back the bile burning in my throat. "I'd prefer to be with him." I took my father's hand and squeezed it,
but it was disturbingly limp and lifeless in my grasp. "Please,
just take off the bloodstone. I only want to talk to him, to let
him know I'm here."

"The stone will be removed soon enough." One of the
guards stepped away from the wall and took my father's arm,

who went in the direction of the dungeon without a fight. I had to hold myself back from going after him.

Ceren led me toward my chambers, though I knew the way all too well. "How is my brother?" he asked, staring at his fingernails as if he didn't really care one way or the other. "He can't be happy that you made a deal with me. I imagine this is exactly what he feared would happen."

"Talin is fine."

"I must say, I'm a bit surprised you aren't married yet. Tell me, is that because of you or him?"

"My relationship with Talin is none of your business," I said flatly.

"So it's you, then. Why are you keeping him waiting? He gave up the crown for you, Nor. If that doesn't prove his love, nothing will."

I wanted to tell him he was completely wrong. Talin had proven his love for me in a hundred other ways that had nothing to do with the crown. But though I had agreed to let Ceren bleed me, he had no right to my inner thoughts or feelings.

"Why haven't you chosen your queen yet?" I asked instead. "I believe you once told me you could have any woman you wanted. I hear Lady Hyacinth is up to the task."

He grunted. "Where did you hear that bit of nonsense?"

"I have my sources," I replied, sensing I had touched a nerve. "She heads your war council, doesn't she?"

He turned toward me. "She does. And any attachment she may feel to me is purely based on her desire for power. Her ruthlessness is exceeded only by my own."

What was I detecting in his voice? I didn't believe Ceren had ever had real feelings for me, though he had tried to woo me in his own sick way. He had even offered me his mother's crown, made from the blood coral and pearls that came from Princess Ilara's body. If I had sacrificed myself then, I may have prevented everything that had come since, though I couldn't possibly have anticipated *this*.

We resumed walking and finally reached my old chambers. I didn't even have Ebb for companionship. As if sensing my thoughts, he turned toward a young woman standing so silently in the shadows I hadn't even noticed her. The bloodstone at her throat lit up as she stepped forward.

"Your lady's maid. She's under my command, which means anything you say or do will be relayed back to me."

Ah, so he didn't really trust me. "You mean she'll be spying on me."

He ignored the remark. "Is there anything else I can get you?"

"I just want to go to sleep." I entered the chamber without saying goodbye and closed the door behind me. The room looked exactly the same as I'd left it. I walked to the carved wooden wardrobe and opened the door.

"It's like I never left," I murmured as I ran my fingers over the familiar fabrics. Why hadn't he destroyed all of these?

I reminded myself that it felt like ages had passed, given everything I'd been through since leaving. But for Ceren, it had only been a few weeks, and almost every one of them had been spent in this castle.

There was a soft knock at the door, and the maid entered a moment later. She was smiling, but it was so unnatural I would have preferred it if she had no expression.

"King Ceren has requested that you join him for dinner in an hour," she stated. "Can I get you anything in the meantime?"

"Requested?"

She stared at me, still smiling that awful smile.

"Never mind. I'd like a bath, if possible." If I had to be at New Castle, I was at least going to take advantage of the one thing I had enjoyed here.

The maid nodded and departed, leaving me alone with my thoughts. At least the Varenians were free. If Talia decided to attack New Castle, they would not be caught in the cross fire. Unless, of course, she decided to use them as soldiers. But I told myself Talin would never allow it, not after what I'd risked to get them free.

I was also in the closest proximity to Ceren I'd been since I learned about the blood bond. If I could get into his study, I could take some of his blood. Then, once I'd found a way to escape New Castle with Father, Adriel could finally perform the spell. I just had to be one step ahead of Ceren at all times. And so far, I'd proven terrible at that.

After my bath, the maid tied me into my corset and helped me dress in a dark purple gown. I smoothed my hands over the fabric, marveling at the fine embroidery and lacework. So much trouble for a gown I would wear once.

I left my hair down and refused the jewelry the maid offered, wondering how I was ever going to get through this meal. The nobles didn't like me before; surely, they would despise me even more now that they thought I'd tried to kill their king. The only allies I'd had were Ebb and Lady Melina. While Ebb was safe, Lady Melina had died to help me get free of this place. I felt tears pricking the backs of my eyes and pressed my hands against them to staunch the flow.

I couldn't waste time on self-pity. Ceren had a war campaign to run, which meant that no matter how much of my blood he drank, he couldn't focus all his attention on me. I already knew where his study was and where Father was being held. Ebb had managed to escape via a cart full of linens. Perhaps the same plan could work for us.

When I reached the dining hall, I was surprised to find it deserted apart from Ceren and a few silent servants.

"Where are the others?" I asked as I took my old seat, to his left. He wore his imposing uniform of black doublet and trousers, but I noticed his posture wasn't quite as straight as it had been. Was there any chance I could kill him before he drank my blood, while he was still weak?

"I thought it would be best to dine alone tonight to ease you back into life at New Castle."

A servant filled my goblet with wine, which I knew better than to drink. I needed my wits about me at all times.

Ceren twisted his goblet in his long fingers and studied me. "You've changed. You're not as nervous as you once were."

"Did you prefer me before, when I found everything new and confusing and you could frighten me with a single glance?"

In lieu of a response, he waved a man forward to serve us dinner. I was relieved there was no liver tonight, just some kind of poultry and vegetables. Perhaps he had finally scaled back on his lavish meals, in preparation for the impending war.

"You've changed, too," I said. "My blood has made you healthy and strong, just like you wanted." I took a delicate bite of food and smiled. "It's a shame that the bloodstones make you so weak."

"Do I seem weak to you, Nor? I controlled every Varenian on that field with my mind. I could have ordered them all to kill themselves, had I wanted to. I am the most powerful man in the kingdom. In the world."

"Power seized by force isn't true power." I thought of Yana, whose power came from respect. Of Roan, whose soldiers were loyal because he led by example. Of the elders, who we relied on for their wisdom and experience. "What happens when you no longer have control over all of those people? What happens when they realize what you've taken from them? One night you're going to wake up with a blade at your throat and no one around to protect you."

He remained impassive. "Has seeing my memories not changed your opinion of me at all?"

"I always felt sorry for the way Talia treated you as a child, Ceren. Even before I saw those memories. But it doesn't excuse the things you have done as an adult. A lot of children are treated horribly, and they all don't grow up to be murderers."

His expression hardened. "If you're finished, perhaps we can go to my study."

Every muscle in my body tightened at the idea of him bleeding me again. The last time, he had done it by force, cutting into my flesh over and over until I passed out from blood loss.

"I'm not going to cut you. Not yet. I want to discuss this blood bond, as you call it. And I'd prefer to do that somewhere private."

I glanced at the servants still milling about in the shadows. Didn't he trust the people he'd surrounded himself with? If most of them were wearing bloodstones, as he'd said before, he should have no reason not to.

I rose stiffly from my chair and followed him down one of the long corridors. We passed a noblewoman who seemed to recognize me from before. She gasped and elbowed the lady next to her, but I didn't spare them a glance. None of these people had done anything to help me or Lady Melina. They had all stood by and watched as she was murdered and I was imprisoned, silent and judging. Then they had stayed at New Castle, knowing what their king was capable of.

Ceren's study looked different from the last time I'd seen it. Gone was the massive breathing apparatus he had created so Varenians could dive for pearls more efficiently. The long table in the middle was covered in small vials of dark red liquid. He must have been bleeding himself daily for weeks. All I had to do was sneak one of those vials into my sleeve. He couldn't possibly miss it.

"That's not all mine," he said, and I wondered if my intentions were that obvious.

"Whose is it, then? I can't imagine you have much of my blood left."

"I've taken it from different sources. I'd like to understand why your blood has the power to heal, while mine needs… replenishment." He bent over one of the vials. From what I could see, there was no obvious system of organization or labeling. Hopefully I'd be able to decipher which was his and not end up taking some random sample with me. "But the truth is, I can't see any difference between my blood and bat blood."

"Not everything in this world can be explained."

His eyes flicked to mine. "I disagree. There is always an explanation. We just have to be wise enough to see it."

"How do you explain the influence the mountain has on Ilarean royals?"

A shadow passed over his eyes as he straightened. "I can't solve every mystery. Running a kingdom at war is fairly time consuming."

"If you find it so tedious, perhaps you should give the throne to the rightful heir. You could spend the rest of your days tinkering in solitude."

"Rightful heir..." He looked down at me with his crystal-line eyes. "The founding rules of Ilara have not applied for quite some time. It may have been a queendom once, but for generations it has been the eldest son who inherits the throne. Why should that be any different now?"

"Because the kings of Ilara were killing off their infant daughters," I said, my voice growing louder than I intended. "Why do you want to be king so badly, anyway? It won't make people love you."

He flinched as if struck, and I instantly wished I could take it back. Before, I would have been locked in my room—or worse—for speaking to him like that. I could see the blood-stones in his crown pulsating faster, in time with my own racing heart.

He stepped forward, catching me by surprise, and took my hand. "Do you feel that?" he asked, placing my fingertips at his throat. "How our hearts beat in time? How can that be?"

I pulled my hand free of his grasp. "You're the one who insists there must be a scientific explanation. There are many who would simply call it magic." I stepped away from him. "Take my blood. I'd rather get it over with than wait around, wondering when you're going to do it."

Ceren reached for a slim silver blade on a tray. "Do it your-self, then."

I eyed him skeptically. "What?"

"I don't get the sense it's the pain you fear. It's the loss of control." He placed a silver bowl beneath my arm. "Now you're the one with control."

Hesitantly, I took the blade from him, sensing some kind of trap. He was being uncharacteristically patient, ignoring my insults and rudeness. If I cooperated and helped him study the blood bond, it would make it far easier to collect some of his blood later on.

I ran the blade along my forearm, deep enough to open a vein, and winced at the pain. I squeezed my fist, the blood dripping into the bowl below. I stopped when my head began to swim.

Ceren wiped away the excess blood with a soft cloth, revealing a wound already knitting together. "Thank you. I suppose I should have let you do it yourself in the first place. It involved far less struggling."

I glared at him in response.

"What will you do with your day tomorrow?" he asked as he poured my blood into a glass vial. "Perhaps a visit to the library?"

It was true the library was the most pleasant room in New Castle, but that wasn't saying much. "I was hoping you might let me see my father."

Without hesitation, he put the vial of blood to his lips and drank. Something about seeing him do it, the way the blood stained the inside of his lips, so stark against his pale skin, made my head spin. I reached for a table to brace myself.

"Nor? Are you all right?" Ceren had always said my name with a Varenian accent, rolling the *r* on his tongue, and I hated how perfect the pronunciation was.

"Don't pretend you care," I spat, forcing myself to straighten. "If you want me to remain compliant, to give you my blood freely and without struggle, then let me see my father. I need to know he's all right. Talia could attack New Castle at any moment, and if anything happens to me, this could be my last chance."

"My brother would never allow that. Not when I have you

as a hostage. Knowing him, he would surrender the entire kingdom for your safe return."

That was probably true, but Talin wasn't the one in charge. "I wouldn't be so sure of that."

"Very well. I'll take you to see him tomorrow. I just want you to be aware, it may be...difficult for you."

"Difficult?" I asked, incredulous. "Do you think any of this is easy for me? Do you think imagining my father's suffering is any worse than seeing it?"

He turned away from me. "He isn't suffering. No more than you were when you first came to New Castle."

"You think I didn't suffer when you brought me here?" I scoffed and headed for the door, then whirled back around. "This is why you'll never be loved, Ceren. You don't care about anyone but yourself."

He towered above me, as fierce and pale as a windwhale. "And why should I? What has anyone ever done for me?"

"If that's the way you approach every relationship in your life, always questioning what the other person can do for you, you will always be alone."

His gray eyes bore into mine the way they did in my visions, and I watched as his expression shuttered. He reached behind me, unlatching the door. "I will take you to see your father tomorrow, after dinner. And, as a warning, it won't just be the two of us. All the nobles are thrilled at the prospect of humiliating an infamous traitor."

I folded my arms across my chest. "Then imagine how excited they'll be when *you* finally fall."

I heard his low chuckle follow me into the hallway, as if he'd just won something.

28

I spent much of the next day pacing over the scattered carpets, still fuming from my conversation with Ceren. I had
briefly considered visiting the library, but the watchful eyes
of servants and nobles were everywhere, and I couldn't stand
their sneers and whispers. Eventually I collapsed onto the large
bed, wishing the day would pass quickly so I could see Father.

When I heard a knock at the door, I realized I had fallen
asleep. I sat up, rubbing the sleep from my eyes. I'd just seen
another painful memory from Ceren's childhood, this time
of him sick in bed with a fever. Talin had come in to check
on him, glowing from a day spent riding with his mother,
who couldn't be bothered to look in on her stepson herself.

"It's time to get ready for dinner," the maid said. She held
a large box in her arms, tied with a satin ribbon.

"What's that?" I asked, eyeing the package with growing
suspicion.

She bobbed a curtsy. "Your gown for this evening. The king said to tell you it's a gift."

I took the box reluctantly from her, holding it away from me just in case Ceren's "gift" was anything like the bat pie he'd made for me at the feast where I danced with Talin. "I'll dress myself," I told the maid, dismissing her.

She stared at me with that frozen smile, barely even blinking. "The king said to tell you that if you don't wear the gown, there will be consequences." She curtsied again, walked to the door, and backed out with that hideous smile never faltering.

Ceren's consequences would no doubt be for my father, if I knew him at all. And if this dress came with a warning, it certainly wasn't a gift. I braced myself before removing the lid from the box and peeling back the layers of soft tissue paper inside.

My breath caught despite myself. It wasn't the first red gown I'd ever seen. That honor went to the dress I'd worn for the choosing ceremony in Varenia. It had once been Mother's own white choosing ceremony dress, dyed a garish blood-red meant to evoke the meaning of my name: coral. At the time, it was the finest thing I'd ever worn, but I had never felt beautiful in it.

I knew that this gown, with its scarlet velvet bodice leading to a skirt made of layer upon layer of crimson chiffon, would make any woman feel beautiful.

I slammed the lid back on the box and pushed it away from me.

Ceren was trying to make a fool of me in front of the court. Among all the somberly dressed men and women, I would stand out like a sore thumb, in flagrant violation of the Ilarean court's rule of wearing mourning clothing. I flipped through my wardrobe and pulled out the simplest black dress I could find, cursing Ceren in increasingly creative ways the whole time.

After I was dressed and my hair was pinned up in a severe, matronly bun, I stopped in front of my door with a sigh. As much as it would be exactly what Ceren deserved, I couldn't go downstairs like this. He would never let me get away with that kind of disobedience. In a childish fit, I threw off the black dress, ripped the pins out of my hair, and changed into the blasted red gown.

The moment I stepped into the dining hall, the roomful of people fell silent. I hadn't planned to arrive so late, but I had struggled to fit the tight corset over my new, fuller frame. Now, my ribs strained against it as I struggled to keep my breathing deep and even.

Ceren rose from his seat at the head of the table, where his father had once sat. The seat next to his was empty, obviously reserved for me.

From the look on Ceren's face, he was pleased with what he saw. My hair was loose around my shoulders, wavy from the braids I'd worn earlier. All of the other ladies present wore their dark mourning clothes, their hair up and powdered, and here I was in my scarlet gown, a traitor brazen enough to break all the rules after nearly assassinating the king.

I forced myself to meet Ceren's gaze. Naturally, he was smirking. I raised my chin, feigning confidence, and strode across the hall toward the seat beside the king.

Who does she think she is? I could hear the other diners' thoughts as if they spoke them aloud. *How dare she sit next to the king? She should be rotting in the dungeon along with the rest of her kind.*

When I reached Ceren, I dropped into my lowest, most graceful curtsy, but my eyes remained insolently trained on his.

To my surprise, Ceren returned the gesture with a flourishing bow. "The dress suits you even more than I'd hoped," he said as I took my seat. "Ah, the first course is ready."

As everyone began to eat their meals, I eyed my goblet warily. I knew better than to drink it, but it was going to be difficult to get through this evening with a clear head.

"You're not thinking of drinking that, are you?" Ceren asked, an amused smile playing on his lips.

"Of course not."

"Good." He took a sip of his own wine. "You have the tolerance of a small child."

A dozen insults came to me, but I managed to bite my tongue. "You knew what this dress would do. How am I supposed to get through a meal with everyone staring at me?"

He waved his hand toward the nobles in one of his typical flippant gestures. "You can hardly blame them. They're a morbidly curious lot, and they do so love a scandal."

"Aren't you worried that this will make you look weak to them?" I asked. "If someone can nearly kill the king and get away with it, what's to stop someone else from trying?"

In answer, he twisted the bloodstone ring on his thumb. I glanced around and realized for the first time that nearly everyone present wore a bloodstone somewhere, either on a necklace, a bracelet, or a hairpin—even an earring in one nobleman's ear. The red stones glimmered in the candlelight like drops of blood.

"Why aren't they acting half-asleep, like the others I've seen?"

"I'm not controlling them at the moment. When I do, it gets rather dull around here."

I glanced at the stone on his finger, the faint pulsating light within. "How do they work?"

"The bloodstones? Ah, that's my little secret, isn't it?"

I took a bite of a small, unidentifiable root vegetable soaked in butter. "You expect me to trust you, but you clearly don't trust me."

Ceren sat back in his chair. "You did try to kill me."

"Technically, you stepped into my blade," I muttered. We ate in silence for a while, until I realized that Ceren was staring at me.

"You're not as thin as you were before." His gaze had drifted somewhere below my neckline.

"I'm not starving anymore," I said flatly, hating how exposed I felt under his scrutiny.

"Now who's being unfair? I hardly starved you while you were here."

"Oh, that's right. I had all the liver and bat pie I could stomach."

Ceren barked a laugh so loud that several nearby lordlings turned to stare at him. He coughed and sipped his wine as if he'd been choking.

I couldn't help smirking as I nibbled on a piece of bread.

"I'm glad you stopped covering your scar," he said.

I was so surprised I nearly choked myself. "Why?"

"Because it's a part of you. The most important part, you might say. You shouldn't be ashamed of it."

He had seen my memory of that day, I remembered. It had certainly been a turning point in my life, as much as coming to Ilara had been. "I was never ashamed of it," I said quietly. "I was raised to be ashamed of it because it meant I could never be chosen to marry you. But I always knew my mother was wrong."

"Tell me," he said, leaning forward on his elbows. "If your mother was so horrible to you, why did you sacrifice yourself for her freedom? I would think you'd be glad that all those people who treated you badly in Varenia were finally being punished. I know I would."

"They weren't being punished for being cruel to me." My eyes found his. "Were they?"

He held my gaze for a moment. "Why do you love it so much?"

"What? Varenia?"

He nodded. "I've always wondered why Talia longed to return there."

"I can't speak for Talia. Perhaps she missed her family, or simply the familiarity of home. It couldn't be more different from New Castle."

Ceren seemed to genuinely consider this. "You went back, though."

"For my family, not for me."

"So you don't feel any affinity for your home?"

"Of course I do," I said, bristling. "It's vibrant and lively and unlike anywhere else I've been. Our houses are painted in the brightest colors, and the water..." A wistful smile curled my lips simply from imagining it. "It's so blue. I haven't seen that color anywhere. Except..." I trailed off and stuffed a bite of food in my mouth. Ceren didn't want to hear about his brother's eyes.

"I have to admit, it was more beautiful than I expected," he said. "I would like to see it again, under different circumstances."

I glanced up from my plate. "Really? I would have thought you'd despise it. It's small and simple, not to mention sunny and warm and in the middle of a massive expanse of water."

He answered with a low chuckle. For a few minutes, we sat in silence, and then he abruptly pushed his chair back from the table. "Why don't I take you to see your father?"

"Now? In the middle of dinner?"

He stepped behind my chair and lowered his face until it was next to mine. "Look around you, Nor."

I turned to the nearest noble. He was staring into the air in front of him, his fork hovering midway to his mouth. I blinked and looked around. Everyone was frozen, as if time had stopped and Ceren and I were the only ones unaffected by it.

"What did you do to them?"

"Nothing. I'm just giving us a moment to make a graceful exit."

"This isn't right," I said as he helped me up from my chair.

He linked his arm through mine. "Do they look upset to you? Think of them as taking a brief catnap."

"It's not a nap," I hissed as we crossed the dining hall to the corridor. Just as we reached the door, the silent room erupted in chatter. I glanced behind me to see the royals resuming their meal as if nothing had happened.

As we made our way deeper into the mountain via the many twisting tunnels of New Castle, my fear began to build. I was going to see Father, I reminded myself. I needed to focus on how I could get him out, should the chance present itself.

"You're shivering," Ceren said as we entered the final tunnel. "I should have provided you with a wrap."

"You did quite enough," I said, referring to the gown. "Where did you get this, anyhow? There's no way your mother wore a dress this color."

"Of course not. I had it made before you left. I thought it would look nice with the coral crown."

He had actually expected me to accept his proposal, I realized. How could he have possibly thought I'd say yes? I looked up and studied his profile. His nose was a little longer than Talin's, his cheekbones slightly more pronounced, but if I dipped Ceren in bronze, it would be a very similar silhouette. "What happened to the crown?" I asked.

"Hmm? Oh, I'm afraid it sustained a bit of damage in our little skirmish."

"What will your queen wear, when you choose one?"

His lip curled in a sneer. "I find myself put off by the idea of marriage of late."

"If you win this war, you'll have to start a family. The throne will need an heir."

He stiffened, and I was glad to know I still had the ability to rile him. That meant he still cared what I thought, and I might be able to use that to my advantage at some point. "I'll worry about that when the time comes. What is Talia's plan, anyhow? A siege? She must know I have enough stores in this mountain to last for years."

Talia had never said anything about a siege. I assumed she would attack the mountain, eliminating the troops at its base before beginning an ascent. "I don't know her plan," I admitted. "She wasn't exactly forthcoming with me."

"No, Talia has never been welcoming to anyone who wasn't a blood relative."

Talin had seen a side of Talia that I would never see, I knew. But the way she distanced herself from everyone but her children would make it much harder for people to respect her as a ruler, even as just a proxy ruler until Zoi came of age. "What is *your* plan? To stay in the mountain and rule from here? Continue to grow your army until you can defeat Talia's?"

"That will depend on some things," he said noncommittally.

We had reached the tunnel leading to the dungeons. Ceren gestured for me to proceed, as the tunnel was too narrow to walk side by side. Turning my back on Ceren felt like turning my back on a shark, but I didn't have much of a choice.

"I'll wait here for you," Ceren said, stopping when we reached the first set of guards.

"Why?" I asked, surprised and not particularly thrilled at the idea of going into the dungeon alone.

"To give you privacy. But try to remember, your father spent all of his time either sleeping or diving. He doesn't know anything that can help Talia or her cause. If I were you, I'd just enjoy the time together."

I ignored him and hurried down the corridor lit with fox-fire torches. They cast green light against the walls of the tunnel, and the shadows of the guards loomed like giants as I made my way past them. Finally, I reached the part of the dungeon where the prisoners were kept in small cells.

"Father?" I called into the dark.

"Nor?"

My breath left me in a rush as I hurried to his cell. The door was wooden, but there was a small window inset with steel bars. As I reached the door, I saw his fingers stretch through the bars, and I immediately grasped them in mine.

"Nor," he said. "I can't believe it's really you."

I could only see his dark eyes and a bit of his proud forehead, but even that glimpse was enough to make me gasp. His skin was lined in a way I'd never seen before, and there were dark circles under his eyes. He had aged ten years in a matter of weeks.

"Are you all right, Father?"

"I'm fine, child. And you? How did you end up here?"

I caught him up on everything that had happened since I'd last seen him as quickly as I could. "I'm going to get you free," I assured him. "Do you know which of the guards has the keys?"

He shook his head. "They never bring torches when they come, so I can't see them. They don't speak, either."

"Oh, Father." I squeezed his fingers in solidarity. "How terribly lonely."

"Have you seen your mother? How are Zadie and Sami?"

"Everyone is fine. The Varenians were all freed when I came." All except us, I thought bitterly. "Zadie and Sami are doing very well, Father."

"That's all that matters," he murmured.

"*You* matter," I told him. "Don't give up on me."

"Listen to me, Nor. We're running out of time." He lowered his voice. "Sometimes, when Ceren was away from the castle, his control over the stones would slip. The Varenians were able to dig a tunnel leading to the outside while they mined. I suspect it's the one you escaped through before. Promise me if you have a chance to go, you'll take it. I'll be fine, knowing you are safe."

I kissed his fingers in gratitude. If Father was correct, that meant we had a way out. But if he thought there was any chance of me leaving without him, he didn't know me at all, and I told him as much.

"How did I raise such a determined daughter?" he mused, his tone a mixture of pride and resignation.

I smiled, feigning cheerfulness. "I should get back. I'll come and visit again as soon as I can."

He squeezed my hand and released it, and suddenly the thought of leaving him was too painful to bear.

"Nor?"

It was Ceren, calling down the corridor for me. I turned back to Father. "I love you so much."

"I love you, too, Nor. Just knowing you're close by makes me stronger."

"Me, too," I whispered. I knew that I would defeat Ceren, somehow. Because even if love was my greatest weakness, it was also the thing that made me strong.

29

The next day, I was invited to meet with Lady Hyacinth for tea. I had no desire to see her; she'd been part of the plan to use the Varenians to dive for pearls, and I had a feeling she was behind the bloodstone mines. But she was also the head of Ceren's war council, which meant she of all people would know his plan of attack.

I had to be careful with how I approached her, though. She was as deceptive as a stingray—soft and placid most of the time, but fully capable of whipping her stinger out at any provocation.

"Lady Nor," Hyacinth said when I entered her chambers. As usual, her natural beauty was obscured by her severe facade. She wore her hair pulled back tight against her skull, and her dress had long sleeves and a high neck, exposing only her hands and face. Her eyes were lined heavily with kohl, a style uncommon in Varenia that made her look even more fierce.

"Lady Hyacinth." I dropped into a polite curtsy, surprised she had used a title when gods knew no one else had bothered.

"Welcome back." She gestured to the three other women in the room. "I'd like you to meet the better half of King Ceren's war council: Ladies Lyra, Dree, and Poppy."

I studied the women with interest. I vaguely recognized two of them from my previous time at New Castle, though none of them had attended Hyacinth's tea parties. The third, Poppy, was completely unfamiliar. It was interesting that half of Ceren's war councilors were women, when he had made it very clear how little he respected them. "A pleasure," I said, taking the offered seat. "May I ask why I was invited today?"

"You may ask whatever you like," Hyacinth said with a high, musical laugh that was clearly fake. Several of the others chuckled, too, but I kept my expression neutral. "Sweet girl. Don't you remember what the first rule of warfare is?"

I remembered what she'd told me all too well. "Know your enemy."

"Exactly! Such a smart one. I always thought King Ceren was underestimating you. I was hardly surprised when you escaped. I wasn't even surprised you stabbed the king." She came to stand behind me, placing her hands on my shoulders. I could feel her long nails—kept that way to show she was above manual labor—pressing against my skin through the holes in my knit wrap. "We are all very fortunate you didn't manage to finish the job."

The other councilmembers were watching me for a reaction, and I wondered what qualified them to advise anyone on warfare. Given their soft hands and smooth skin, they hadn't spent much time outdoors, let alone fighting.

It was difficult to ascertain how much the people in New Castle knew of what had transpired between Ceren and me.

It was no secret that Ceren had kept me in the dungeon and bled me repeatedly for "research," but I couldn't imagine him telling everyone he'd been drinking my blood. It wouldn't do much for his image to admit that the person who nearly killed him was also the person who had made him strong.

"It wasn't for lack of trying," I said finally.

She barked a mirthless laugh. "No, I suppose not. We were all shocked by his miraculous recovery and the discovery of the bloodstone vein. I must say, your people are so hard-working. Even the elders and children." She pushed away from my chair and walked back to her seat, then steepled her fingers, clicking those awful claws together.

I glanced at the other ladies. "How did you become members of the war council?" I asked, figuring I might as well find out whatever I could while I was here.

"I was raised in Galeth," Lady Poppy said. "I came to Ilara when I was still a girl, but King Ceren finds my knowledge useful."

Lyra lifted her chin. "I have something of a knack for design and building. I'm helping with weaponry."

"I learned strategy from my father, who was general of the king's guard before Prince Talin," Dree explained.

I tried not to let my concern show on my face. Ceren was surrounding himself with the right people, much to my surprise.

"Speaking of dear Prince Talin," Hyacinth said. "I could have sworn you'd be married by now. And yet here you are, wearing your old clothes, sleeping in your old room. Even dining with the man you tried to assassinate."

"I am loyal to Talin and to my family," I ground out. "I came to free them, not to help Ceren."

"Ah, but he's already had more of your blood. So you have helped him, haven't you?"

She knew he was drinking my blood, then. They all did. "You're one to talk about helping Ceren," I growled, no longer able to pretend I didn't despise her. "You head his war council." Why question my loyalties, I wondered, when she knew they were in exact opposition to hers?

Unless they weren't. I stared at Lady Hyacinth for a moment. "You said I was free to ask anything I want," I began.

"Yes, of course."

"What exactly do you want for this kingdom?"

"We all want the same thing as you: a strong Ilara, united and whole."

My pulse began to speed up, and I wondered if somewhere in the castle, Ceren felt it. I glanced around the room to see if there were any of the spying holes I had in my chambers, the ones Ceren or his guards could use to listen in on me. This had all the makings of a trap.

Know your enemy, she had said when I asked why she invited me. And she had implied that I was helping Ceren, perhaps willingly. Did that mean she thought I was on Ceren's side? If so, would that make me her enemy?

Hyacinth glanced at the other ladies, who all gave tight nods. "Tell me, Nor. How much do you know about the bloodstones?"

I wasn't about to tell her about Adriel's book and the spell we had uncovered, but I also couldn't pretend I was completely ignorant, or she would know I was lying. "I know they come from the blood of Ilarean royals and only Ilarean royals can use them."

She nodded. "That's true. But it's also true that King Xyrus had a few pieces of bloodstone jewelry that were never destroyed by Queen Ebbeela, and they never worked for him—or Ceren, for that matter. You might recall a ring he used to wear, with a red stone in it?"

I thought back to when I'd first met Ceren. I vaguely remembered a ring of that description, though it had meant nothing to me at the time. "I think so."

"It wasn't until after he drank your blood that the stones began to work, Nor."

That was new, and definitely interesting, information. "But why? I'm not an Ilarean royal."

Hyacinth sat down next to me, so close our thighs were touching. "No, but the Varenians are the only people in our kingdom, as far as we know, who still have a spiritual and physical connection to the natural world. Your blood is special, Nor."

Where are all the bloodstones now? I had asked Ebb once.

Gone, milady. Scattered to the edges of the world. They say there was once power in the blood of men, but we abused that power, and the gods took it back.

I thought of Adriel, how her people buried their dead to grow the bone trees, with their deadly fruit. If the Galethians had magic, they would never know it as long as they burned their dead.

"So you're saying that without my blood, Ceren would have no command over the bloodstones?" I asked. I knew he needed my blood to remain strong enough to wield so many stones, but I would never have suspected that he couldn't use them at all without me.

"That's correct. Ceren is the last of the pure-blooded Ilarean royals. If he dies, the bloodstones die, too."

I had considered that before, but if my blood was part of the equation, that meant we didn't have to kill Ceren; we merely had to break the blood bond. Which meant, no matter what, I had to get a vial of his blood back to Adriel.

My pulse was beginning to race, and I took a deep breath, trying to calm myself. I didn't want Hyacinth to suspect my plans. But if she was trying to trick me somehow, this was a strange way to go about it. Ceren already knew what I thought of him and that I would never help him willingly. Nothing I had admitted today was new information to him.

But Hyacinth had given *me* useful information. I looked at the other women, who were watching me coolly for a reaction. Was it possible I had allies in this castle after all? "Can you get me a key to Ceren's study?" I asked.

She raised an eyebrow. "Why?"

"Do you want my help or not?"

She glanced at Dree, who nodded. "I'll get you the key," Hyacinth said.

Finally, I was getting somewhere. "Good. I only have one more question."

She gestured for me to go on.

"Why are you helping me?"

Her eyes glittered behind the kohl like cut gemstones. "Have you ever stopped to consider that there are other women besides Talia who are tired of having a kingdom, Nor? That this place has slowly deteriorated with men in power? It's only a matter of time before Ceren gives us a choice: wear the bloodstones or die. At that point, it will be too late."

I was summoned to dinner again that night, and the thought of spending any time under Ceren's shrewd observation was rattling me. I had information I could use against him finally, and I needed to keep it close.

Ceren had ordered me to wear the red gown again, though

I wasn't given a reason why. Tonight, I let the maid curl my hair and arrange it with a few gold pins.

"All finished, my lady," the maid said behind me.

I turned to face her. "What's your name?"

"Elspeth," she replied without hesitation. She had the high forehead and narrow face of a lookdown fish, with ash-brown hair and a sallow complexion. I wondered how she had ended up with the task of caring for the Varenian traitor.

"Where are you from, Elspeth?"

The frozen smile widened. "I'm from a little village near the Lakes, my lady."

It was very likely her family would be impacted by the impending war, if they weren't already. I felt a stab of pity for her, and a wave of gratitude that Ebb had managed to escape this fate. "How did you come to work at New Castle?"

"My parents couldn't pay their taxes, so they sent me instead." The smile wobbled slightly; the bloodstone pulsed faintly at her throat. It was a painful reminder of what the bloodstones did to people, how she couldn't even experience her true emotions while Ceren had control of her.

"What if I asked you to do something for me, Elspeth? Would you be able to, do you think?"

"As long as it doesn't go against the king's orders, I'd be happy to help you, my lady."

I hated using a human being like this, but while I was at dinner with Ceren, it was the perfect time for Elspeth to get the key to Ceren's study. I gave her instructions to retrieve a package from Lady Hyacinth without telling her what it was and made my way to dinner.

I was surprised to find the long table set for just two people. Ceren sat at the head, idly twirling a small box in his fingers and ignoring the few servants who milled about on the periphery of the hall.

I cleared my throat and Ceren immediately put the box in his pocket, then rose from his seat and bowed. His silken blond hair fell forward, obscuring his features.

I curtsied out of habit and went to my chair, but Ceren insisted on pulling it out for me. I watched him from the corner of my eye.

"Thank you for coming," he said as I sat down. "And for wearing the gown."

I turned to look up at him. "Where is everyone else?"

"Perhaps I sent them all to bed without supper," he retorted. "What does it matter?"

I shrugged. "It doesn't."

He took his seat and waved one of the servants forward. She filled his wine goblet without him having to ask. "I have some bad news to share, unfortunately. I'm afraid Talia has decided not to wait any longer to start this war. She's bringing her canons up to the base of the mountain as we speak."

My stomach sank at his words. I had hoped we would have more time, that Talin might convince Talia to delay. "Then what are you doing? Shouldn't you be preparing for battle?"

He tossed a long, silky lock of hair over his shoulder. "I have plenty of time for that," he said, draining his goblet of wine and rising from his chair. "I have a gift for you." The small box was in his hand again, procured from his pocket when I wasn't looking.

I turned my head to look at him. "I don't want any more gifts from you."

"But I had it made especially for you."

Just as I started to rise, he lifted his hands over my head. I saw a flash of something stretched between them, like a rope, and I was sure he was going to strangle me in my seat. I surged backward, hoping to catch Ceren off guard, but he pressed me down with his forearms. A scream died in my throat as I felt cold metal against my breastbone, and a matching chain against my neck. I reached up to touch the pendant, my fingers finding the facets of a jewel.

I peered down at my chest, where a red gem pulsated with light.

"Before you ask, I'm not going to use it on you," Ceren said. "But I wanted you to have it." He pulled my hair away from my neck, out of the chain. The cold slide of his fingers on my bare skin sent a chill down my spine. "You're free to take it off yourself. But you should know it looks beautiful on you."

I could feel something thrumming in my veins, like the distant crash of waves on shore, a sound I'd only heard briefly in my life. Ceren went back to his seat, still gazing at me intently. The servants stood like statues against the walls, clearly under Ceren's control, their bloodstones pulsating in a slow, rhythmic beat, in time with my heart. I wondered if they felt the same warm rush of blood through their bodies that I did, as if there were a dozen hearts in my chest, instead of one.

"Nor."

The voice sounded far away. I struggled to focus on it.

Ceren was smiling at me. "It takes a bit of getting used to, I know."

I shook my head, trying to clear it. "What are you doing, Ceren?"

His long, pale fingers were reaching across the table for mine, and it was as if I was watching from above, no longer in my own body. "I thought you hated me when you stabbed me in the crypt. I was going to find you and kill you no matter what it took. But then the visions started, and I saw your memories of what you went through as a child. I started to realize that we weren't so different after all. I was wrong to try to force you to marry me. I knew it then. But I didn't believe there was any other way."

The pleasant buzz in my head was beginning to recede, replaced by a sick feeling in my stomach. "Ceren—"

"You wouldn't have come back if you hated me, Nor."

It was an effort not to close my eyes and succumb to that lovely thrumming in my veins. "I didn't come back willingly," I whispered. "You forced me."

His fingers circled my wrist, immediately finding my pulse. Whatever he found there seemed to satisfy him. "I was so relieved when you returned. I hated seeing you weak and starving in the dungeons." His eyes met mine. "I hope you know that I would do anything for you, Nor. I would give you the blood in my veins, if I thought it would help."

Something about his words cut through the fog in my mind. Moving was like struggling against a tide, but I forced myself to my feet.

Sit down, Nor.

It was a command, not a request. He was trying to control me with the bloodstone, despite his promise. But if he was using the same force on me as he did everyone else, it wasn't having the desired effect. I reached up to my neck and fumbled at the chain, searching vainly for the clasp with numb fingers.

"Don't you understand?" I asked, though my voice sounded slurred in my head. "This isn't how it works. You can't force someone to love you."

"You think I don't know that? If I could, Talia would

have loved me like the mother I never had. Instead, she despised me."

It was easy to think of him as the same Ceren I'd known before, weakened by the mountain. But he loomed above me, a mountain in his own right. I could see the frustration on his face as I began backing toward the exit, as if he was mentally commanding me to stop. But his voice in my head was nothing but a low buzz, and with every step, I pushed it farther away.

Some of the feeling was coming back into my limbs. I glanced around at the guards, but they were still frozen in place. Two stood before the exit, blocking my escape route.

"So you attempted to kill Talia for not loving you?" I asked, trying to distract Ceren from controlling his men. He may not be able to stop me with his mind, but Ceren was still physically capable of overpowering me.

"I lived with that woman for years knowing she despised me. If she hadn't gotten pregnant, everything could have gone on that way forever."

I stared at him, my mouth open as I searched for words. "So you decided to kill your own sibling? You didn't even know it was a daughter."

"Talia always knew it was a girl. And whether or not anyone else would believe that girl had a legitimate claim to the throne over me, my father would have. He was always going to choose Talia over me."

He had stepped within a foot of me, and though he towered over me, I could still see the broken child in his eyes, begging to be accepted and finding nothing but rejection. I could have loved that boy.

But I could find nothing but disdain for this man.

"I'm sorry," I said, as I turned to leave.

The guards at the door drew their swords.

I turned back to Ceren, more weary than surprised. I was tired of fighting, of giving this man chance after chance to do the right thing. I should have realized long ago that he never would. "Don't do this."

"You've given me no choice, Nor."

Tears spilled free of my lashes as the memories of all the horrible things Ceren had done washed over me. Threatening me, bleeding me, killing Lady Melina, cutting off my family's water, imprisoning the Varenians. It had been foolish to hope there was some scrap of compassion left in Ceren.

But he had been foolish to underestimate me again.

I reached out to the guards with my mind, following the warm tether of our heartbeats. It was the strangest sensation, but I knew that we were all linked through this bloody web. How was Ceren wielding hundreds of these strings daily? It must be taking everything he had not to go mad.

I had no idea if it would work, but I was out of options. Hesitantly, I sent out my first command.

Stop him.

The guards turned their swords on Ceren. His wide eyes went straight past them to me.

"Goodbye, Ceren," I said. And then I ran.

30

I clutched the bloodstone in my fist, still reeling from the fact that the guards had followed my command. I knew that the bloodstone wasn't working on me as Ceren had hoped. Otherwise, I would never have been able to walk away from him. Lady Hyacinth had been right: whatever powers Ceren had were in my blood, too. Not only that—the guards had defied a direct order from Ceren and obeyed me instead.

But as I ran, I could feel my control over the men I'd left behind slipping. I didn't know if it was the lack of proximity or that I was too panicked to focus my thoughts, but soon I heard Ceren behind me, his boots ringing out on the stone floors. Even if I could command the people guarding the exits, I wasn't going to leave without my father, and Ceren knew it.

"Nor," Ceren called, his voice bouncing off the stone walls around me. "You're trapped, silly bird."

I hadn't made it far before I was knocked off my feet by a tremor that seemed to shake the entire mountain. I landed hard on my hip and rolled onto my back, the wind knocked out of me. Talia's assault on New Castle had begun, and any hope I had that she would take precautions to prevent casualties was gone. Talia didn't want New Castle at the end of all of this; she wanted Ceren dead.

I pushed shakily to my feet and stumbled through the great hall toward the massive doors leading to the stairs down from New Castle. There were more men posted there, and I saw the bloodstones flare to life as I neared, but whatever command Ceren had given wasn't working. They stayed where they were as I passed them and shoved my way through the small door.

I found myself on the very same platform where Lady Melina had died and Talin had given up the throne to save me. The wind was always strong this high up, and it whipped through my hair and skirts icily. I ran to the edge and looked down at the field that stretched from here to the main road leading to Old Castle.

A battle unlike anything I'd ever seen raged below me. Massive cannons fired at the mountain itself, and I gripped the railing to keep from falling again.

Ceren's soldiers were lined up on the field, easily identified by their black armor, but they didn't move. Feebly, I tried reaching out through the web to find their minds, but there were too many of them. I turned around suddenly, realizing that I had no idea where Ceren had gone.

Talia's army was advancing toward New Castle, the cavalry riding out first. I couldn't spot Talin from this distance, but knowing him, he was out in front of his troops. What must he be thinking, knowing that I was inside? Was he planning some foolish rescue, or had he decided his mother's cause was more important than one life?

My eyes darted to the stone steps leading down the mountain. I could leave right now and rescue Father later. At least then Ceren wouldn't be able to use me to get to Talin, assuming he was still willing to risk everything for me.

But it was more important that I stopped Ceren from reaching his troops. There were thousands of them, far more than Talia had, lined up like statues before New Castle, and I suspected Ceren had more elsewhere. Talia might manage to win this war, but not without losing hundreds of lives in the process.

And if Ceren wasn't leaving New Castle through the main doors, that meant he had found another way out.

I turned and ran back inside, calling out to the nearest guard. "Where did the king go?"

He raised an arm and pointed, deeper into the castle.

Cursing my stupid gown and slippers, I broke into a run, following the outstretched arms of guards as I passed, all pointing in the same direction. It was a strange feeling to have complete control over them, coming so easily it would have disturbed me had I stopped long enough to think about it. A part of me could understand why Ceren enjoyed this so much; he was that broken child again, surrounded by toys. Only now, no one could refuse to play with him.

It wasn't until I was lower in the castle that the guards began to seem more alert. Ceren must be attempting to control them as he passed. At least that meant I was getting closer.

"No one goes down to the mine," one man said, stepping in front of me.

The bloodstone on his neck was pulsating in time to my heartbeat.

Let me pass.

Wordlessly, he stepped aside.

Exhilaration coursed through me. A man who could have taken me down with one blow had moved out of my way without argument. I hurried past him and down the dark, dank corridors. I could smell the underground lake before I neared it. The lunar moss torches were glowing fairly brightly, but as I approached the entrance of the cave, I could feel my breaths starting to come more rapidly. My body would always remember everything that had happened here: the first time Ceren had nearly caught me spying and had brutally killed the salamander; the fight with the giant monster, Salandrin, that had nearly cost me my life; and my desperate escape after Ceren impaled himself on my knife. I closed my eyes and tried to slow my heart rate.

As I entered the cavern, I saw someone emerge from the water on the other side in the glow of the torches. Ceren was taking the route I had used to escape, which led to an exit on the side of Mount Ayris.

I stopped, unsure what to do. I had promised not to leave this mountain without Father. If something happened to me out there, would anyone be able to get back into New Castle to rescue him? Would they forget he was there, suffering? But the farther Ceren got, the greater the likelihood of him attacking, and the smaller the chance of my plan working.

With a silent prayer that Father would understand, I shed the red gown like a creature emerging from a shell that no longer fit. I took a deep breath and dove into the lake. This time, I was the one in pursuit of Ceren. I saw him turn as I rose for my first breath, and I was glad he knew I was coming. Let him experience being the prey for a change.

By the time I reached the small opening leading outside, my shift was partially dried. I stumbled into the sunlight just in time to see Ceren mounting his black horse. As I had suspected, there were thousands more troops waiting, though these weren't wearing the black armor of his trained soldiers. They were villagers, I realized, like Jerem had been before he was conscripted. They carried everything from rakes to shovels to scythes, and every one of them wore a bloodstone at their throat.

"Please work," I whispered as I removed one of the golden pins from my hair. It was in the shape of a swallow. I knew Ceren well enough to know that he had given me bird-shaped hairpins for a reason. He had called me a little bird in the dungeon, when he caught me in his arms and told me I was trapped.

I understood why Talin's arms had felt like a cage these past weeks, why the idea of being constrained by a person, a place, or even a corset, was so intolerable. They were all a reminder of the powerlessness I'd felt as Ceren's prisoner. But I wasn't powerless anymore. I tore a piece of cloth from my hem and stepped onto the field.

I might not have the kind of control Ceren had with the bloodstones, but I could still feel the link between the two of us as strong as ever. I screamed his name through the bond.

He turned to face me, and the confusion I saw there made it clear he had not figured out what I had. He may have created a blood bond between us, but he didn't know how to break it. Why would he have concerned himself with that, when this bond was what had given him everything he ever wanted?

I dragged the sharp edge of the swallow's wing across my forearm, deep enough to draw blood, and quickly tied the strip of cloth around the broken skin.

If my guess was correct, I didn't need Adriel for this. I didn't need anyone.

If I really had Ceren's blood in my veins, then maybe, just maybe, I had enough magic to cast a spell.

I was afraid I wouldn't be able to remember the words Adriel had read to me—it had only been once, and I had never considered repeating them myself—but I felt something rise up from deep inside, and the words fell from my lips as easily as a lullaby.

"'Two hearts beating now as one; the bond must break to come undone.'" I untied the bandage from my arm and gripped it between my fists. "'Free them from the spell they're under; what was made now tear asunder.'"

I ripped the blood-soaked fabric down the center as I spoke.

Nothing happened, and for one heart-stopping moment, I doubted everything. Who had I thought I was, to cast a spell? I wasn't a witch like Adriel or a healer like Elder Nemea. I had never been chosen, the way Zadie was. I was just a girl with a scar from a tiny village in the middle of the sea.

In that moment, I realized that Adriel was right. I hadn't just been judging myself by Ilarean standards of beauty; I had been judging myself by the opinions of people who didn't even know me, let alone care about me. I always tried to see the best in the people who had wronged me, but I never saw the best in myself.

I had learned to look in the mirror and accept myself, scars and all, but I hadn't done that for the scars I bore on the inside.

Bonds of blood will not be broken, 'less the blood spell...

What had Adriel said the rest of the line was? My hold on the bloodstone began to slip as I tried to remember the rest of the words. Ceren began to move toward me on his massive stallion. *What was the rest of the line?*

Twice is spoken. It was as if Adriel had whispered the words into my ear herself. I repeated the spell, knowing if it didn't work, it would be too late. Ceren was nearly upon me.

Pain radiated through my skull, as if a piece of me really was being ripped apart, and I fell to my knees, a wave of loss unexpectedly rushing over me.

I watched as the veins in Ceren's neck bulged, his face contorting in a combination of agony and rage, followed by what looked strangely like relief. A howl eerily similar to the one he made when I stabbed him erupted out of him.

By some miracle, the spell had worked. It was a lucky guess. Adriel said I needed Ceren's blood in my veins for a bond to form, and though I hadn't believed her then, something about Ceren saying he would give me the blood from his veins had sparked a memory.

The liver stew he'd given me in the dungeon. It had revolted me at the time, but I'd forced myself to eat it to regain the strength lost in the bleedings. The metallic taste had been overwhelming; Ceren could easily have mixed his own blood into the stew without me realizing.

The feeling of loss was subsiding now. I hadn't realized how much the blood bond had taken from me, but I felt stronger and more alive than I had in months. I watched, breathless, as one by one the people on the field awakened. Some screamed, some collapsed, and others stared at the weapons in their hands in confusion.

Ceren was riding among them, barking commands, but no one obeyed him. Instead, many turned to look at him, and there were hints of recognition on their faces, of memories coming back from the last moment of clarity before they put on the bloodstones. First one man raised a pitchfork over his head and sprinted toward Ceren, then another, holding aloft a scythe.

Suddenly realizing that he was surrounded by thousands of armed men he had forced into submission, Ceren fled.

I couldn't imagine he would get very far, with his body weakened by the broken bond and both Talia's army and his own after him. My priority had to be making it clear to everyone that the fighting could cease. I would send someone to free Father and the other prisoners soon after.

Still clad in my slippers and shift, I found a horse wandering riderless among the turmoil and climbed into the saddle.

The battlefield was chaos, with a vast majority of the people present not entirely sure what they were doing there. The last thing they remembered was Ceren putting a bloodstone necklace on them, and now they were awakening to find themselves in combat. Fortunately, the confusion allowed me to make it to Talia's side of the battlefield.

It wasn't hard to spot Talin. Xander was massive, and there was a wide swath of clear ground around him. I was relieved to see he had stopped fighting, but there were men and women still going after Ceren's guards, who had continued to fight even without their master's command.

When Talin spotted me, he screamed my name, and I dug my heels into the horse's sides. We flew toward each other, both dismounting simultaneously. This time, when he pulled me into his arms and held me, as if he never wanted to let go, it didn't cause my chest to tighten with dread.

"Thank the gods you're all right," he breathed against my hair. His face was streaked with dirt and blood, but all I could see were his ocean eyes, searching mine.

"I broke the blood bond. Ceren fled. We need to tell your mother right away."

He nodded and kissed the top of my head. "Of course. Let's get you back to your family."

"My father," I said. "He's still in the dungeon. Someone needs to free him."

"I'll see to it as soon as we're back at Old Castle."

"No, it can't wait that long."

"Nor." He smoothed my hair from my face. "You're trembling, love. You're in shock. Your father will be all right for a little while longer. Right now, we need to take care of you."

I was too exhausted to argue. I let him lift me onto Xander, and when he climbed up behind me, I slumped against him, struggling to remain conscious. I was asleep before we left the battlefield.

I woke in the room I shared with Adriel.

"Nor." Zadie rose from a chair and hurried over to me. "Thank Thalos you're okay."

"Zadie." We hugged each other tightly. There were a few candles lighting the room, but it was dark outside. "What's happening? Where's Talin?"

"He found his mother. She brought her troops back to Old Castle for the night. Tomorrow we'll assess the damage."

Memories of the battlefield rushed in. "Has anyone seen Ceren?"

"There are people searching for him, but so far, he hasn't turned up."

I shouldn't have been concerned. Ceren was weak and alone, vulnerable outside the shell of the mountain. But the thought of him creeping about like a pale spider made me nervous.

I glanced down and realized I'd been changed into a clean shift. "How are Mother and Father? Can I see them?"

Zadie nodded, gently urging me to lie back against the

pillows. "Everyone is fine. You'll see them in the morning, after you've had some rest."

There was a light knock on the door, and a moment later, Adriel entered.

"You're a sight for sore eyes," she said as she came to give me a hug. "I heard you broke the blood bond all on your own."

I smiled sheepishly. "You don't sound particularly surprised."

She shrugged and sat down on the opposite side of the mattress from Zadie. "I always knew you had an affinity for magic. You just needed to realize it for yourself."

I told Zadie and Adriel everything that had happened in New Castle, ending by showing them the bloodstone pendant still around my neck. It felt like nothing more than a cold piece of metal and stone.

"Will it still work?" Zadie asked.

"The stone? I don't think so," I said, though I made no attempt to test it out. "I think whatever power made Ceren and me capable of wielding the stones was lost when the bond broke. Something about our combined blood must have made them work."

"The combination of royal blood and witch blood, if I had to guess," Adriel said.

My eyes widened involuntarily. "Witch blood?"

"Call yourself a healer if that makes you feel better." She stared at me with those unnerving eyes. "Either way, you're one of us now."

"Really?"

She nodded. "You have a great deal of potential, Nor, but you have a lot of studying to do as well."

Zadie squeezed my hand, sensing I was becoming overwhelmed. "You should get some more sleep. I imagine to-morrow will be a big day for everyone."

I nodded and nestled deeper into my pillow. I hoped I would feel relieved, but Ceren's scream still echoed in my ears when I closed my eyes and fell into a deep, blessedly dreamless sleep.

31

I woke to a scream so primal and desperate I bolted upright in bed, my heart pounding, convinced I was back in New Castle—or perhaps I'd never left. But then Adriel sat up in her bed, immediately lighting the candle on her nightstand.

"What was that?" she asked, getting out of bed and padding barefoot to the hall.

I shook my head and joined her. As we peered into the hallway, we heard people shouting in the distance and heavy footsteps pounding down the corridor. We ducked back as a soldier ran past our room. Fear crept over my body like frost, making my exposed skin prickle. Ceren shouldn't be on my mind anymore. The bond was broken, and he was gone. But as I dressed in a tunic and breeches, the looming dread that chased me into sleep returned.

"Where are you going?" Adriel asked as I entered the hall and headed toward Talia's chambers.

"To see what happened."

She sighed, reaching for me. "Can't you stop being a heroine for five minutes? Whatever it is, someone else can take care of it."

But I evaded her grasp and darted into the hall, my pace quickening as my worry grew. There was a commotion coming from Talia's chambers, and no one stopped me from entering. I found Talia weeping in her son's arms, inconsolable. Seeing the warrior queen crying and desperate made me feel sorry for Talia, something I hadn't thought possible.

"What happened?" I asked Talin as he passed his mother to the waiting arms of the nursemaid.

"My sister is missing," he said quietly. "We've searched the entire castle grounds, but Mother is certain Zoi wouldn't have left on her own."

"She's a curious little girl. It's possible she decided to go exploring," I said, but even I wasn't convinced by my words.

Talin shook his head and lowered his voice. "The guards would have seen her if she'd gone anywhere."

"Assuming they're loyal." I hadn't meant to say the words out loud, but Talin's eyes flew to mine.

He pulled me aside so his mother couldn't hear us, though I doubted she was aware of anything beyond her own wailing. "Why would you say something like that?"

"I'm sorry. It's just that your mother conscripted people who had no interest in fighting a war, Talin. She tore people away from their families, and some of them probably lost loved ones in the battle yesterday." I softened my tone, not wanting to hurt him. "Besides, anyone can be bought if the price is right."

His brow furrowed, first in doubt, then concern.

"You have to admit it's possible," I pressed.

After a moment, he turned to Osius, who had just entered the room. "Did you find anything?"

Osius shook his head.

Talin nodded, setting his jaw. "Round up everyone on duty tonight. I want each of them searched and questioned."

"Of course." Osius nodded and left immediately.

Talia looked up from the nursemaid's shoulder to address Talin. "You don't really think one of my men had something to do with this."

I didn't want to be the one to mention his name, but someone had to. "Ceren is still on the loose. If he was able to bribe one of the guards, someone could have taken Zoi to him."

"Let's not jump to conclusions," Talin said, but Talia was already drying her tears with a handkerchief and ushering everyone out of the room.

"Perhaps Nor is wrong, but the longer we wait, the farther away Zoi might be." She ordered a maid to fetch her clothing, and I headed to my own room to prepare for a search. By the time I was dressed in my riding clothes, the sun was beginning to rise, and Osius had called Talin, Talia, and me to join him.

"Nor was right," he said as he led us to a small room where the guards were being interrogated. "A guard named Dru was approached outside the castle walls last night. The stranger had offered him a bag full of red gems in exchange for Zoi. Dru thought they looked valuable."

From the look in Talin's eyes, he was ready to kill the guard, but Talia got to him first.

"What did you do?" she screamed at Dru, who was shackled and cowering against the wall. "Who took her?"

It was unnerving to see Talia, the most composed woman I'd ever met, so rattled. Perhaps she loved her daughter more than I realized.

"Mother," Talin said gently, though he took a firm hold of her arms. "Please. Let me handle this."

She was trembling with rage, but she let him take her place. "What did the man look like?" Talin asked Dru.

He was a large man, but his voice shook as he answered. "H-he was wearing a cloak, so I didn't get a good look at him. But he was very pale, with strange eyes like two full moons."

Talin and I exchanged a glance. "We need to go," I said.

Talin rubbed his jaw between his fingers. "We have no idea where he took her. We need to keep our heads and think about this logically."

"Logically, Ceren is the one person who has a reason to harm Zoi," I murmured. "If your mother was going to surrender for anything, this is it."

Talin nodded and squared his shoulders. "We'll get the hounds on the scent right away. He won't have gone back to New Castle, not when it has already been occupied by our men."

"We should split up," Osius said. "We can cover more ground that way."

Talin issued a few more orders, then turned to his mother. "I know you want to help, but I think you should stay here, in case Zoi comes home."

She adamantly shook her head no. "If she manages to get away from Ceren and hears a bunch of strangers calling her name, she could very well stay in hiding."

Talin looked doubtful, but he nodded. "Very well. Try not to worry, Mother. We'll find her."

I could only think that Ceren must be more desperate than ever before, to risk coming here and kidnapping Zoi. Still, she was no use to Ceren dead, and without my blood or our bond to strengthen him, we just might be able to catch him.

We all went to the stables to prepare our horses. In the distance, I could hear dogs baying in anticipation of the search. The guard had admitted to slipping into Talia's room and taking Zoi as she slept, bundling her in a cloak and somehow sneaking past the others. He estimated it had been about five hours ago.

Talin divided everyone into groups of three, keeping Talia and me with him. Talia was riding her white mare, and, though she seemed to have calmed down, she looked exhausted.

"Why would he do this?" she asked as we rode out from Old Castle. "He must see that he's lost. Harming a child won't change that."

"I believe he did it to get to you," I replied. "This is his final attempt to claim the throne."

Talia's voice was a disconcerting rasp. "I'll die before I let that man take my daughter's throne."

I cast a glance at Talin, but we had stopped at a fork in the main road. One went north, toward Galeth. The other went west, to the ocean.

Where would Ceren go? I wondered. Not north, surely. Galeth wasn't going to help him, and Pirot had never been loyal to Ceren. Meradin, even less so. South was Talia's territory, so that seemed even less likely.

Unconsciously, I found myself reaching for the bond that was no longer there. Like it or not, I knew Ceren better than most, and the only indication he'd given me that he wanted to see anything outside the walls of New Castle was his comment about how he would like to see Varenia again someday.

If my hunch was wrong, we would end up wasting time. But if it was right and he reached the ocean before we did,

he could take Zoi on a ship and be on another continent before we realized he'd left Ilara.

"I think he's going to Varenia," I said.

Talin turned to look at me in surprise. "What? Why would
you think that?"

"When I was at New Castle, he mentioned he wanted to
see it again."

Talia fixed me in her narrowed gaze. "I find it strange that
Ceren would say something like that to the woman who tried
to kill him, of all people. It almost makes me wonder if you
didn't have something to do with this."

"Mother!" Talin wheeled Xander around to face her. "Nor
would never dream of hurting Zoi. You're frightened and
overwhelmed, understandably. But if you can't learn to dif-
ferentiate your friends from your enemies, you'll never be able
to help Zoi. Not just now, but when she becomes queen."

I was grateful to Talin for defending me, but this wasn't just
about the fact that I would never hurt a child. "I spent quite
a bit of time connected to Ceren," I said to Talia, "through
no choice of my own. I do know him, whether I want to or
not. And I also know that we don't have time to waste on
petty accusations when every moment, Ceren is getting farther away from us."

I doubted Talia was capable of looking chastened, but she
pressed her heels into her mare's sides and took off down the
road toward the ocean. Talin and I followed at a reasonable
canter. I didn't want to wear Titania out when we had a lot
of ground to cover.

"I know you're frustrated," Talin said to me after a long
time had passed in silence. "But I wish you could be more
understanding with my mother. She's been through a great
deal."

"We all have. And I have supported your cause because I believe you wouldn't do anything corrupt or selfish. But I can't say I have those same convictions when it comes to your mother."

Despite my anger, I was afraid I'd gone too far and Talin wouldn't answer. But finally, he looked at me. "I know she isn't perfect, Nor. I know she's made mistakes and her methods for building an army were questionable at best. But I still believe in her cause. I still believe Zoi belongs on the throne and Ilara will be far better off under a female ruler. We've all seen how well things have gone with men running the kingdom for hundreds of years."

He wasn't wrong, and someday Zoi might make an excellent ruler. But in the meantime, I wasn't sure Talia was all that different from Ceren. Would a woman who had been prepared to endanger the lives of all Varenians really see to it that they had somewhere safe to live? Would the united, stable Ilara so many had dreamed of really become a reality?

When we reached the River Ilara, I was hopeful we'd find some sign that Ceren and Zoi had come this way. While we dismounted to let the horses drink and rest, Talin went in search of information from the soldier at the nearest bridge.

"Go on, girl," I said to Titania, releasing the reins so she could drink. I estimated we were farther north than when I had first gone to Ilara, but whether we were as far north as Riaga was impossible to guess.

"No one fitting Ceren's description has crossed the bridge today," Talin said when he returned. "But the soldier thinks it's entirely possible Ceren crossed the river during the night. There are places where crossing is relatively easy on horseback."

Talia mounted her mare and started toward the bridge. "Come on, then. We're wasting time."

We crossed without incident and followed the road through Pirot, where we were soon surrounded by pine forest. There were plenty of fresh hoofprints in the soil, but that meant little, with such an oft-used road. It was late afternoon, and the sun was already beginning to set. I was starting to worry that my guess had been wrong after all.

Suddenly, Titania tensed, her ears pricking forward in alarm. I raised a hand, signaling for Talia and Talin to stop.

"The sun will be down soon," a voice said in the distance. "We should stop for a few hours, get some rest."

The man who answered was clearly in charge. "We'll ride until we reach Old Castle," he said. "We can water the horses at the river."

I recognized the stubborn tone immediately. Without explaining myself, I urged Titania forward through the trees.

"Someone's coming," a female voice said. "Arm yourselves."

"It's me! It's Nor!" I came around a bend in the road to find a dozen crossbows trained on me, but I was too happy to see who was holding them to worry.

"Nor?" Roan leaped from Kosmos's back and hurried toward me. "What in the world are you doing here?"

"It's good to see you, too, Roan." I pulled him into a hug, grateful for this reunion.

When I finally released him, his eyes searched mine. "I mean it, Nor. What are you doing here? Shouldn't you be at Old Castle?"

"Shouldn't you be in Galeth, enjoying your independence?" I raised my eyebrows pointedly, still a little hurt that he had left when we needed him, although I was no longer angry. He had been right to question Talia's motives.

"I would be, if we hadn't run into one of Ceren's patrols on our way home." Roan pulled a waterskin off his saddle and took a long drink. "They had Landrey. Ceren's soldiers must have captured her at some point, probably when she was in Riaga. She had one of those bloodstones on her neck. We tried to convince her to come back with us, but she didn't even recognize us. Then the other soldiers attacked, and we fled."

I felt relief for Landrey and Roan, as well as a tiny bit of disappointment that Titania's rider would likely be asking for her back. "Where is she?"

He shook his head. "We don't know."

"Why didn't you go to Galeth after that? Staying in Ilara couldn't have been the safest decision."

"Of course not. This place is crawling with men who work for Talia or Ceren, and none are happy to see a Galethian this far south. But after witnessing what those bloodstones did to one of our own…" He shuddered at the memory. "We'll never acknowledge Talia as a monarch, Nor, but you were right. This affects all of us."

"I managed to break the blood bond with Ceren before the fighting got too bad," I explained. "The bloodstones don't work anymore. There's a very good chance that Landrey is safe."

I relayed everything as fast as I could, ending with the fact that we were pursuing Ceren. Or that we hoped we were, anyway.

"We haven't crossed paths with him," Roan said when I'd finished. "But we'll help you look. Won't we?" he asked the others.

The Galethians nodded their assent, and I turned to where Talin and Talia waited from a distance, waving them forward.

"Talia," Roan said with a tight nod. "We've offered to assist in the search for your daughter, if you'll accept our help."

She surprised me by bowing her head in response. "We will do so gratefully. I'll repay you however I can. I just want to get my daughter back."

32

We stopped for the night when it grew too dark to see the road, the moonlight diminished by a thick veil of clouds. The Galethians camped with their horses, and I did the same, grateful to have Titania as long as I could. If Landrey came to claim her, keeping her might not be a matter of choice. Roan had said a horse would never forsake its First Rider, and that was something I could never be for Titania.

I was tired from so many hours in the saddle, but it was a relief to have the Galethians with us and to know that Roan and I were on solid footing once again. I left the others talking as they settled down for the night and went to refill my waterskin at a small creek meandering through the woods.

A branch snapped somewhere close by, and the skin on my arms prickled as I straightened and looked around. Ceren could still have men patrolling these woods. As quietly as possible, I headed toward the firelight and safety of camp.

A figure emerged on the trail ahead of me, nearly causing

me to drop the waterskin. In the darkness, it was difficult to make anything out, but as my eyes adjusted, I realized they were wearing skirts, unlike all the other members of our party.

"What do you want, Talia?" I asked, resuming my walk back to camp as if she hadn't just scared the wits out of me.

"I wanted to talk to you alone," she said.

I snorted. "The last time we talked alone, you asked me not to pursue my relationship with Talin and held the safety of my family over my head. I think we both know how that worked out."

She fell in step with me, not making a sound on the fallen leaves on the trail. That broken branch I heard must have been deliberate. I wondered what the last four years had been like for her, raising a small child in exile. Somehow, despite starting a new life with nothing but the clothing on her back, she had grown a network of followers who were willing to risk their lives for her. True, not all her troops were loyal, but there were many who had joined her cause of their own volition. They must have seen something in her that inspired enough confidence to risk the consequences of an uprising that was by no means guaranteed to succeed.

"I do," she admitted. "And I'm grateful you chose not to tell Talin. You were right, of course. He never would have stood for it, not if it wasn't coming from you." She cleared her throat, looking uncharacteristically discomfited. "The truth is, I have seen very little of genuine love in my life. My parents' marriage was not a happy one. And though I cared for my late husband, it was not the kind of love you and Talin have for each other. I was wrong about you, Nor."

The best I could offer her was a tight nod of acknowledgment. I wasn't about to thank her.

"And the truth is, I owe you a debt for ending this war,"

she continued. "We might have won without you, but at the cost of many more lives."

I stopped and turned to face her. "I didn't do it for you, Talia. I did it for my parents, the Varenians, and all the innocent Ilareans who would have died if you'd had your way. I did it for the good of the kingdom."

"I understand," she said, annoyingly unflappable.

"Besides, I'm not even sure if the war really *is* over. Ceren asked me what it was you loved so much about Varenia and why you wanted to go back. And I honestly couldn't answer him. I don't know what you want, Talia. Is it to see your daughter on the throne because you think she'll be a wise and fair ruler? Or is it simply because you're as blinded by power as every other royal?"

She sighed and looked away, but not before I saw her brow furrow like Talin's, a timely reminder that he was her son, no matter her flaws. And while her cold detachment and ruthless pursuit of power hadn't been passed on to her son, I knew that the things I loved most about him—his loyalty, his selflessness, his compassion—had come from her.

"I don't know what you want to hear, Nor. Ruling is a messy business. Peace, as you seem to envision it, isn't real."

The last thing I wanted to do was agree with her, but what if she was right? What did I know about ruling? I had seen several different ways of governing of late, and any system that put few people in control of many was going to have flaws. I could acknowledge that there were others with far more wisdom and experience who could make these sorts of decisions, but did I really want to spend my life with someone so close to all this? If I married Talin, I would never be able to escape the drama and danger of court politics.

"What will you do when we find Zoi?" I asked finally. "What if Ceren demands the crown in return?"

She shook her head. "I would think you would understand better than anyone, Nor. I have spent my life obeying the commands of men. First to leave Varenia, then to marry Xyrus, then to bear his children, and then to sit by while my stepson rose to the throne, even though it wasn't his by right. Why should I give up anything else? Why shouldn't I have everything a man has?"

"Of course I understand all that. But that's not a good enough reason to rule a kingdom or to force people to follow a cause they may not even believe in."

She placed her hand on my arm. "At the end of this, Nor, someone will be responsible for Ilara and all the people in it. You need to ask yourself who that someone should be. And if you don't believe in me, at least try to believe in my children."

"I'll try," I said, then returned to the camp alone.

We rose before the sun to resume our chase. Several of the Galethians had searched the woods through the night, their surefooted horses capable of navigating the road in the dark. But they circled back by midday, having seen nothing. When the road wound north, toward Riaga, Talin brought our party to a stop.

"Would he go into the city?" Roan asked Talin, his hand shading his dark eyes from the sun. "Seems to me he'd be far too conspicuous there."

Talin said something in response, but I barely heard him. Something was calling me forward, off the road and toward the horizon. I rode ahead silently, as if I was being reeled in by an invisible thread. Titania was more alert as well, her nostrils flaring as she breathed heavily, but I wasn't sure if that had to do with me or whatever I was sensing.

The horizon blurred, and suddenly I was no longer looking at land but a wide strip of blue. Just the sight of the ocean released something inside of me, and I breathed in until my ribs ached, letting the salt air fill my lungs. We had come to the edge of a cliff overlooking the Alathian Sea, stretched out in all its glory as far as the eye could see. There was no sign of Ceren, and it seemed unlikely he could have commandeered a ship. We were still miles from the port.

"Don't move, or I'll kill her."

Titania pivoted on her hind legs before the words registered. Somehow, Ceren had managed to come up behind me on foot. I froze the moment I saw the bundle in his arms.

Talin and the rest of our party were on the other side of Ceren. "Put her down," Talin demanded. The Galethians had their crossbows trained on Ceren, but Talin hadn't drawn a weapon. I wondered how he thought he'd convince his brother to do anything in his current state.

Ceren was spinning back and forth like a caged animal with Zoi cradled in his arms, unconscious or asleep, I hoped. There was a wild look in his eyes that I'd only seen when I stabbed him in New Castle.

"Let her go," I urged, sliding off Titania's back slowly. "Please. She's just an innocent child."

I raised my palms and took a step closer. He was wearing a black cloak, but the hood had fallen back, revealing his blond hair, tangled and matted like I'd never seen it before. His ashen skin was pulled taut over his cheekbones, and the shadows around his eyes and in the hollows of his cheeks reminded me of the skeletons in the New Castle crypt. His gray eyes darted between us, as if he thought one of us might make a sudden move.

"This war is over," I said softly. "Hurting your little sister isn't going to change that."

He turned to me, his lips twisted in a sneer. "And what is she to you? Did she give you jewels and gowns, as I did? Did she offer you a crown? Would she have promised you a kingdom, Nor?"

How could he still not understand that none of that mattered to me, that I had no use for gowns and jewels, or even power? As he spoke, his grip on Zoi had tightened, and she whimpered quietly. "Ceren, please."

"Your betrayal is the worst of all." The hurt in his silver eyes was painfully genuine. So many years of anguish had brought him to this moment. I wished I could have known him before it was too late.

"I never betrayed you," I said. "You violated me in unspeakable ways. You hurt my family, you killed innocent people, and you forced a bond between us by feeding me your blood. I had every right to break that bond."

He was slowly sidestepping north, but we kept pace with him easily. He was trapped, and the only option left to him now was surrender. I didn't believe he really wanted to hurt Zoi. What could that possibly accomplish?

My eyes flicked briefly past Ceren, to Talin. He was getting closer to his brother while I distracted him. If I could just keep his guard down, Talin might be able to reach Zoi. "I am sorry that you suffered, Ceren. I truly am. But your sister is just as innocent as you were. Perhaps if you tell us what you want, we can come to some kind of an agreement."

Ceren laughed, and Zoi began to sob quietly. "An agreement? I think we're past the point of negotiations, Nor. Talia can have the throne, or she can have her daughter. It's simple."

"You'll never have the throne!" Talia screamed. She dug her heels into her mare's sides, heading straight for Ceren.

Suddenly, with a burst of speed I hadn't expected, he made for the cliff. I sprinted toward him, hoping to intercept him, but I could see he was going to reach it before I did, despite his weakened state. As he neared the edge, I heard a horse's sharp whinny behind me.

"Stop!" Talia dismounted and fell to her knees.

Ceren froze, just feet from the cliff's edge. Zoi was crying at the sight of her mother, struggling with so much force I worried she'd accidentally knock Ceren over the edge. Perhaps she had believed she was calling Ceren's bluff before, but now, seeing her daughter's terror, Talia was in tears. "I'm sorry. You can have the throne. You can have the entire bloody kingdom. Just give me my daughter."

Ceren set Zoi down, but his grip on her arms didn't soften. "Do you mean it?" His eyes lit up in desperate hope.

"Yes," Talia cried. "You have my word."

We all stood breathless, waiting to see what Ceren would do. I didn't know if I believed Talia myself. I knew her love for her daughter was real, but she could easily tell Ceren anything he wanted to hear right now. There was no way to ensure she would hold up her end of the bargain. Ceren might be armed, but the second he released Zoi, the Galethians could put an arrow straight through his heart. He took a step backward, his lips peeled in a triumphant smile, and I gasped, wondering if there was any chance I could reach Zoi before it was too late.

Then, to my shock, Ceren released her. She ran straight into her mother's open arms, seemingly uninjured. Mother and daughter rocked together, Talia on her knees, Zoi stretched on tiptoe, and for the first time since I'd met her, I had faith that Talia was not lost to power the way Ceren was, that she could actually help steer this kingdom into a safe harbor.

I had stopped a few yards from Ceren when I thought he might drop Zoi over the cliff, and while everyone's attention was on the girl, he was looking directly at me. The setting sun behind him was as bright as the gems in his crown, lighting up the sky and Ceren's hair like flames. Even the water looked scarlet for a moment, an entire ocean of blood.

I slowly stepped closer to Ceren, palms still out to show him I meant no harm. The smile had faded from his lips, as if he knew as well as everyone that he wasn't capable of running a kingdom anymore. "Come away from the edge, Ceren."

"I can't," he said, his heels edging perilously close to the drop. I couldn't tell how far it was to the ocean, but there were likely rocks in the water below. A fall from here would most certainly kill him, and while a part of me believed it was the fate he deserved—he had sent other people, including Lady Melina, to eerily similar deaths by throwing them from Mount Ayris—it was also a coward's death, a way to escape without ever facing the consequences of his actions.

I realized then he had known Talia wasn't going to give him the throne. She would put him in the dungeon, probably for the rest of his life. He had crimes to answer for, and he was a danger to everyone, including himself. But perhaps just hearing her surrender was enough; maybe he had doubted Talia as much as I had, and in his own bizarre, misguided way, was testing her.

Or maybe he'd wanted to see for himself what a mother's love was supposed to look like.

He opened his mouth to speak, and foolish as I was, I

thought he might apologize for everything he'd done. Maybe, finally, he could acknowledge his mistakes. I didn't imagine he cared about forgiveness, and I wasn't even sure I was capable of granting it. I just wanted to believe that the little boy was still in there, and if he asked for help, he would finally receive it.

But the next thing I knew, he fell backward, and with nothing but the flapping of his cloak in the wind, he was gone.

33

Later, when I had been reunited with my family and was safe back in Old Castle, Father would try to explain Ceren's death was the justice he deserved.

"Ceren took too much from the sea, Nor," he said to me as we sat under the stars in the courtyard with Zadie and Mother. We'd been back for two days, and even though I was wearing layers of clothing and had wrapped myself in a thick throw, I still couldn't get the chill out of my bones that had crept in the moment Ceren died. Adriel thought it might be the lingering effects of the broken bond, but I didn't believe it was that simple. I knew well enough now that nothing ever was.

Varenians believed that Thalos was a hungry god, one who demanded sacrifices from our people. Perhaps Father was right, and Ceren's fate *was* a kind of justice. But believing his downfall would bring me some kind of resolution had been foolhardy. I was relieved to know he wasn't immortal, at least. But I felt just as unsettled as I had when my journey began.

There was much to be grateful for, of course. Zoi was healthy, and while the kidnapping had been frightening and confusing, I hoped she was young enough that the memory would fade over time. The wounds would still be there, of course. They were for all of us. But if we were lucky, they would heal over stronger than before, fading into scars that reminded us of everything we had survived.

As if sensing my turmoil, Mother squeezed my hand in hers. The tension between us would always be there, I knew. But it had eased in the face of far more important things. She understood what I had gone through to help the Varenians—they all did, having lived through some of it themselves. Earlier in the day, Governor Kristos, Elidi, and the elders had formally apologized to me on behalf of Varenia, and while I appreciated the gesture, it didn't bring me the satisfaction it might once have. Even seeing Sami reunited with his family couldn't erase the pain our community had caused him.

Zadie wrapped her arm around me. I rested my head on her shoulder and looked up at the sky, at the same stars that just recently had represented infinite possibilities for the future, and wondered why I couldn't imagine even one.

Two days later, Talin convened the first council of the new, hopefully unified Ilara. Roan had stayed behind with several other Galethians, while the rest of our original traveling party returned to report back on what had happened. The de facto leaders of Pirot and Meradin were there as well, along with the remnants of Ceren's war council, including Lady Hyacinth.

Governor Kristos and Samiel were there to represent Varenia, and Talin, in a gesture that surprised even me, had invited Adriel to represent her own people, however few remained scattered in other lands. All in all, there were more than a dozen leaders at the long table in Old Castle's hall, including me.

Talin had named me a special envoy, though it wasn't a title I wanted or necessarily believed I deserved. But the rest of the council had voted on it unanimously, and I couldn't refuse their invitation.

Now, as the meeting began, I fidgeted nervously, my fingers drumming on my bouncing legs. Adriel cast me a pointed glance, and I did my best to sit still as Talin took his place at the head of the long table.

He had been elected as Zoi's regent, though not unanimously. There were several Galethians, and one or two Meradians, who believed Zoi should be represented by a leader from each territory in Ilara. But there had been surprisingly little dispute over the rightful woman king of Ilara. It seemed everyone was tired of fighting, at least for now.

"Thank you all for coming," Talin said, looking regal despite his lack of royal insignia. Ilara was being recreated from scratch, in some ways, and the symbols of this new land hadn't yet been discussed. "Our first matter of business is to decide where Zoi's castle will be built. There are some who would like to return to New Castle." He glanced at Lady Hyacinth, who I was happy to see didn't look quite so smug these days. "And others who would prefer we build the castle in their territory."

At least seven heads nodded. It seemed most of the leaders were hesitant to give anything up.

"But I propose we build an entirely new castle, just south of Riaga," Talin continued. "The port has always been neutral territory, and if we include Varenia as part of Ilara, it's the most central part of the kingdom. It's also good for trade."

"What about Princess Zoi?" Roan asked. "Where does she want to live?"

To my shock, Talia hadn't asked to be a member of the new council. I wondered if she was too afraid to let Zoi out of her sight or if she had actually realized that her aims might not be the same as the kingdom's. She would see her daughter on the throne one day, if all went well, and I hoped that truly would be enough for her. Zadie had volunteered to be the little girl's governess, and Zoi had taken to my sister as easily as a whale calf to water.

"She said she wants to live near the sea," Talin said with a laugh. "I guess it's the Varenian blood in her."

"Then we will build the castle on the cliffs overlooking the ocean, north of Riaga," a lord from Meradin said.

"She has also asked for it to be made of pearls and jewels," Talin added with a smile. "I told her we'd do our best."

A few chuckles came from the other councilmembers. Governor Kristos rose when the room had quieted. "I'd like to ask what is to become of my people, now that we are no longer exiled. I believe some of our citizens will choose to return to Varenia, but others have requested to stay on land."

"Of course," Talin replied. "Any Varenian who wishes to remain in Ilara will be given a small plot of land. We will divide them evenly among the territories, to be equitable. If anyone is opposed to this, please speak up."

I was relieved when no one protested. My own parents had surprised me by expressing interest in splitting their time between Varenia and Ilara, preferably near the castle so they could be close to Zadie and Sami. And Governor Kristos and Elidi had decided to return to Varenia for the time being.

When the council dispersed, I found myself next to Adriel,

who wrapped an arm around my shoulder with a relaxed familiarity that I had come to appreciate.

"How are you?" she asked as we walked toward our chambers. "You've been quiet this week."

I shrugged and forced a smile. "I've had a lot on my mind."

"You know, you're always welcome to come and stay with me for a bit. I could use the help catching up with my patients, and I know Foxglove would be grateful for the company."

I smiled. "Foxglove will be grateful for *your* company, and I'm sure the people of Galeth will be happy to have you back. But I don't know if it's the right place for me. Besides, I have Zadie and Talin to consider."

Adriel paused outside her room and turned to face me. "You don't owe anyone anything, Nor. And you don't have to decide today."

"I know," I said, though I was still plagued with doubts. Talin had made it abundantly clear that he wanted me by his side, but I knew Governor Kristos would need some help in Varenia, considering it had been nearly abandoned for weeks. And of course, there was Zadie to think of. She would be busy with Sami and Zoi, but I also couldn't stand the thought of being away from her for long. Above all, I couldn't forget about my parents. My father would not be able to farm his land alone, and it would take some time before they had an income that would allow them to travel back and forth.

"Just think about it," Adriel said, embracing me.

"I will. Say goodbye before you leave."

"Of course."

I found Zadie looking through a stack of books in her chambers. She glanced up as I entered, her entire face lighting up. I'd never seen her look more beautiful or happy.

"There you are," she said, gesturing for me to sit. "How was the council meeting?"

"It went well. We're moving the castle to the coast, north of Riaga."

Zadie's grin spread. "Oh, Zoi will be delighted!"

I sighed and dropped my chin onto my fist. "Is this going to work, Zadie? Can Ilara really be ruled by all these people with completely different agendas overseen by a little girl?" She couldn't even read, for Thalos's sake.

"Talin is a strong leader, Nor. He will make sure things are done fairly."

"I have every faith in Talin. It's the others I worry about."

She raised an eyebrow. "Like Roan?"

"Roan has been remarkably well behaved," I conceded. "He seems the most concerned about Zoi of everyone, other than Talin."

"And how is Talin?" she asked, coming to sit next to me. "He looked exhausted when I saw him at breakfast."

"He isn't sleeping well. I suppose that's to be expected. He's been through a lot."

Zadie took my hand in hers. "So have you."

"I don't understand it," I said, swiping the tears from my cheeks. "Why should I be sad about a man who tried to kill me more than once, who tried to kill Zoi and Talin and enslaved everyone I love?"

"Because you have a very generous heart," she said, smoothing my hair back from my face. She pulled me against her side, and I allowed myself to cry for Ceren for the first time since his death. Not for the tyrant who had used everyone in his path for his own selfish gains and revenge, but for the little boy standing at a rain-streaked window, for the man who had stared up at me from the lakeside after I saved him from drowning, the one who wanted to see the ocean again one last time.

That person was worthy of forgiveness.

"Auntie Nor!"

I turned away from the ocean to see Zoi running toward me. I was in the main room of the manor we were living in until the castle was built, standing as I often did on the wide veranda overlooking the sea. It was early winter, and the air was cold and sharp against my cheeks, but I welcomed it. The biting cold was a reminder that I was still here.

"What is it?" I asked, scooping Zoi up in my arms. She had come out of her shell over the past month, easing into a far more settled existence than she'd ever known. Between her mother, her nursemaid, Zadie, and Talin, she was rarely alone, and she seemed to thrive on the routine they'd created for her. In the afternoons, she rode her little white pony along the cliffs with Talin, and I accompanied them on Titania from time to time.

For reasons I still didn't understand, Landrey had been allowed to return to Galeth from her banishment. I never knew why she'd been sent away in the first place, but Roan told me that Yana had been a different person since her sister came home, and they were considering ending the use of banishment as a punishment. And in an even more surprising twist, Landrey had let Titania stay with me. It was the best gift I could have asked for.

Adriel and Roan had returned to Galeth, though they would be visiting next month for the council meeting. It would be months, maybe years, before the castle was complete, but the large manor Talin had chosen for us as living quarters in the meantime was far more beautiful than New

Castle or Old Castle. The expansive windows let in sunshine even in the winter, and it was surrounded by lush moors on three sides, the ocean on the other.

"Look what my brother had made for me!" Zoi gestured to Talin, who had entered the room behind her.

"What is it?" I asked.

Talin held up the long, narrow object in his hand. It was a scepter, I realized, though too small to belong to a king, and too large for a diminutive princess.

I set Zoi down as Talin passed it to me. It was crafted from a warm rose gold, engraved with coral and studded with pearls and jewels.

"It's beautiful," I said to Talin. "Where did you get it?"

"The other councilmembers had it made for Zoi," he whispered in my ear, "but please don't tell her that. She's convinced it was my idea."

I ran my fingers over the engravings and smiled. "A consolation prize for a jewel-encrusted palace, perhaps?"

"Zoi!"

Zadie stepped into the room and paused on the threshold. "There you are. You're late for your lessons." She glanced at me and sighed wearily. "It's like trying to tutor a very wiggly, very naughty eel," she said.

"What's an eel?" Zoi took the scepter from my hands and ran to show it to Zadie without waiting for an answer. Zadie made such a show over how beautiful it was that even Zoi rolled her eyes.

"Back to work," she said, giving me a meaningful smile as she escorted Zoi out of the room. "Ilara's future leader must be clever *and* disciplined."

I turned back to the window and felt Talin's arms wrap

around my waist. I leaned back against his shoulder, breathing in the salty sea air and Talin's own warm, familiar scent.

"What's wrong?" he asked against my neck. "You haven't been yourself for ages."

"I'm fine," I insisted, turning to face him. "Really."

"But fine isn't good enough. I want you to be happy."

I shrugged as well as I could in his arms. "I will be."

His eyes searched my face. "Not here, though."

"Don't say that. I do feel restless, but it's not because of the house, or you, or anyone. I don't know what it is."

He kissed me softly. His nightmares had all but faded in the past couple of weeks, and he seemed happier than I'd ever seen him. Ruling suited him, though he was far busier than I would have liked. We only really had time to talk at night, and he was usually so exhausted he fell asleep quickly.

But I lay awake at night feeling oddly unsettled. I had slept better on the road, in fact. "I think," I began, hoping I could convey my thoughts without hurting him, "that I don't feel like I have a purpose here. You, Zadie, Adriel, and Roan all have important jobs. I am grateful for my seat on the council, but I don't represent anyone or anything."

Talin waited patiently for me to finish.

"I thought I would be satisfied when all the people I cared about were safe. But I still find myself wondering what else is out there beyond the horizon."

"Of course you do," he said, pressing a kiss to my forehead. "You have the soul of an adventurer. That doesn't just go away."

I gazed up at him uncertainly. "No?"

"No. So tell me, what do you want to do?"

"I want to learn about healing from Adriel. I want to see if we can improve our diplomatic relationship with Kuven.

Without you marrying their princess," I added hastily. "I'd like to visit the Penery Islands, and train with the Galethians, and find out if anyone else has the same ties to nature as the Varenians."

His eyes crinkled at the corners. "Then what are you waiting for?"

"It's not that simple, Talin. I want to be with *you*, too. I want to be with the people I love." I chewed my lip, hesitant. Knowing what I wanted was one thing; admitting it to Talin was another. But I couldn't keep denying the truth that had been buried in me since the day the Ilarean boy gave me the wandering crab. I took a deep breath. "And I want freedom."

His face was so open with understanding that my heart felt like it might burst from loving him. "Then go, my love. We'll be waiting for you when you get back."

Tears of relief sprang free of my eyes. "You'd better be," I said, the tightness in my chest already easing. I should have known Talin would never try to hold me back. I stood on tiptoe to kiss him, in no hurry to let him get back to his duties. When the time was right, I would go forward with my eyes wide open, no longer afraid of the unknown, no longer afraid of goodbye.

Most importantly, I was no longer afraid that my freedom depended on the whims or constraints of others. I would carry the people I loved with me, whether I chose to stay in Ilara permanently or visit other lands.

Because that was what it meant to be free: I could *choose*.

When we broke apart, I turned back to the ocean, finally understanding what it meant to be content. Ceren had said love was my weakness, once. But I knew now that love was the strength that would sustain me out there in the world, and it was the bond that would ensure I always came back.

The warmth in my chest radiated through me like golden light over the water. I had found the place I belonged, and it wasn't a cottage or a village or a country: it was right here, inside of me.

Finally, I was home.

★ ★ ★ ★ ★

Acknowledgments

Writing a sequel is a little like having a second child; I thought I knew what to expect, but it somehow managed to take me completely by surprise. I'm so fortunate to once again have the support of an entire village behind me.

To my agent, Uwe Stender, and my foreign rights agent, Brent Taylor: thank you for getting my words out into the world and for continuing to make Team Triada such a warm, welcoming home. There's no one else I'd want steering this ship.

To my editor, Connolly Bottum, I am so grateful for your enthusiasm, encouragement, and insight. Writing can sometimes feel like being lost in the woods, but working with you turned out to be "just right." I'm so glad our journey together is only beginning.

To Lauren Smulski, who first saw the potential in this series, and Abby Ranger, who provided more than just edits; I learned so much from you in our brief time working together.

To Bess Braswell, thank you for your unwavering support

of my books and career. I'm so grateful to be an Inkyard Press author, and I can't wait to see what the future holds.

Thanks to Mary Luna, Allan Davey, and Kathleen Oudit for another stunning cover. I know how important that first impression is, and you all nailed it. Thanks also to Brittany Mitchell, Laura Gianino, and the rest of the Inkyard team for your hard work.

As always, so much love to my critique partners: Elly Blake, who is so loyal and generous she volunteered to read the first draft of this novel (bless you!), and Nikki Roberti Miller, who came to the rescue with her title and tagline genius. And to the rest of the Pitch Wars 2014 Table of Trust, you remain the best writers group out there.

To my friends all around the world, but especially my Belgrade girls, thanks for keeping me sane(ish). I am so lucky to have found you.

To the entire Embassy Belgrade community: thank you, thank you, thank you. From buying my books, listening to me whine about revisions, and waving to me in the café while I'm hunkered down with my headphones, you all make me feel like a real author. More importantly, you make this place feel like home.

Special thanks to Tate for the character name auction idea, Heidi for bidding far above my expectations, and Alex for finding me a compatible plug adapter at a crucial revision moment. To Leena (owner of the real Mr. Fox) and Malina, who are both amazing writers in their own right, thanks for being such loyal fans. Jelisaveta and Marko, my little book community here in Belgrade, thanks for your friendship and support (and for pretending I'm not literally twice your age).

To my family near and far—Mom, Dad, Aaron, Elizabeth, Amy, Jennifer, my amazing nieces and nephews, Patti, and the rest of the Rutherford crew—I love you guys and can't wait till we can be together again. And to my twin sister, Sarah, my first call whether the news is good or bad, thank you for always being there with words of wisdom and without judgment. You are truly my North Star.

To my husband, John, who makes up for in hugs what he lacks in writing advice. Thank you for working so hard to provide us with this beautiful life, for keeping us all fed, and for still being as silly as you were when I met you twenty years ago (even if I'm the only one who gets to see it). I love you so very much.

To my boys, Jack and Will: you inspire me every day with your imagination, resilience, and sheer capacity for weirdness. There are no other kids in the world I'd want to ride out a pandemic with. I'm so proud to be your mom.

To Mishka, my dogter, who keeps our hearts (and feet) warm and cozy.

And finally, to all the readers who blogged, bookstagrammed, posted, reviewed, tweeted, messaged, and shared your love for this series, thank you for continuing on this adventure with me. You may not realize it, but you are the most important part of this village. I would not be here without you, and I never take that for granted.